DINOSAUR EXPLORERS

PAPERCUT𝒁

DINOSAUR EXPLORERS
#5 LOST IN THE JURASSIC

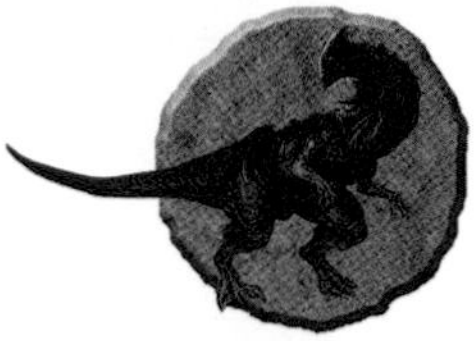

REDCODE and ALBBIE — Story
AIR TEAM (KINO, XENO, SAMU, NEKO, ESTHER, and VEZILL) — Art
REDCODE and SAMU — Cover Art
MAX — Cover Color
FUNFUN, MAX, and EVA — Interior Color
KENNY CHUA and KIAONG — Art Direction
ROUSANG — Original Design
REDCODE, ESTHER, KA CHEONG and CLAZ'ROOM — Illustration
BALICAT and MVCTAR AVRELIVS — Translation
ROSS BAUER — Original Editor
SPENSER NELLIS — Editor
JEFF WHITMAN — Managing Editor
JIM SALICRUP
Editor-in-Chief

ISBN HC: 978-1-5458-0315-8
ISBN PB: 978-1-5458-0316-5

Printed in India
July 2019

Papercutz books may be purchased for business or promotional use. For information on bulk purchase please contact Macmillan Corporate and Premium Sales Department at (800) 221-7945 x5442

Distributed by Macmillan.
First Papercutz Printing.

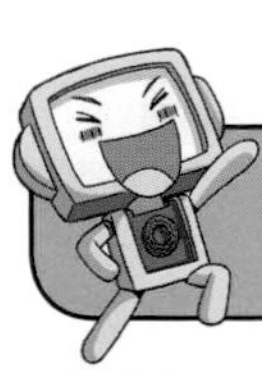

DINOSAUR EXPLORERS Reading Guide and Lesson Planner available at:
http://papercutz.com/educator-resources-papercutz

DINOSAUR EXPLORERS

#5 LOST IN THE JURASSIC

REDCODE & ALBBIE – WRITERS

AIR TEAM – ART

PAPERCUTZ
NEW YORK

FOREWORD

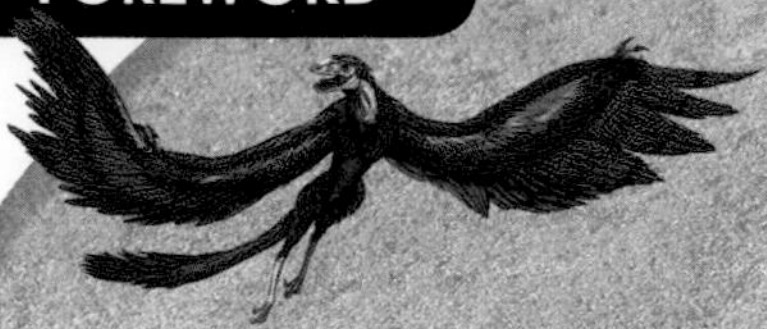

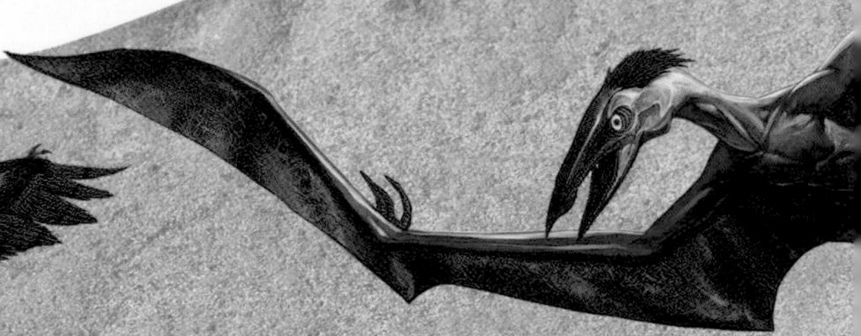

Our planet is more than 4.5 billion years old, but we have only been around for 2 million! What strange creatures inhabited the Earth before we did?

While the DINOSAUR EXPLORERS series does refer to dinosaurs, this first book focuses on where they came from—and the creatures even dinosaurs would call prehistoric! This series contains as much fun as scientific information and you will see how our planet was transformed from a dry, barren ball of space rock into the haven it is today. See how the Earth's surface and seas formed, how single-celled microorganisms became complex multi-celled creatures, how bones evolved, and how we are not descended from monkeys, but fish!

Oh, yes, dinosaurs are the stars of the series, —from the magnificent pterosaurs, to the terrifying Tyrannosaurus rex, to the seafaring Icthhyosaurs; all mighty beasts of fact and legend. But even they had to start somewhere, and that is what we are going to discover!

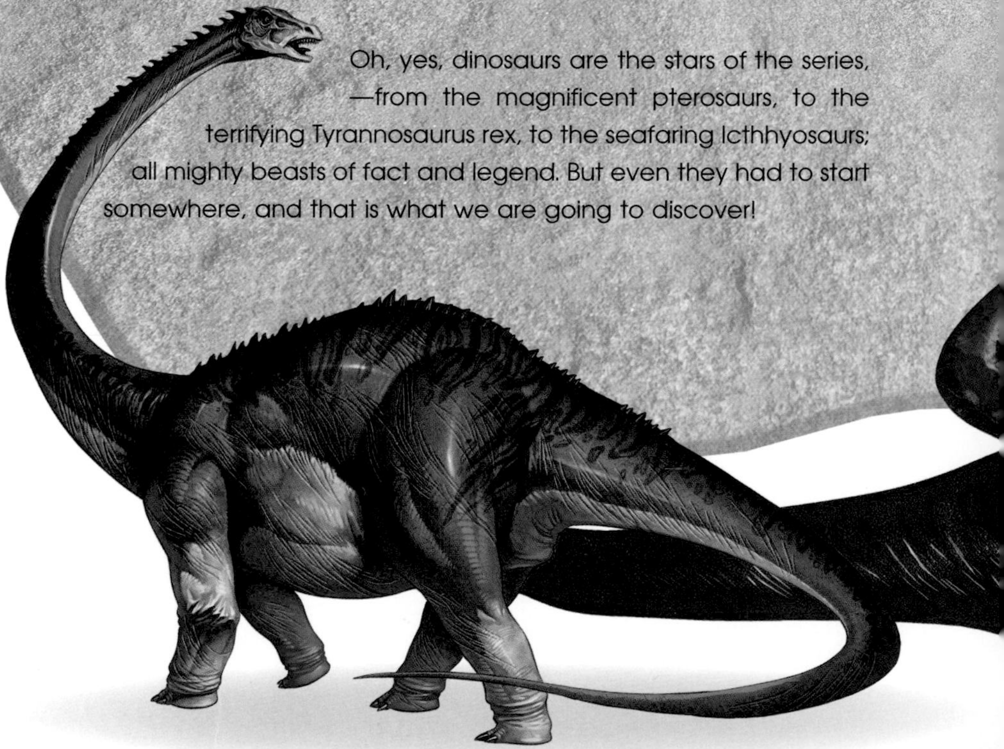

And that just describes what was in the first volume of DINOSAUR EXPLORERS! As our heroes try to make their way back to the present, they've been "Puttering in the Paleozoic" (in volume 2), "Playing in the Permian" (volume 3), "Trapped in the Triassic" (volume 4), and now they're "Lost in the Jurassic." They're in the early to mid-Jurassic period, and once they're no longer lost, they'll be "Exploring the Jurassic" (in volume 6). With great stories and science that will wow your friends and teachers,this Papercutz graphic novel series is something not to be missed.

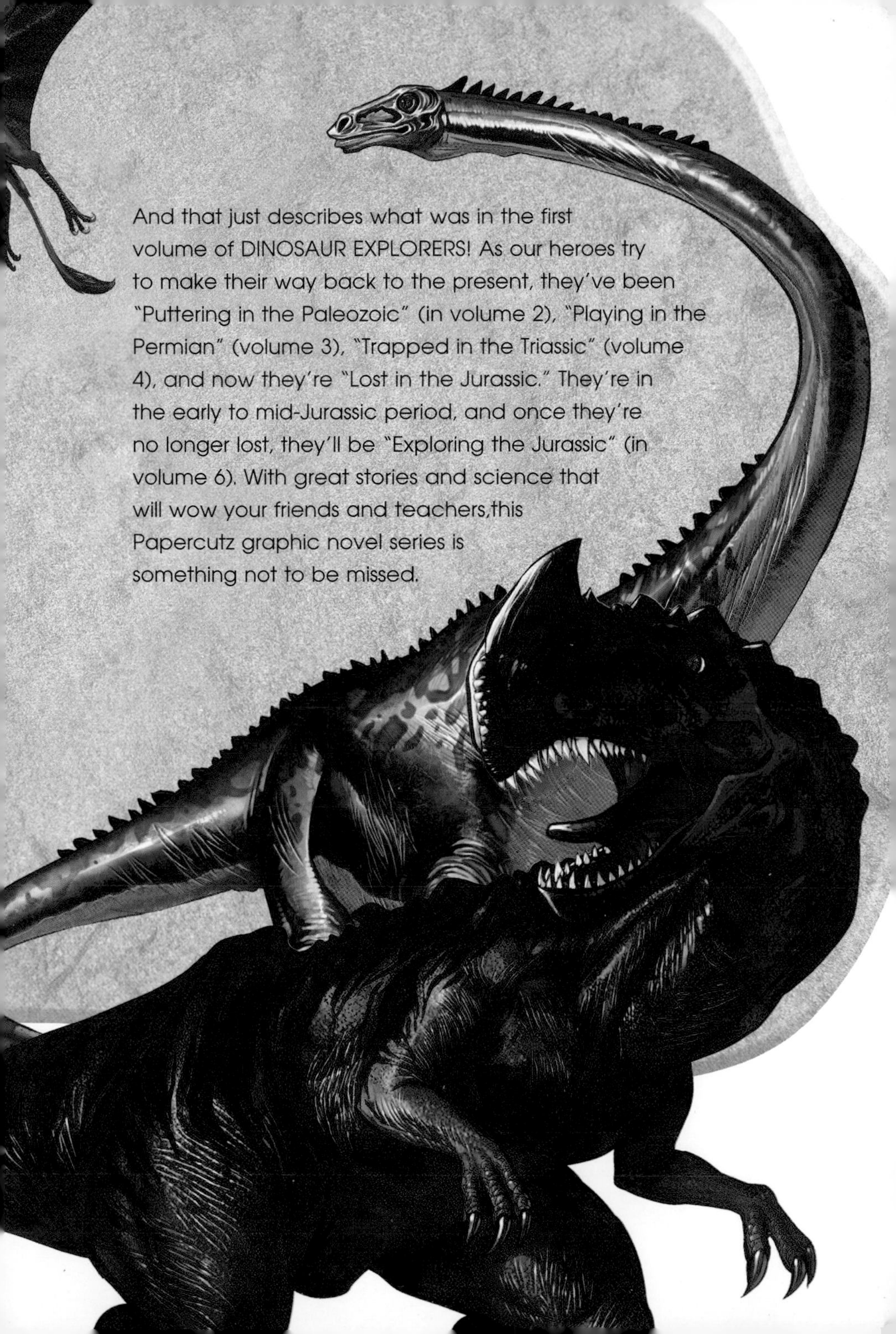

HOW THE EARTH WAS FORMED

We know the Earth is the third planet in the solar system, the densest planet, and so far, the only one capable of supporting life (although new evidence is emerging that Mars may also be able to support various forms of life). But how did that happen?

1 The Sun's formation

Way, way back, there was a patch of space filled with cosmic dust and gases. Slowly, gravity (and a few nearby exploding stars) forced some of this dust and gases together into clumps—the gases formed into a massive, pressurized ball of heat which became the Sun, while the dust settled into planets, the Earth being one of them.

2 Formation of the Earth

As the Earth formed, its gravity grew stronger. Heavier molecules and atoms fell inward to the Earth's core, while lighter elements formed around it. The massive pressures from the external material heated up the Earth's interior to the point where it was all liquid (except for the core, which was under so much pressure it could not liquify). These settled down into the Earth's 3 layers: the crust, mantle, and core.

While we cannot say for sure just when these dust clouds solidified to form the Earth, nor when they came into being in the first place, we can tell that it took place more than 4.5 billion years ago.

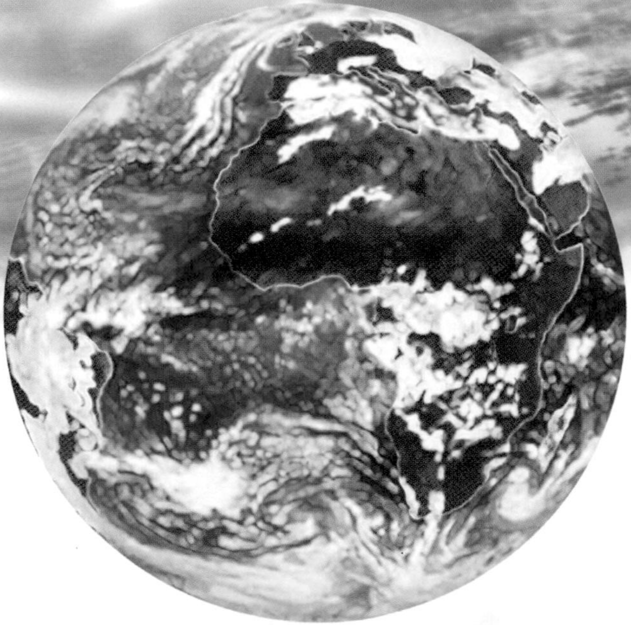

6 The Earth today

Even now, our Earth changes with time; its tectonic plates still move about on the lava bed of the mantle, pushing and pulling continents in all directions.

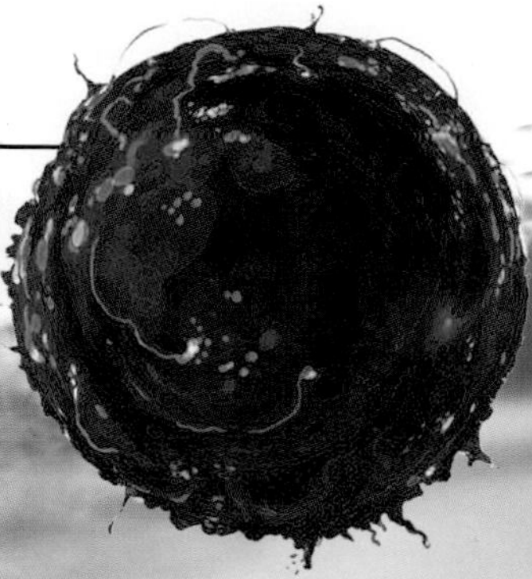

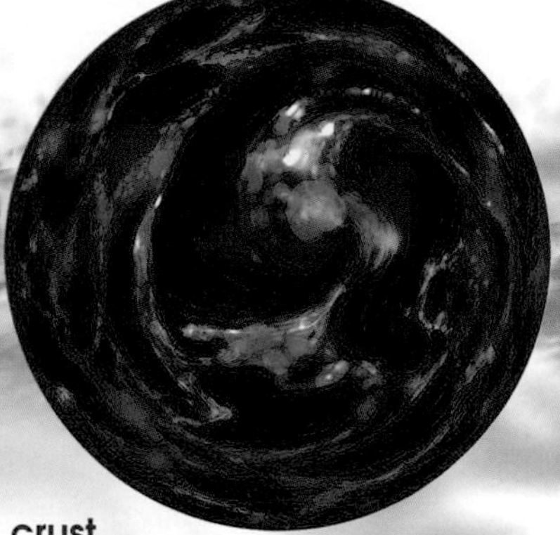

3 The crust

The crust was created around 4 billion years ago, as cooled, solid rock floating on the molten lithosphere merged. Even today, as the continental plates shift away from and against each other, some of this rock and molten material might still change place.

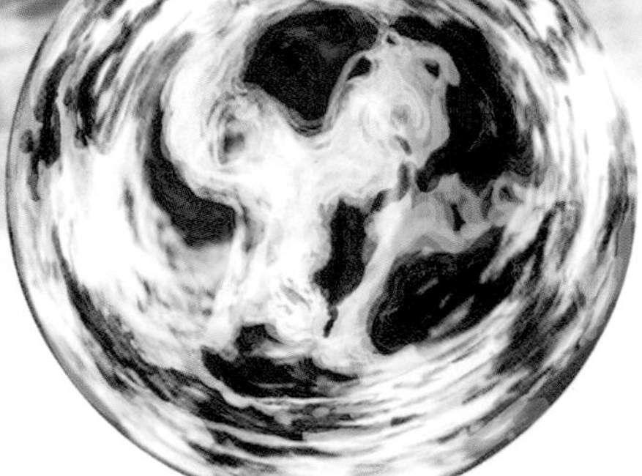

4 The formation of the atmosphere

After our crust solidified, volcanic gases formed our atmosphere. The cooling surface allowed the formation of water vapor and bodies of water.

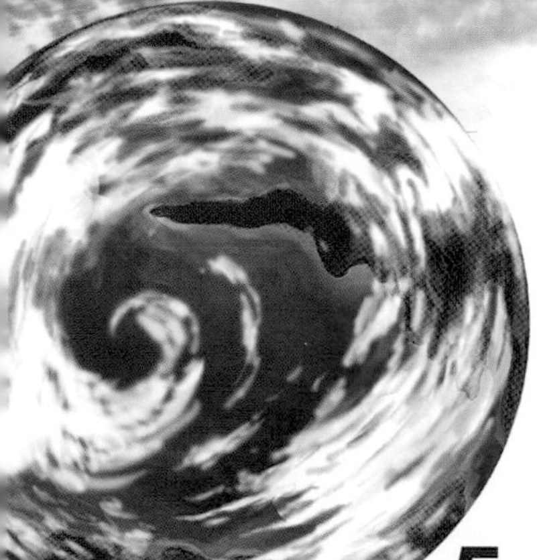

5 Land forms

Around 3.5 billion years ago, several land masses rose above the global ocean, giving rise to the continents we know today.

Geological Time Spiral

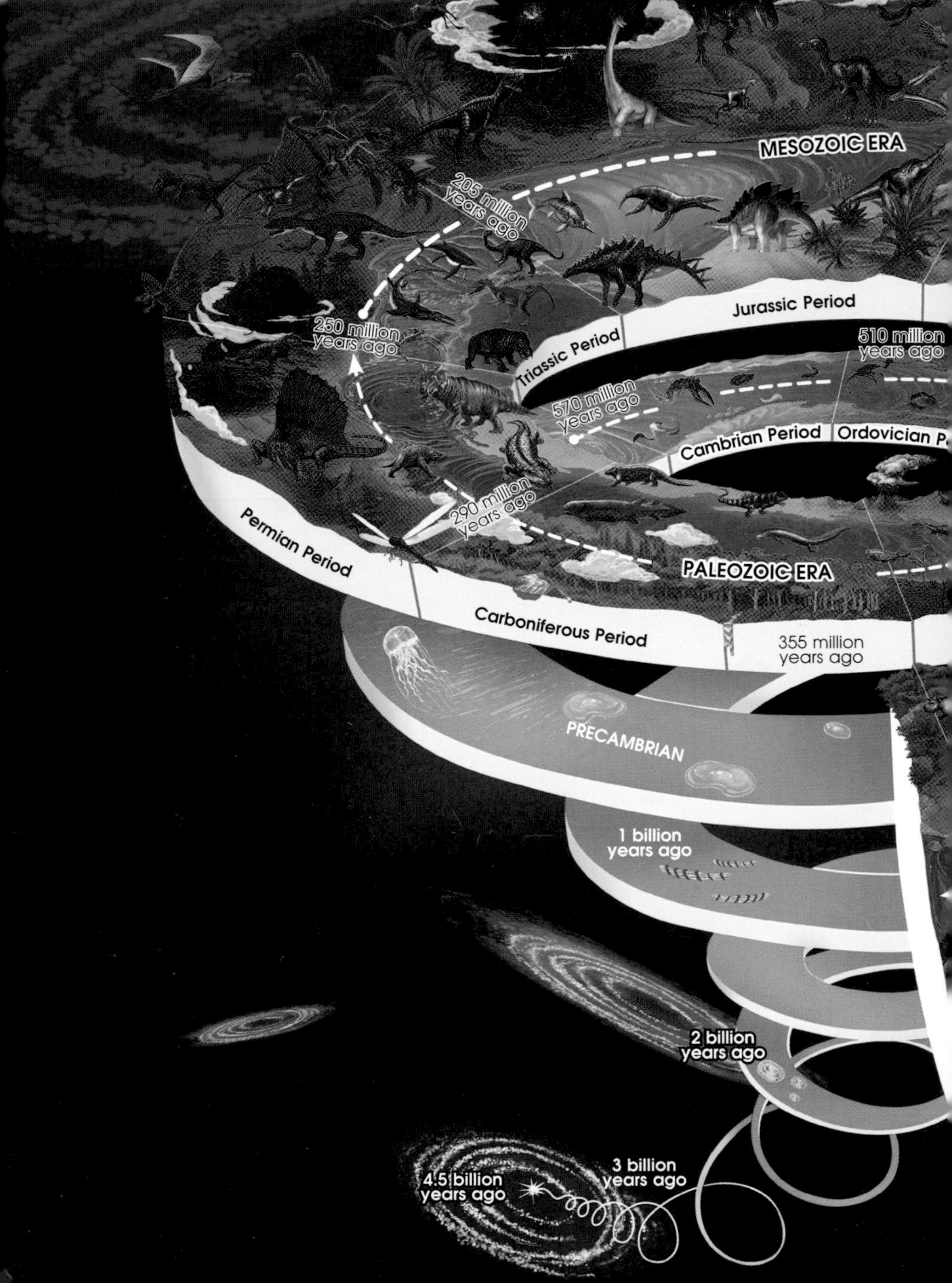
MESOZOIC ERA
205 million years ago
250 million years ago
Triassic Period
Jurassic Period
510 million years ago
570 million years ago
Cambrian Period
Ordovician P
290 million years ago
Permian Period
PALEOZOIC ERA
Carboniferous Period
355 million years ago
PRECAMBRIAN
1 billion years ago
2 billion years ago
3 billion years ago
4.5 billion years ago

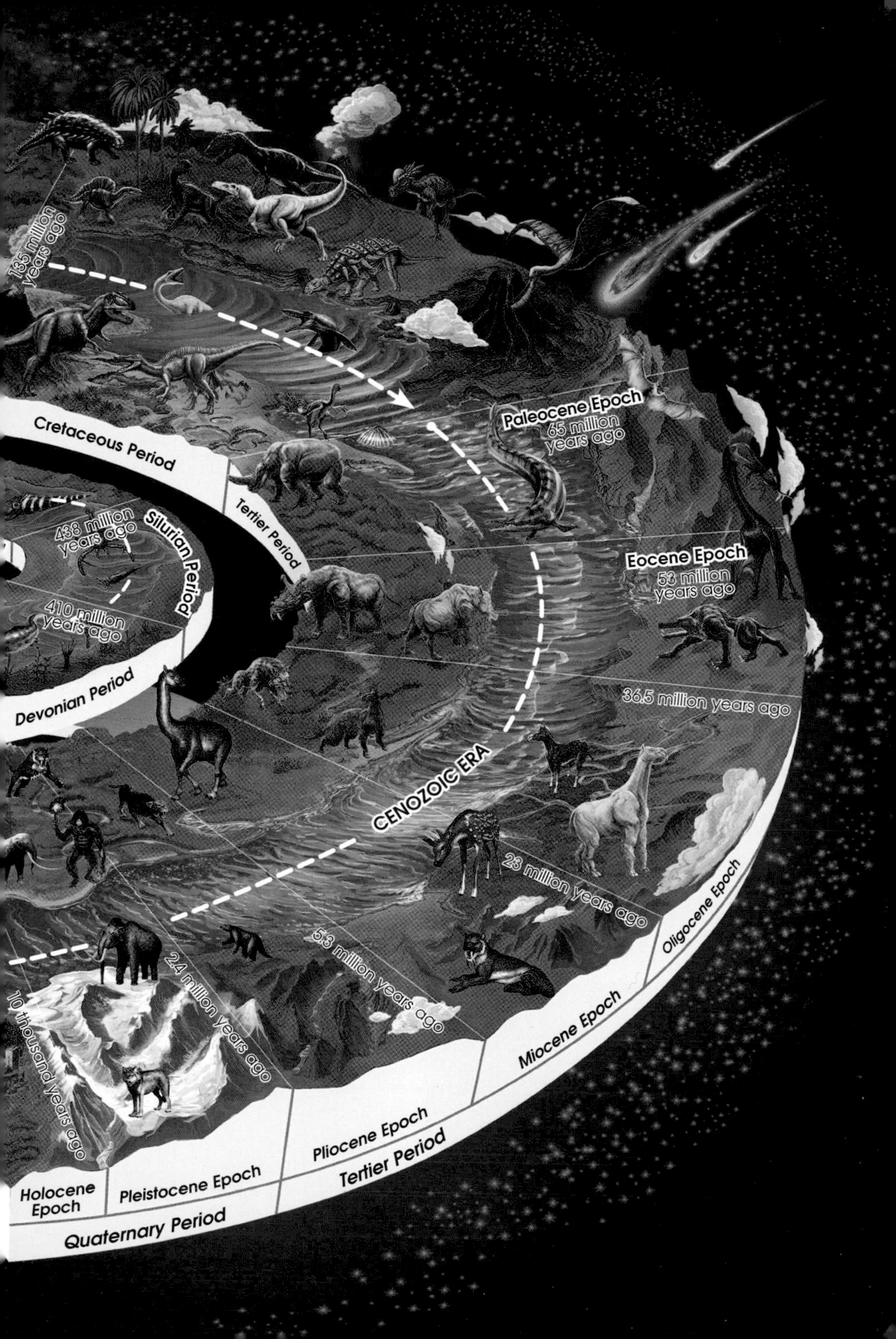
135 million years ago
Cretaceous Period
438 million years ago
Silurian Period
410 million years ago
Devonian Period
Tertier Period
Paleocene Epoch
65 million years ago
Eocene Epoch
53 million years ago
36.5 million years ago
CENOZOIC ERA
23 million years ago
Oligocene Epoch
5.3 million years ago
2.4 million years ago
10 thousand years ago
Miocene Epoch
Pliocene Epoch
Tertier Period
Holocene Epoch
Pleistocene Epoch
Quaternary Period

GEOLOGIC TIME SCALE

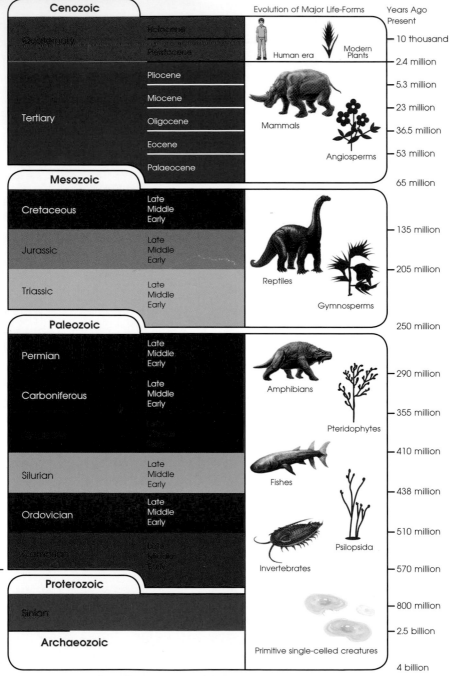

Cenozoic			Evolution of Major Life-Forms	Years Ago
				Present
Quaternary		Holocene	Human era / Modern Plants	— 10 thousand
		Pleistocene		— 2.4 million
Tertiary		Pliocene	Mammals / Angiosperms	— 5.3 million
		Miocene		— 23 million
		Oligocene		— 36.5 million
		Eocene		— 53 million
		Palaeocene		
Mesozoic				65 million
Cretaceous		Late / Middle / Early	Reptiles / Gymnosperms	— 135 million
Jurassic		Late / Middle / Early		— 205 million
Triassic		Late / Middle / Early		
Paleozoic				250 million
Permian		Late / Middle / Early	Amphibians / Pteridophytes	— 290 million
Carboniferous		Late / Middle / Early		— 355 million
				— 410 million
Silurian		Late / Middle / Early	Fishes	— 438 million
Ordovician		Late / Middle / Early		— 510 million
Cambrian		Late / Middle / Early	Invertebrates / Psilopsida	— 570 million
Proterozoic				
Sinian				— 800 million
Archaeozoic			Primitive single-celled creatures	— 2.5 billion
				4 billion

Phanerozoic

Proterozoic

Archaean

CONTENTS

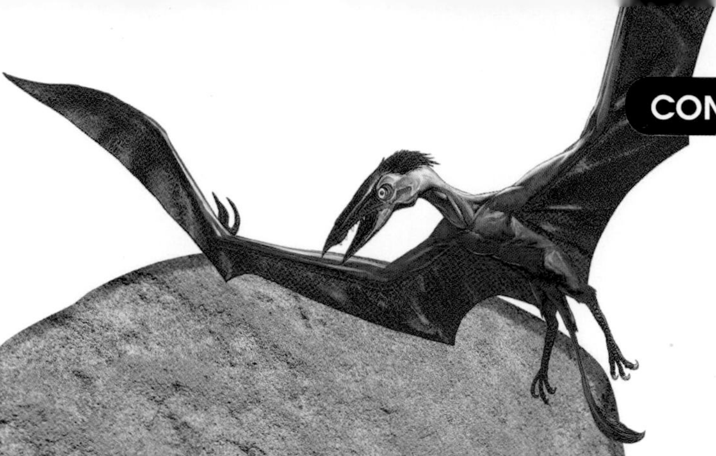

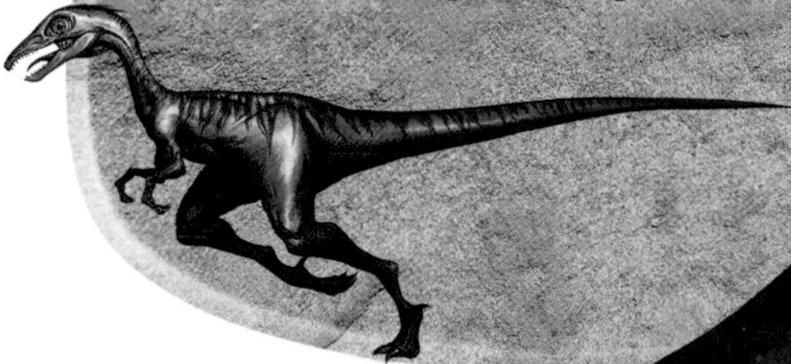

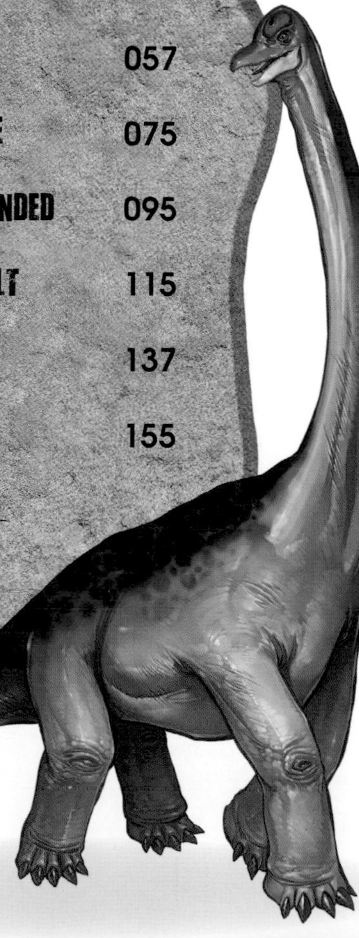

Cast

Sean (Age 13)
- Smart, calm, and a good analyst.
- Very articulate, but under-performs on rare occasions.
- Uses scientific knowledge and theory in thought and speech.

Stone (Age 15)
- Has tremendous strength, appetite, and size.
- A boy of few words but honest and reliable.
- An expert in repairs and maintenance.

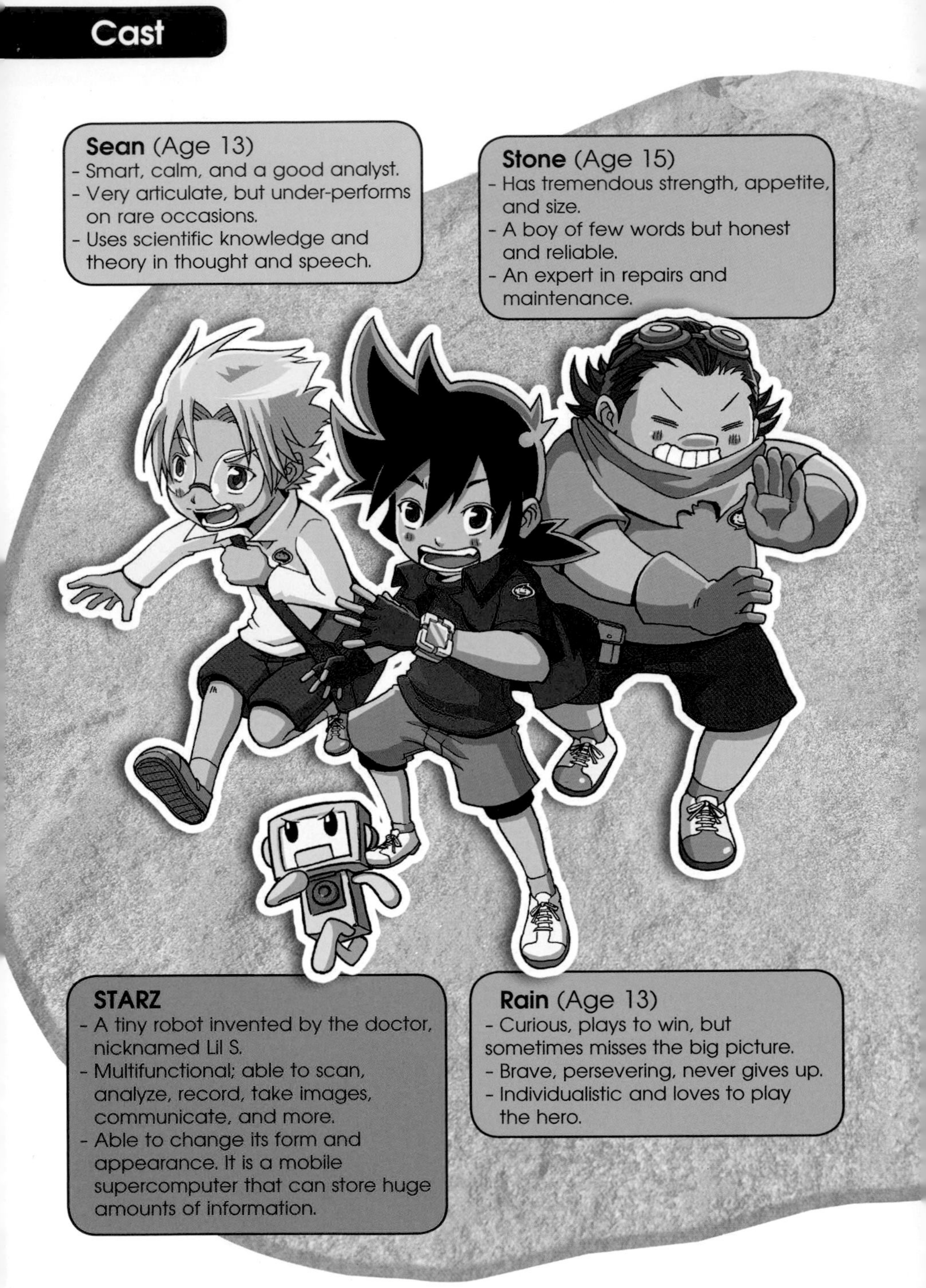

STARZ
- A tiny robot invented by the doctor, nicknamed Lil S.
- Multifunctional; able to scan, analyze, record, take images, communicate, and more.
- Able to change its form and appearance. It is a mobile supercomputer that can store huge amounts of information.

Rain (Age 13)
- Curious, plays to win, but sometimes misses the big picture.
- Brave, persevering, never gives up.
- Individualistic and loves to play the hero.

Dr. Da Vinci (Age 60)
- A professor at the National Scientific Research Institute.
- A genius inventor.
- Highly knowledgeable, loves adventure, but lazy by nature.

Diana (Age 30)
- Research-based Administrator, the Doctor's helpful assistant.
- A mature, beautiful, and capable lady.
- Good at problem solving.

Emily (Age 13)
- Smart, responsible, and adaptive.
- Calm under pressure, slightly vain.
- Computer savvy.

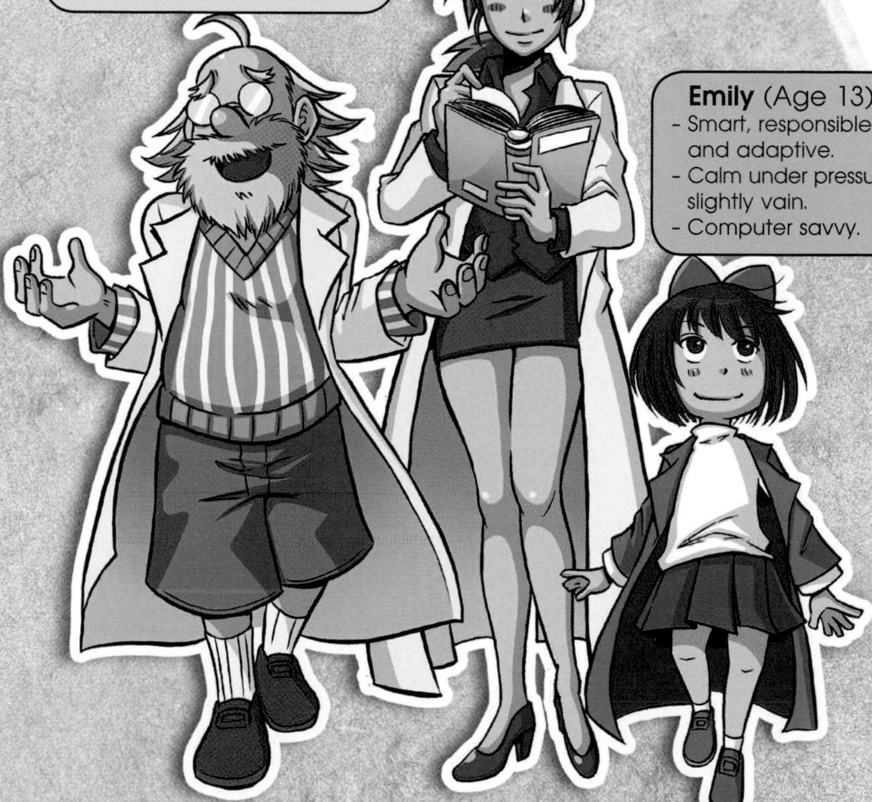

Particle Transmitter
- One of Dr. Da Vinci's most important inventions.
- Able to teleport the team to any period of time and space to execute their missions.
- Able to send urgently needed items to the team at any time.

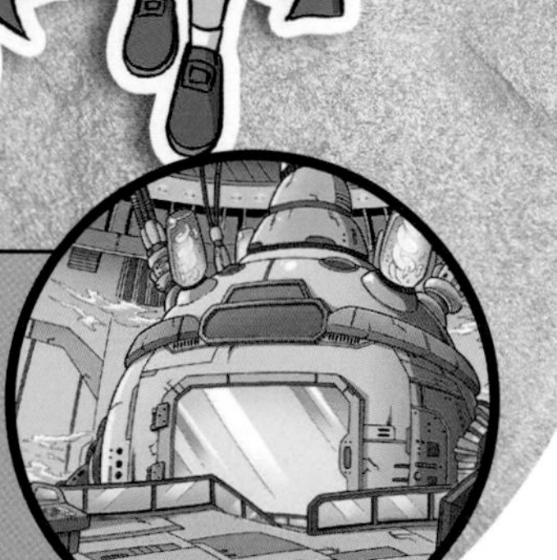

PREVIOUSLY...

A massive earthquake sent the DINOSAUR EXPLORERS team millions of years into the past, and when they first emerged in the Cambrian, they didn't know what to do! Though they managed to jump away in time (literally!) to avoid sinister Silurian sea life, they found that their Particle Transmitter only allowed them to jump several million years at a time – a problem when you're over 500 million years in the past!

Cambrian

Ordovician

Silurian

Devonian

This came to a head in the Silurian when their worries and despair drove them to fight among themselves. Incensed by Rain's behavior, Emily decided to set out with the DINOSAUR EXPLORERS to prove herself – and prove herself she did, facing everything from giant squid to sand-burrowing sea scorpions with guts and gusto!

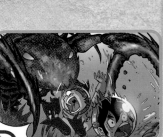

Thankfully, our seven surprise time travellers managed to escape the Silurian, only to end up facing the Devonian's major maulers, the Ichthyostega and Placodermi! Only a large dose of luck and dried fish saw them make their escape!

014

Things only got worse in the Carboniferous when our gang nearly became Happy Meals for some super-sized bugs! Giant spiders, huge dragonflies and enormous frogs (they might not have been bugs, but they were BIG!) all stood in their way as they attempted to study and escape this perilous period.

They then found themselves in the Permian, stuck with the proto-reptiles that would evolve into dinosaurs! Things only got more complicated when they discovered that their latest assignment included babysitting. Though not much for escort missions, our heroes successfully pulled it off in time to jump... to the Triassic!

| Carboniferous |
| Permian |
| Triassic |
| Jurassic |
| Cretaceous |
| Tertiary |
| Quaternary |

The Triassic saw our heroes face their greatest challenge yet– themselves! Tensions in the group caused the bonds of friendship between them to fray, and things got worse when dinosaurs entered into the mix! Thankfully, they managed to patch things up before they had to patch themselves up, and made their escape from some of history's earliest predatory dinosaurs!

*The size of this graphic novel's critters are exaggerated, and do not really represent the true sizes of the creatures.. Hey, it makes for a more visually exciting story!

CHAPTER 1
PAST, PRESENT, FUTURE!

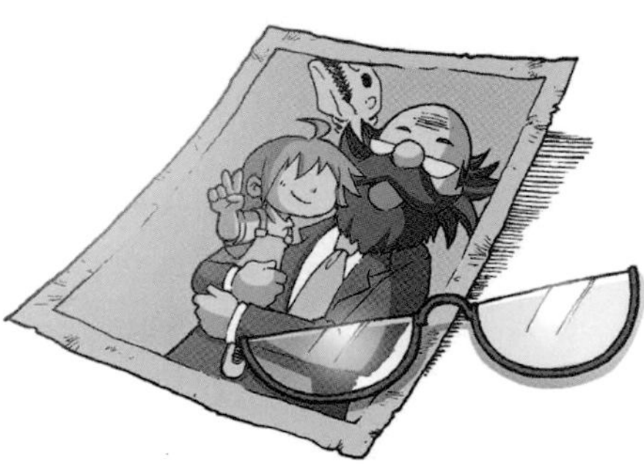

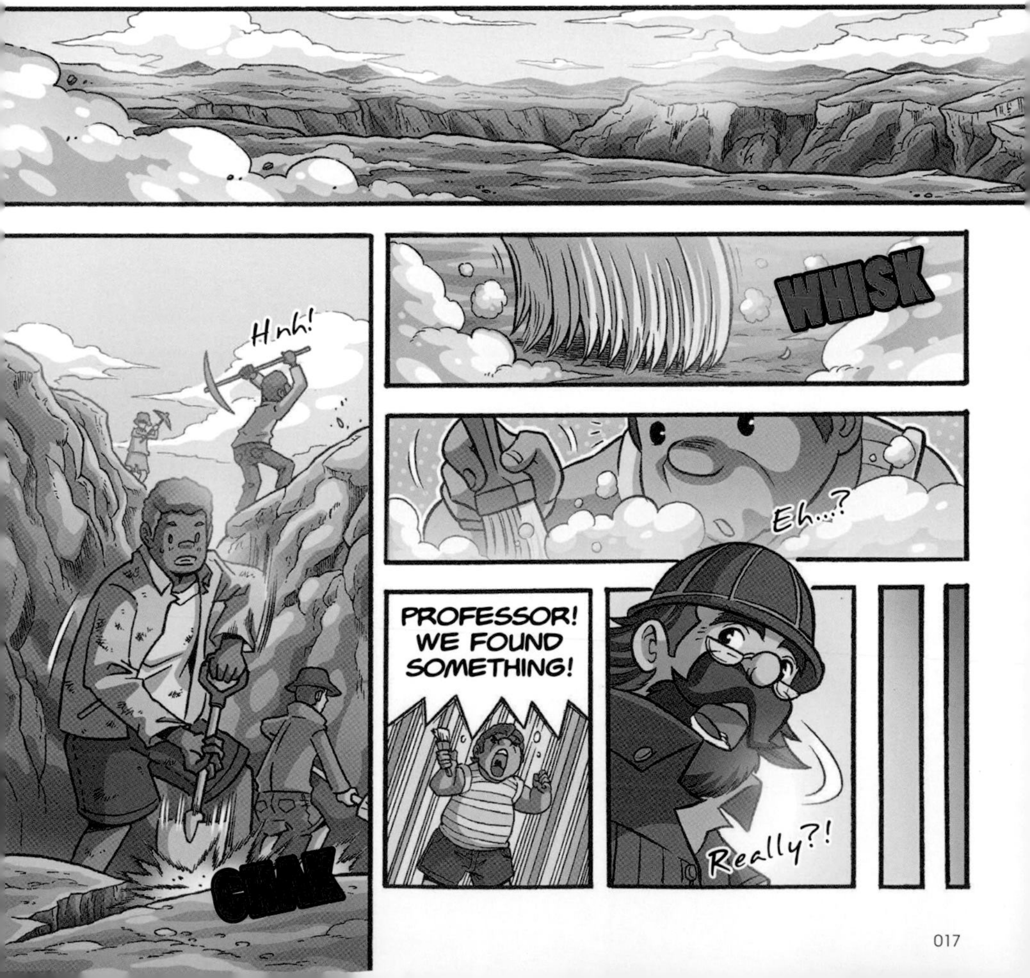

Hnh!
CHAK
WHISK
Eh...?
PROFESSOR! WE FOUND SOMETHING!
Really?!

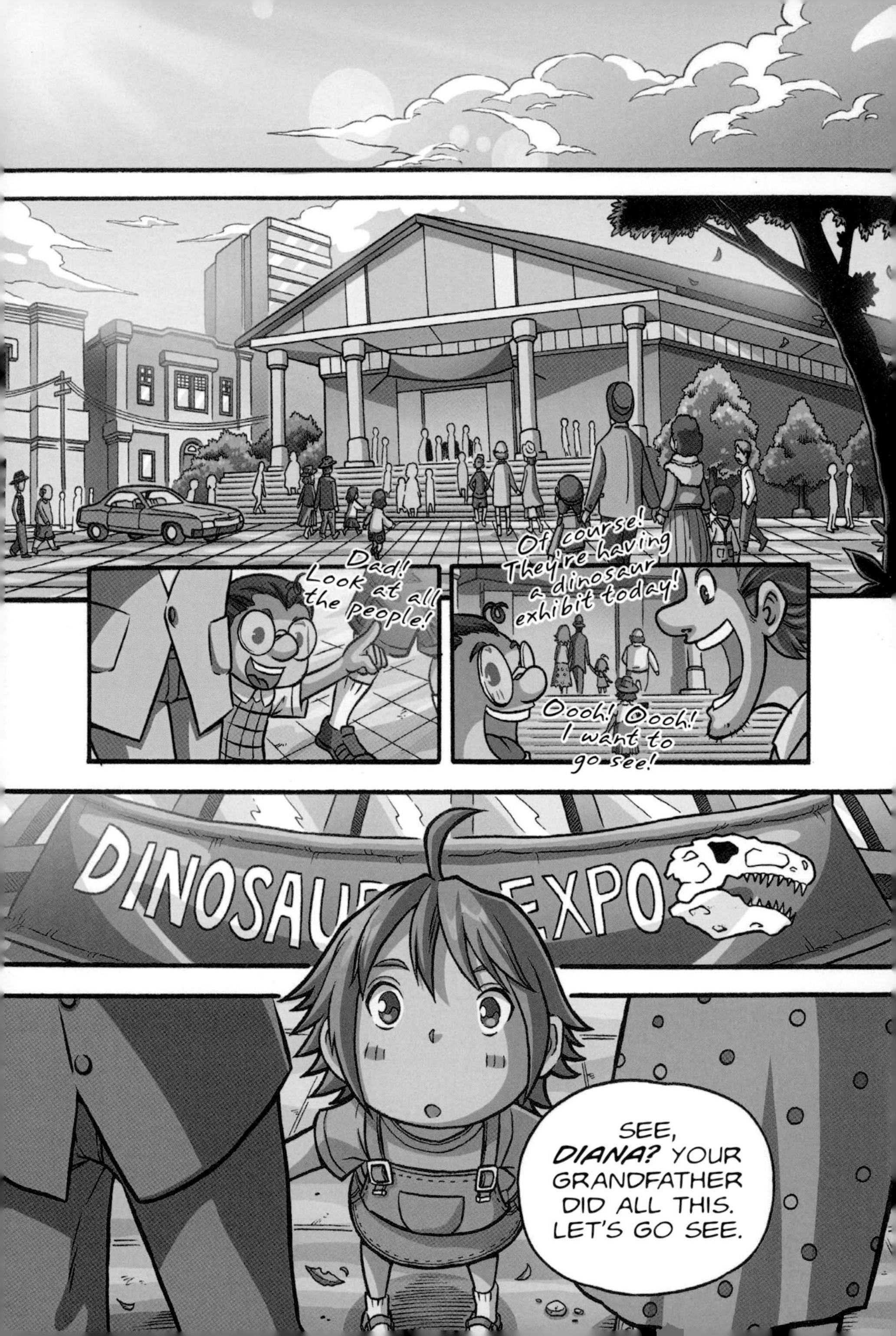
Dad! Look at all the people!
Of course! They're having a dinosaur exhibit today!
Oooh! Oooh! I want to go see!
DINOSAUR EXPO
SEE, DIANA? YOUR GRANDFATHER DID ALL THIS. LET'S GO SEE.

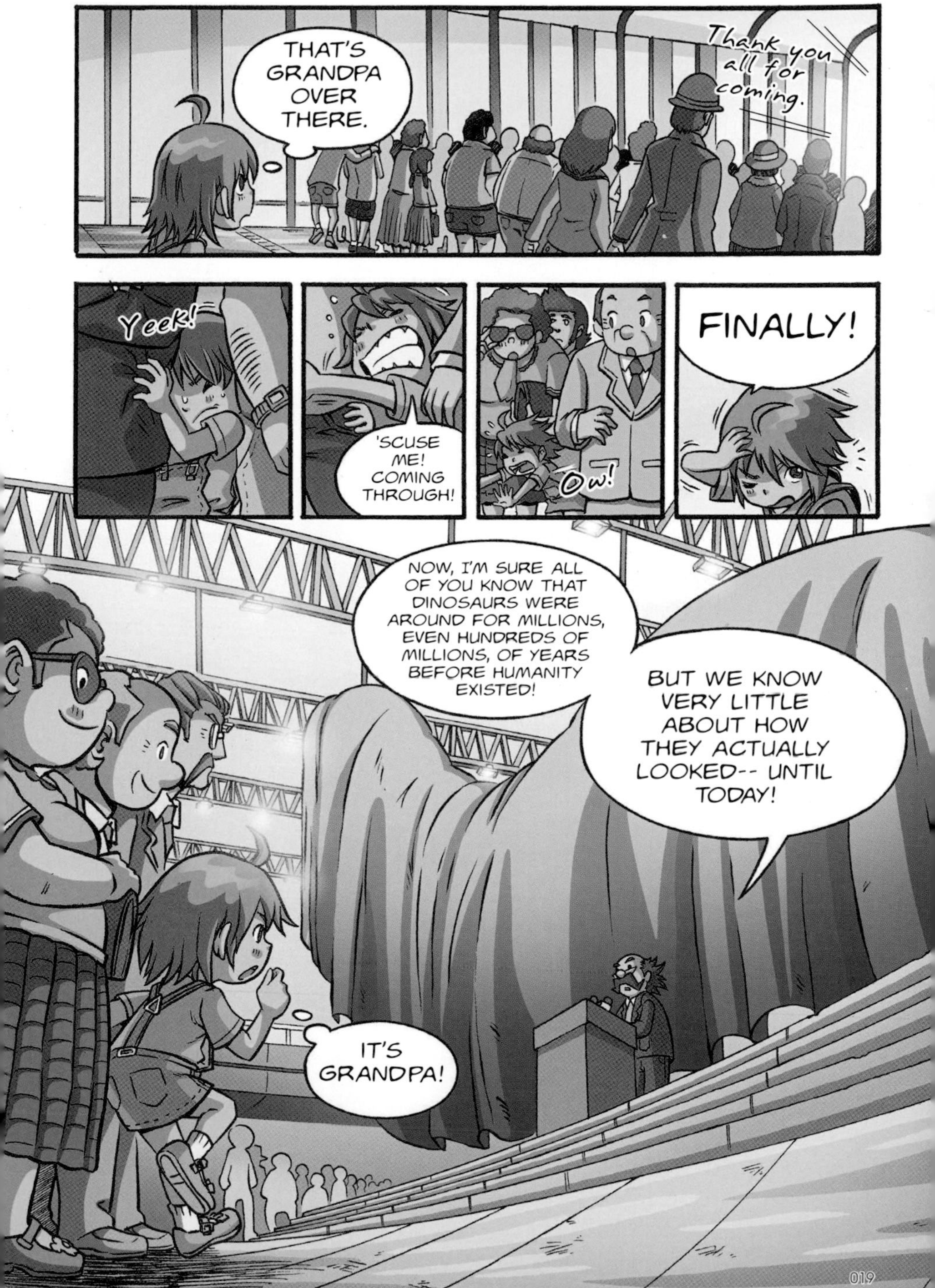
THAT'S GRANDPA OVER THERE.
Thank you all for coming.
Yeek!
'SCUSE ME! COMING THROUGH!
Ow!
FINALLY!
NOW, I'M SURE ALL OF YOU KNOW THAT DINOSAURS WERE AROUND FOR MILLIONS, EVEN HUNDREDS OF MILLIONS, OF YEARS BEFORE HUMANITY EXISTED!
BUT WE KNOW VERY LITTLE ABOUT HOW THEY ACTUALLY LOOKED-- UNTIL TODAY!
IT'S GRANDPA!

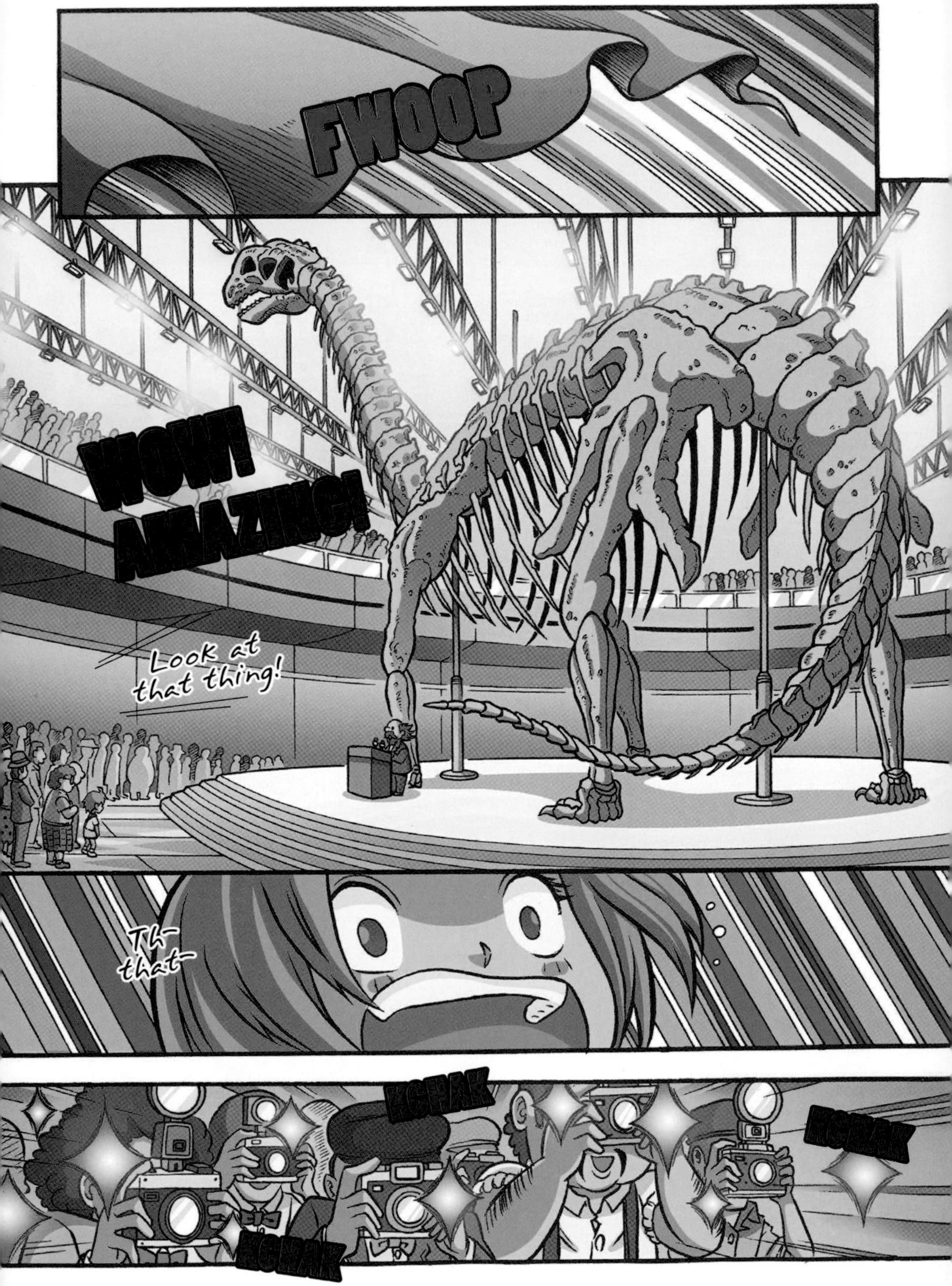
FWOOP
WOW! AMAZING!
Look at that thing!
Th-that-
KCHAK
KCHAK
KCHAK

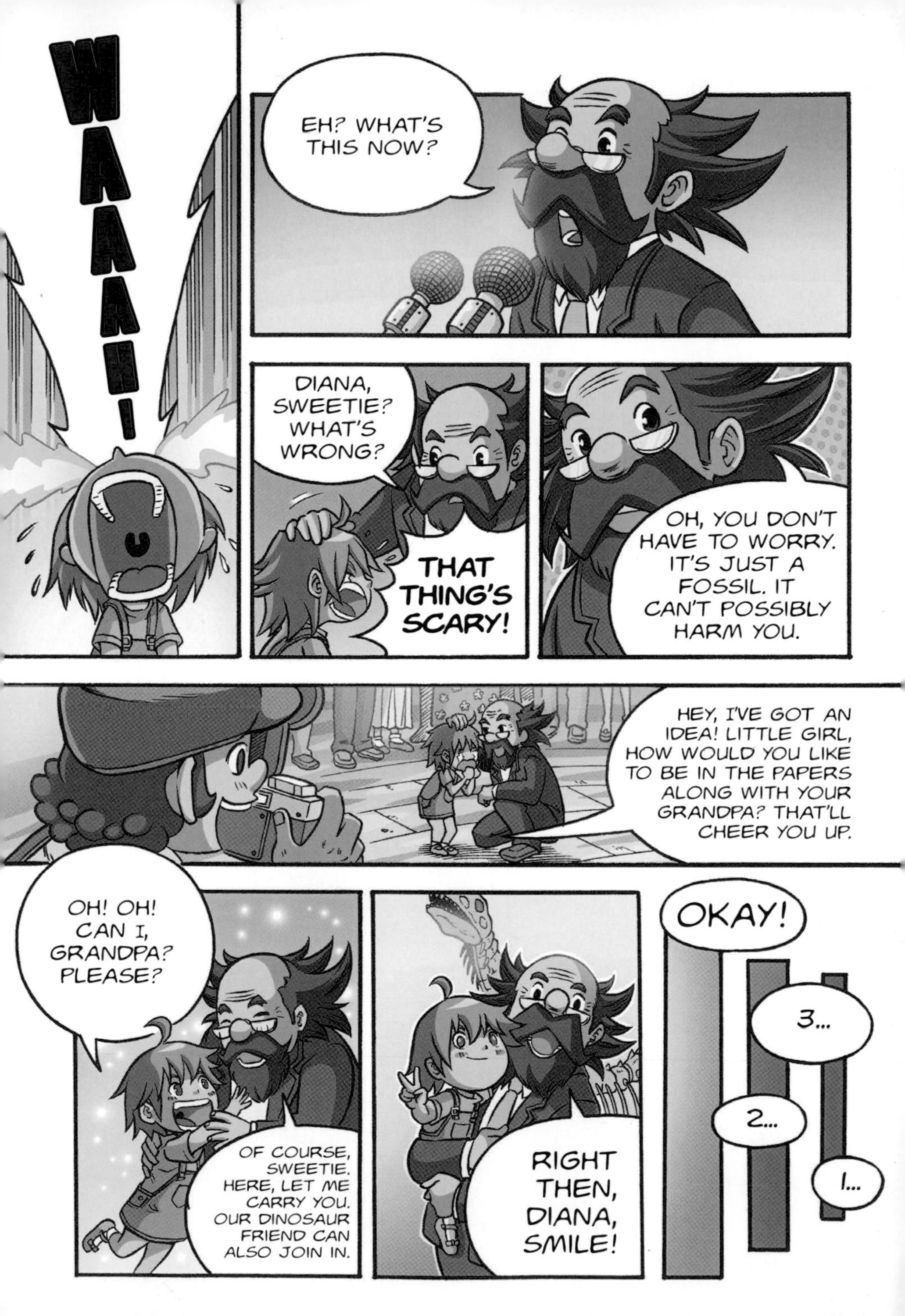
WAAAAH!
EH? WHAT'S THIS NOW?
DIANA, SWEETIE? WHAT'S WRONG?
THAT THING'S SCARY!
OH, YOU DON'T HAVE TO WORRY. IT'S JUST A FOSSIL. IT CAN'T POSSIBLY HARM YOU.
HEY, I'VE GOT AN IDEA! LITTLE GIRL, HOW WOULD YOU LIKE TO BE IN THE PAPERS ALONG WITH YOUR GRANDPA? THAT'LL CHEER YOU UP.
OH! OH! CAN I, GRANDPA? PLEASE?
OF COURSE, SWEETIE. HERE, LET ME CARRY YOU. OUR DINOSAUR FRIEND CAN ALSO JOIN IN.
RIGHT THEN, DIANA, SMILE!
OKAY!
3...
2...
1...

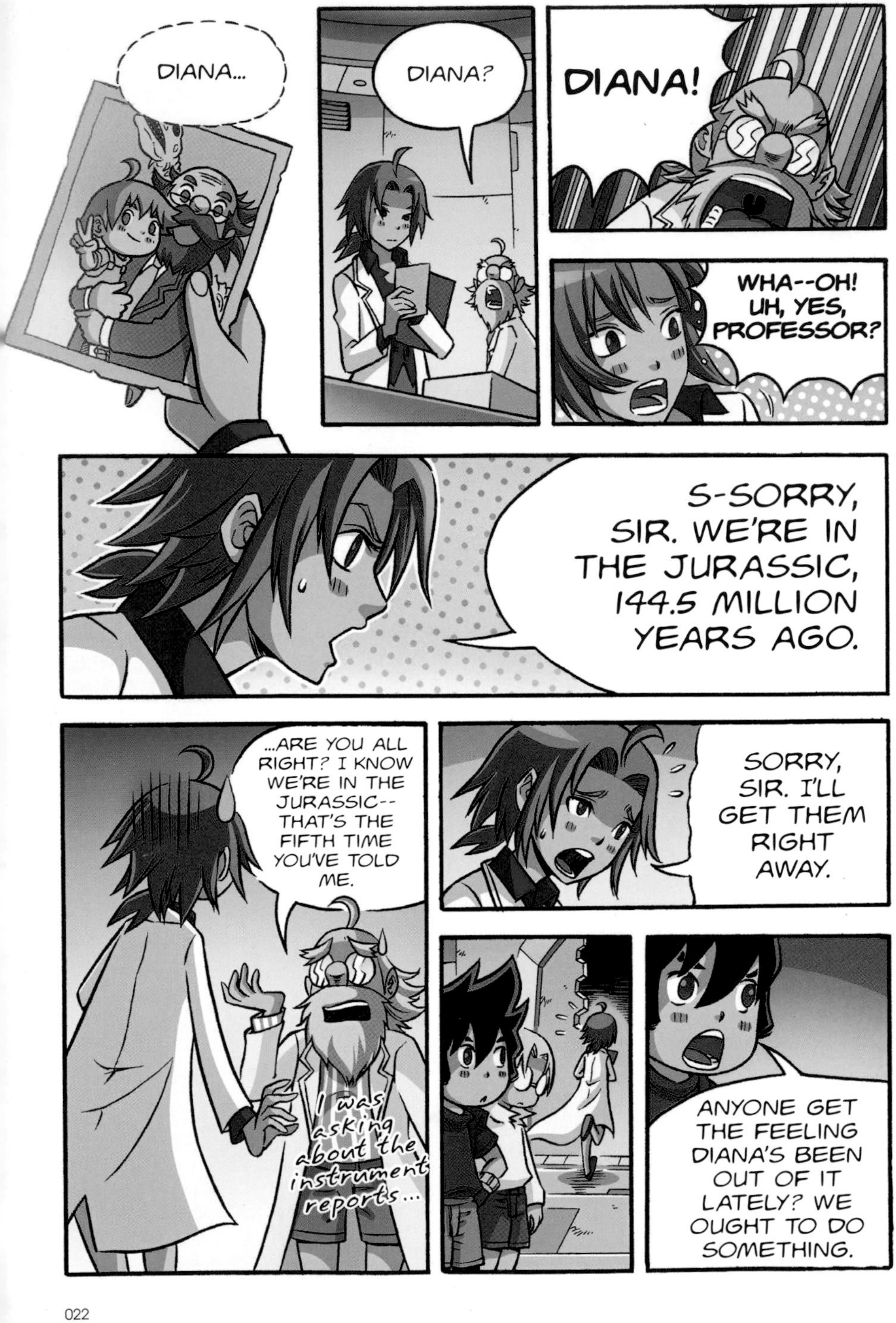
DIANA...
DIANA?
DIANA!
WHA--OH! UH, YES, PROFESSOR?
S-SORRY, SIR. WE'RE IN THE JURASSIC, 144.5 MILLION YEARS AGO.
...ARE YOU ALL RIGHT? I KNOW WE'RE IN THE JURASSIC-- THAT'S THE FIFTH TIME YOU'VE TOLD ME.
I was asking about the instrument reports...
SORRY, SIR. I'LL GET THEM RIGHT AWAY.
ANYONE GET THE FEELING DIANA'S BEEN OUT OF IT LATELY? WE OUGHT TO DO SOMETHING.

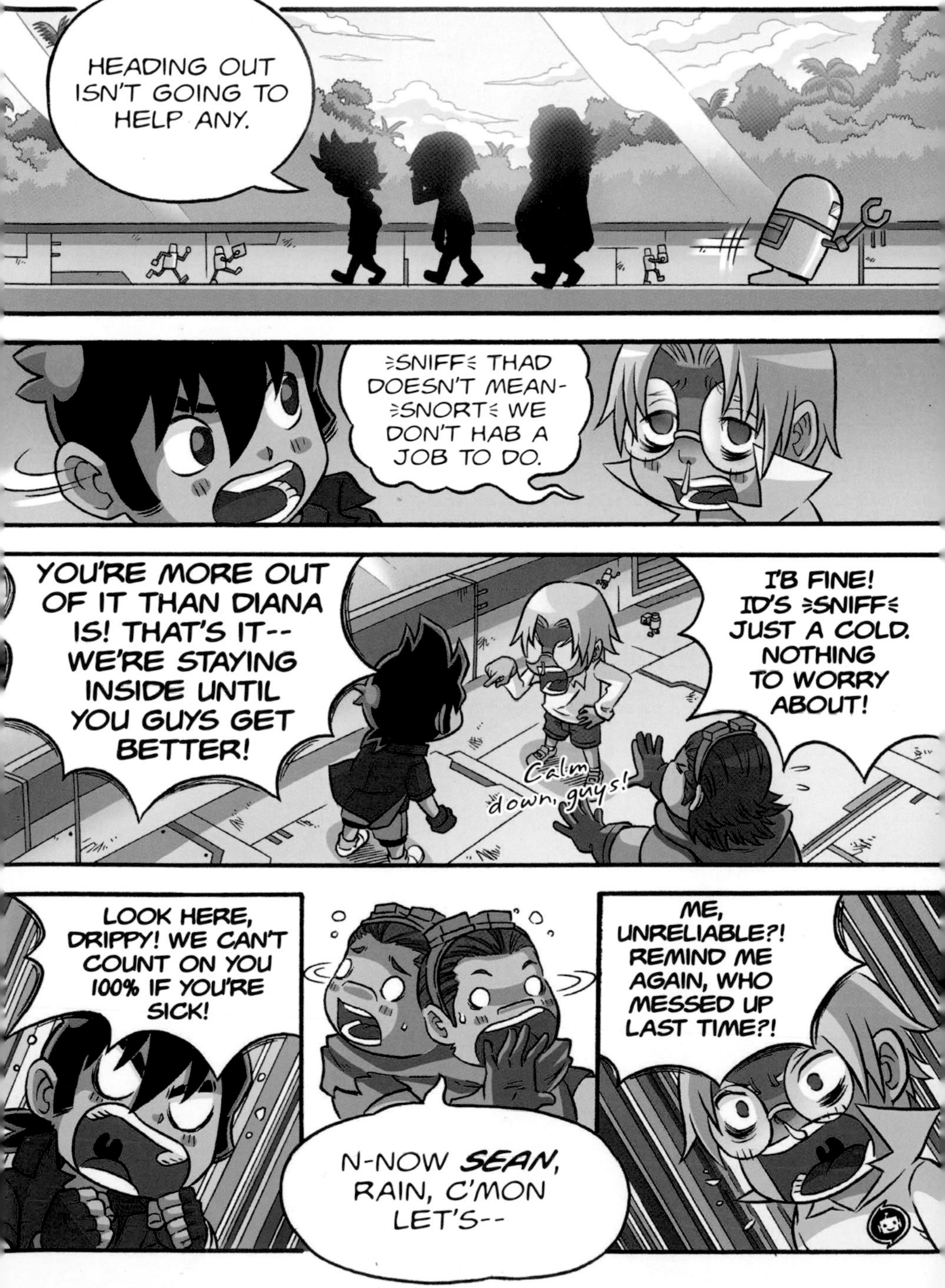
HEADING OUT ISN'T GOING TO HELP ANY.
⪫SNIFF⪪ THAD DOESN'T MEAN- ⪫SNORT⪪ WE DON'T HAB A JOB TO DO.
YOU'RE MORE OUT OF IT THAN DIANA IS! THAT'S IT-- WE'RE STAYING INSIDE UNTIL YOU GUYS GET BETTER!
I'B FINE! ID'S ⪫SNIFF⪪ JUST A COLD. NOTHING TO WORRY ABOUT!
Calm down, guys!
LOOK HERE, DRIPPY! WE CAN'T COUNT ON YOU 100% IF YOU'RE SICK!
ME, UNRELIABLE?! REMIND ME AGAIN, WHO MESSED UP LAST TIME?!
N-NOW SEAN, RAIN, C'MON LET'S--

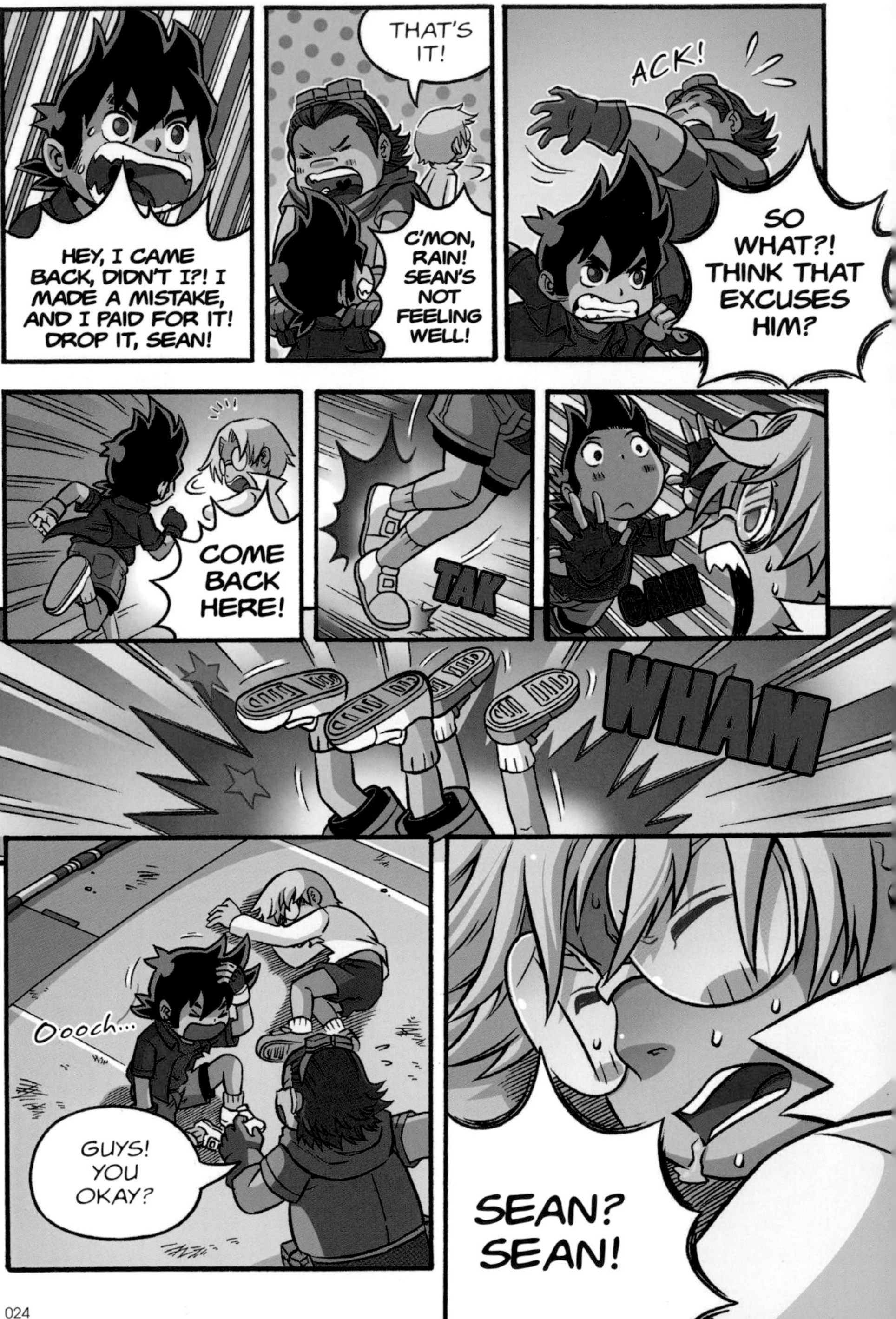
HEY, I CAME BACK, DIDN'T I?! I MADE A MISTAKE, AND I PAID FOR IT! DROP IT, SEAN!
THAT'S IT!
C'MON, RAIN! SEAN'S NOT FEELING WELL!
ACK!
SO WHAT?! THINK THAT EXCUSES HIM?
COME BACK HERE!
TAK
WHAM
Oooch...
GUYS! YOU OKAY?
SEAN? SEAN!

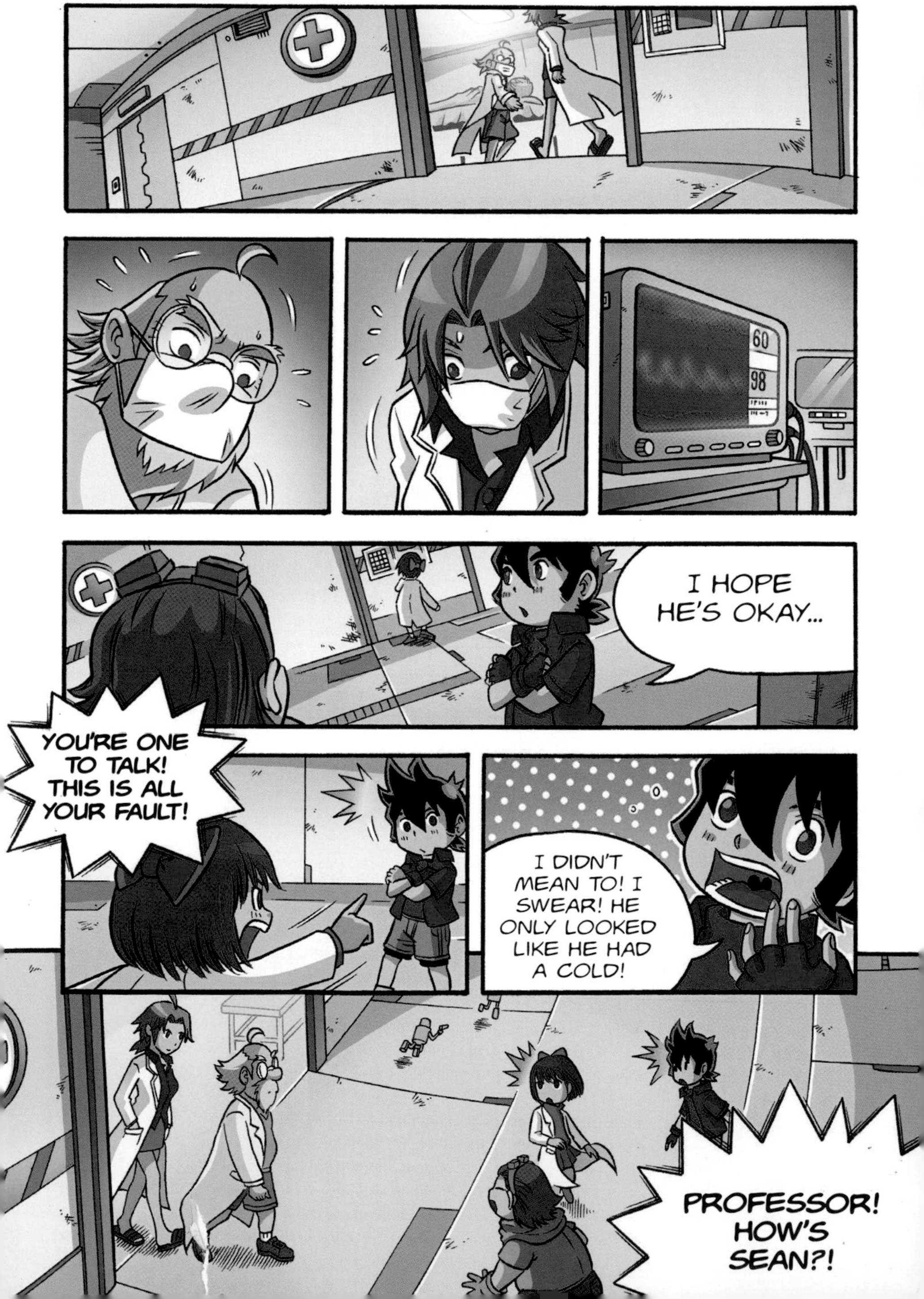
I HOPE HE'S OKAY...
YOU'RE ONE TO TALK! THIS IS ALL YOUR FAULT!
I DIDN'T MEAN TO! I SWEAR! HE ONLY LOOKED LIKE HE HAD A COLD!
PROFESSOR! HOW'S SEAN?!

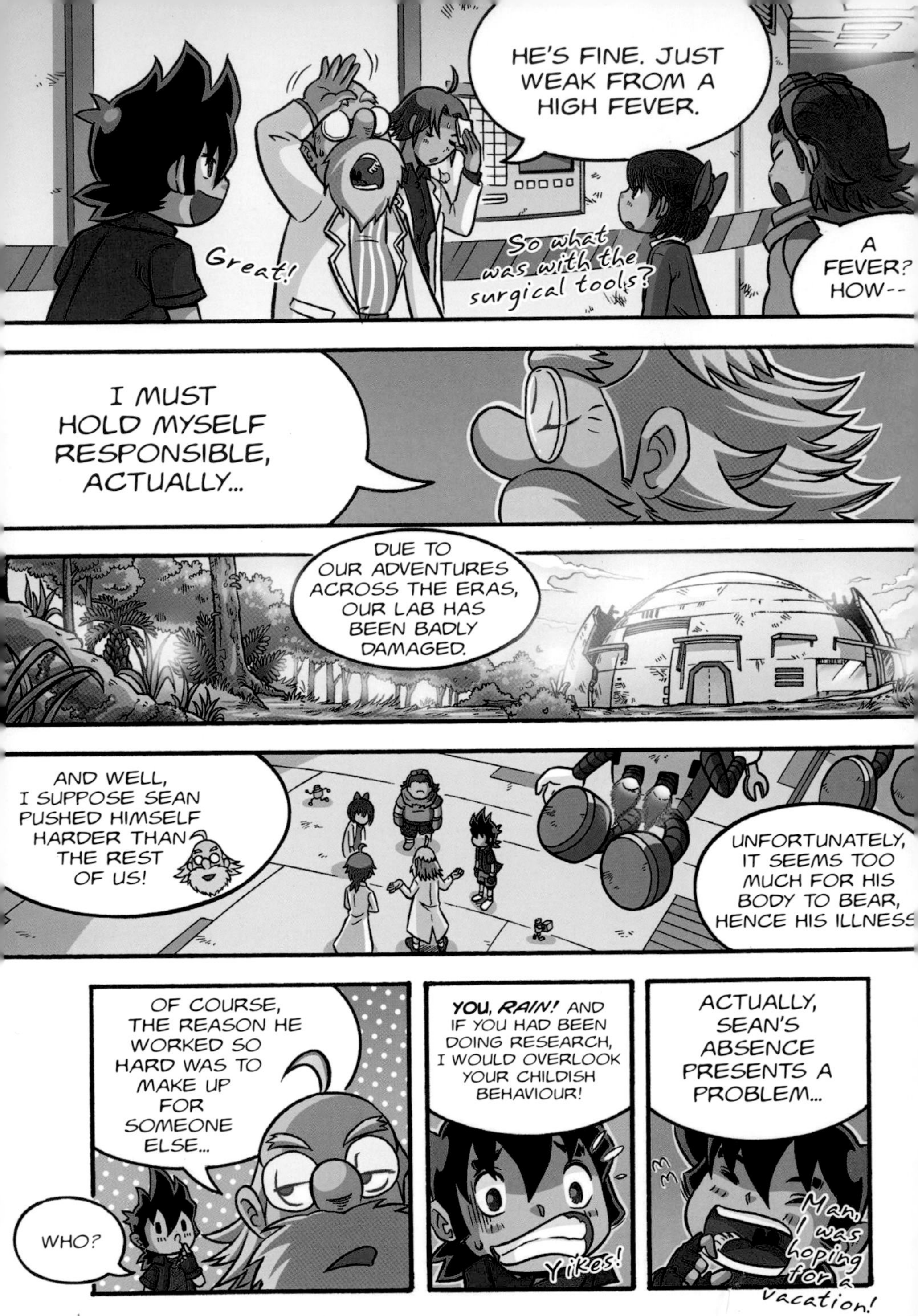
HE'S FINE. JUST WEAK FROM A HIGH FEVER.
Great!
So what was with the surgical tools?
A FEVER? HOW--
I MUST HOLD MYSELF RESPONSIBLE, ACTUALLY...
DUE TO OUR ADVENTURES ACROSS THE ERAS, OUR LAB HAS BEEN BADLY DAMAGED.
AND WELL, I SUPPOSE SEAN PUSHED HIMSELF HARDER THAN THE REST OF US!
UNFORTUNATELY, IT SEEMS TOO MUCH FOR HIS BODY TO BEAR, HENCE HIS ILLNESS
OF COURSE, THE REASON HE WORKED SO HARD WAS TO MAKE UP FOR SOMEONE ELSE...
WHO?
YOU, RAIN! AND IF YOU HAD BEEN DOING RESEARCH, I WOULD OVERLOOK YOUR CHILDISH BEHAVIOUR!
Yikes!
ACTUALLY, SEAN'S ABSENCE PRESENTS A PROBLEM...
Man, I was hoping for a vacation!

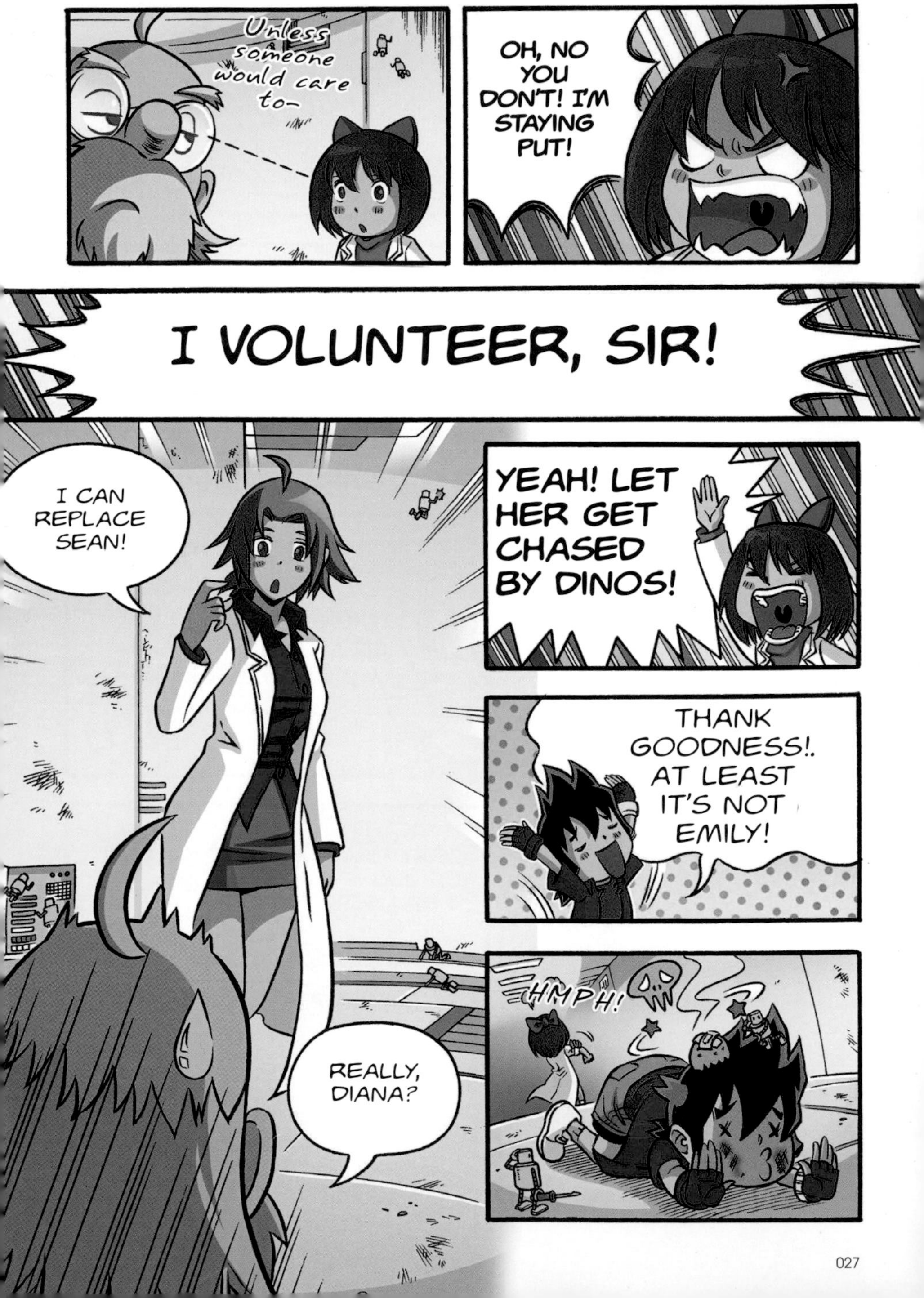
Unless someone would care to-
OH, NO YOU DON'T! I'M STAYING PUT!
I VOLUNTEER, SIR!
I CAN REPLACE SEAN!
YEAH! LET HER GET CHASED BY DINOS!
THANK GOODNESS!. AT LEAST IT'S NOT EMILY!
REALLY, DIANA?
HMPH!

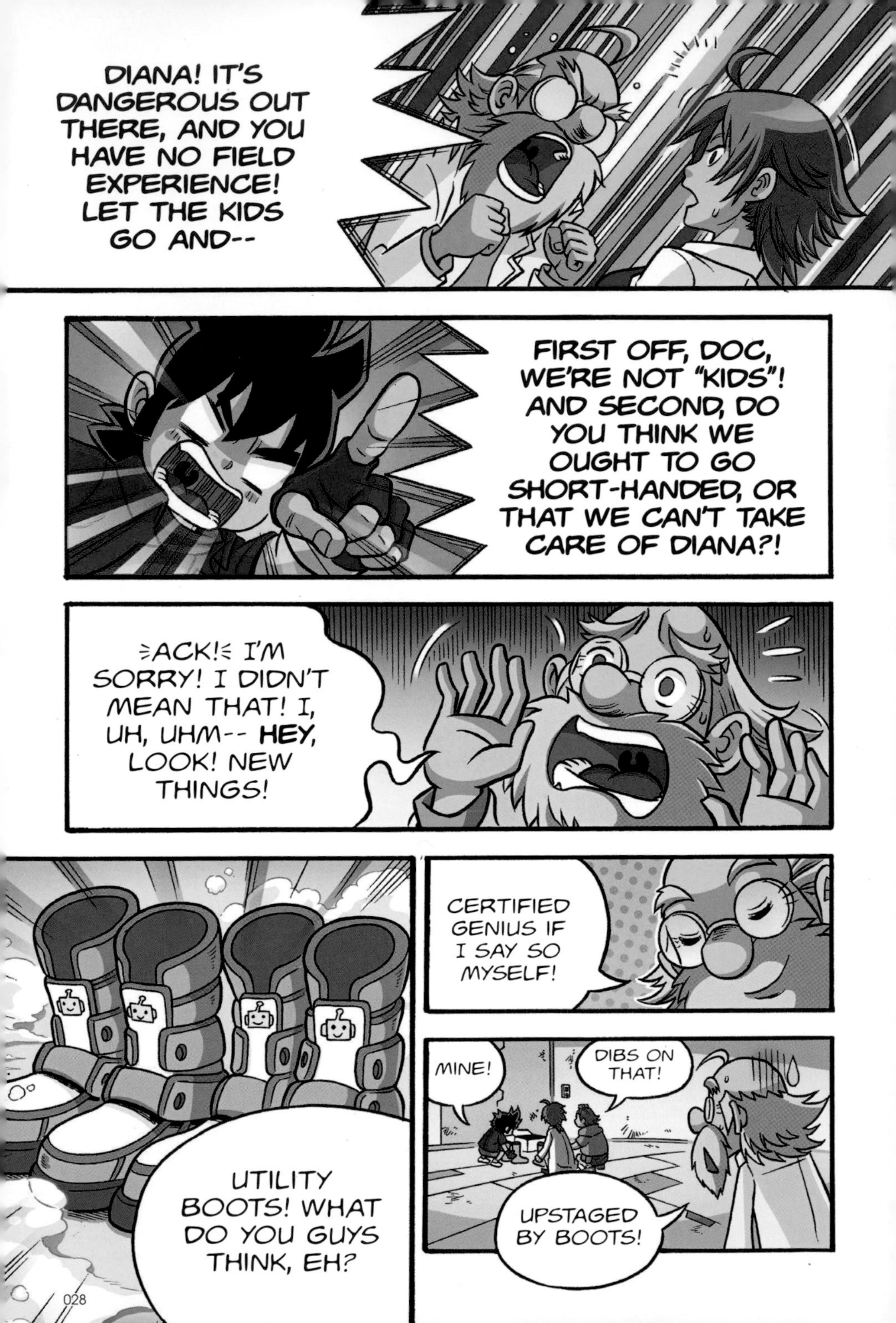

DIANA! IT'S DANGEROUS OUT THERE, AND YOU HAVE NO FIELD EXPERIENCE! LET THE KIDS GO AND--
FIRST OFF, DOC, WE'RE NOT "KIDS"! AND SECOND, DO YOU THINK WE OUGHT TO GO SHORT-HANDED, OR THAT WE CAN'T TAKE CARE OF DIANA?!
ACK! I'M SORRY! I DIDN'T MEAN THAT! I, UH, UHM-- **HEY**, LOOK! NEW THINGS!
UTILITY BOOTS! WHAT DO YOU GUYS THINK, EH?
CERTIFIED GENIUS IF I SAY SO MYSELF!
MINE!
DIBS ON THAT!
UPSTAGED BY BOOTS!

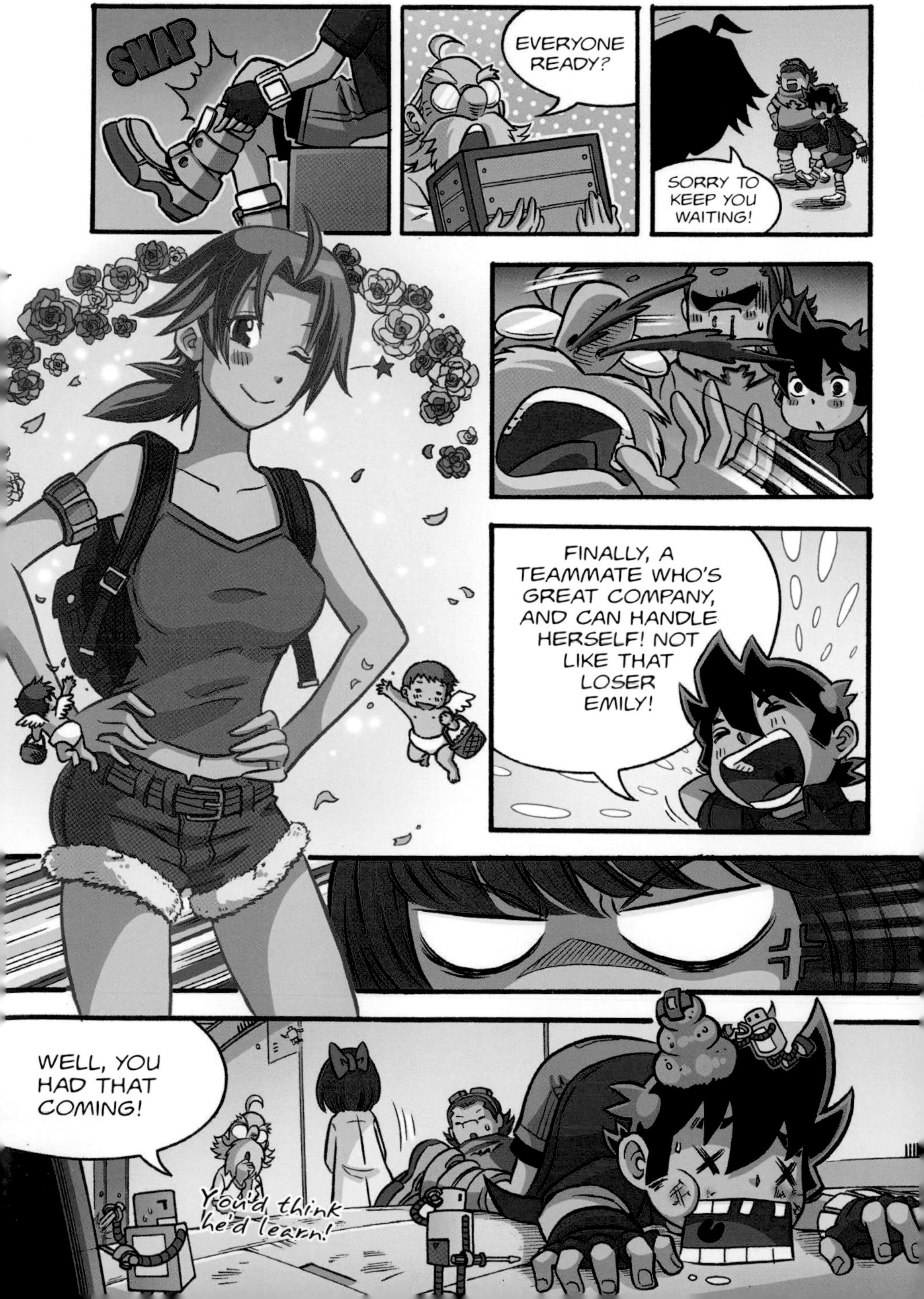
SNAP
EVERYONE READY?
SORRY TO KEEP YOU WAITING!
FINALLY, A TEAMMATE WHO'S GREAT COMPANY, AND CAN HANDLE HERSELF! NOT LIKE THAT LOSER EMILY!
WELL, YOU HAD THAT COMING!
You'd think he'd learn!

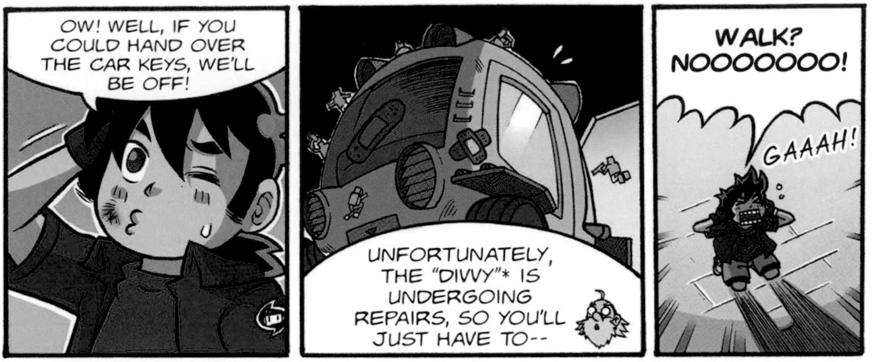
OW! WELL, IF YOU COULD HAND OVER THE CAR KEYS, WE'LL BE OFF!
UNFORTUNATELY, THE "DIVVY"* IS UNDERGOING REPAIRS, SO YOU'LL JUST HAVE TO--
WALK? NOOOOOOO!
GAAAH!

*A SPECIAL SOLAR-POWERED CAR INVENTED BY DR. DA VINCI.

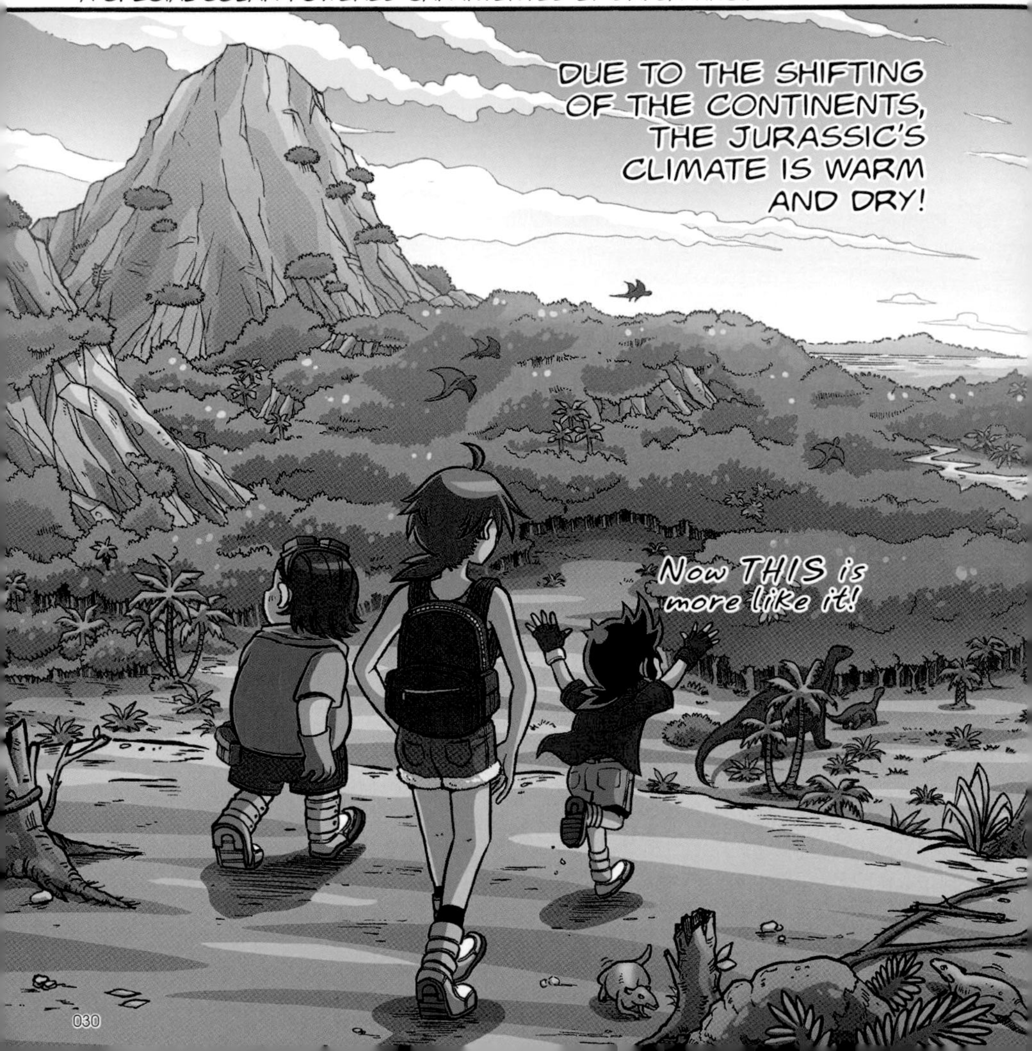
DUE TO THE SHIFTING OF THE CONTINENTS, THE JURASSIC'S CLIMATE IS WARM AND DRY!
Now THIS is more like it!

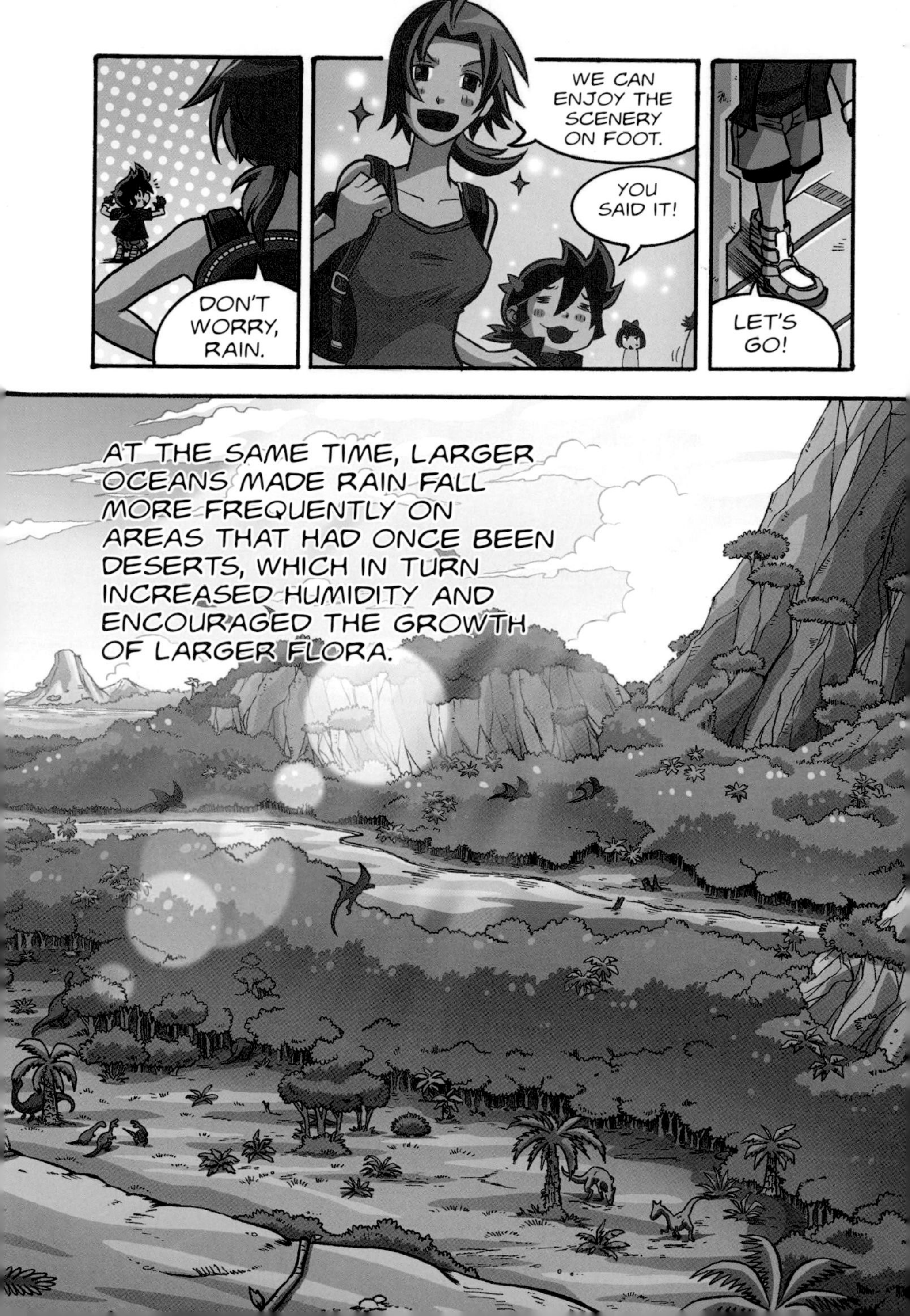
DON'T WORRY, RAIN.
WE CAN ENJOY THE SCENERY ON FOOT.
YOU SAID IT!
LET'S GO!
AT THE SAME TIME, LARGER OCEANS MADE RAIN FALL MORE FREQUENTLY ON AREAS THAT HAD ONCE BEEN DESERTS, WHICH IN TURN INCREASED HUMIDITY AND ENCOURAGED THE GROWTH OF LARGER FLORA.

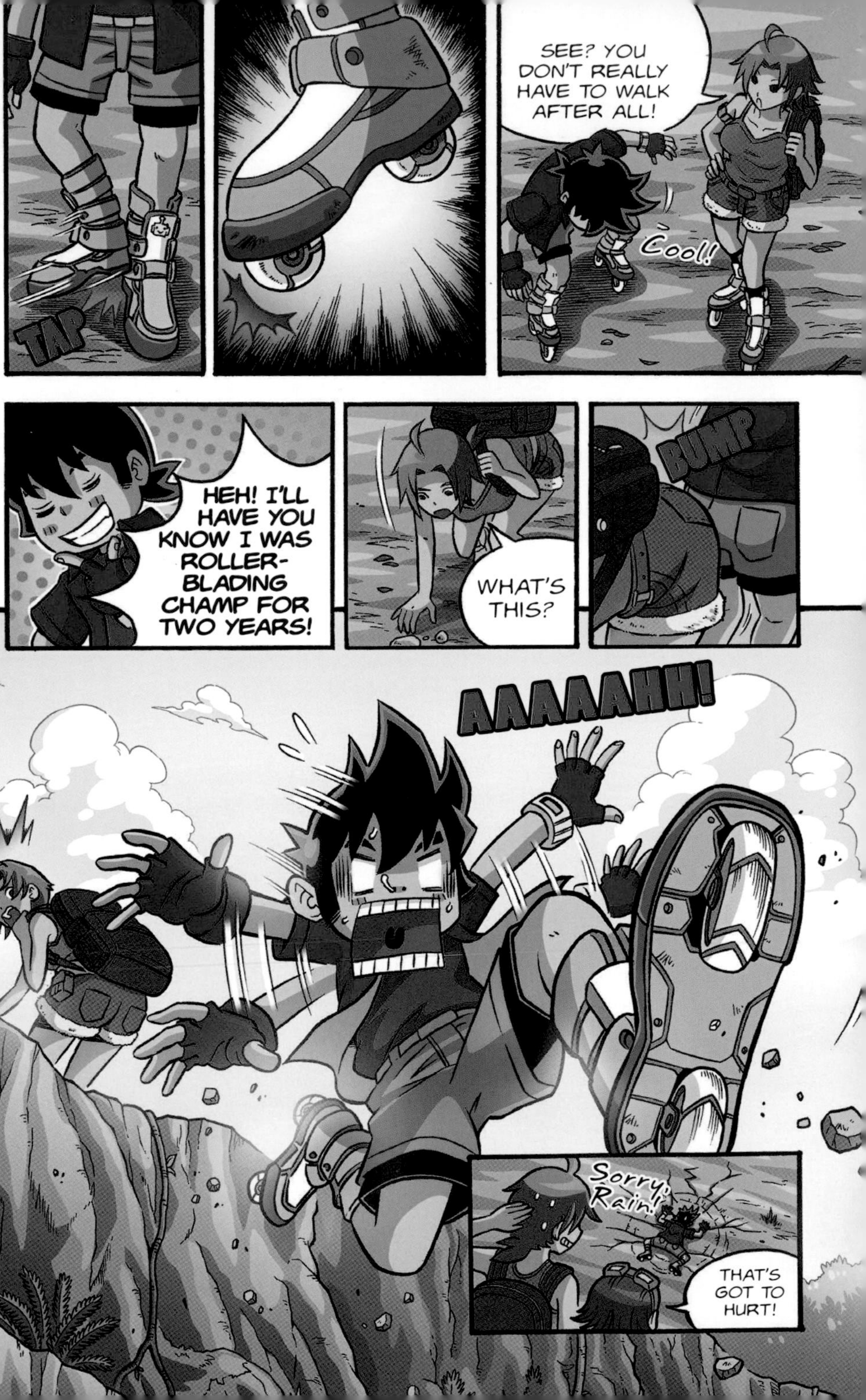
TAP
SEE? YOU DON'T REALLY HAVE TO WALK AFTER ALL!
Cool!
HEH! I'LL HAVE YOU KNOW I WAS ROLLER-BLADING CHAMP FOR TWO YEARS!
WHAT'S THIS?
BUMP
AAAAAHH!
Sorry, Rain!
THAT'S GOT TO HURT!

CONTINENTS OF THE JURASSIC

In the early Jurassic, the Pangaean supercontinent began breaking up into the northern continent of Gondwana and the southern continent of Laurentia; these two continents would later split as well and form today's continents. The future Atlantic, dividing Africa and North America, also began to expand and Antarctica, India, and Australia began to take shape.

Ancient Mediterranean
Pangaea

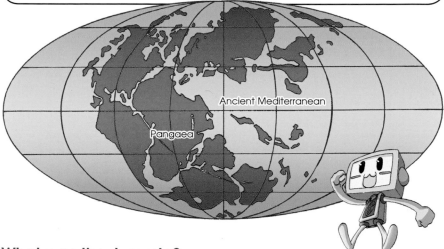

What was the Jurassic?

The Jurassic was the second period of the Mesozoic, some 199.6 to 145.5 million years ago, though when it ended, is still hotly debated, due to different clues offered by ancient rock formations. That said, the advent of the Jurassic can be traced to a major occurrence called the Triassic-Jurassic extinction event. This wiped out most of the organic life present during the Triassic, paving the way for the dinosaurs.

What animals were around back then?

Dinosaurs dominated the Jurassic, most were from the orders Ornithischia and Saurischia. There were also insects and smaller reptiles galore, with a few small mammals as well. Marine reptiles predominated, and pterosaurs ruled the skies.

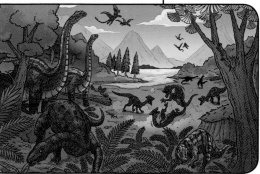

What does "dinosaur" mean?

Though fossils have been discovered prior the 19th century, people saw them as the bones of monsters. It was not until the 19th century that British paleontologist Gideon Mantell published his findings – that these were the bones of extinct creatures. In 1842, another British paleontologist named Richard Owen dubbed them "dinosaurs," from the Latin, "dinosauria," meaning "terrible lizards."

How do we know they were dinosaurs and not fantasy creatures?

By measuring the level of radioactive isotopes in fossils as well as the geological layers of soil where they were found, and applying their knowledge of anatomy, paleontologists are not only able to tell just how long ago these creatures lived, but also how their bodies were put together.

How fossils are formed

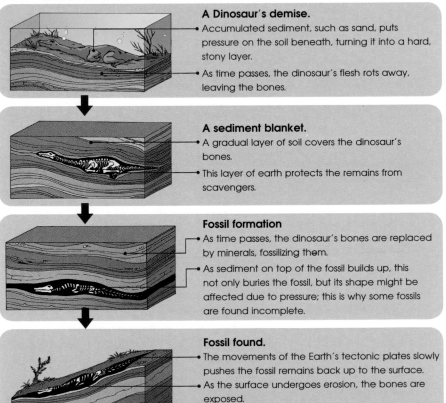

A Dinosaur's demise.
- Accumulated sediment, such as sand, puts pressure on the soil beneath, turning it into a hard, stony layer.
- As time passes, the dinosaur's flesh rots away, leaving the bones.

A sediment blanket.
- A gradual layer of soil covers the dinosaur's bones.
- This layer of earth protects the remains from scavengers.

Fossil formation
- As time passes, the dinosaur's bones are replaced by minerals, fossilizing them.
- As sediment on top of the fossil builds up, this not only buries the fossil, but its shape might be affected due to pressure; this is why some fossils are found incomplete.

Fossil found.
- The movements of the Earth's tectonic plates slowly pushes the fossil remains back up to the surface.
- As the surface undergoes erosion, the bones are exposed.
- These fossils are delicate; they require careful excavation and extensive preservation, without which they could be irreparably damaged.

What other fossils are there?

Bones are not the only things that are fossilized; dinosaur dung and footprints are other key examples, and although obviously difficult (if not impossible) to tell what specific dinosaur made these tracks without bones nearby, such fossils are valuable clues on their own.

Typical dinosaur footprints

Carnosaur footprint

Large bipedal (walks on two legs) carnivores usually leave distinctive footprints with three clawed toes in front and one at the back.

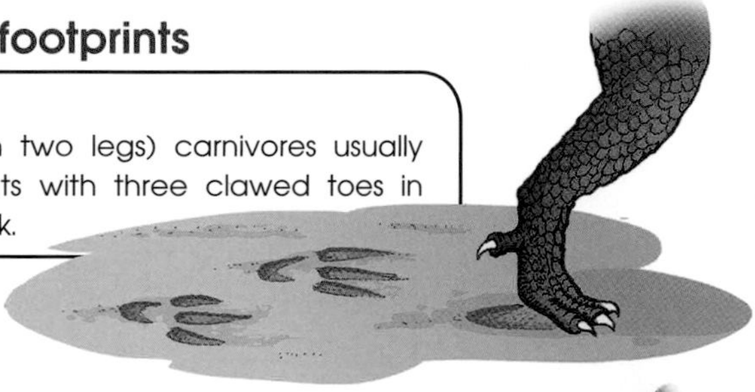

Coelurosaur footprint

With their light bodies, coelurosaurs left birdlike footprints.

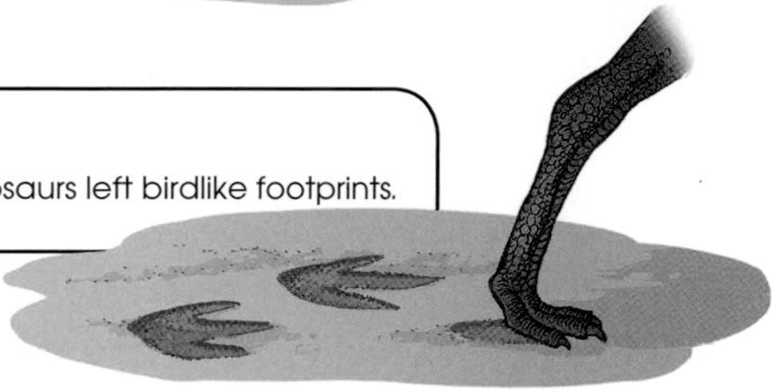

Ceratopsid footprints

Heavy quadrepedal (walks on four legs) dinosaurs, ceratopsids (such as the Triceratops and Microceratus) left deep footprints that showed their front legs being shorter than their hind legs.

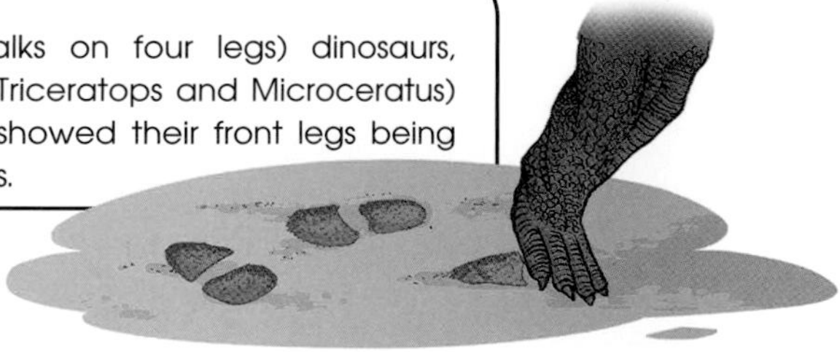

Sauropod footprint

Heavier than ceratopsids, sauropods left huge, deep, rounded footprints

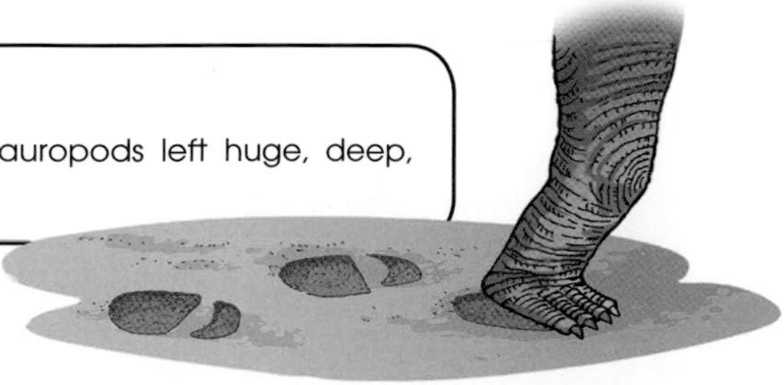

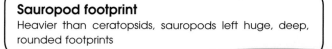

Know your dinos!

Ceratosaurus was a powerful bipedal theropod carnosaur of the late Jurassic. Its powerful hind legs and muscles gave it an edge in hunting its prey.

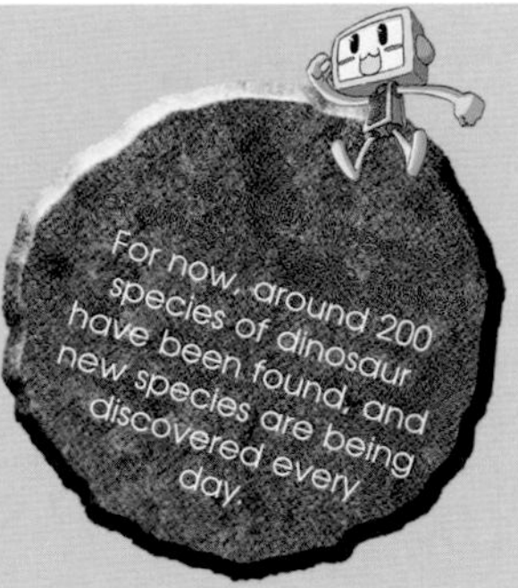
For now, around 200 species of dinosaur have been found, and new species are being discovered every day.

Skin

Though no samples of dinosaur skin survive today, we can theorize about them based on what we know about modern-day climates and animals; some fossils even have imprints of skin. For the most part, dinosaurs might have been camouflaged, and their skins should have been thick enough to withstand insect and parasite attacks, as well as the sun. Some dinosaurs even had armored skin.

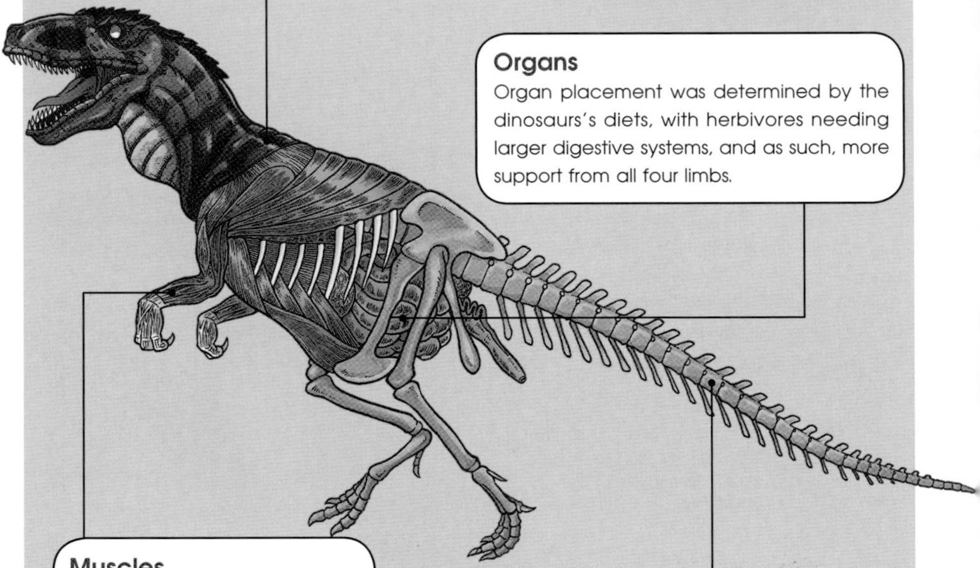

Organs

Organ placement was determined by the dinosaurs's diets, with herbivores needing larger digestive systems, and as such, more support from all four limbs.

Muscles

Large dinosaurs also needed a great deal of muscle mass to move. Unfortunately, their large size meant that most of their strength was used simply to keep them moving and upright, which made them prime targets for smaller, more agile dinosaurs.

Bones

Another component necessary to support a body's weight, many dinosaur bones were hollow to varying degrees just so they would not be too heavy to move. Each species of dinosaur had specially adapted bones to facilitate daily activity, and identifying these bones is necessary for paleontologists to perform proper classification.

CHAPTER 2

DIANA'S BIG DAY OUT

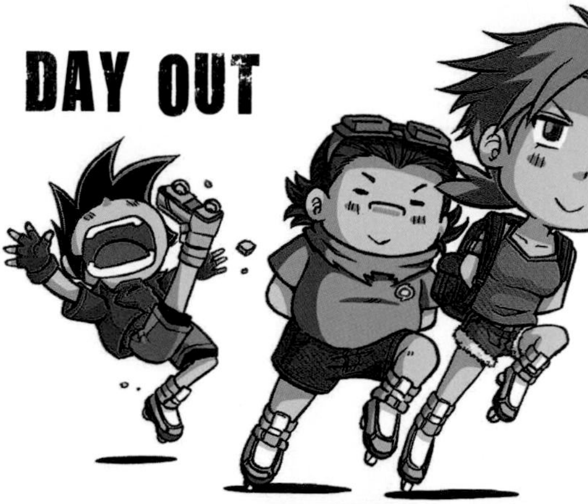

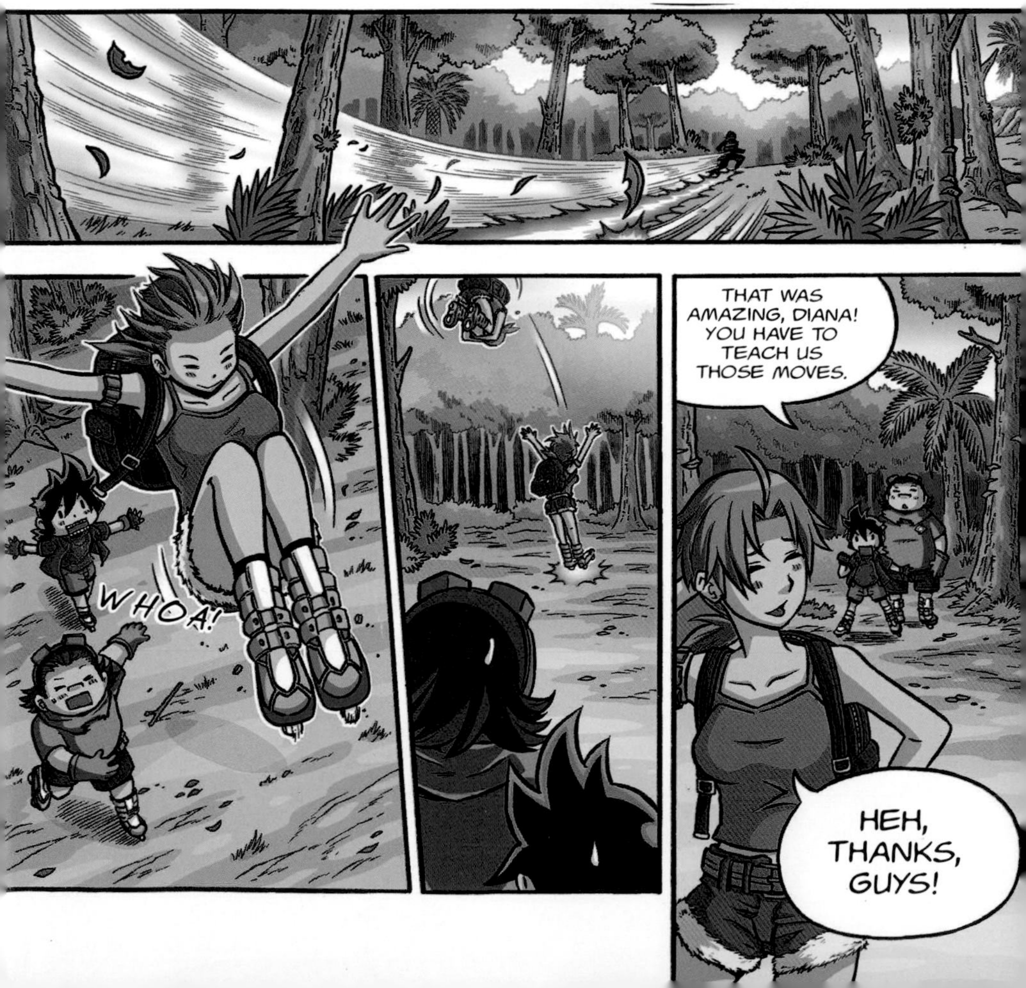
WHOA!
THAT WAS AMAZING, DIANA! YOU HAVE TO TEACH US THOSE MOVES.
HEH, THANKS, GUYS!

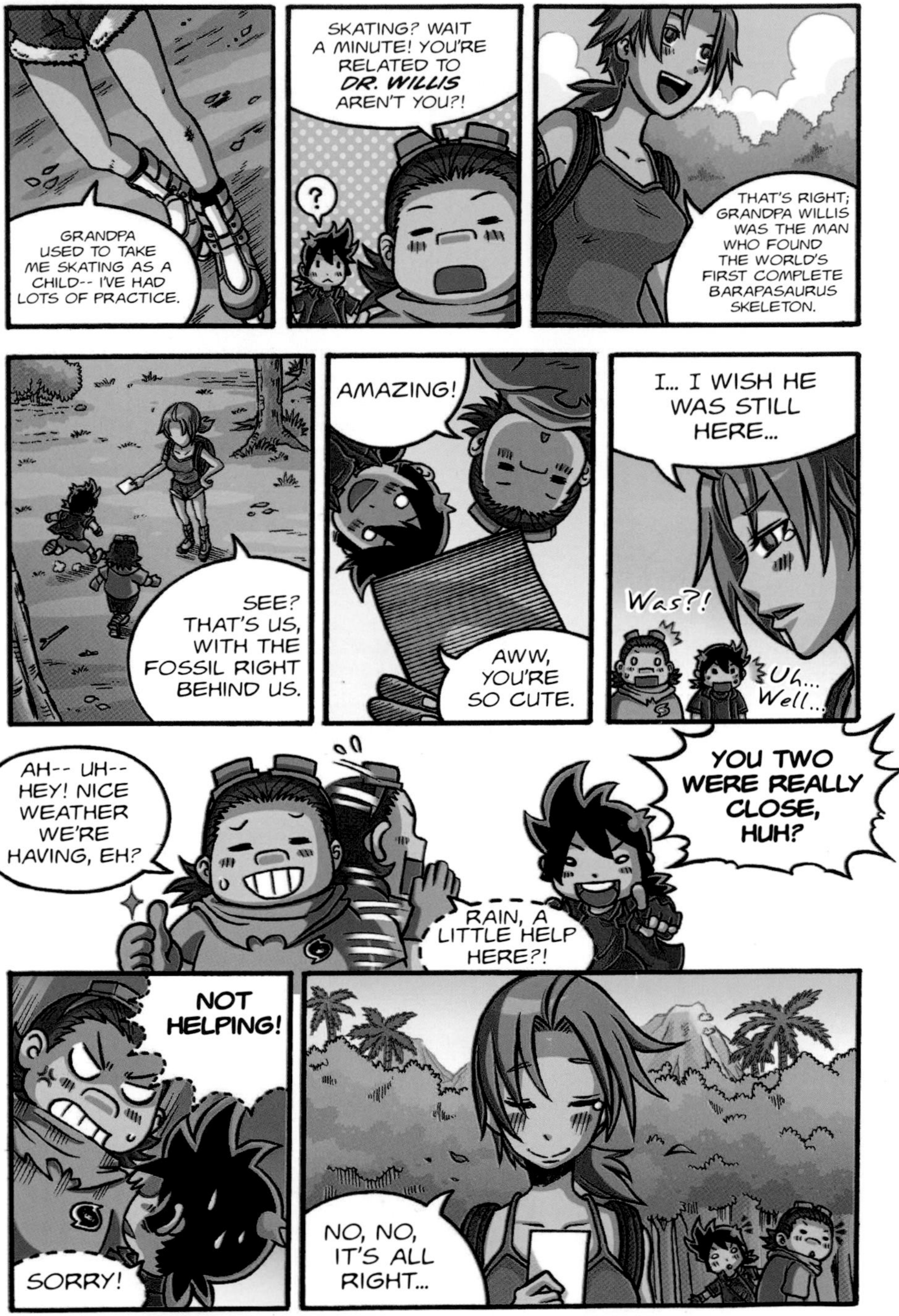
GRANDPA USED TO TAKE ME SKATING AS A CHILD-- I'VE HAD LOTS OF PRACTICE.
SKATING? WAIT A MINUTE! YOU'RE RELATED TO DR. WILLIS AREN'T YOU?!
?
THAT'S RIGHT; GRANDPA WILLIS WAS THE MAN WHO FOUND THE WORLD'S FIRST COMPLETE BARAPASAURUS SKELETON.
SEE? THAT'S US, WITH THE FOSSIL RIGHT BEHIND US.
AMAZING!
AWW, YOU'RE SO CUTE.
I... I WISH HE WAS STILL HERE...
Was?!
Uh... Well...
YOU TWO WERE REALLY CLOSE, HUH?
AH-- UH-- HEY! NICE WEATHER WE'RE HAVING, EH?
RAIN, A LITTLE HELP HERE?!
NOT HELPING!
SORRY!
NO, NO, IT'S ALL RIGHT...

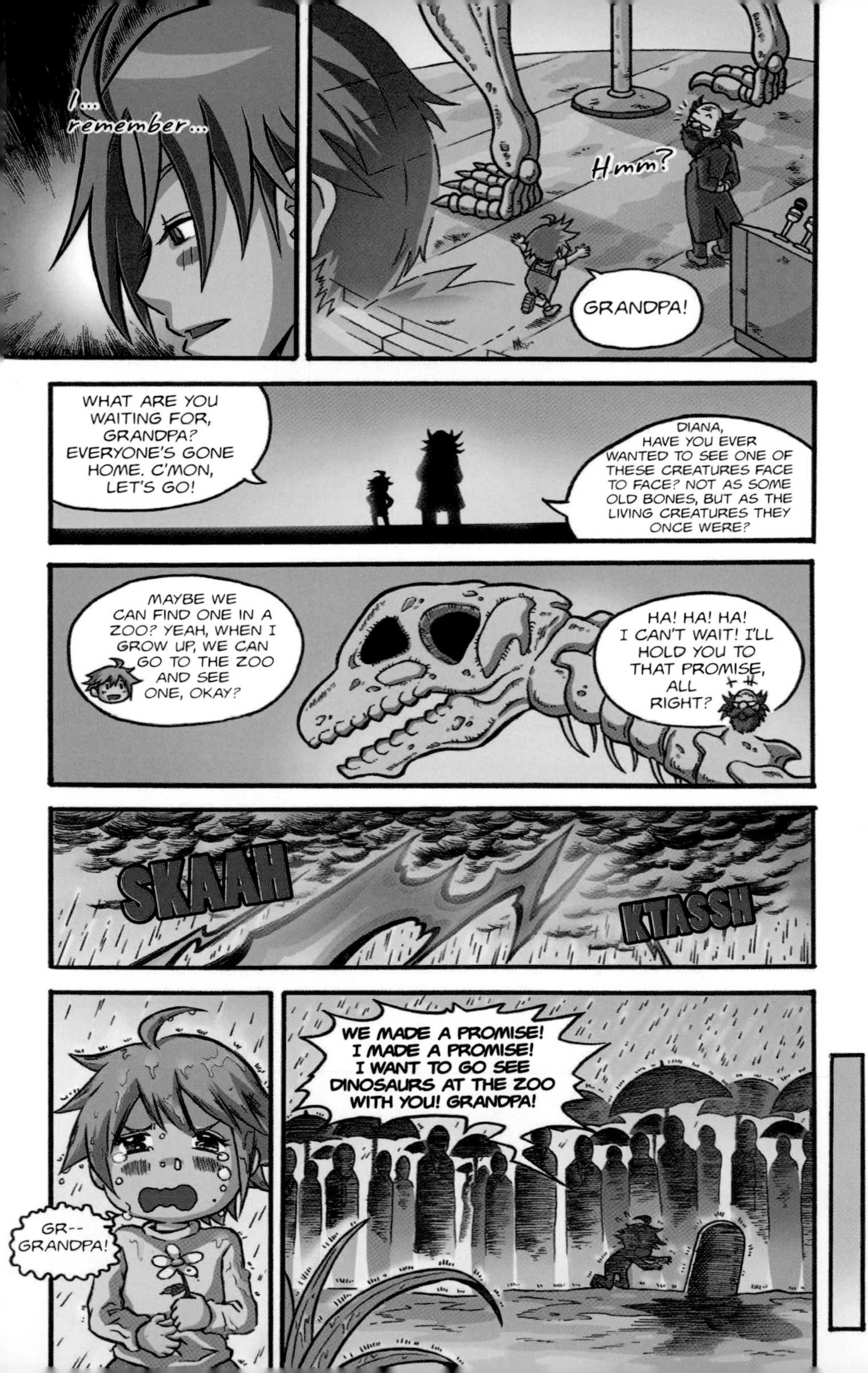
I... remember...
Hmm?
GRANDPA!
WHAT ARE YOU WAITING FOR, GRANDPA? EVERYONE'S GONE HOME. C'MON, LET'S GO!
DIANA, HAVE YOU EVER WANTED TO SEE ONE OF THESE CREATURES FACE TO FACE? NOT AS SOME OLD BONES, BUT AS THE LIVING CREATURES THEY ONCE WERE?
MAYBE WE CAN FIND ONE IN A ZOO? YEAH, WHEN I GROW UP, WE CAN GO TO THE ZOO AND SEE ONE, OKAY?
HA! HA! HA! I CAN'T WAIT! I'LL HOLD YOU TO THAT PROMISE, ALL RIGHT?
SKAAH
KTASSH
GR-- GRANDPA!
WE MADE A PROMISE! I MADE A PROMISE! I WANT TO GO SEE DINOSAURS AT THE ZOO WITH YOU! GRANDPA!

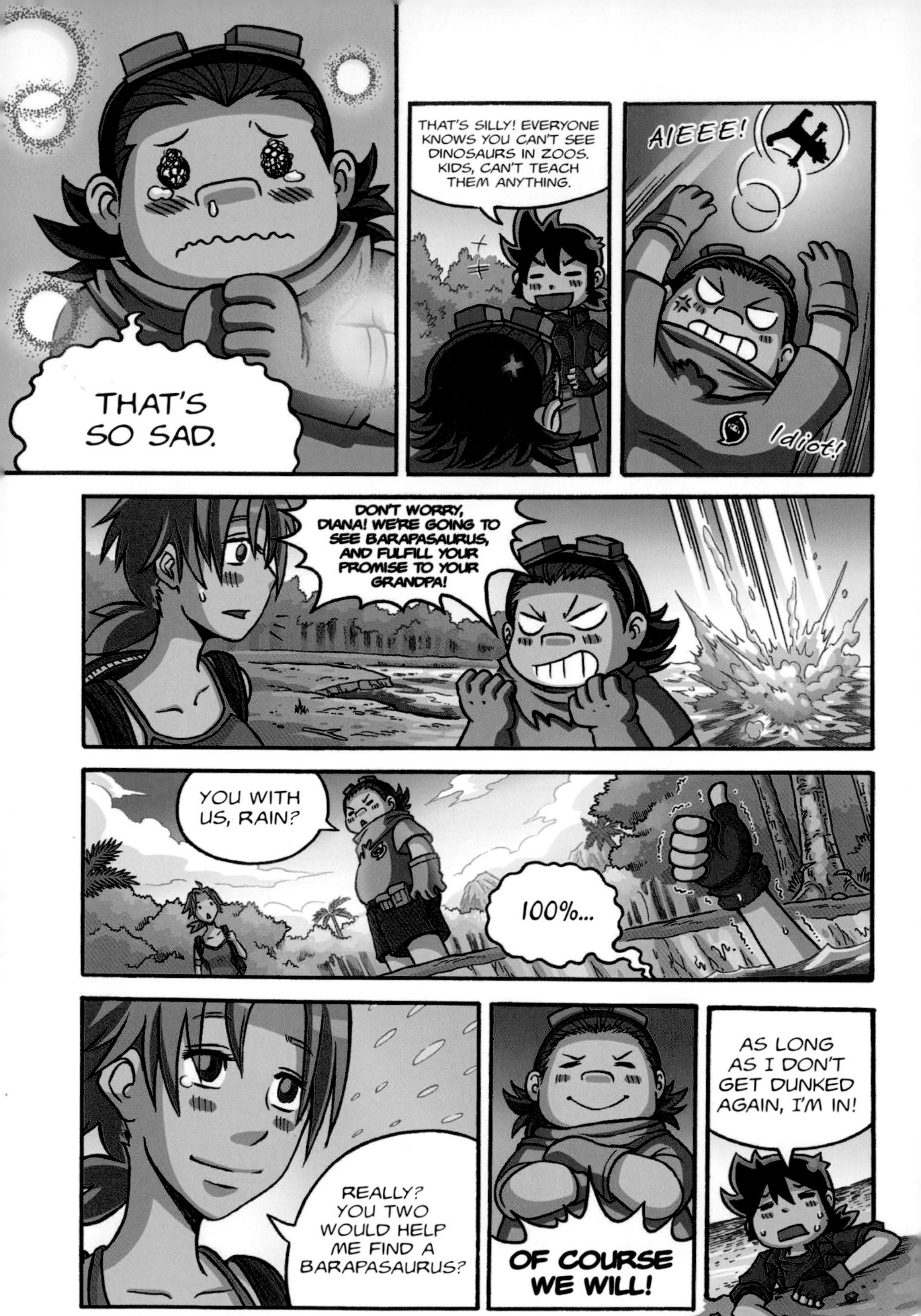
THAT'S SO SAD.
THAT'S SILLY! EVERYONE KNOWS YOU CAN'T SEE DINOSAURS IN ZOOS. KIDS, CAN'T TEACH THEM ANYTHING.
AIEEE!
Idiot!
DON'T WORRY, DIANA! WE'RE GOING TO SEE BARAPASAURUS, AND FULFILL YOUR PROMISE TO YOUR GRANDPA!
YOU WITH US, RAIN?
100%...
REALLY? YOU TWO WOULD HELP ME FIND A BARAPASAURUS?
OF COURSE WE WILL!
AS LONG AS I DON'T GET DUNKED AGAIN, I'M IN!

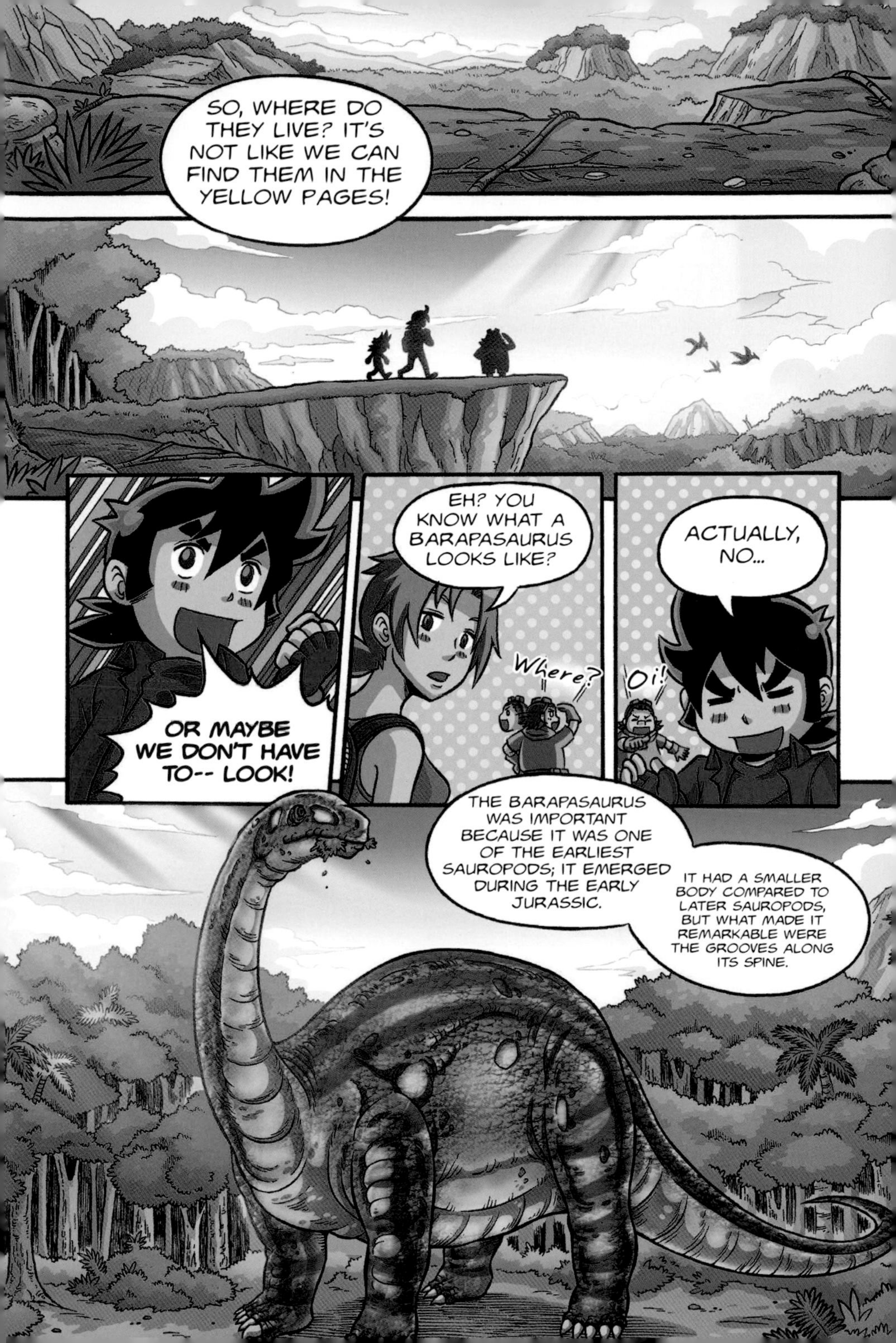
SO, WHERE DO THEY LIVE? IT'S NOT LIKE WE CAN FIND THEM IN THE YELLOW PAGES!
OR MAYBE WE DON'T HAVE TO-- LOOK!
EH? YOU KNOW WHAT A BARAPASAURUS LOOKS LIKE?
Where?
ACTUALLY, NO...
Oi!
THE BARAPASAURUS WAS IMPORTANT BECAUSE IT WAS ONE OF THE EARLIEST SAUROPODS; IT EMERGED DURING THE EARLY JURASSIC.
IT HAD A SMALLER BODY COMPARED TO LATER SAUROPODS, BUT WHAT MADE IT REMARKABLE WERE THE GROOVES ALONG ITS SPINE.

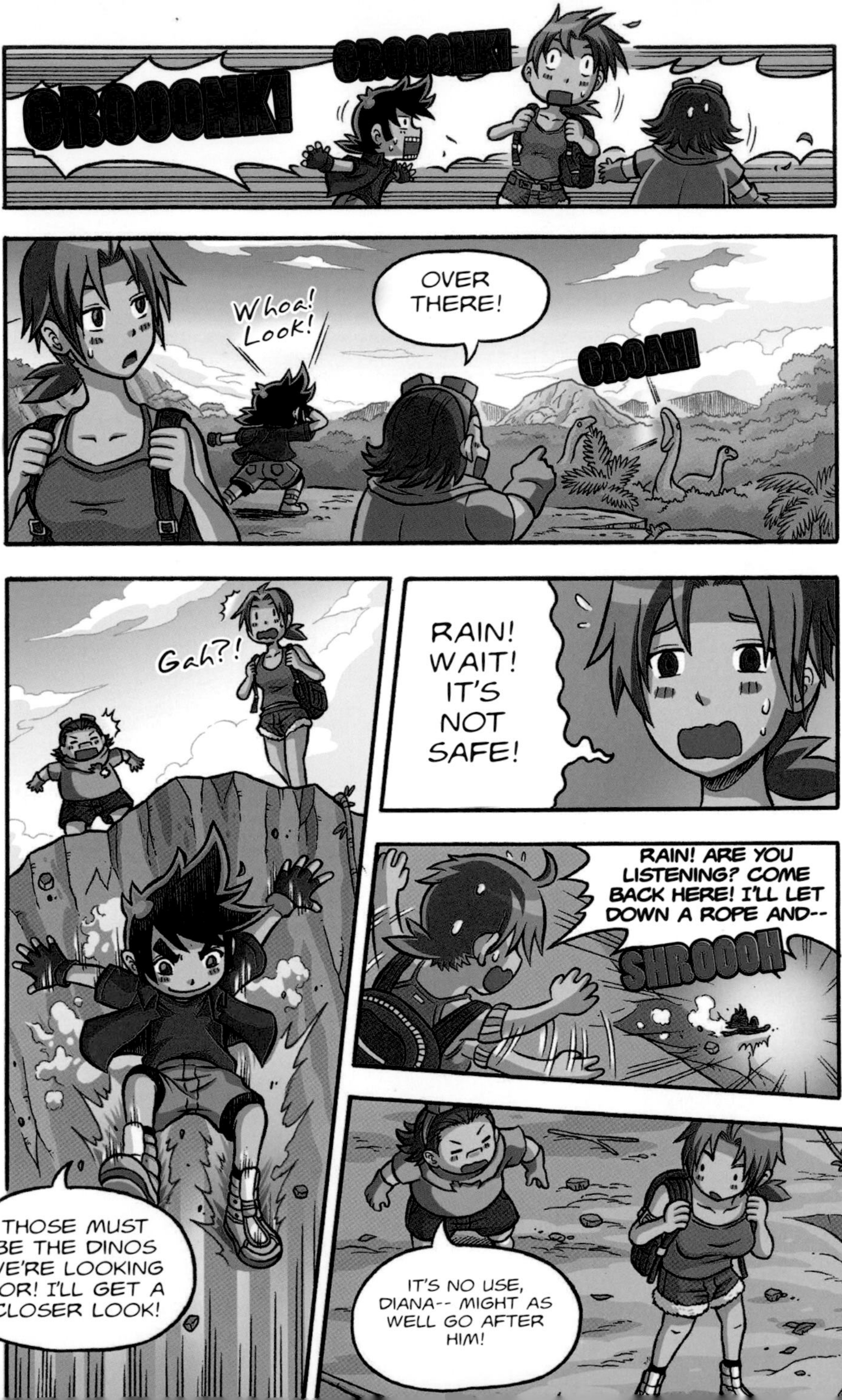
GROOONK!
GROOONK!
Whoa! Look!
OVER THERE!
CROAH!
Gah?!
RAIN! WAIT! IT'S NOT SAFE!
RAIN! ARE YOU LISTENING? COME BACK HERE! I'LL LET DOWN A ROPE AND--
SHROOOH
THOSE MUST BE THE DINOS WE'RE LOOKING FOR! I'LL GET A CLOSER LOOK!
IT'S NO USE, DIANA-- MIGHT AS WELL GO AFTER HIM!

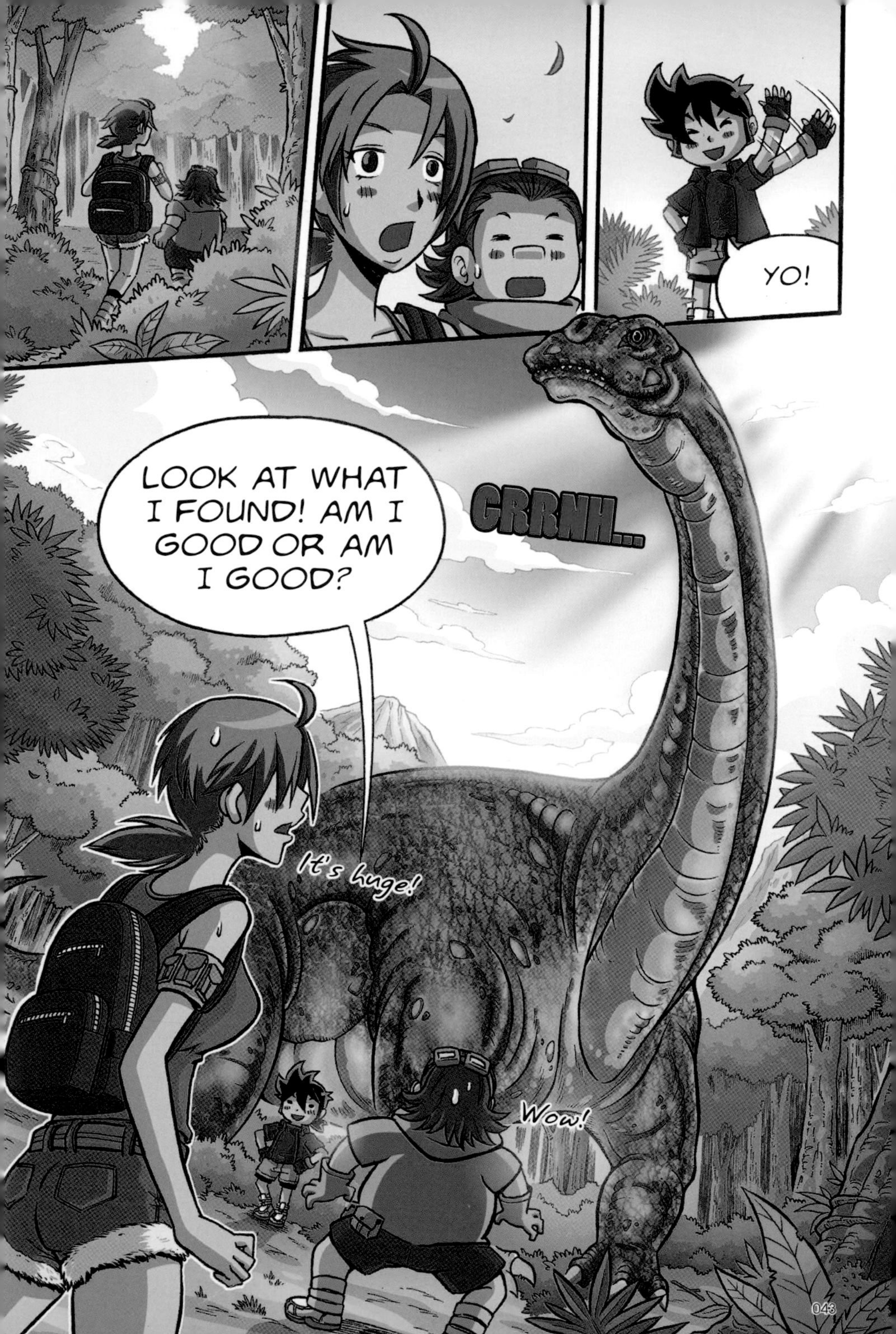
YO!
LOOK AT WHAT I FOUND! AM I GOOD OR AM I GOOD?
GRRNH...
It's huge!
Wow!

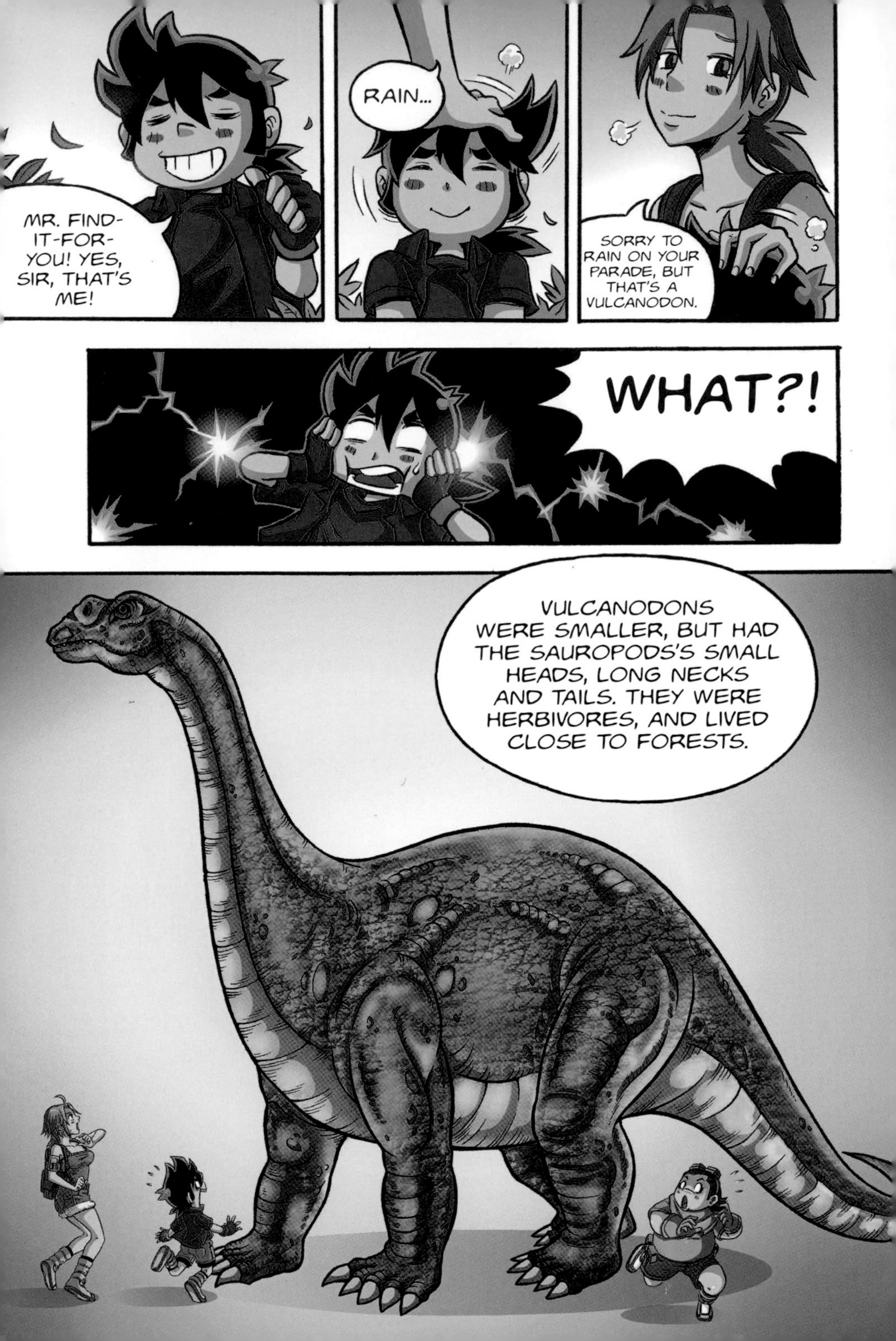
MR. FIND-IT-FOR-YOU! YES, SIR, THAT'S ME!
RAIN...
SORRY TO RAIN ON YOUR PARADE, BUT THAT'S A VULCANODON.
WHAT?!
VULCANODONS WERE SMALLER, BUT HAD THE SAUROPODS'S SMALL HEADS, LONG NECKS AND TAILS. THEY WERE HERBIVORES, AND LIVED CLOSE TO FORESTS.

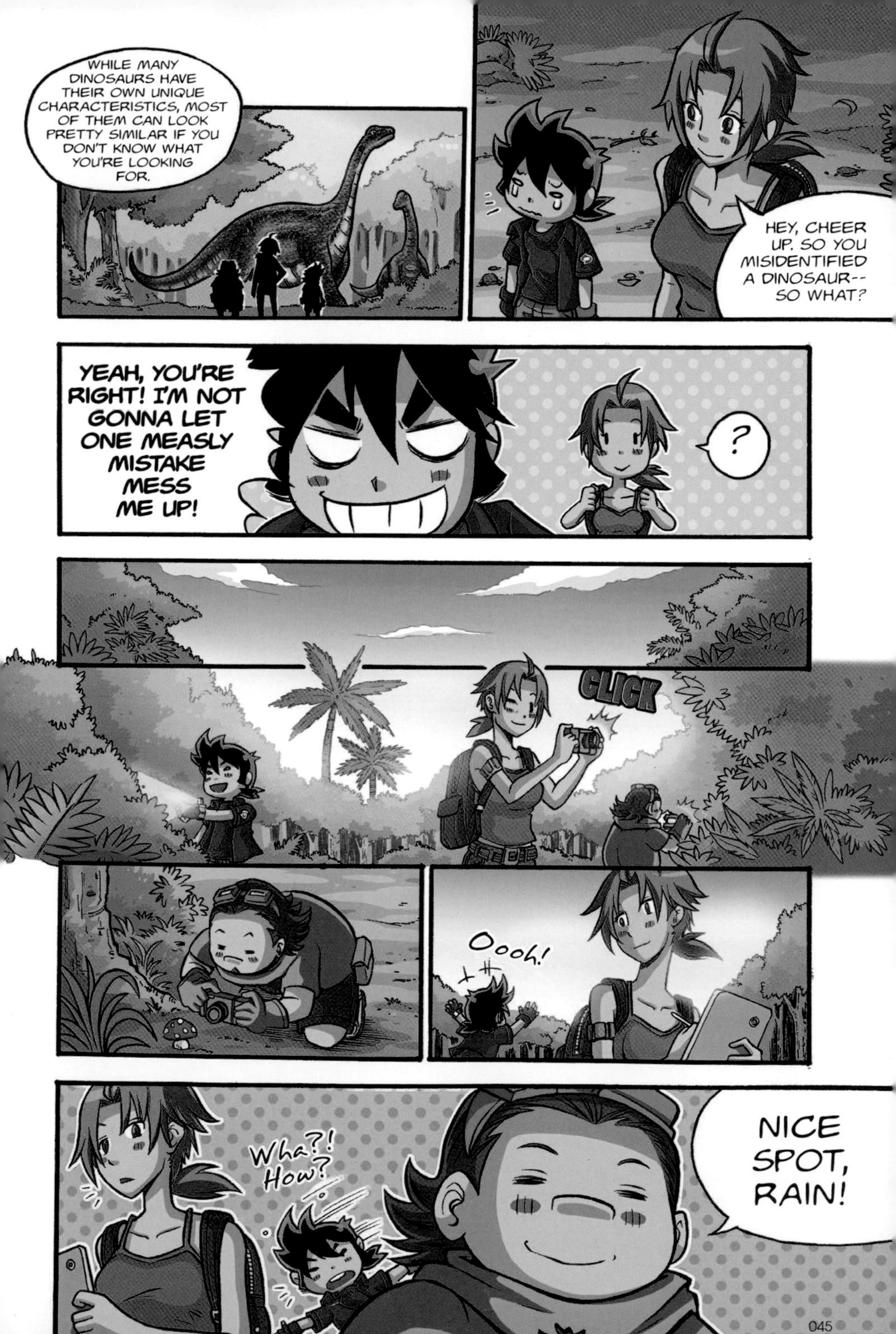
WHILE MANY DINOSAURS HAVE THEIR OWN UNIQUE CHARACTERISTICS, MOST OF THEM CAN LOOK PRETTY SIMILAR IF YOU DON'T KNOW WHAT YOU'RE LOOKING FOR.
HEY, CHEER UP. SO YOU MISIDENTIFIED A DINOSAUR-- SO WHAT?
YEAH, YOU'RE RIGHT! I'M NOT GONNA LET ONE MEASLY MISTAKE MESS ME UP!
?
CLICK
Oooh!
Wha?! How?
NICE SPOT, RAIN!

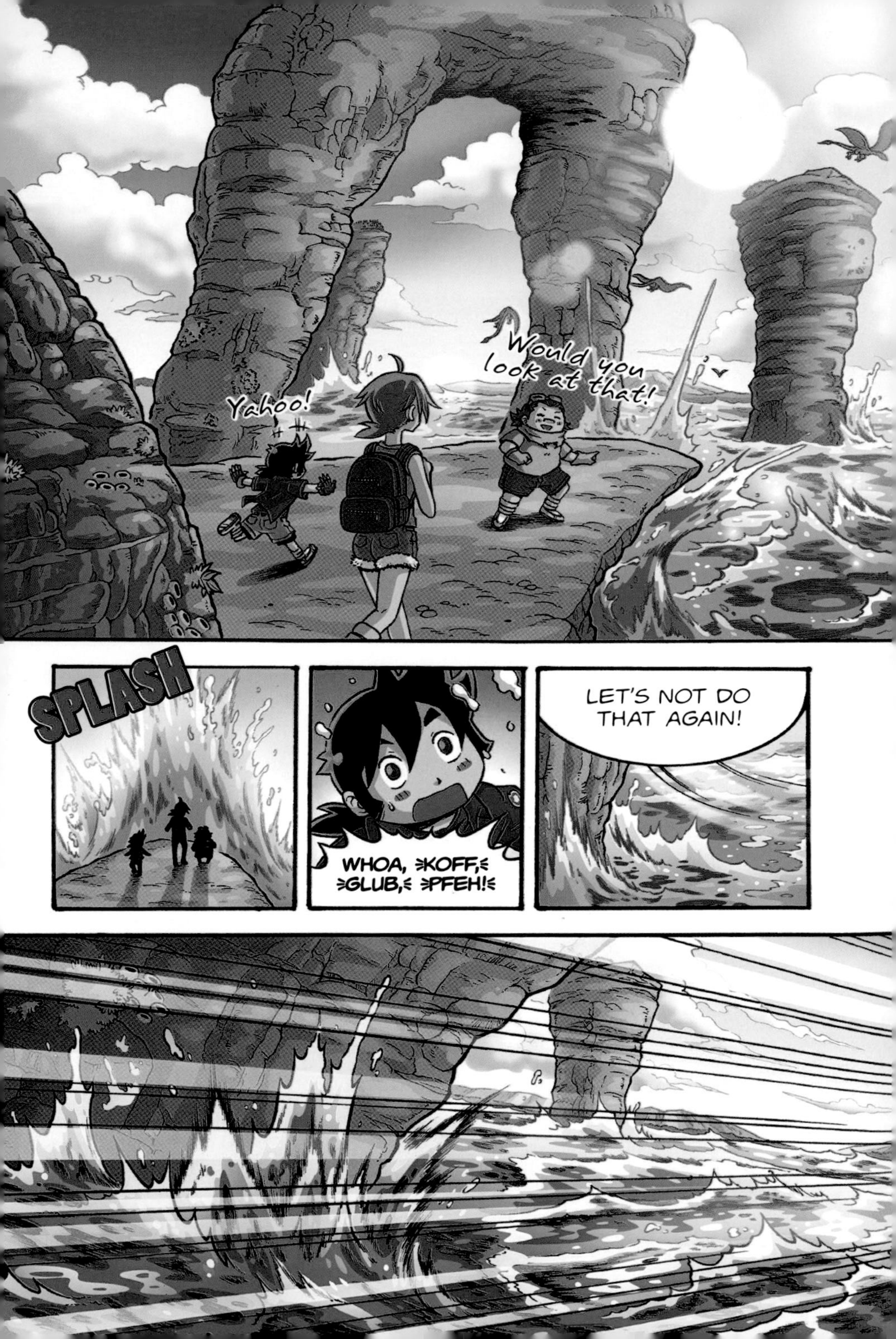
Yahoo!
Would you look at that!
SPLASH
WHOA, KOFF, GLUB, PFEH!
LET'S NOT DO THAT AGAIN!

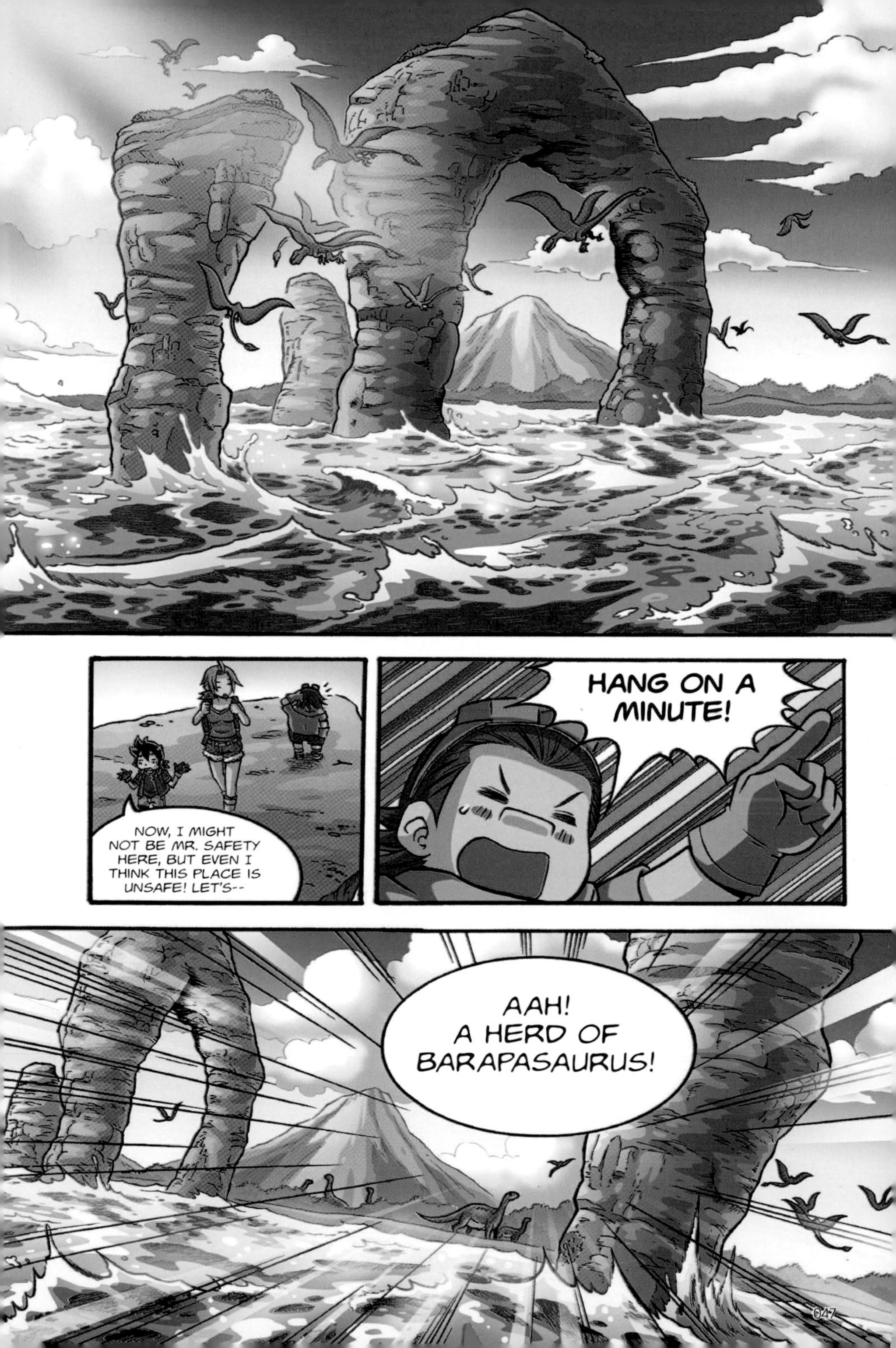
NOW, I MIGHT NOT BE MR. SAFETY HERE, BUT EVEN I THINK THIS PLACE IS UNSAFE! LET'S--
HANG ON A MINUTE!
AAH! A HERD OF BARAPASAURUS!

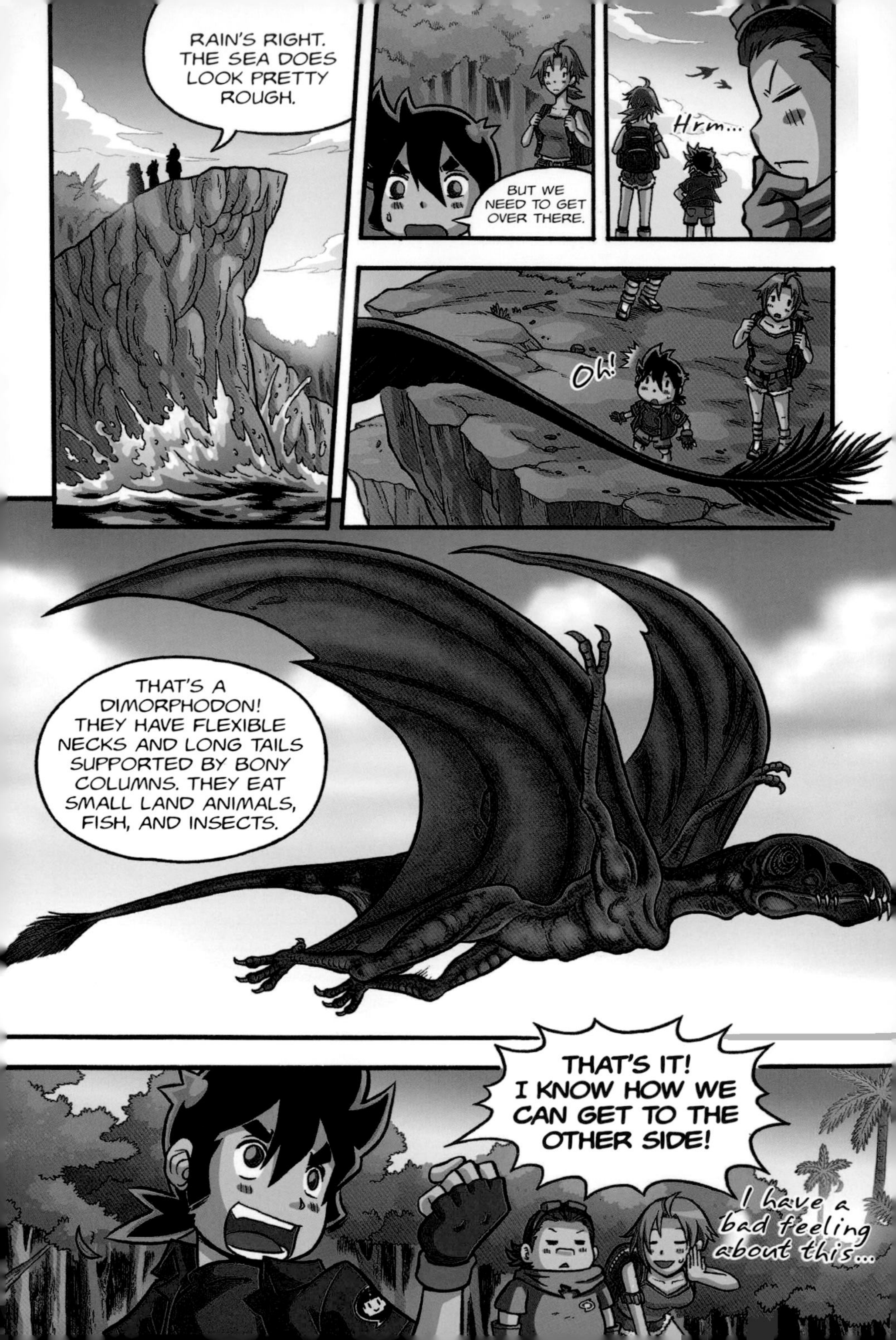
RAIN'S RIGHT. THE SEA DOES LOOK PRETTY ROUGH.
BUT WE NEED TO GET OVER THERE.
Hrm...
Oh!
THAT'S A DIMORPHODON! THEY HAVE FLEXIBLE NECKS AND LONG TAILS SUPPORTED BY BONY COLUMNS. THEY EAT SMALL LAND ANIMALS, FISH, AND INSECTS.
THAT'S IT! I KNOW HOW WE CAN GET TO THE OTHER SIDE!
I have a bad feeling about this...

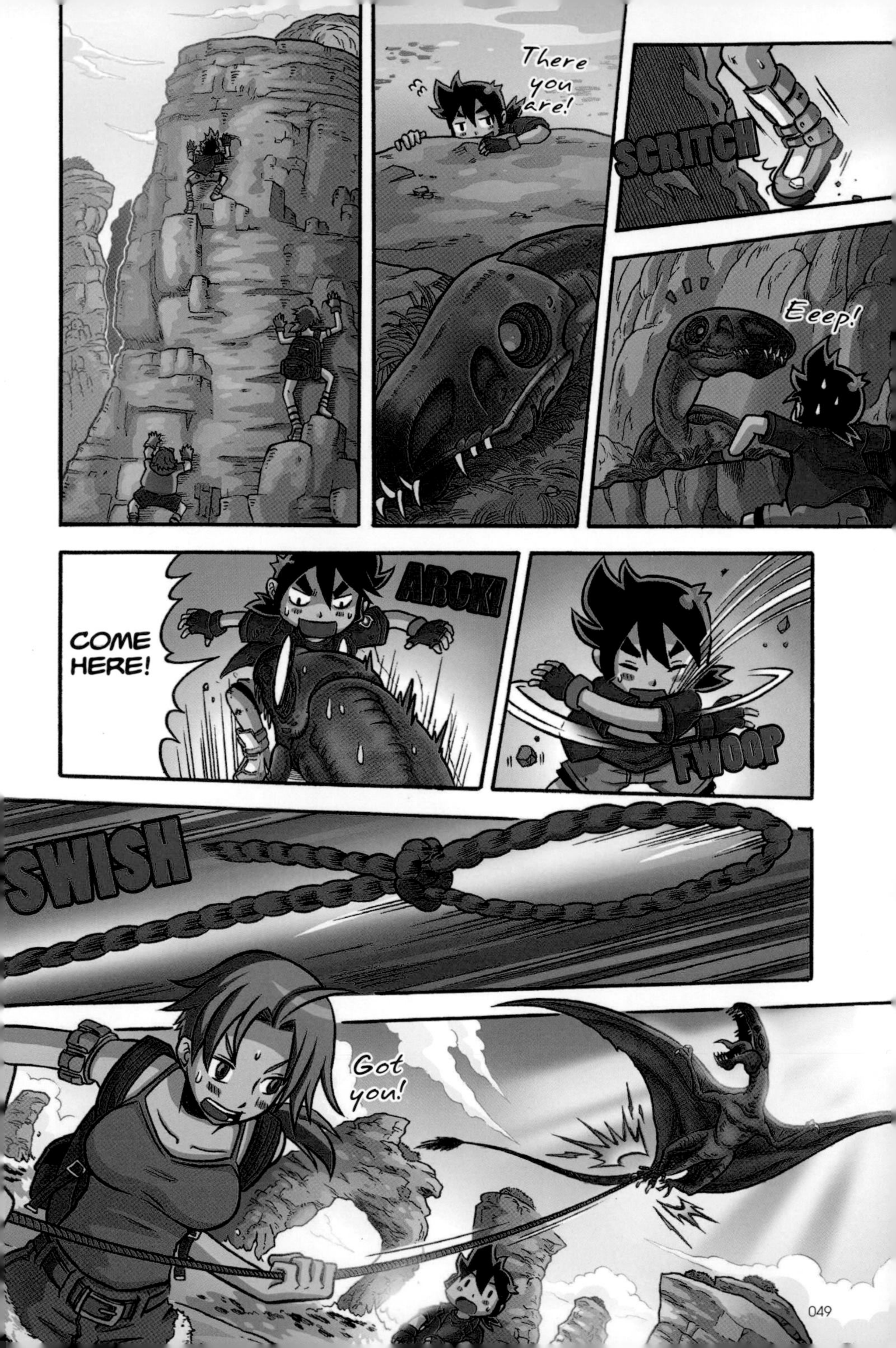
There you are!
SCRITCH
Eeep!
AACK!
COME HERE!
FWOOP
SWISH
Got you!

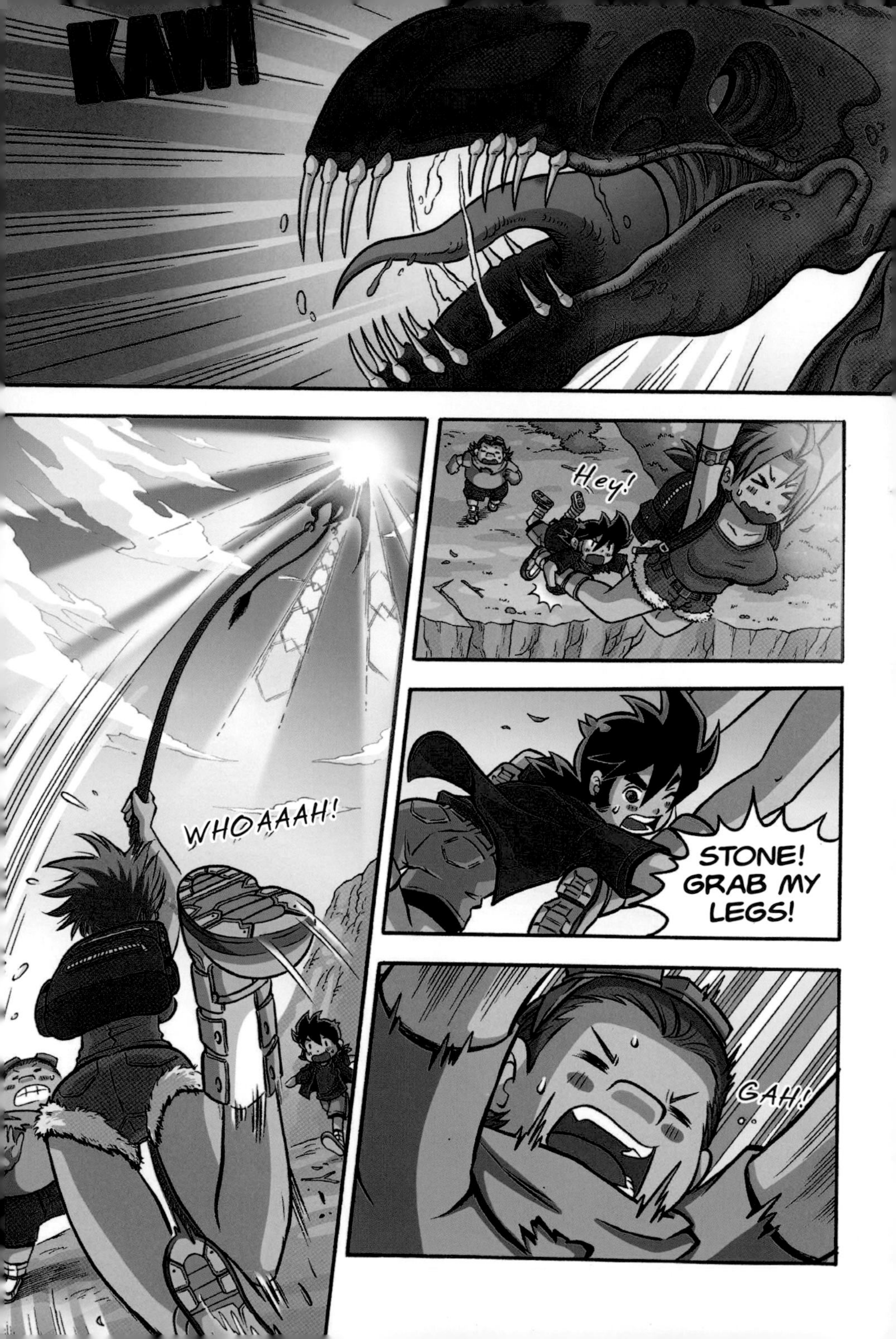
KAW!
WHOAAAH!
Hey!
STONE! GRAB MY LEGS!
GAH!

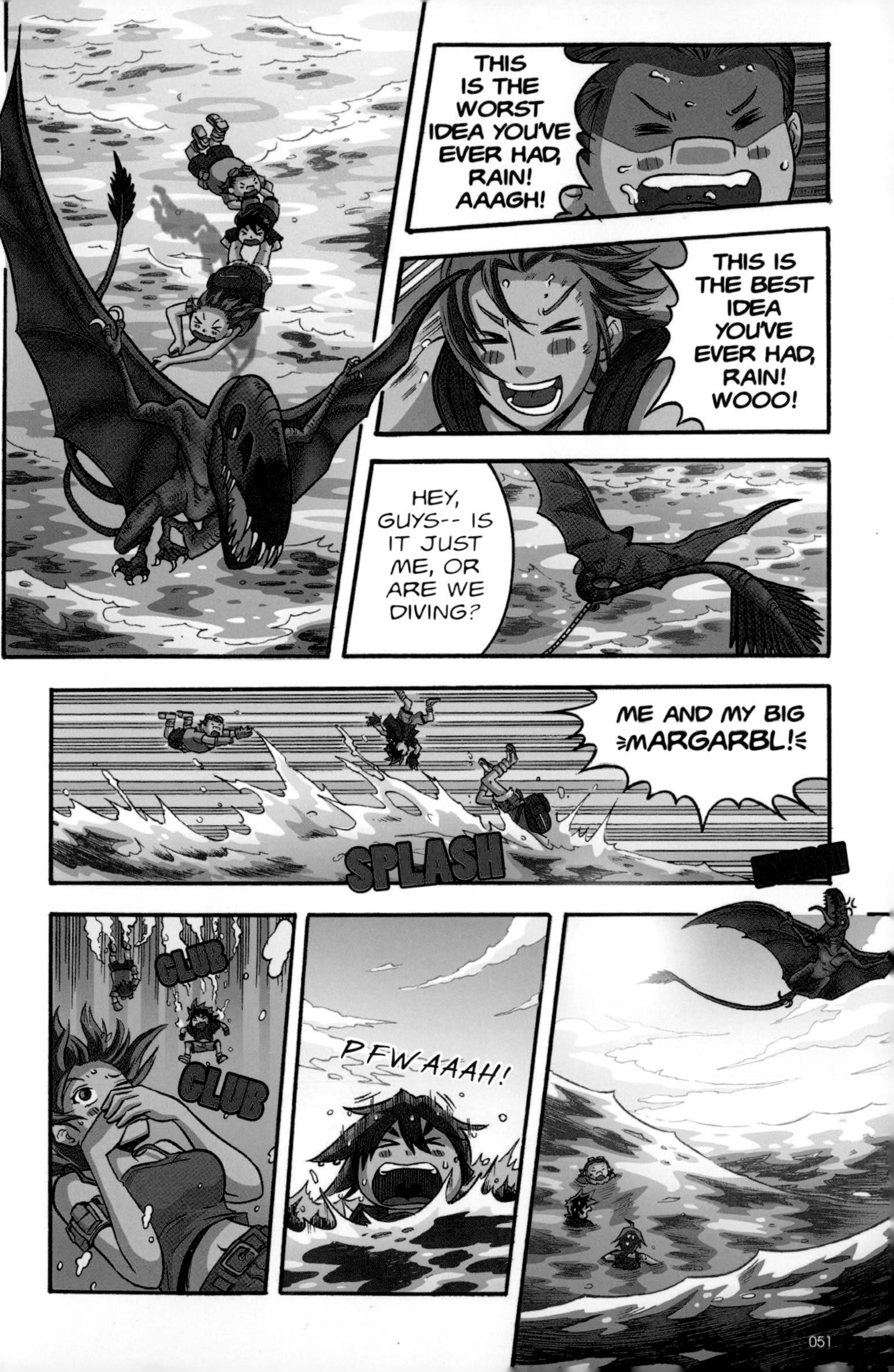

THIS IS THE WORST IDEA YOU'VE EVER HAD, RAIN! AAAGH!
THIS IS THE BEST IDEA YOU'VE EVER HAD, RAIN! WOOO!
HEY, GUYS-- IS IT JUST ME, OR ARE WE DIVING?
ME AND MY BIG MARGARBL!
SPLASH
CLUB
CLUB
PFW-AAAH!

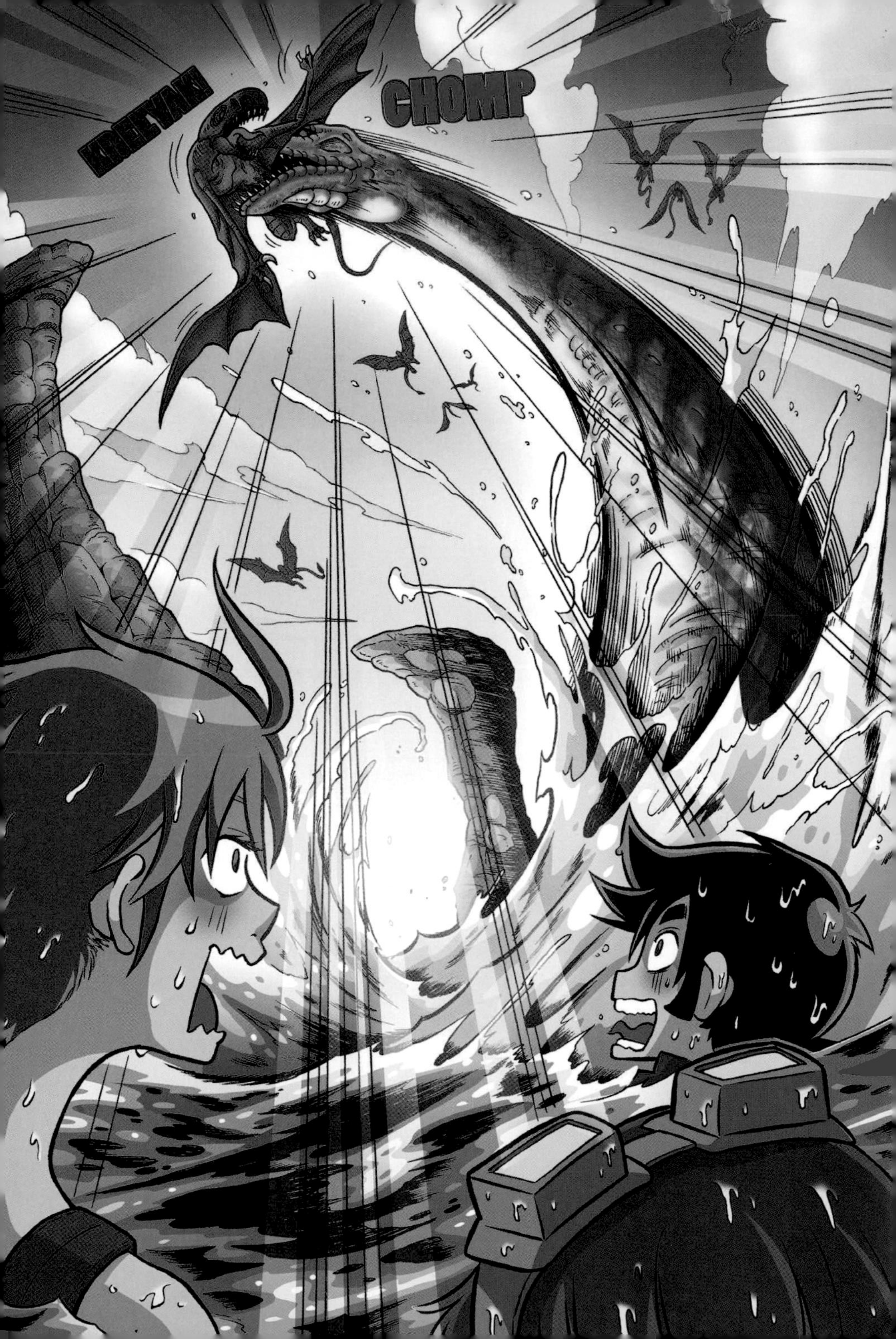
KREEYAK!
CHOMP

JONESING FOR THE JURASSIC

Vulcanodon

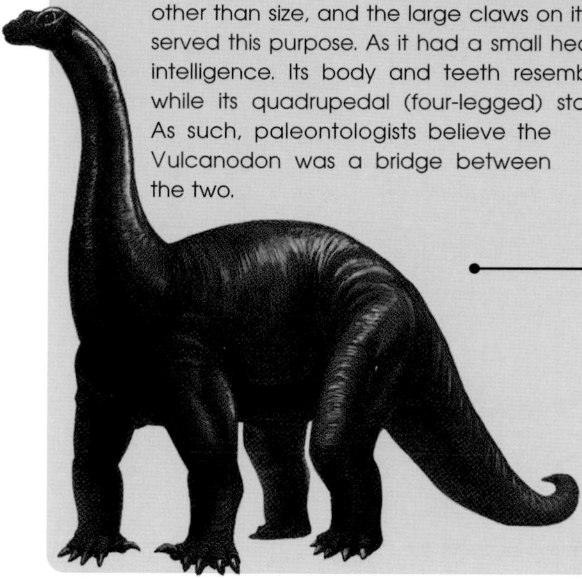

Vulcanodon was small for a sauropod; as such, it needed defenses other than size, and the large claws on its forelegs are thought to have served this purpose. As it had a small head, it is believed that it lacked intelligence. Its body and teeth resembled that of a prosauropods, while its quadrupedal (four-legged) stance resembled a sauropod. As such, paleontologists believe the Vulcanodon was a bridge between the two.

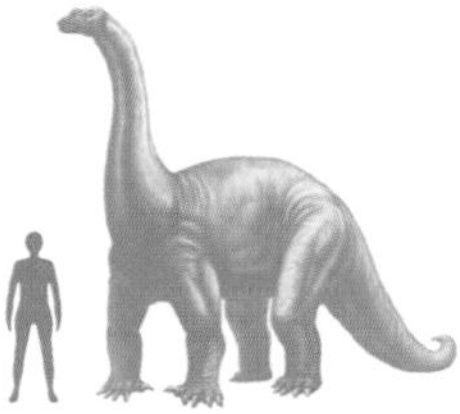

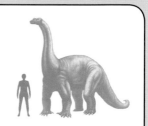

Scientific name: Vulcanodon
Length: 21.3 feet
Diet: Herbivore
Habitat: Forest outskirts
Discovered: South Africa
Era: Early Jurassic

JONESING FOR THE JURASSIC

Massospondylus

A prosauropod, Massospondylus was a small dinosaur compared to the larger Plateosaurus, but like its bigger cousin, could stand up on its hind legs to reach high leaves. Smooth rocks have been found with Massospondylus fossils, which indicated that it swallowed stones to help it digest food. While it is believed to have been herbivorous, its long, sharp, serrated front teeth might indicate a meat-eating diet as well.

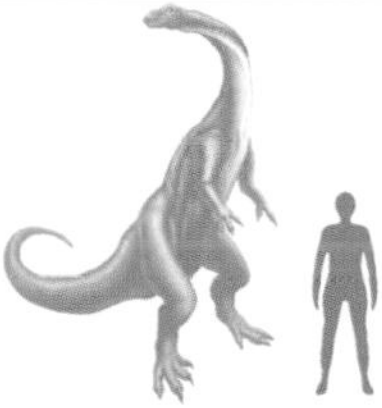

Scientific name: Massospondylus
Length: 16.4 feet
Diet: Herbivorous; might have been omnivorous
Habitat: Forest outskirts, dry areas
Discovered: South Africa, United States
Era: Early Jurassic

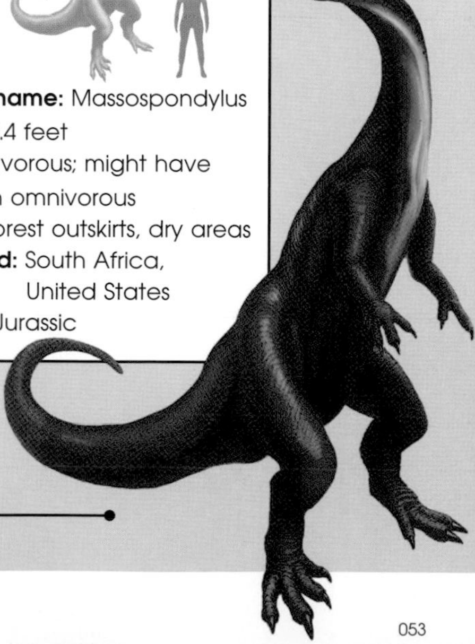

SAURISCHIAN CLADOGRAM

The saurischians were one of two large dinosaur groupings. Their traits included a longer second digit on each forelimb, longer necks than ornithischians, and air sacs connected to their lungs. Saurischians were divided into subgroups based on their diets. Some of them managed to escape the great extinction (called the Cretaceous–Paleogene extinction event) at the end of the Cretaceous, and later evolved into birds.

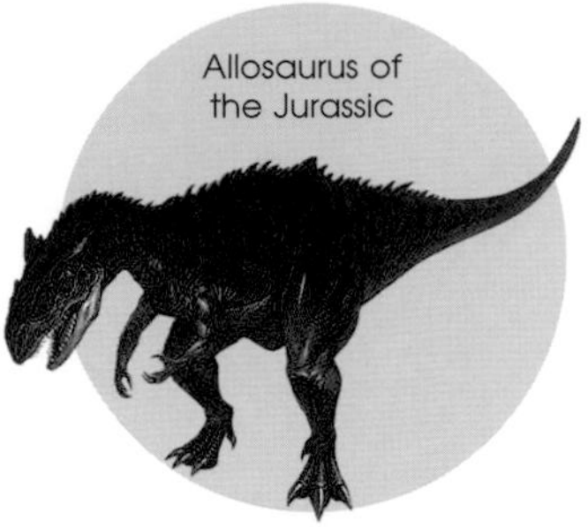
Allosaurus of the Jurassic

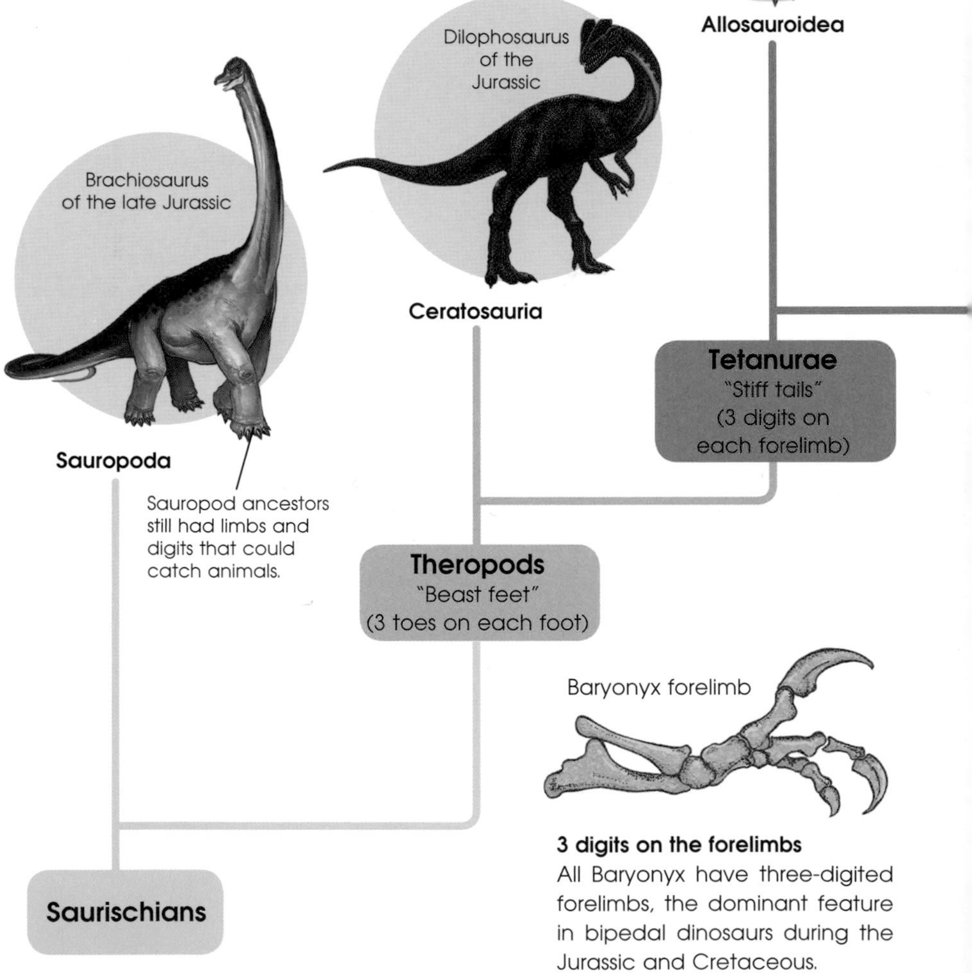
Allosauroidea
Dilophosaurus of the Jurassic
Brachiosaurus of the late Jurassic
Ceratosauria
Tetanurae
"Stiff tails"
(3 digits on each forelimb)
Sauropoda
Sauropod ancestors still had limbs and digits that could catch animals.
Theropods
"Beast feet"
(3 toes on each foot)
Baryonyx forelimb
Saurischians

3 digits on the forelimbs
All Baryonyx have three-digited forelimbs, the dominant feature in bipedal dinosaurs during the Jurassic and Cretaceous.

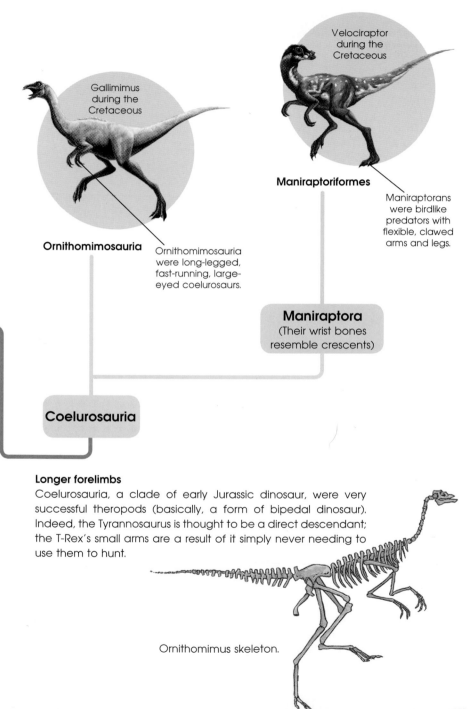

Velociraptor
during the
Cretaceous

Gallimimus
during the
Cretaceous

Maniraptoriformes

Maniraptorans
were birdlike
predators with
flexible, clawed
arms and legs.

Ornithomimosauria   Ornithomimosauria
were long-legged,
fast-running, large-
eyed coelurosaurs.

Maniraptora
(Their wrist bones
resemble crescents)

Coelurosauria

Longer forelimbs

Coelurosauria, a clade of early Jurassic dinosaur, were very successful theropods (basically, a form of bipedal dinosaur). Indeed, the Tyrannosaurus is thought to be a direct descendant; the T-Rex's small arms are a result of it simply never needing to use them to hunt.

Ornithomimus skeleton.

JONESING FOR THE JURASSIC

Dimorphodon

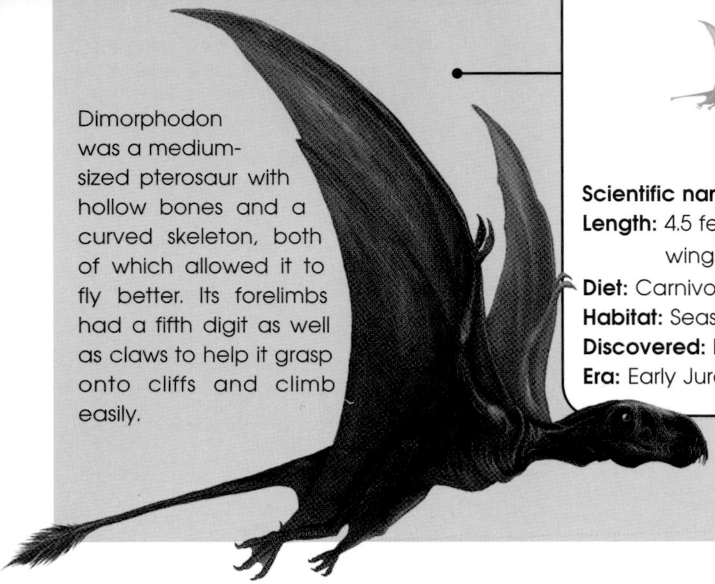

Dimorphodon was a medium-sized pterosaur with hollow bones and a curved skeleton, both of which allowed it to fly better. Its forelimbs had a fifth digit as well as claws to help it grasp onto cliffs and climb easily.

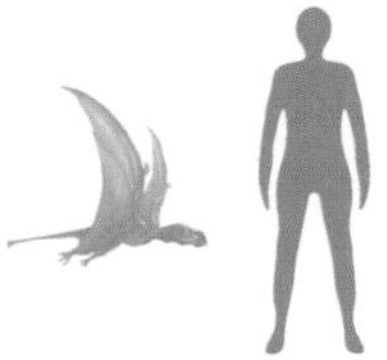

Scientific name: Dimorphodon
Length: 4.5 feet (8.2 feet with wings open)
Diet: Carnivorous
Habitat: Seaside and riversides
Discovered: Europe, North America
Era: Early Jurassic

JONESING FOR THE JURASSIC

Rhamphorhynchus

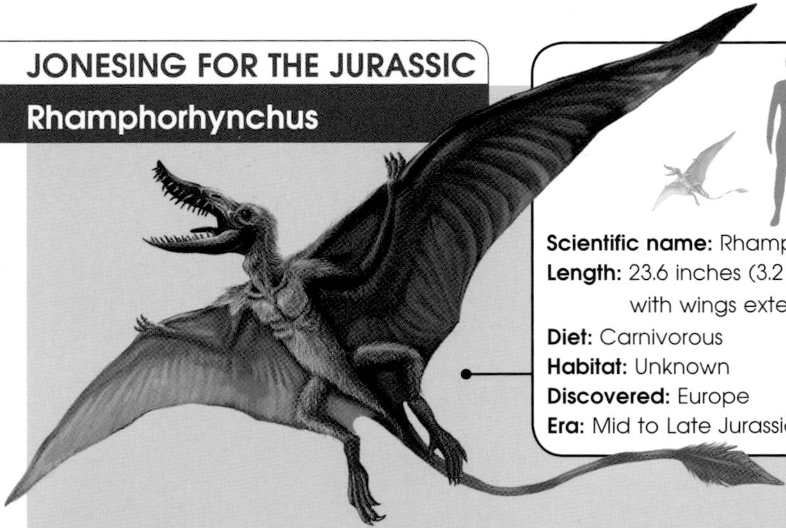

Scientific name: Rhamphorhynchus
Length: 23.6 inches (3.2 feet with wings extended)
Diet: Carnivorous
Habitat: Unknown
Discovered: Europe
Era: Mid to Late Jurassic

The fourth digit of each of Rhamphorhynchus forelimbs became the main structure of its wings, while its feet became smaller. It had sharp teeth that slotted together closely when it closed its mouth, an invaluable tool for catching thin, slippery fish. A broad, leaf-shaped membrane at the tip of its tail helped it steer.

CHAPTER 3

OCEANIC FLIGHT

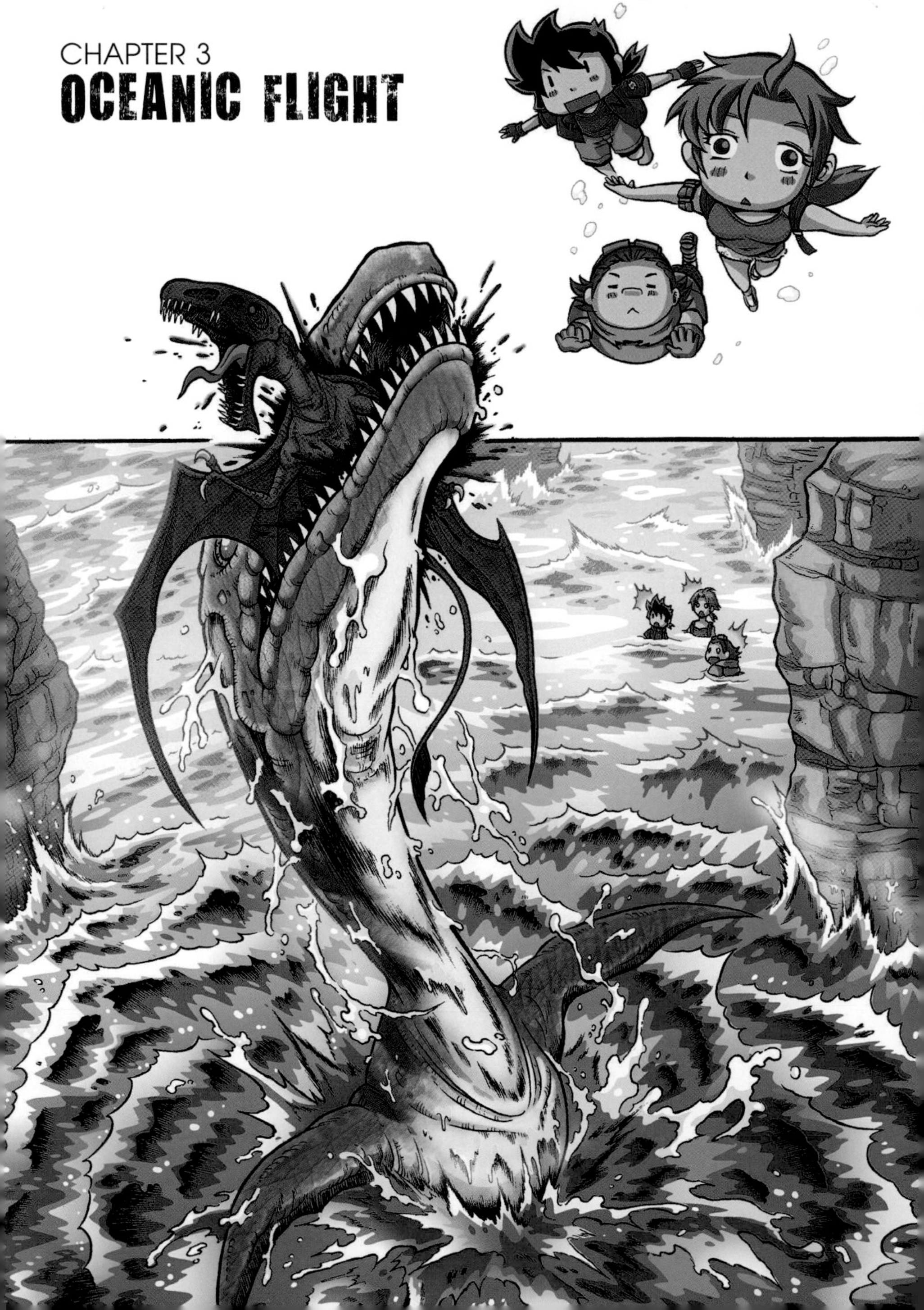

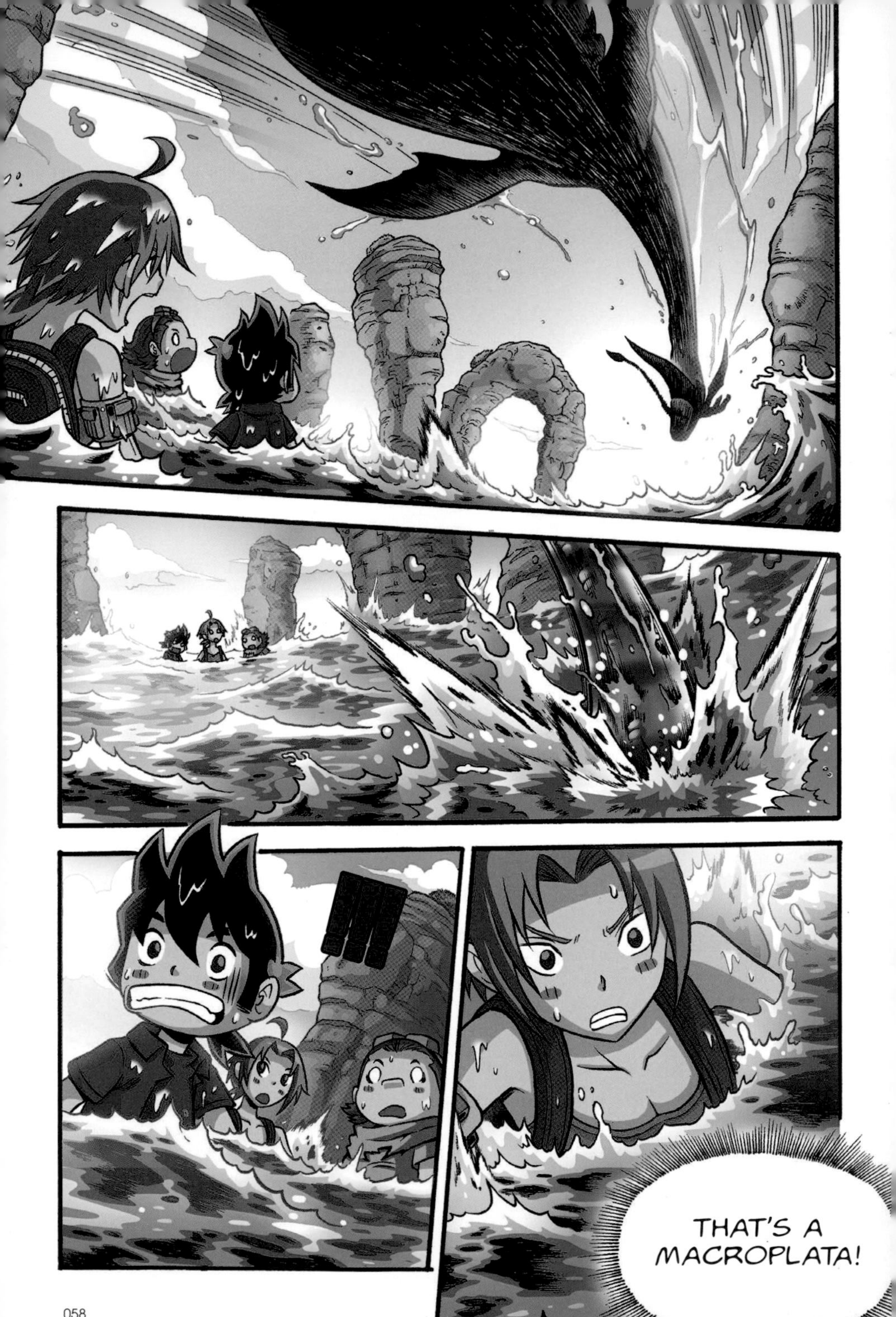
THAT'S A MACROPLATA!

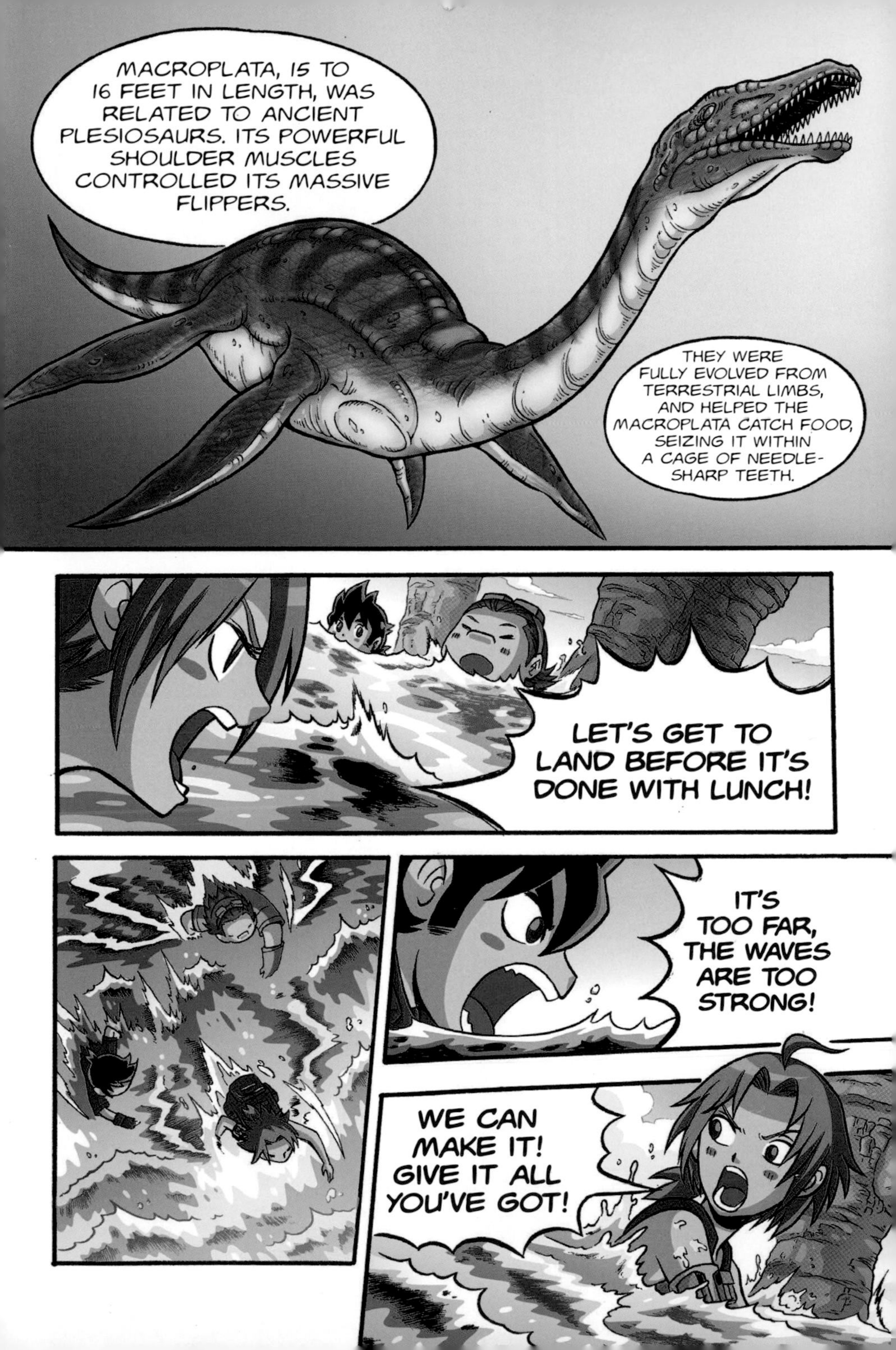
MACROPLATA, 15 TO 16 FEET IN LENGTH, WAS RELATED TO ANCIENT PLESIOSAURS. ITS POWERFUL SHOULDER MUSCLES CONTROLLED ITS MASSIVE FLIPPERS.
THEY WERE FULLY EVOLVED FROM TERRESTRIAL LIMBS, AND HELPED THE MACROPLATA CATCH FOOD, SEIZING IT WITHIN A CAGE OF NEEDLE-SHARP TEETH.
LET'S GET TO LAND BEFORE IT'S DONE WITH LUNCH!
IT'S TOO FAR, THE WAVES ARE TOO STRONG!
WE CAN MAKE IT! GIVE IT ALL YOU'VE GOT!

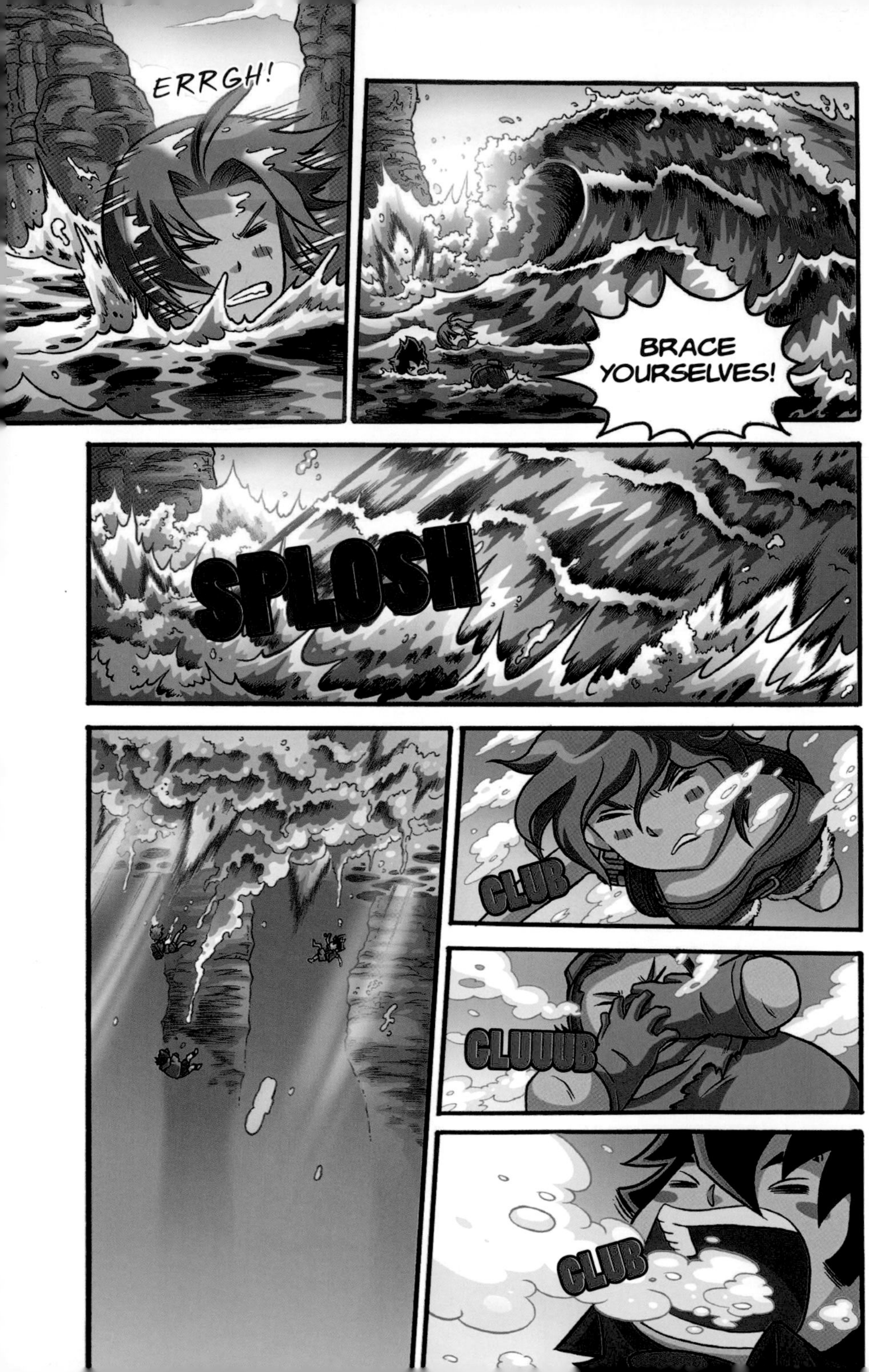
ERRGH!
BRACE YOURSELVES!
SPLOSH
CLUB
CLUUUB
CLUB

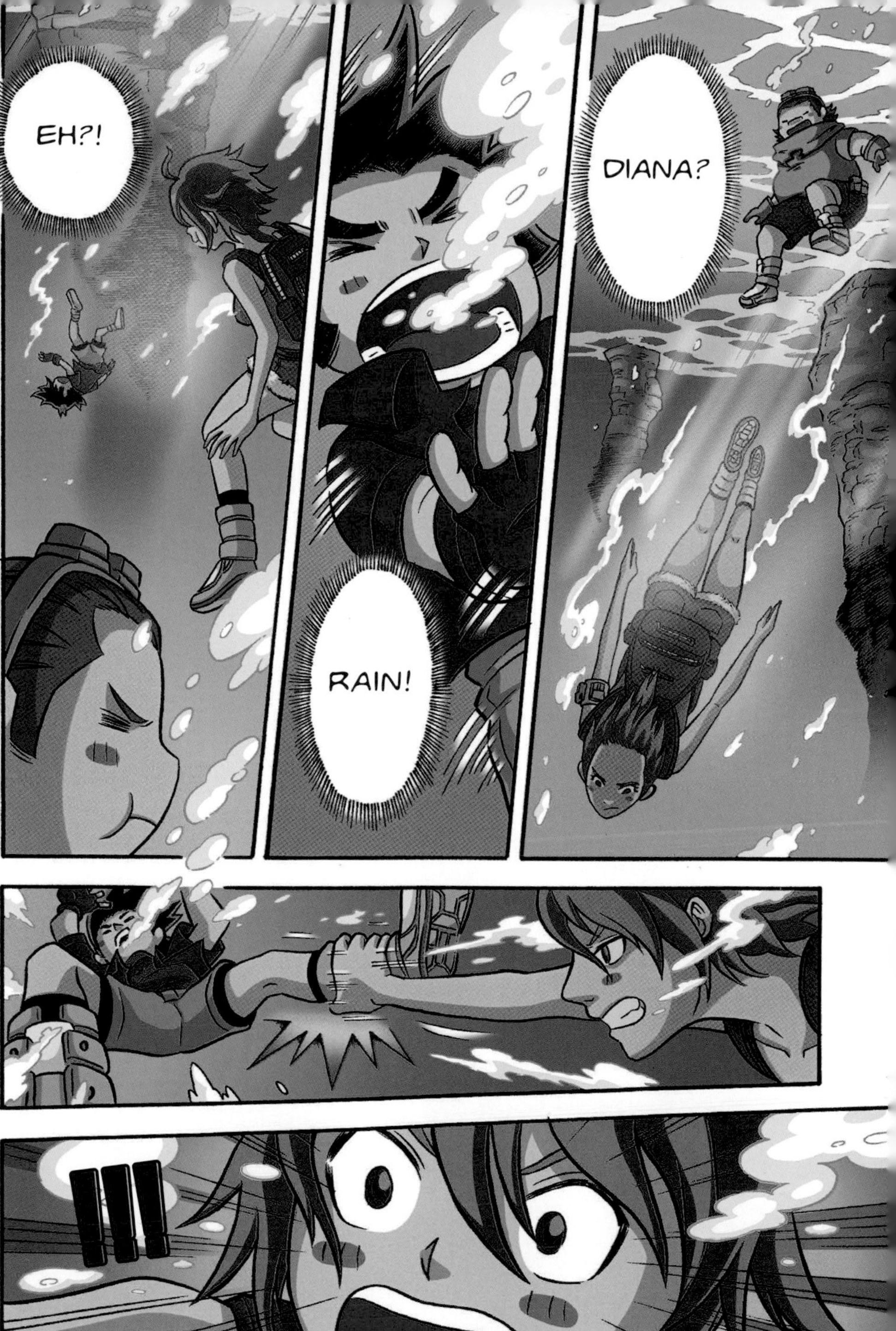
EH?!
RAIN!
DIANA?
!!!

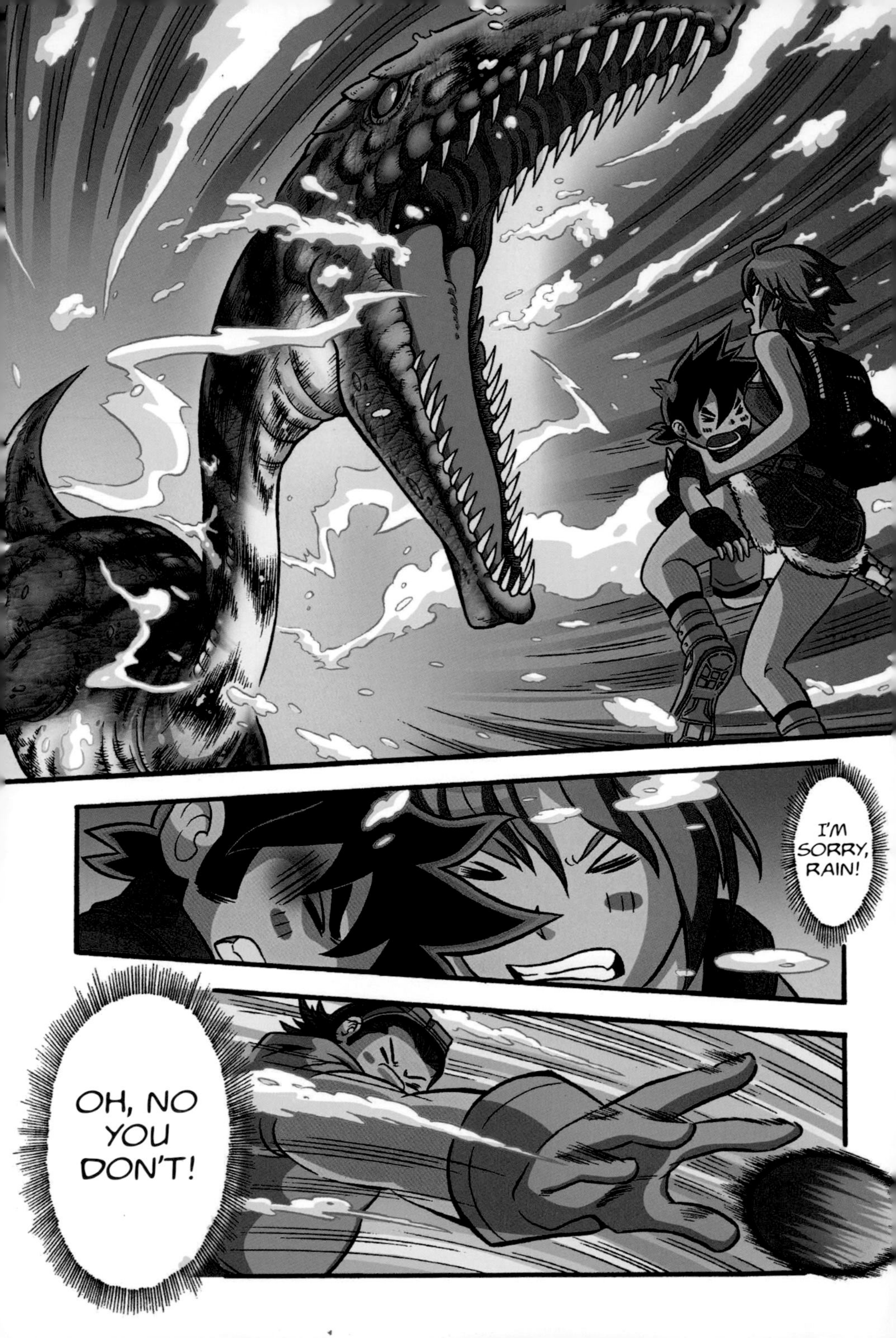
I'M SORRY, RAIN!
OH, NO YOU DON'T!

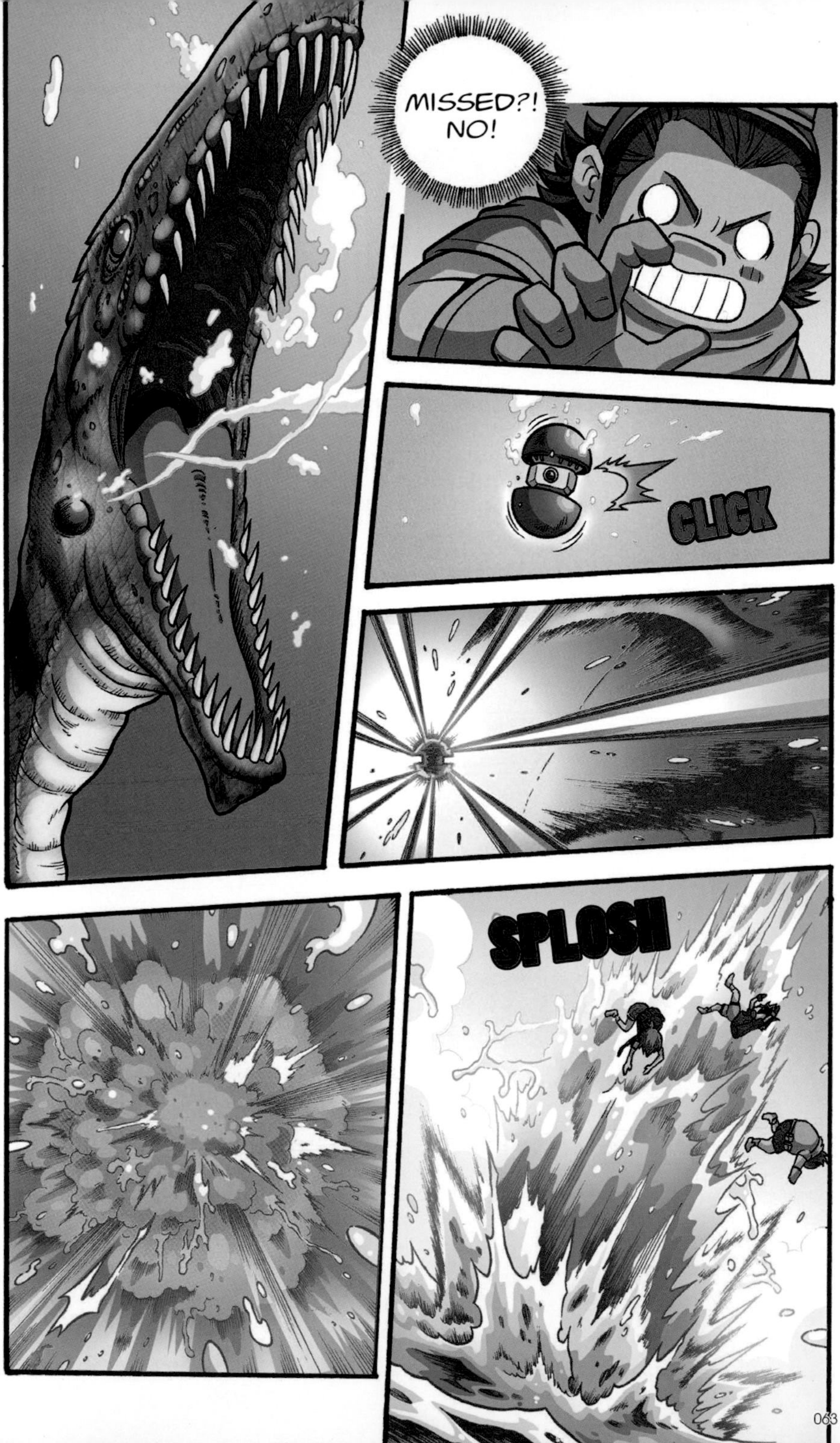
MISSED?! NO!
CLICK
SPLOSH

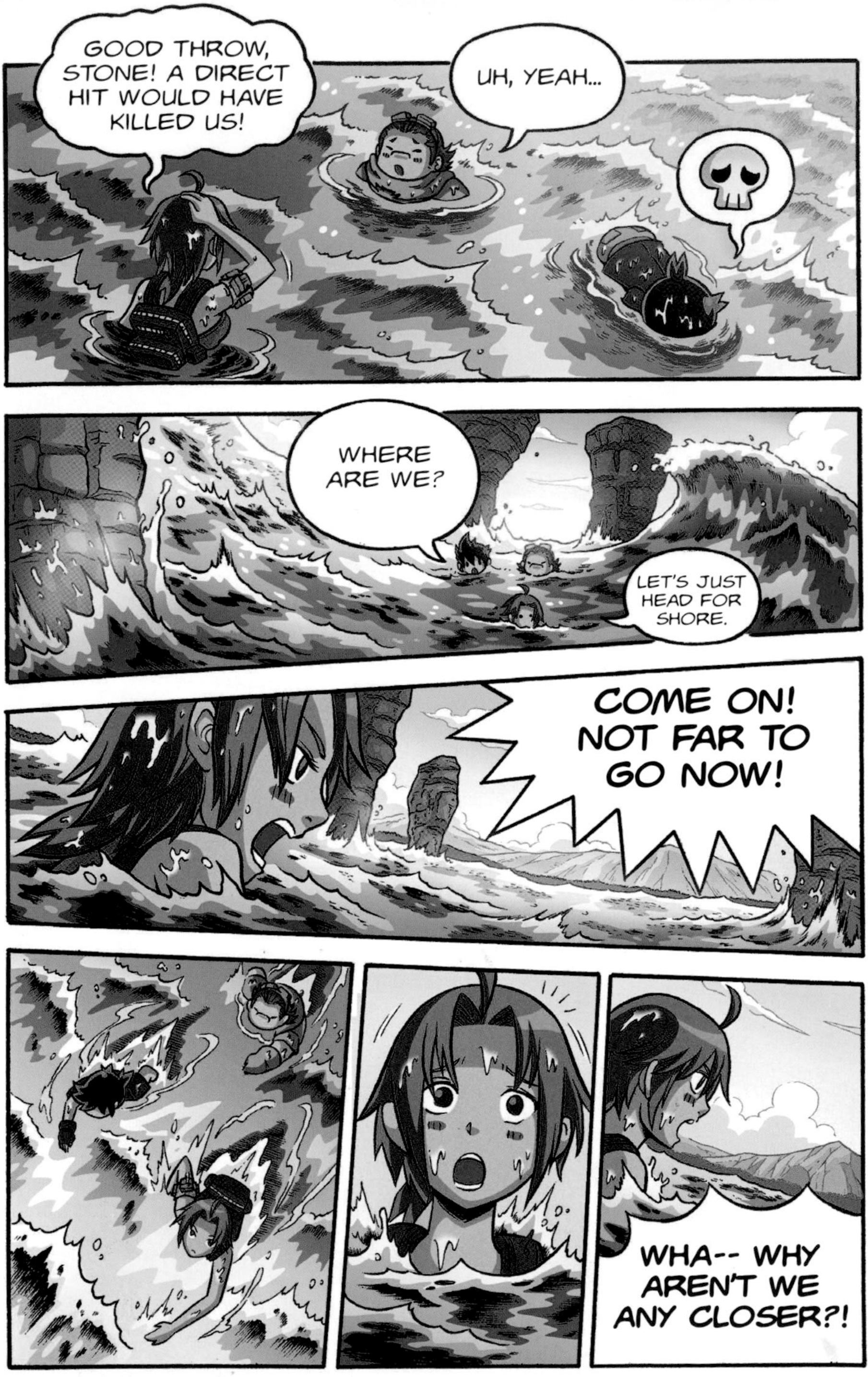
GOOD THROW, STONE! A DIRECT HIT WOULD HAVE KILLED US!
UH, YEAH...
WHERE ARE WE?
LET'S JUST HEAD FOR SHORE.
COME ON! NOT FAR TO GO NOW!
WHA-- WHY AREN'T WE ANY CLOSER?!

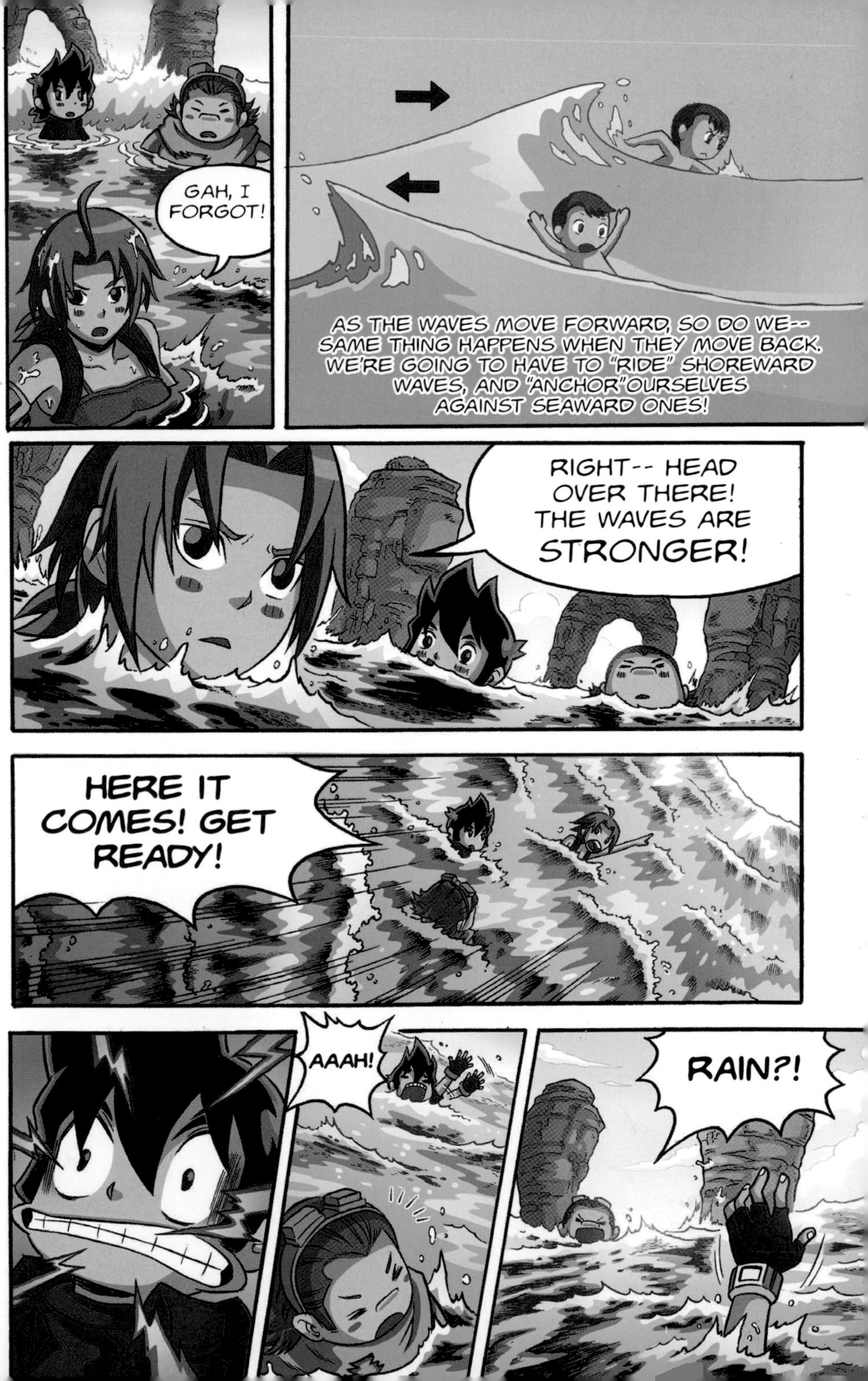

GAH, I FORGOT!
AS THE WAVES MOVE FORWARD, SO DO WE-- SAME THING HAPPENS WHEN THEY MOVE BACK. WE'RE GOING TO HAVE TO "RIDE" SHOREWARD WAVES, AND "ANCHOR" OURSELVES AGAINST SEAWARD ONES!
RIGHT-- HEAD OVER THERE! THE WAVES ARE STRONGER!
HERE IT COMES! GET READY!
AAAH!
RAIN?!

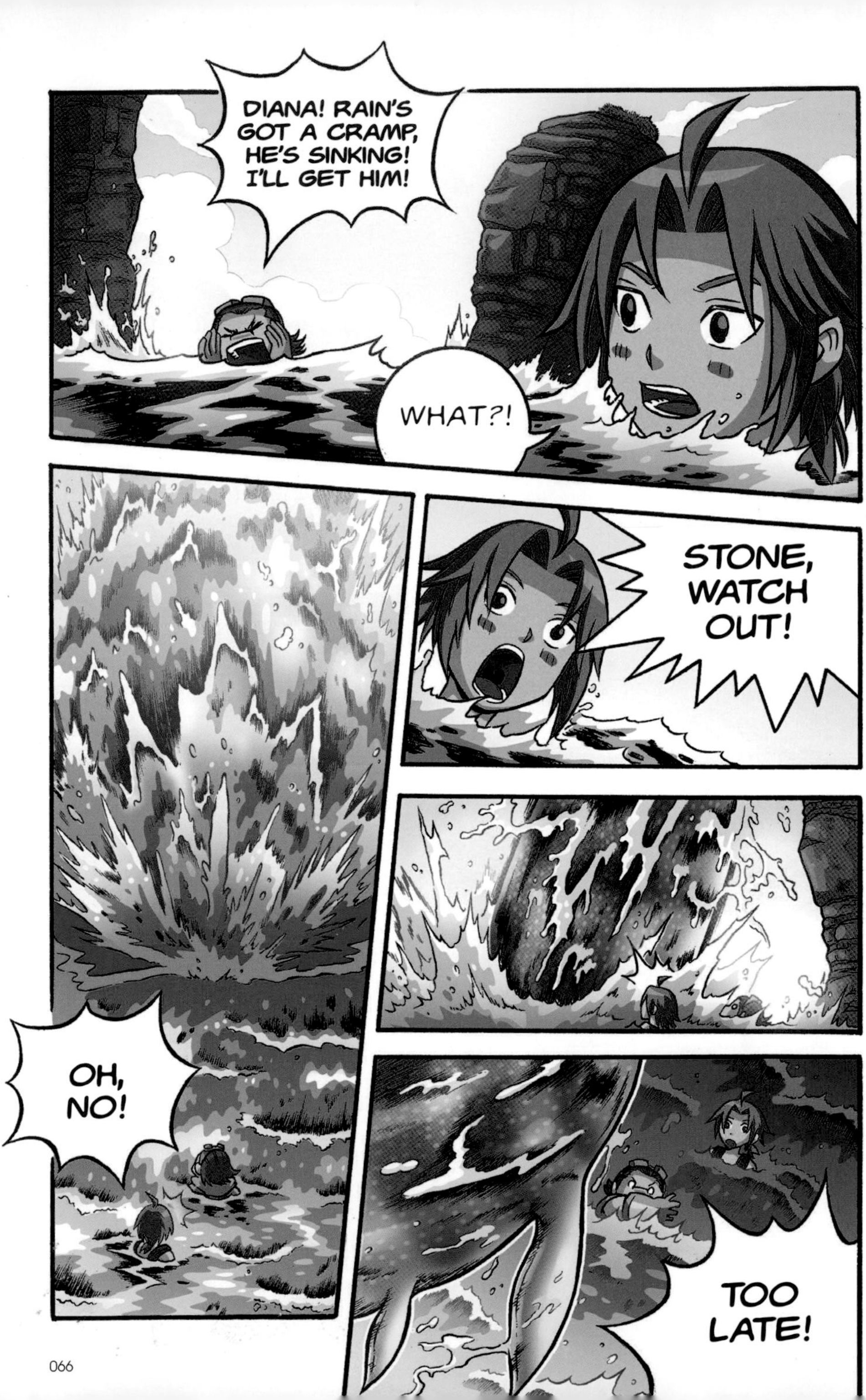
DIANA! RAIN'S GOT A CRAMP, HE'S SINKING! I'LL GET HIM!
WHAT?!
STONE, WATCH OUT!
OH, NO!
TOO LATE!

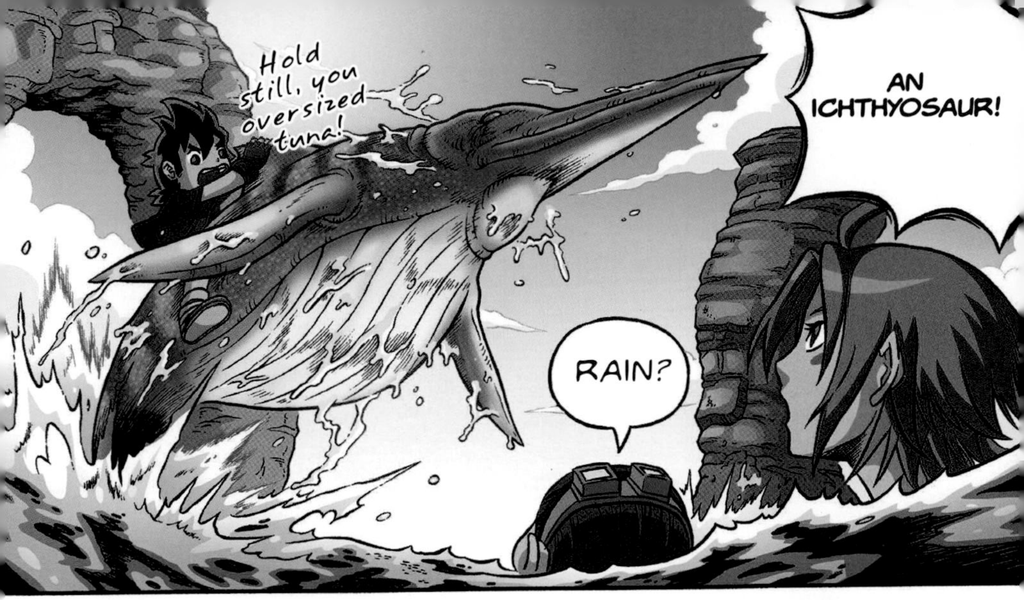
Hold still, you oversized tuna!
AN ICHTHYOSAUR!
RAIN?

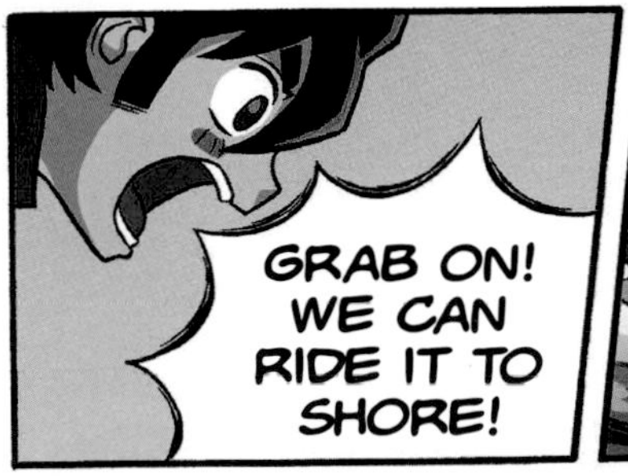
GRAB ON! WE CAN RIDE IT TO SHORE!

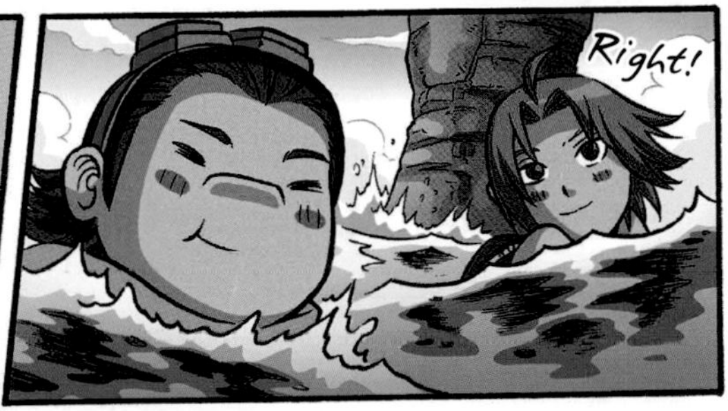
Right!

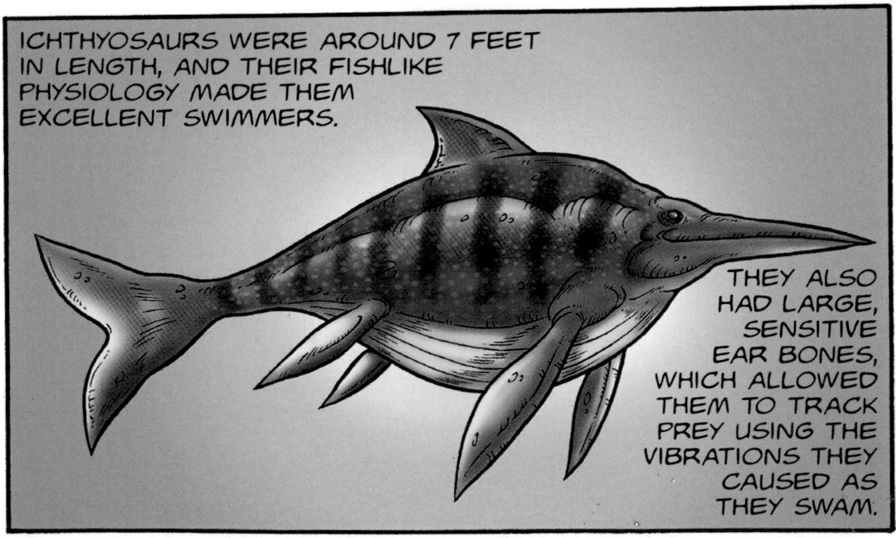
ICHTHYOSAURS WERE AROUND 7 FEET IN LENGTH, AND THEIR FISHLIKE PHYSIOLOGY MADE THEM EXCELLENT SWIMMERS.
THEY ALSO HAD LARGE, SENSITIVE EAR BONES, WHICH ALLOWED THEM TO TRACK PREY USING THE VIBRATIONS THEY CAUSED AS THEY SWAM.

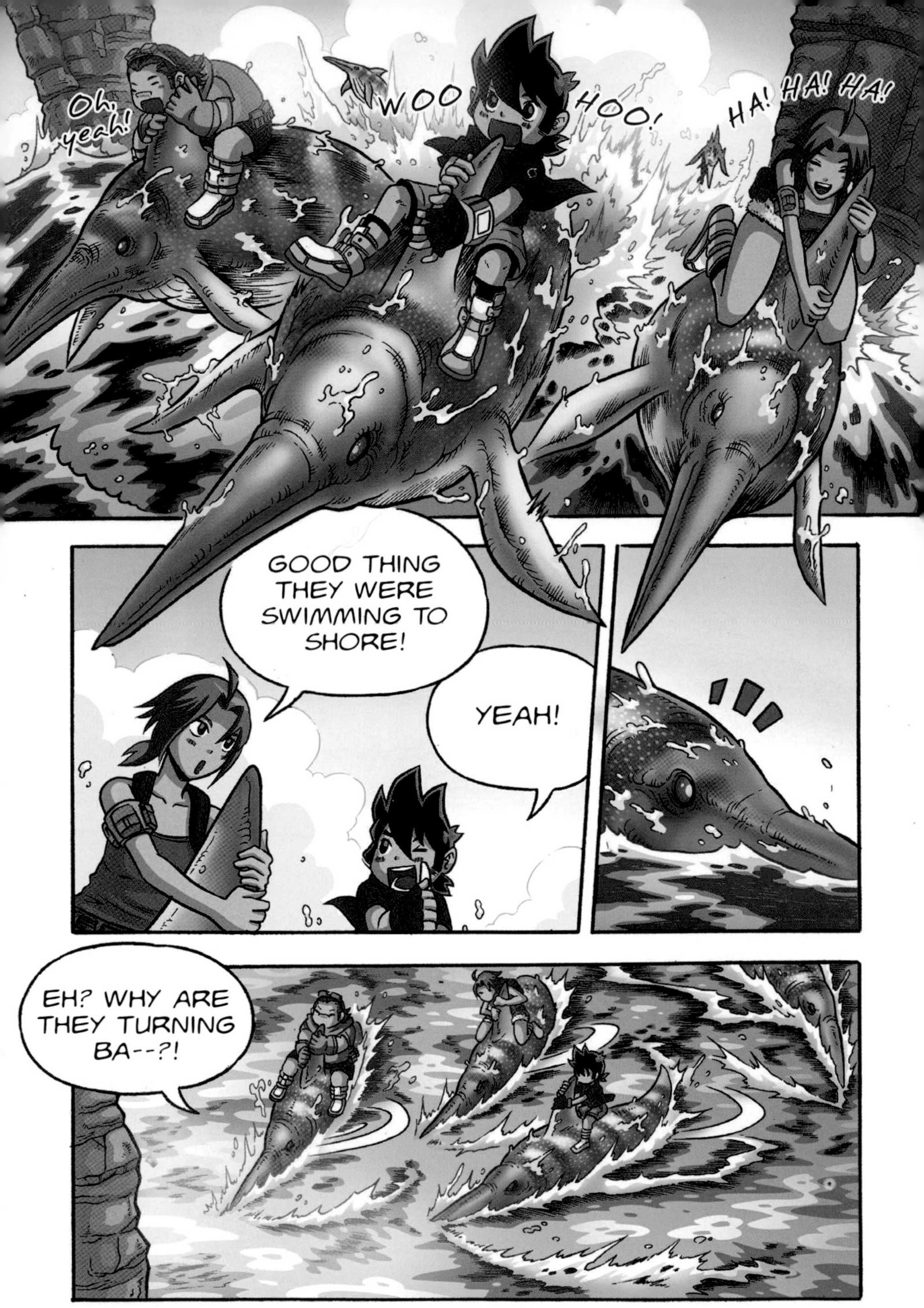
Oh, yeah!
WOO HOO!
HA! HA! HA!
GOOD THING THEY WERE SWIMMING TO SHORE!
YEAH!
EH? WHY ARE THEY TURNING BA--?!

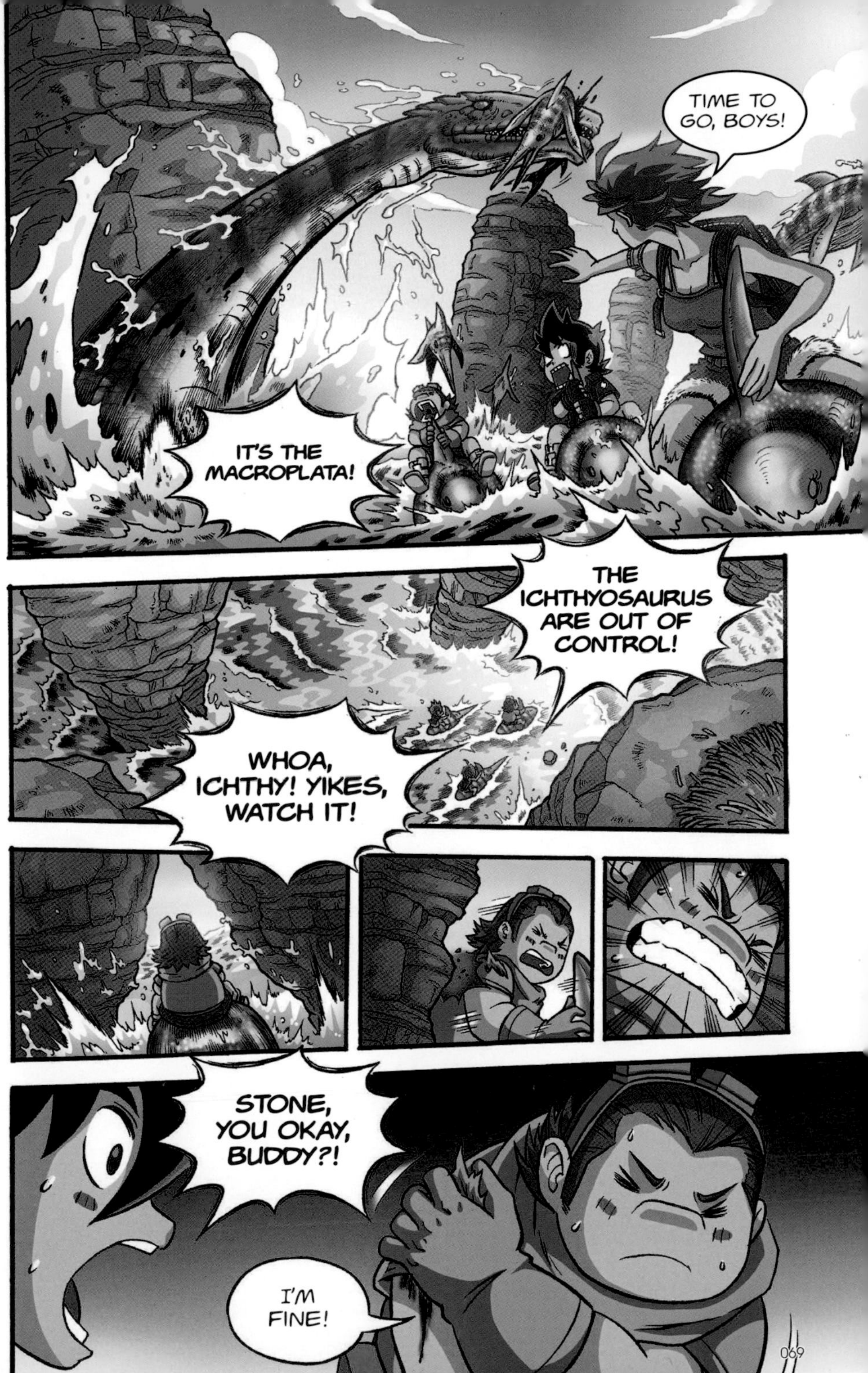
TIME TO GO, BOYS!
IT'S THE MACROPLATA!
THE ICHTHYOSAURUS ARE OUT OF CONTROL!
WHOA, ICHTHY! YIKES, WATCH IT!
STONE, YOU OKAY, BUDDY?!
I'M FINE!

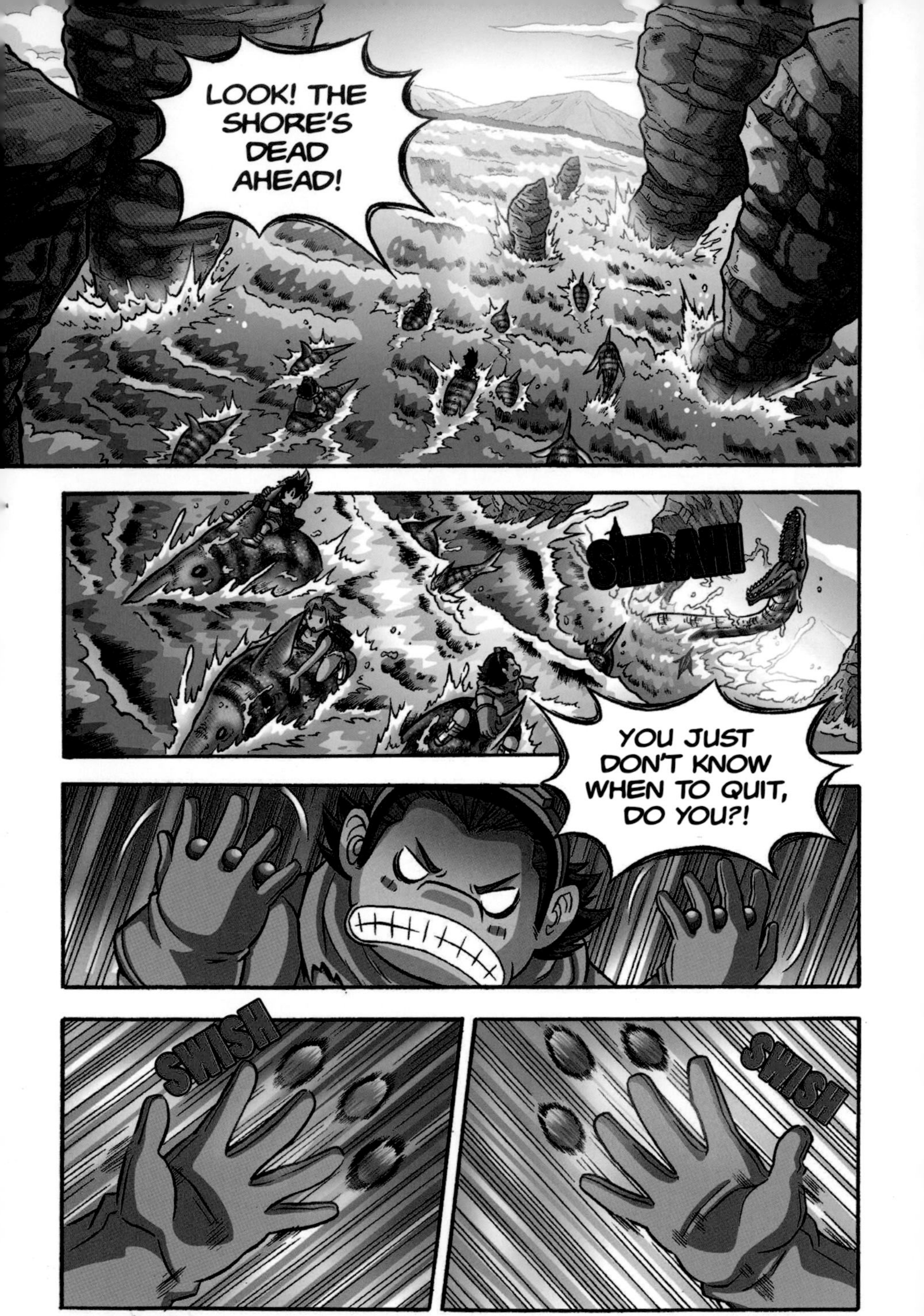
LOOK! THE SHORE'S DEAD AHEAD!
SHRAHH
YOU JUST DON'T KNOW WHEN TO QUIT, DO YOU?!
SWISH
SWISH

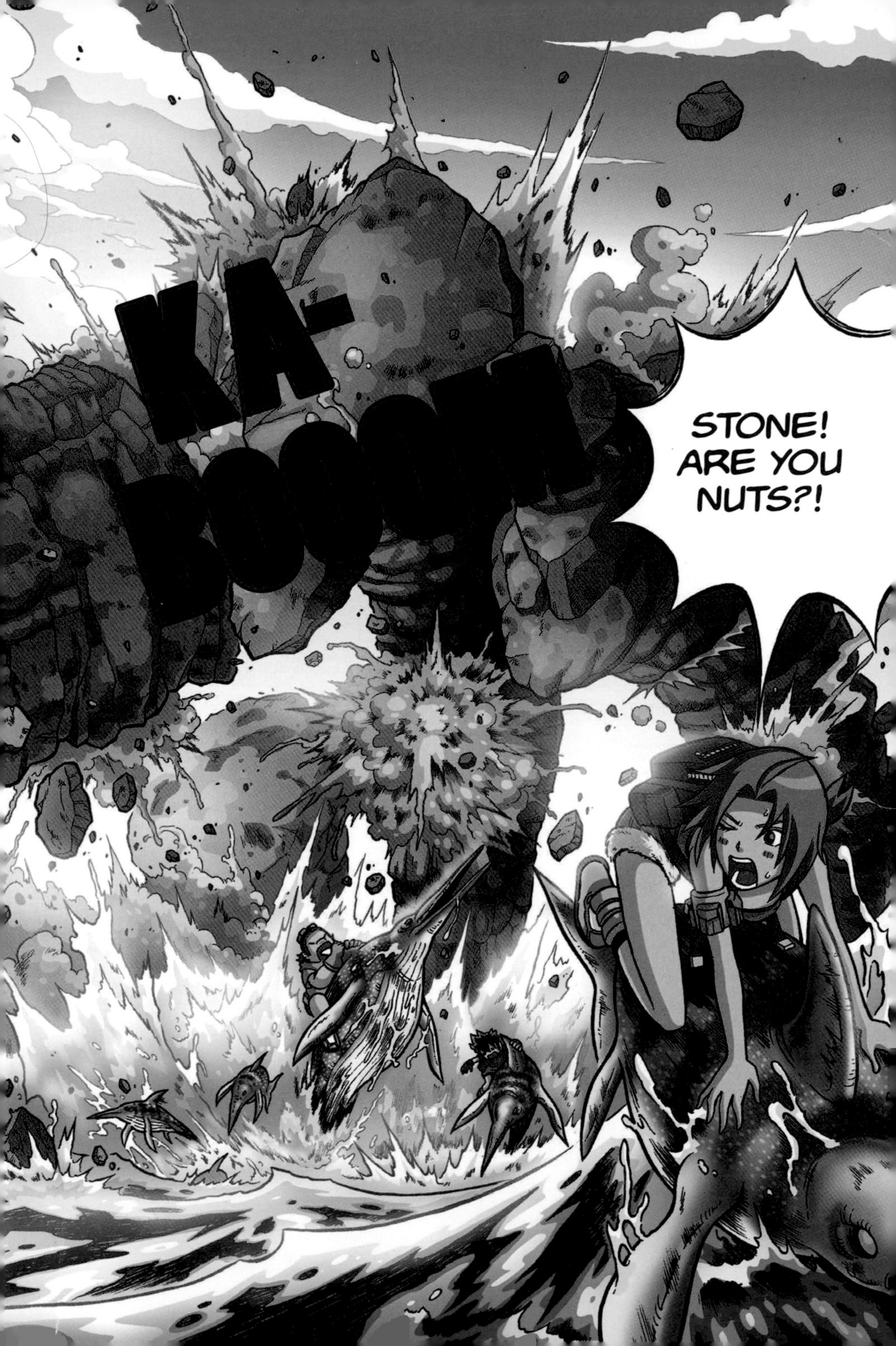
KA-BOOOM!
STONE! ARE YOU NUTS?!

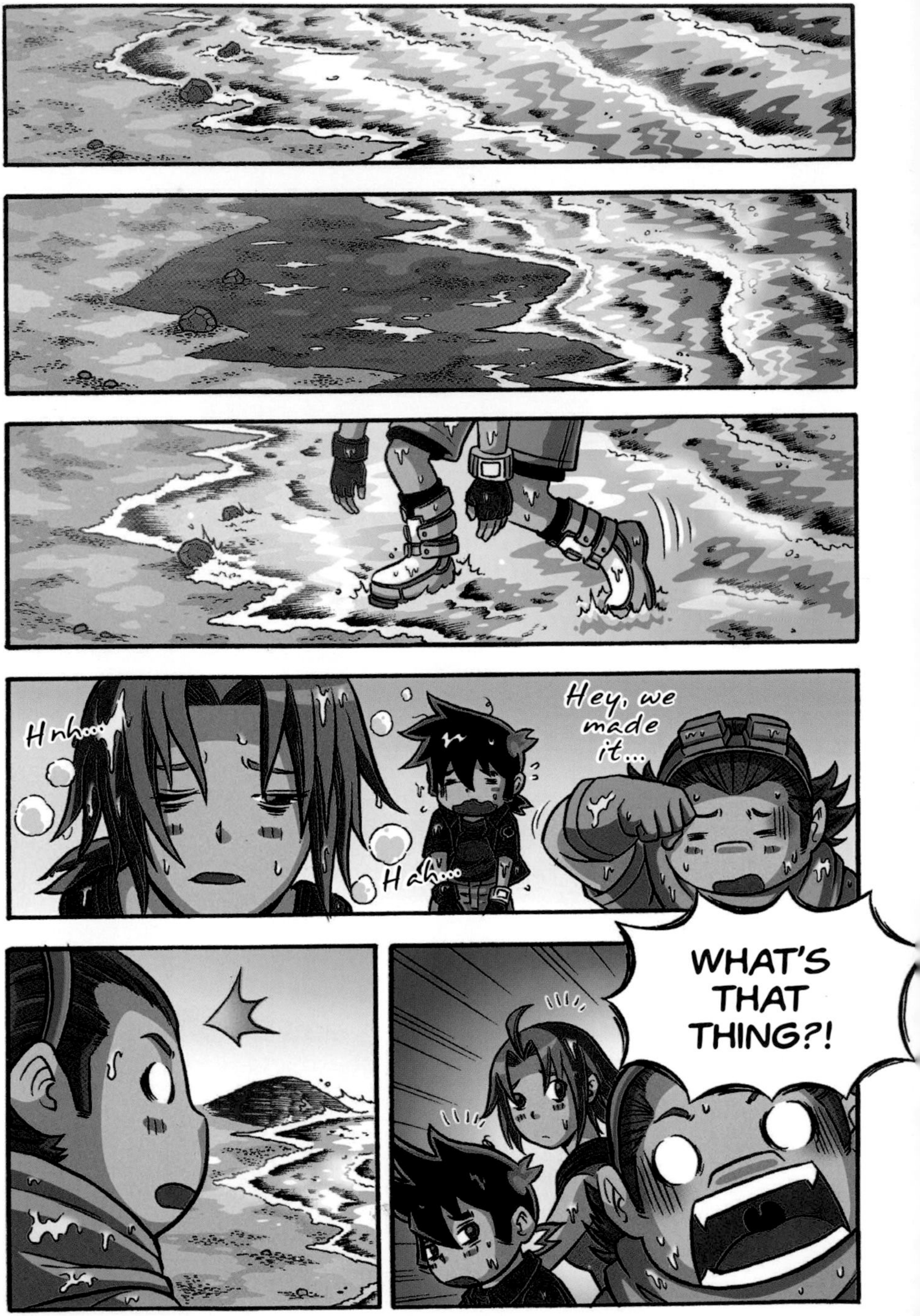
Hnh...
Hah...
Hey, we made it...
WHAT'S THAT THING?!

JONESING FOR THE JURASSIC

Macroplata

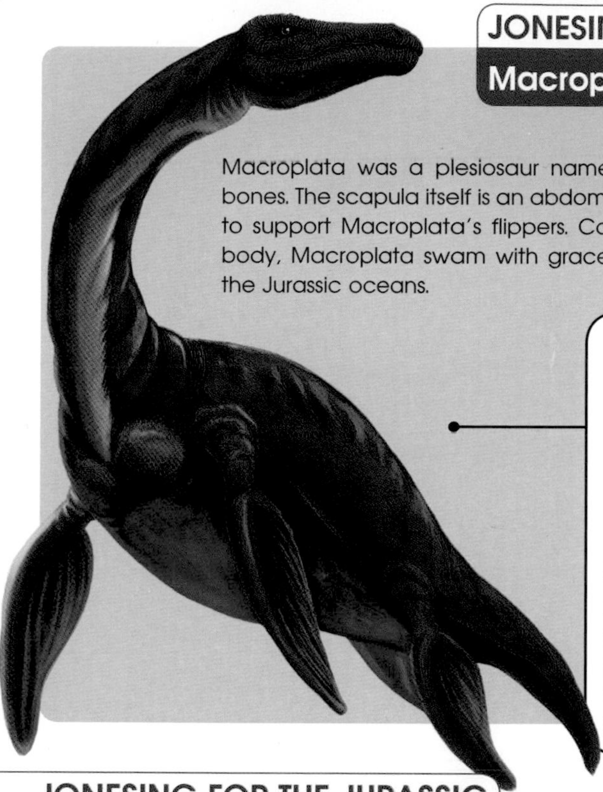

Macroplata was a plesiosaur named after their large scapula bones. The scapula itself is an abdominal bone plate that evolved to support Macroplata's flippers. Combined with its streamlined body, Macroplata swam with grace, speed and agility through the Jurassic oceans.

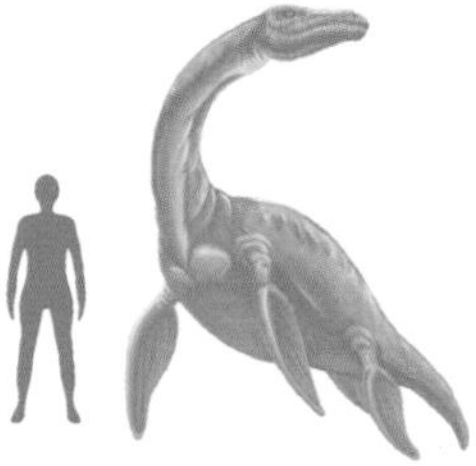

Scientific name: Macroplata
Length: 16.4 feet
Diet: Carnivorous
Habitat: Oceans
Discovered: Unknown
Era: Early Jurassic

JONESING FOR THE JURASSIC

Stenopterygius

Looking like a modern dolphin, Stenopterygius was built for speed rather than agility (though it was still quite manouvrable). It is theorised that it had senses similar to those of modern sharks and dolphins as well, which allowed it to sense food from great distances.

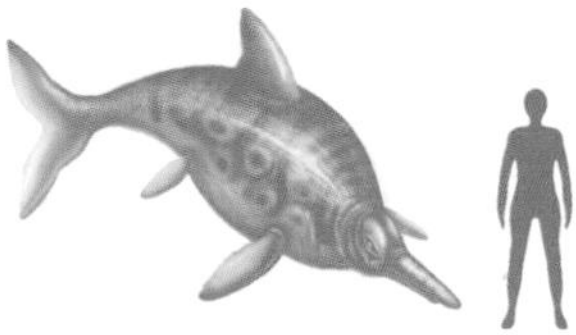

Scientific name: Stenopterygius
Length: 13.1 feet
Diet: Carnivorous
Habitat: Oceans
Discovered: Europe
Era: Mid to Late Jurassic

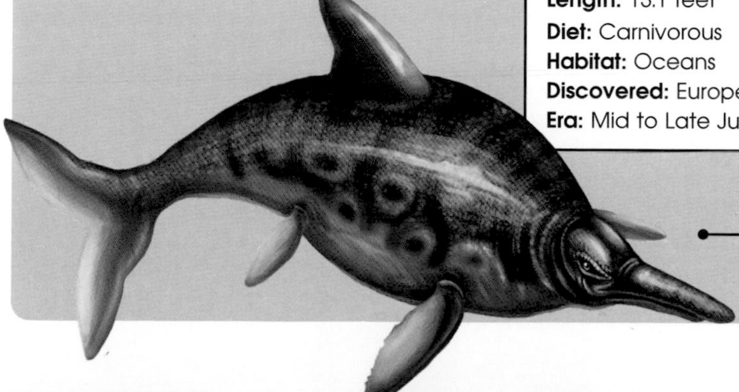

JONESING FOR THE JURASSIC

Ichthyosaurus

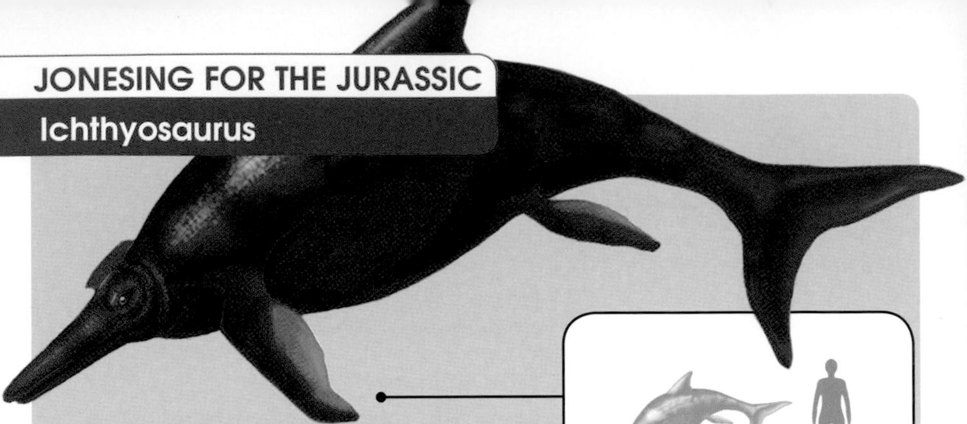

Ichthyosaurus was one of the best-researched aquatic reptiles in existence, due to the common occurence of its fossils, which were almost always found intact. As such, it has been observed that, apart from being supremely adapted to underwater life, its fin structure and smooth skin allowed it great flexibility while underwater. It also had large ears, which were probably used more than its sense of smell to find prey underwater.

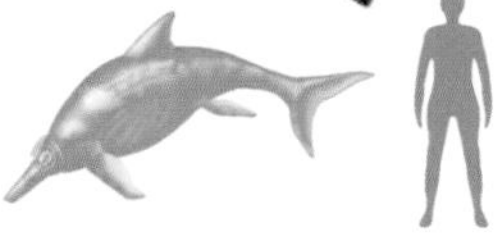

Scientific name: Ichthyosaurus
Length: 6.5 feet
Diet: Carnivorous
Habitat: Oceans
Discovered: Europe
Era: Jurassic

JONESING FOR THE JURASSIC

Temnodontosaurus

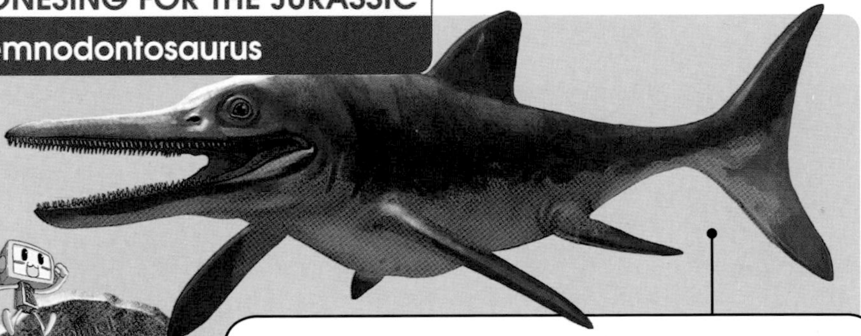

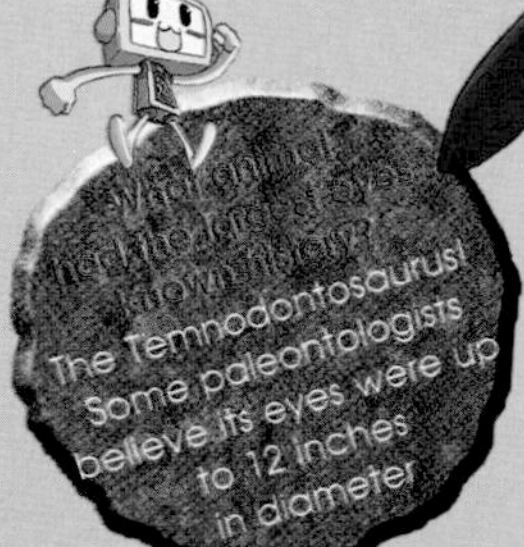
The Temnodontosaurus!
Some paleontologists
believe its eyes were up
to 12 inches
in diameter

Scientific name: Temnodontosaurus
Length: 29.5 feet
Diet: Carnivorous
Habitat: Shallow oceanic areas
Discovered: Europe
Era: Early Jurassic

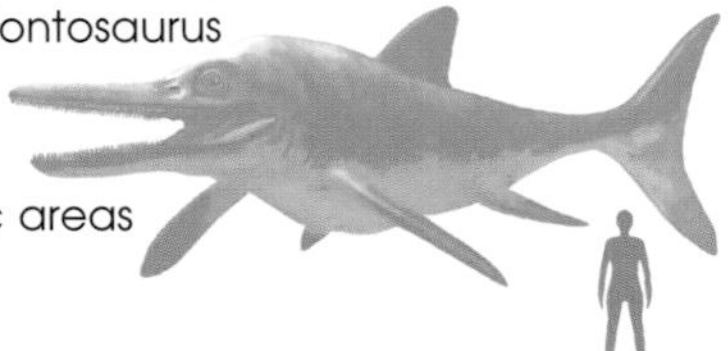

The dolphinlike Temnodontosaurus might have had a mouth full of sharp teeth and a sensitive nose, but its eyes were the main subjects of informed speculation. With eyes around 12 inches in diameter on average Temnodontosaurus; sensitive eyes would have helped it find food even in the dark depths.

CHAPTER 4
KEEPING A PROMISE

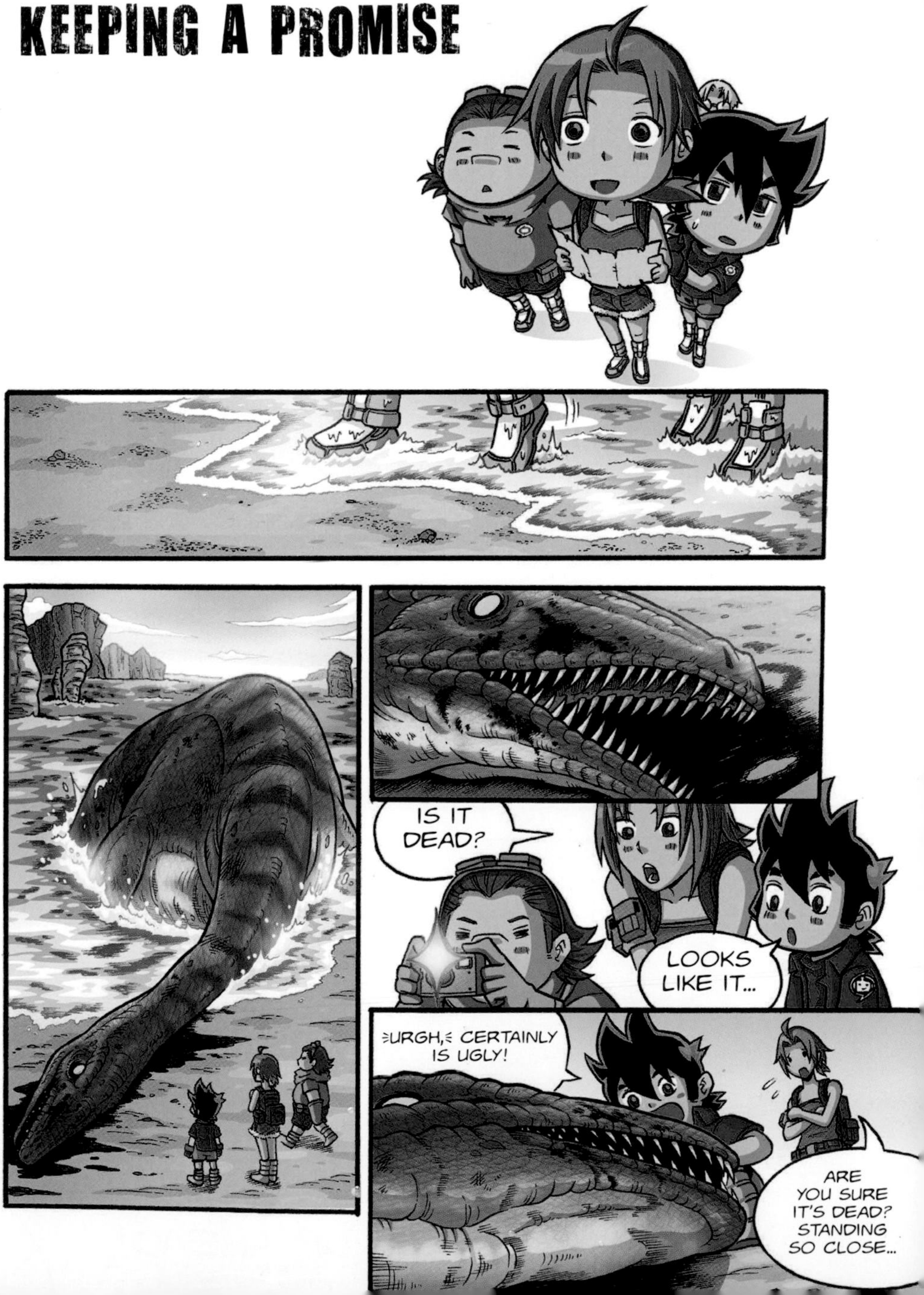

IS IT DEAD?
LOOKS LIKE IT...
≶URGH,≶ CERTAINLY IS UGLY!
ARE YOU SURE IT'S DEAD? STANDING SO CLOSE...

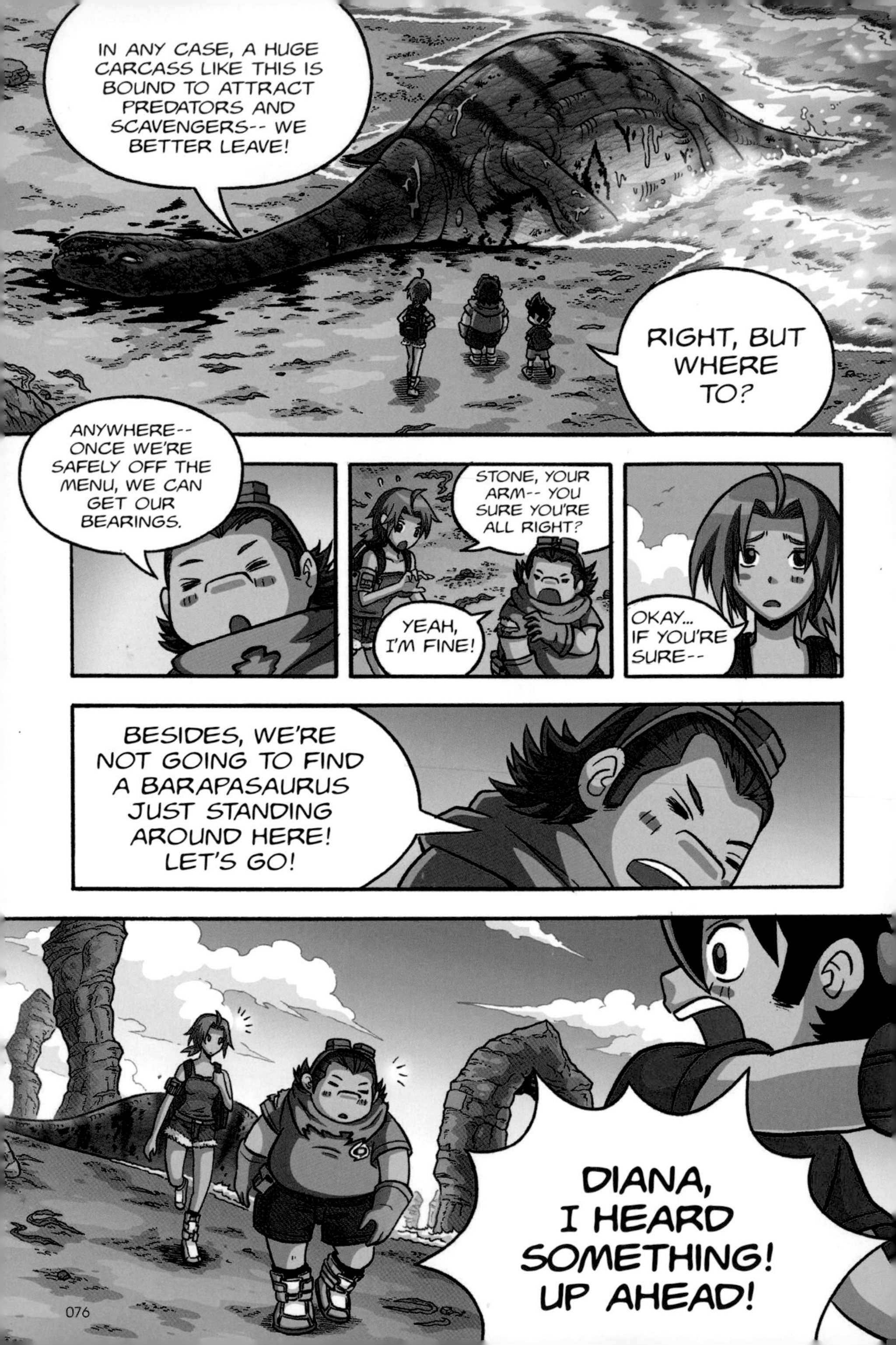
IN ANY CASE, A HUGE CARCASS LIKE THIS IS BOUND TO ATTRACT PREDATORS AND SCAVENGERS-- WE BETTER LEAVE!
RIGHT, BUT WHERE TO?
ANYWHERE-- ONCE WE'RE SAFELY OFF THE MENU, WE CAN GET OUR BEARINGS.
STONE, YOUR ARM-- YOU SURE YOU'RE ALL RIGHT?
YEAH, I'M FINE!
OKAY... IF YOU'RE SURE--
BESIDES, WE'RE NOT GOING TO FIND A BARAPASAURUS JUST STANDING AROUND HERE! LET'S GO!
DIANA, I HEARD SOMETHING! UP AHEAD!

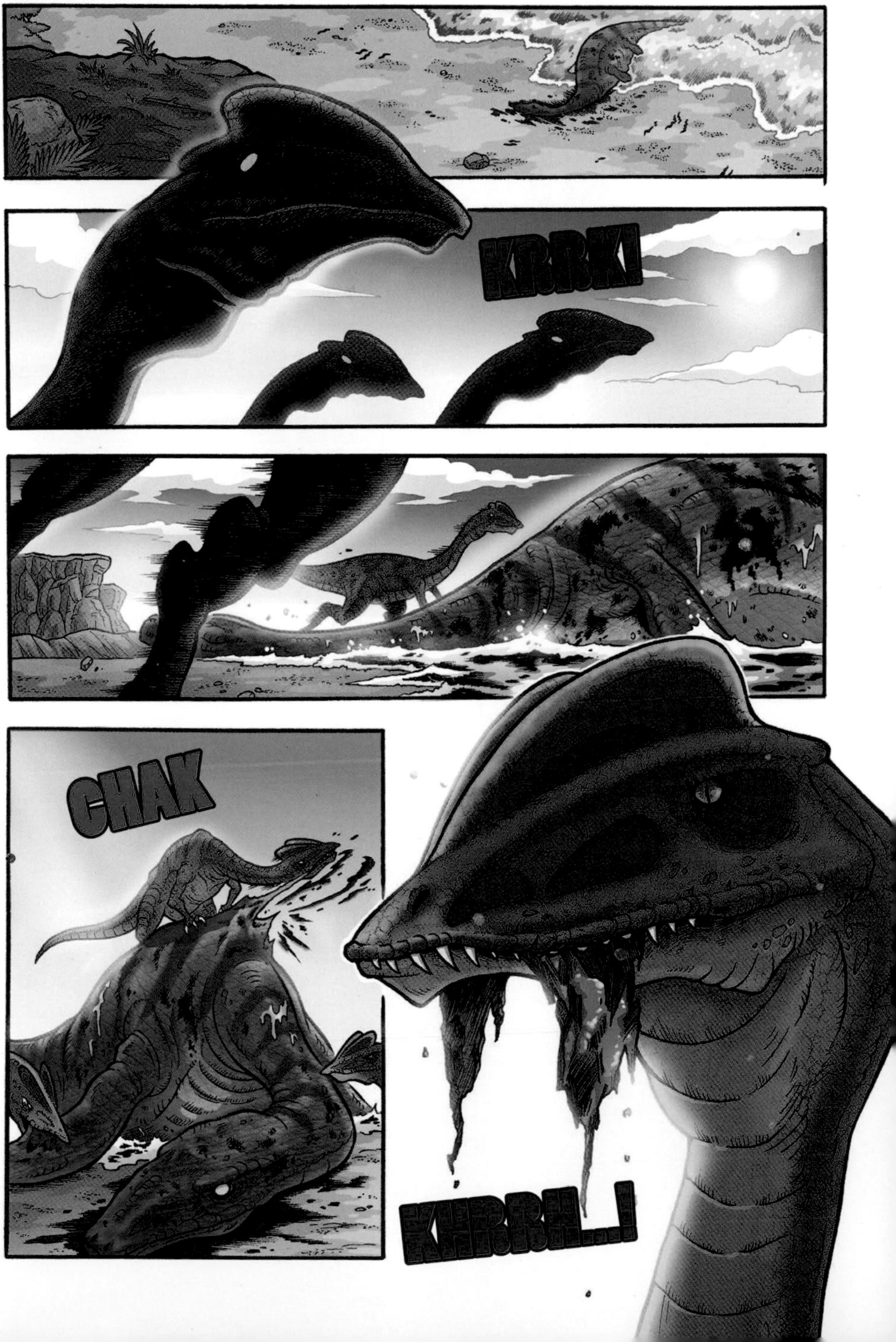
KRRK!
CHAK
KHRRH...!

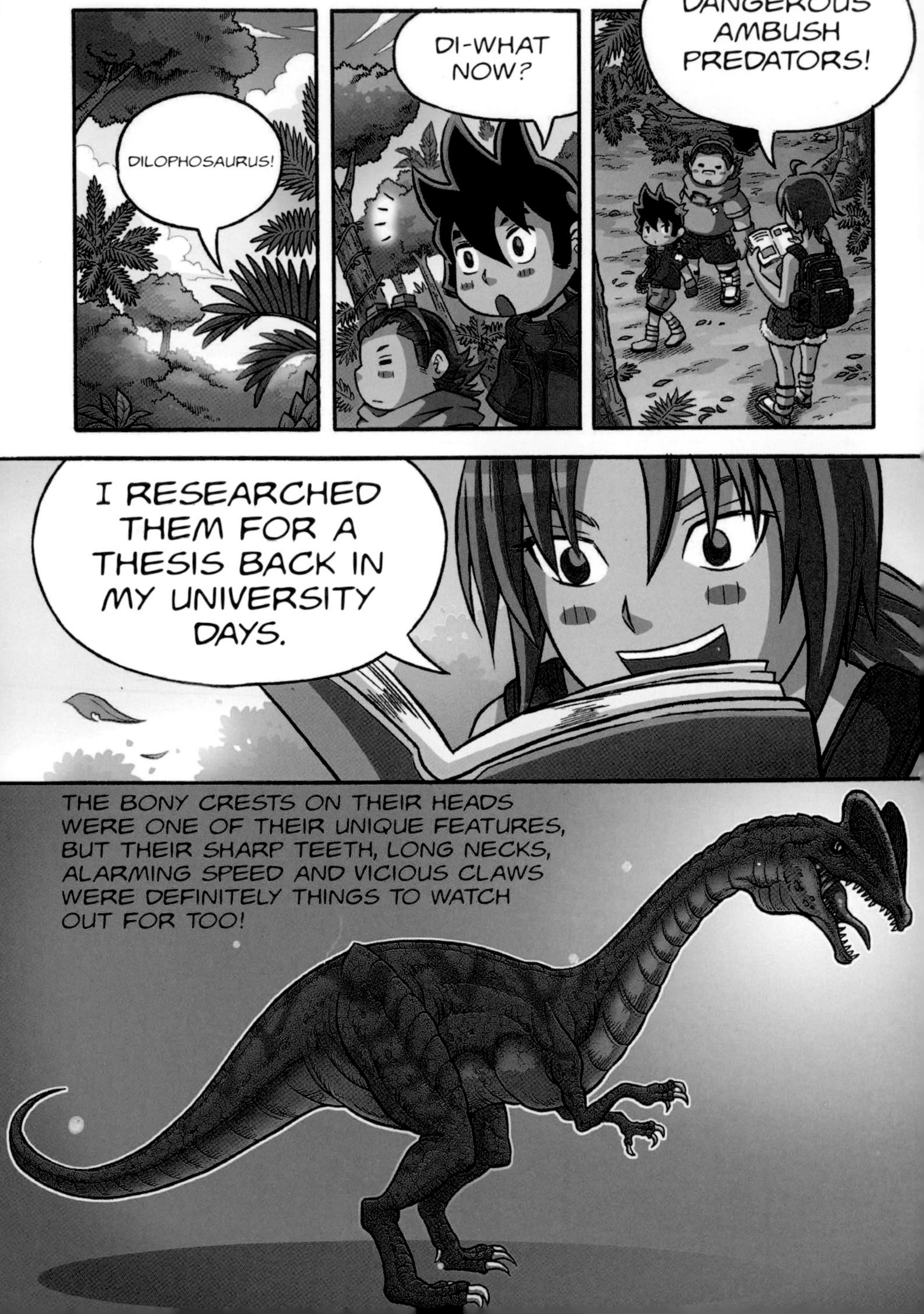
DILOPHOSAURUS!
DI-WHAT NOW?
DANGEROUS AMBUSH PREDATORS!
I RESEARCHED THEM FOR A THESIS BACK IN MY UNIVERSITY DAYS.
THE BONY CRESTS ON THEIR HEADS WERE ONE OF THEIR UNIQUE FEATURES, BUT THEIR SHARP TEETH, LONG NECKS, ALARMING SPEED AND VICIOUS CLAWS WERE DEFINITELY THINGS TO WATCH OUT FOR TOO!

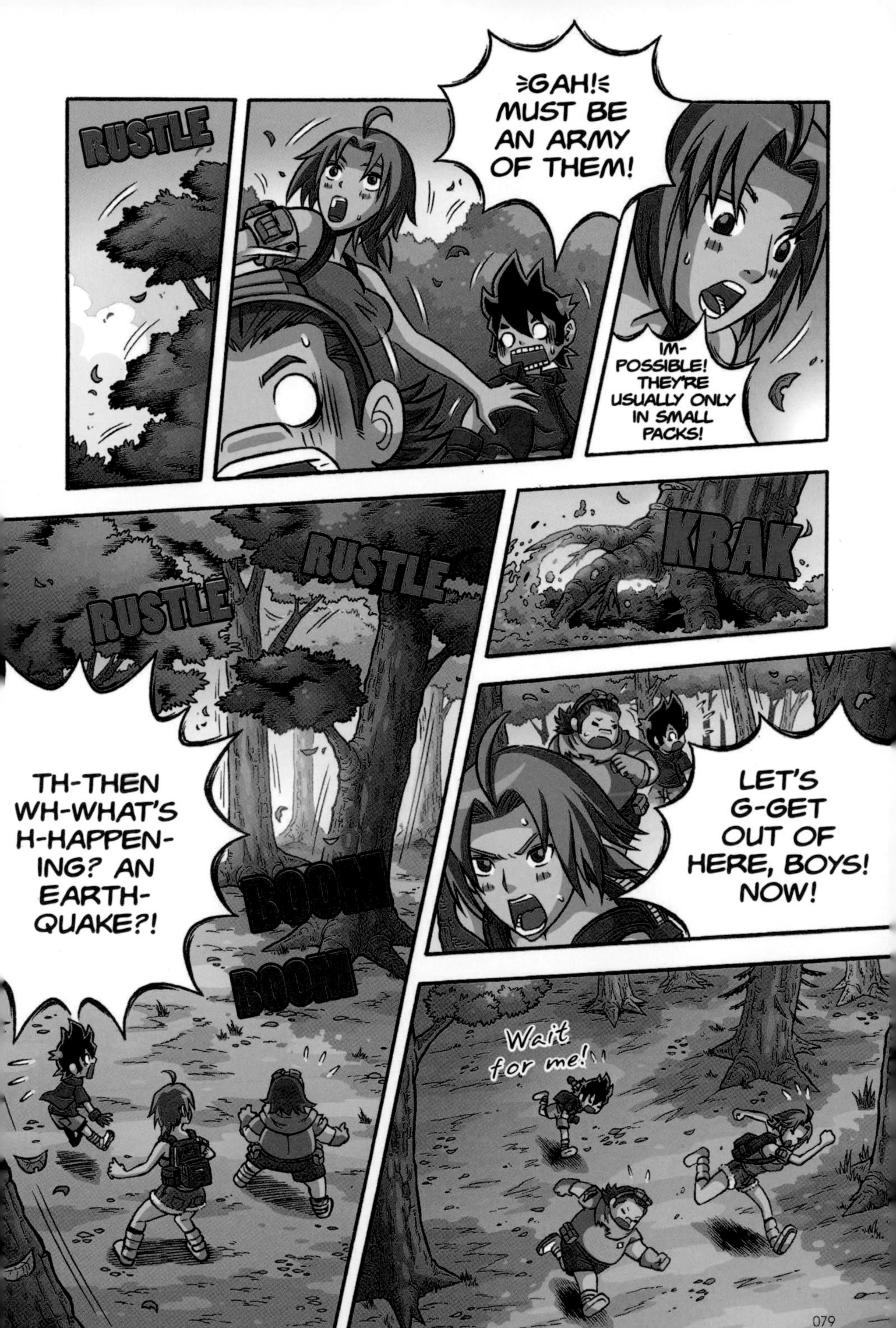
RUSTLE
GAH! MUST BE AN ARMY OF THEM!
IM-POSSIBLE! THEY'RE USUALLY ONLY IN SMALL PACKS!
RUSTLE
RUSTLE
KRAK
TH-THEN WH-WHAT'S H-HAPPEN-ING? AN EARTH-QUAKE?!
LET'S G-GET OUT OF HERE, BOYS! NOW!
Wait for me!

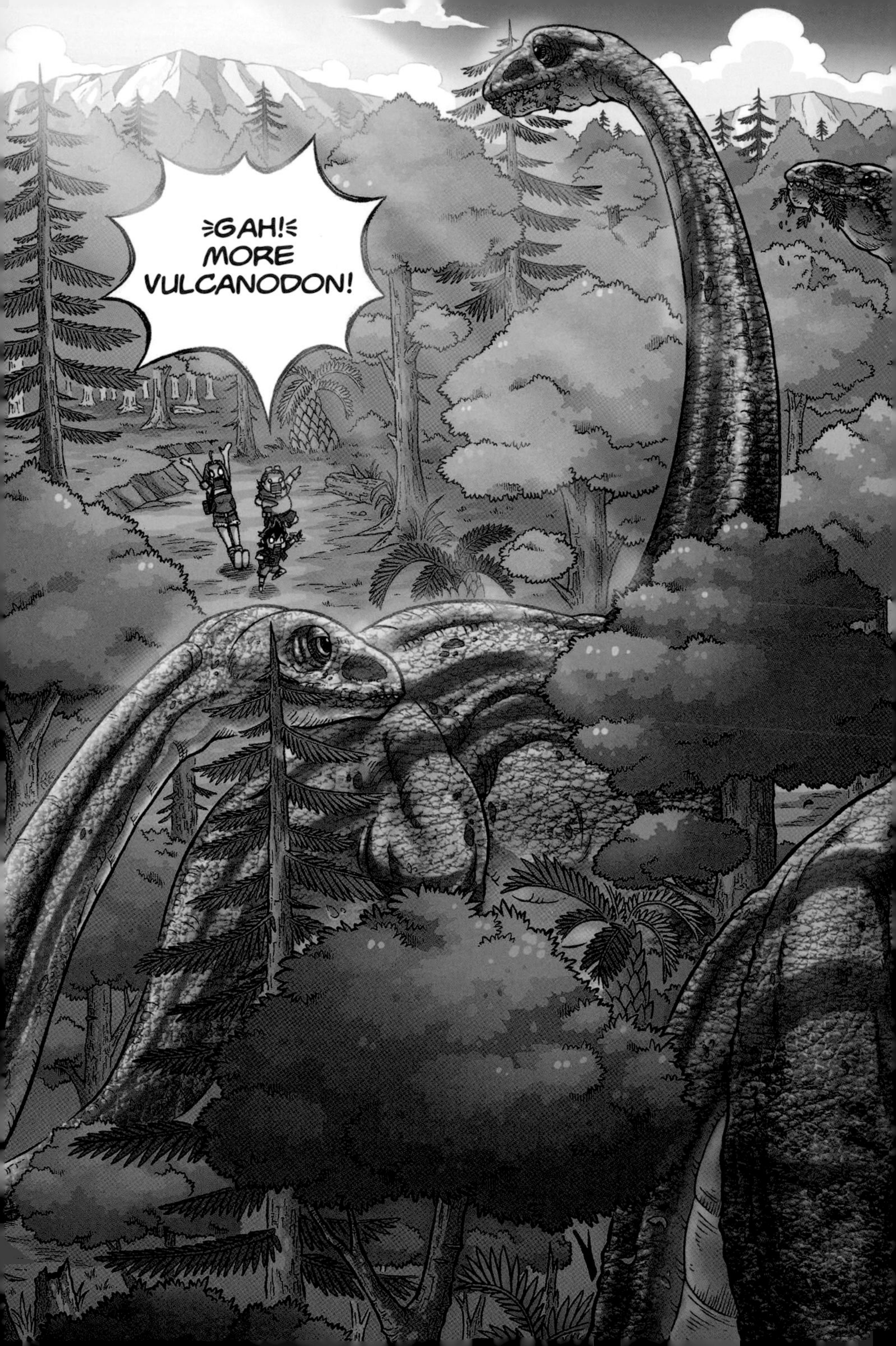
GAH! MORE VULCANODON!

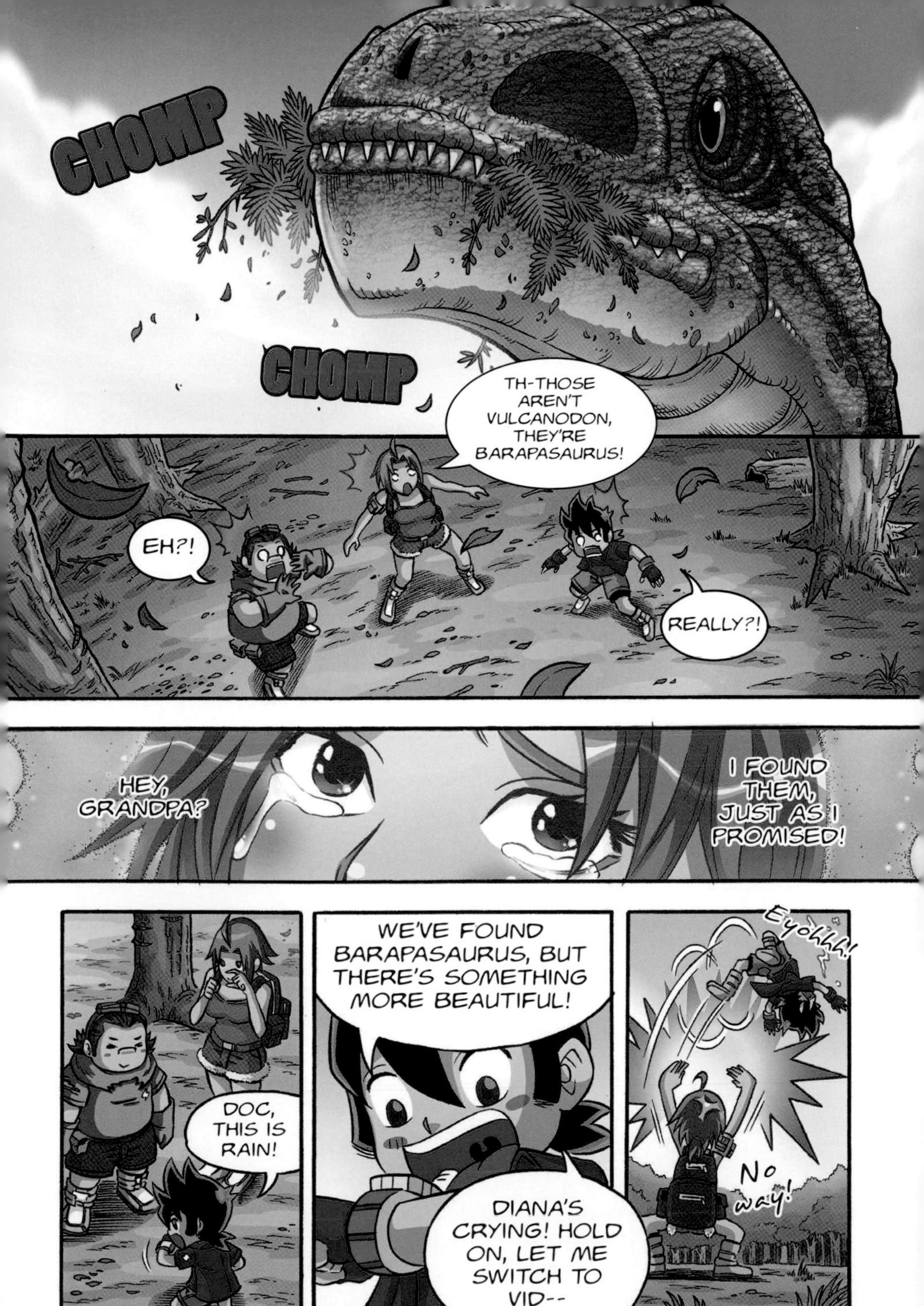
CHOMP
CHOMP
TH-THOSE AREN'T VULCANODON, THEY'RE BARAPASAURUS!
EH?!
REALLY?!
HEY, GRANDPA?
I FOUND THEM, JUST AS I PROMISED!
DOC, THIS IS RAIN!
WE'VE FOUND BARAPASAURUS, BUT THERE'S SOMETHING MORE BEAUTIFUL!
DIANA'S CRYING! HOLD ON, LET ME SWITCH TO VID--
Eyohhh!
No way!

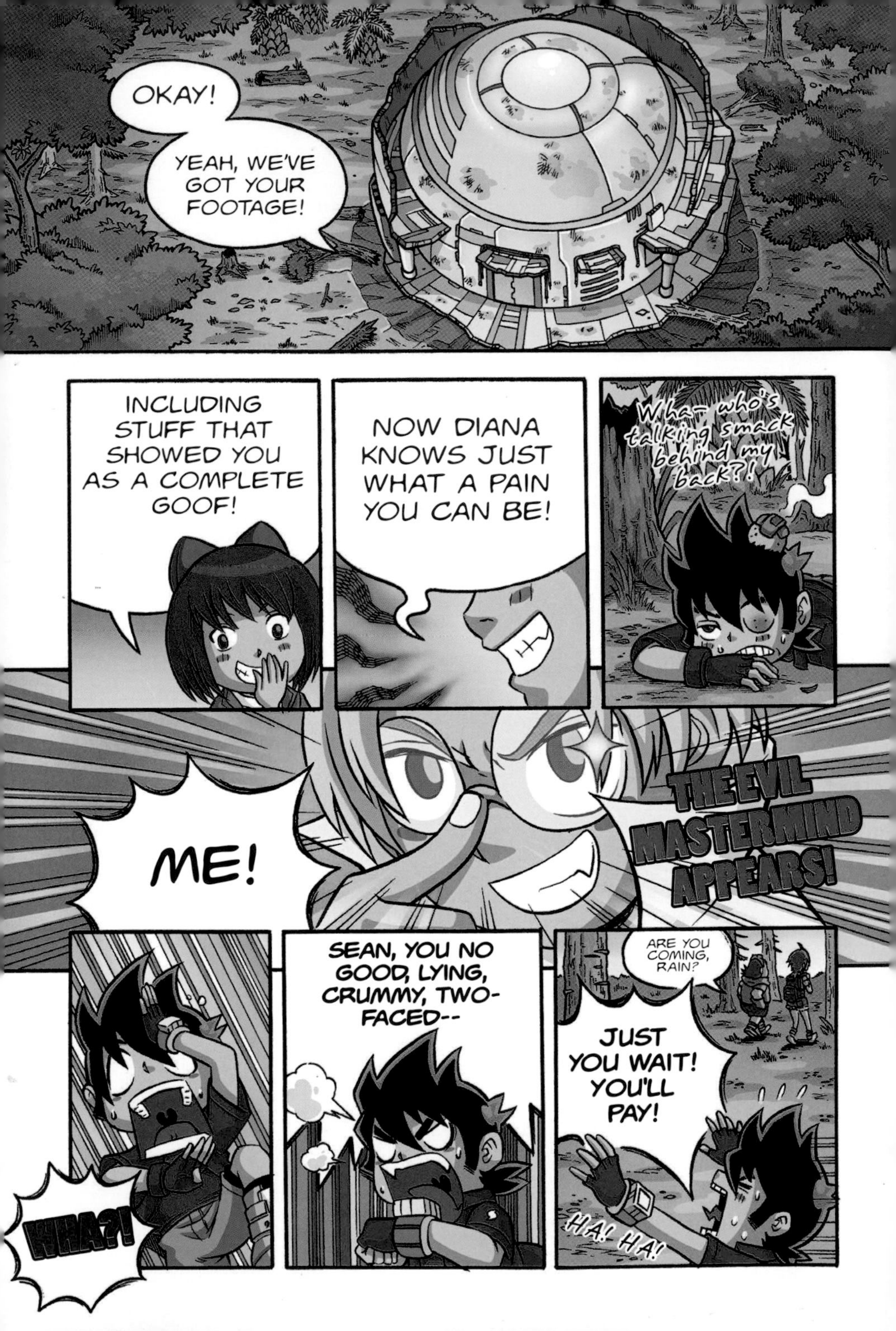
OKAY!
YEAH, WE'VE GOT YOUR FOOTAGE!
INCLUDING STUFF THAT SHOWED YOU AS A COMPLETE GOOF!
NOW DIANA KNOWS JUST WHAT A PAIN YOU CAN BE!
Wha- who's talking smack behind my back?!
ME!
THE EVIL MASTERMIND APPEARS!
WHA?!
SEAN, YOU NO GOOD, LYING, CRUMMY, TWO-FACED--
ARE YOU COMING, RAIN?
JUST YOU WAIT! YOU'LL PAY!
HA! HA!

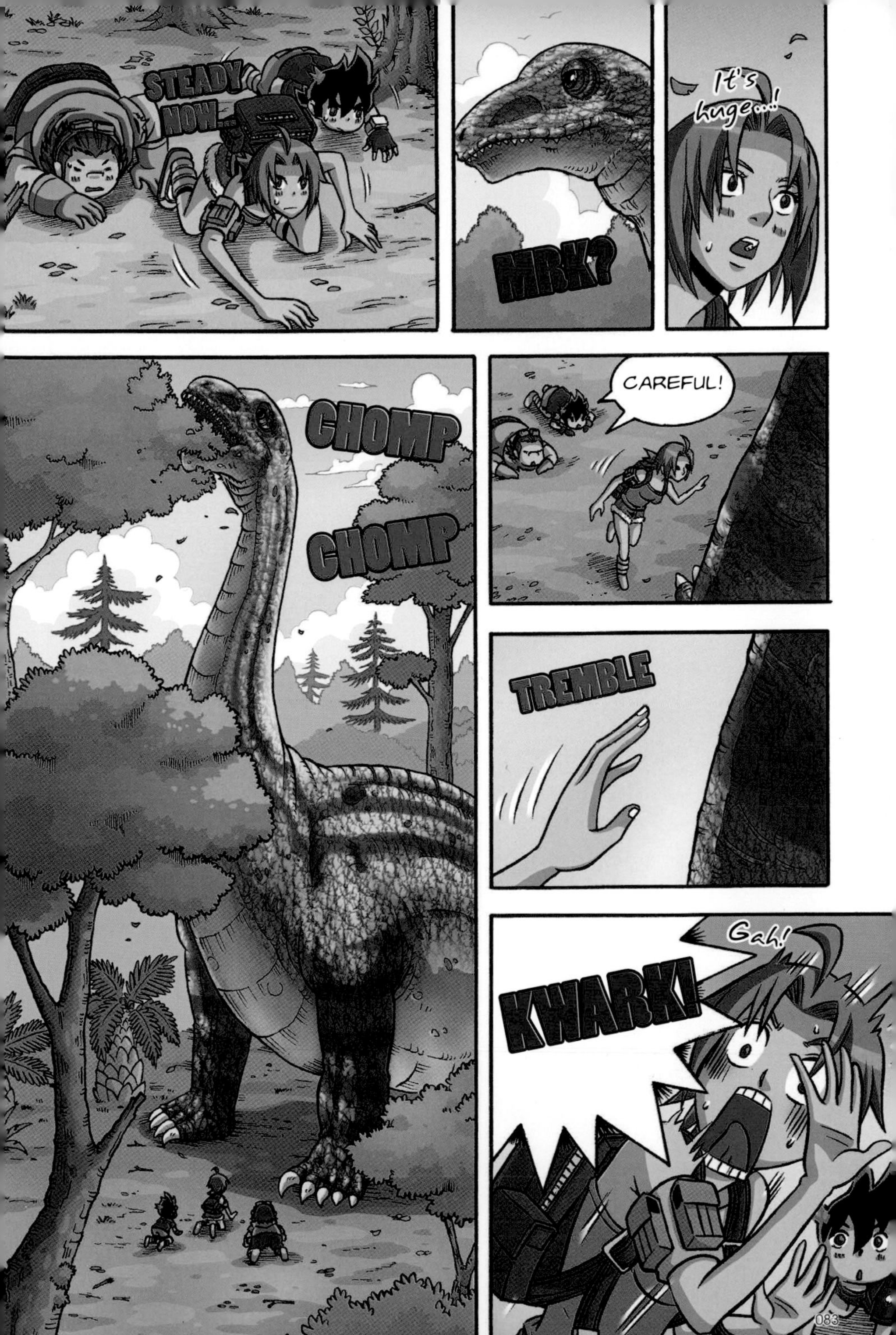
STEADY NOW...
MRK?
It's huge...!
CHOMP
CHOMP
CAREFUL!
TREMBLE
Gah!
KWARK!

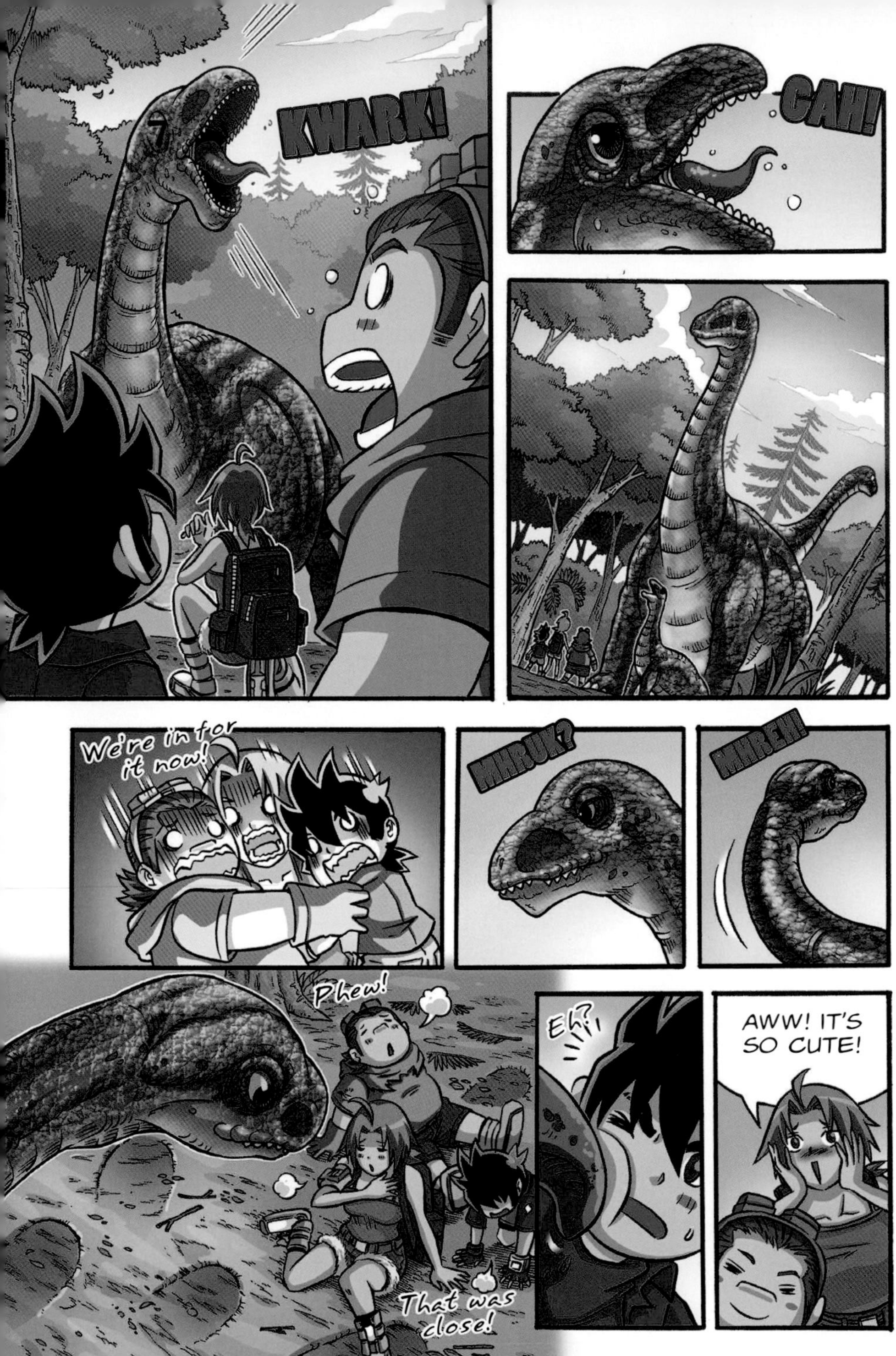
KWARK!
GAH!
We're in for it now!
MHRUK?
MHREH!
Phew!
That was close!
Eh?
AWW! IT'S SO CUTE!

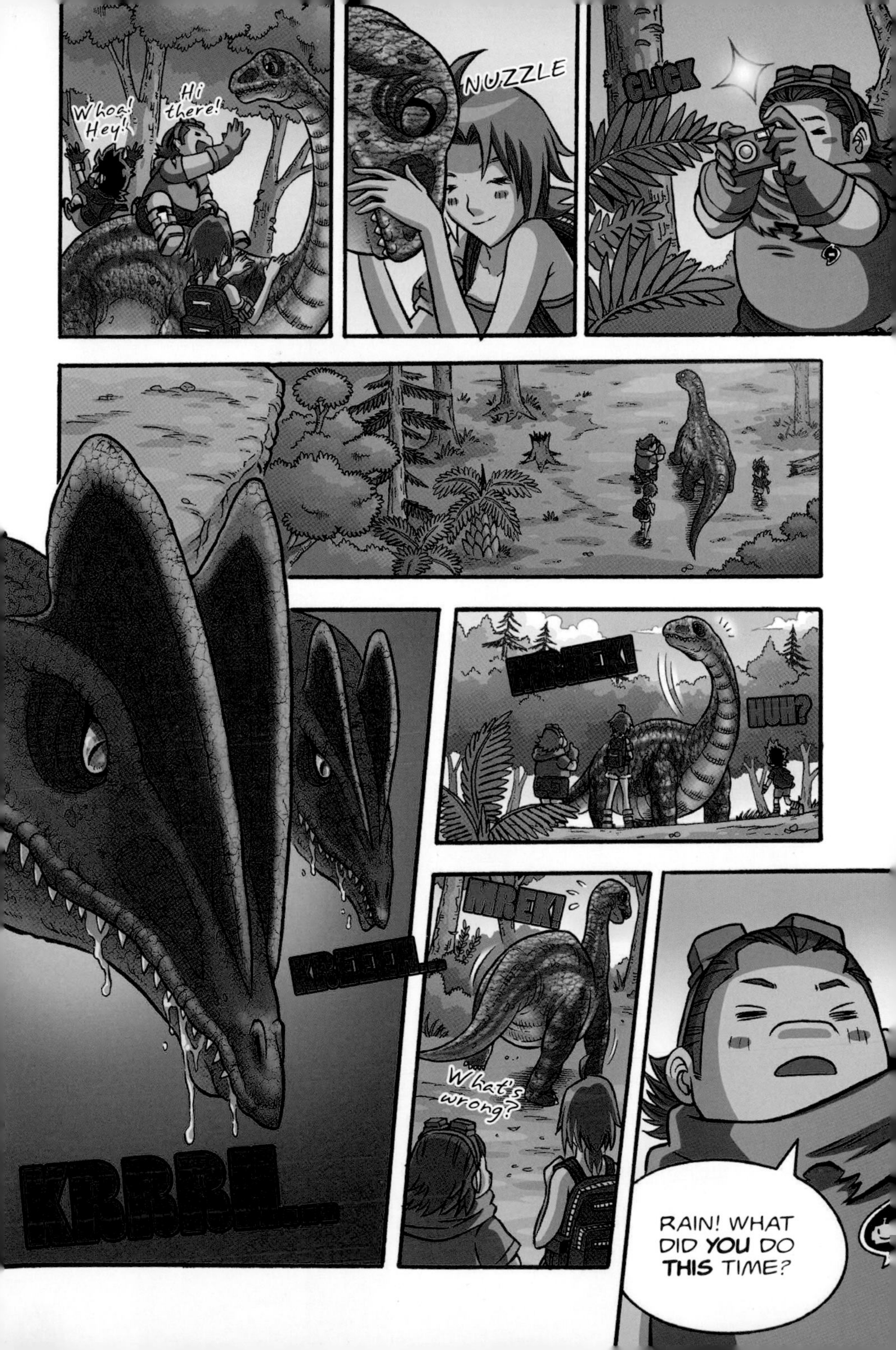
Whoa! Hey!
Hi there!
NUZZLE
CLICK
HUH?
MREK!
What's wrong?
RAIN! WHAT DID YOU DO THIS TIME?

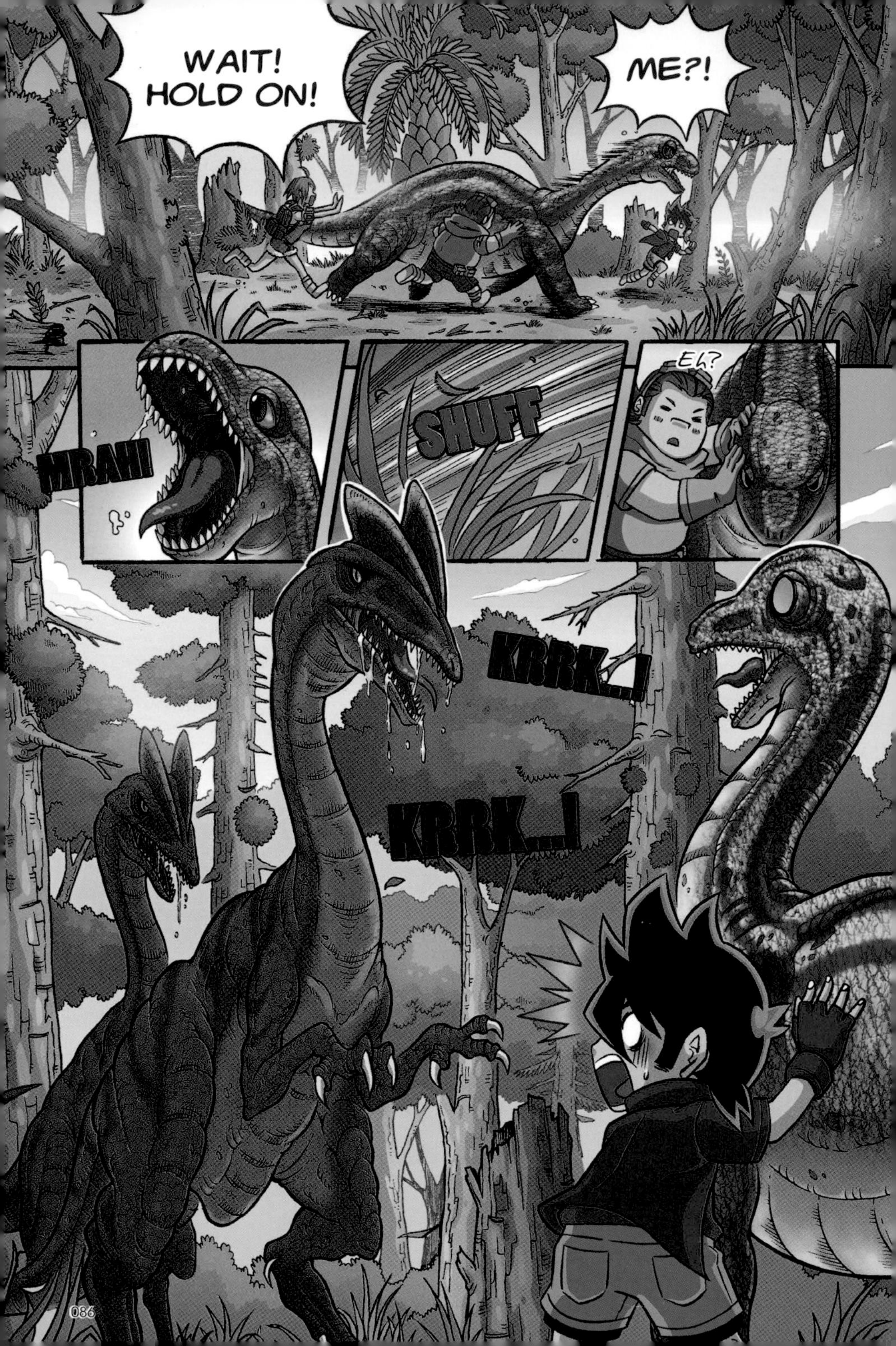
WAIT! HOLD ON!
ME?!
MRAH!
SHUFF
Eh?
KRRK...!
KRRK...!

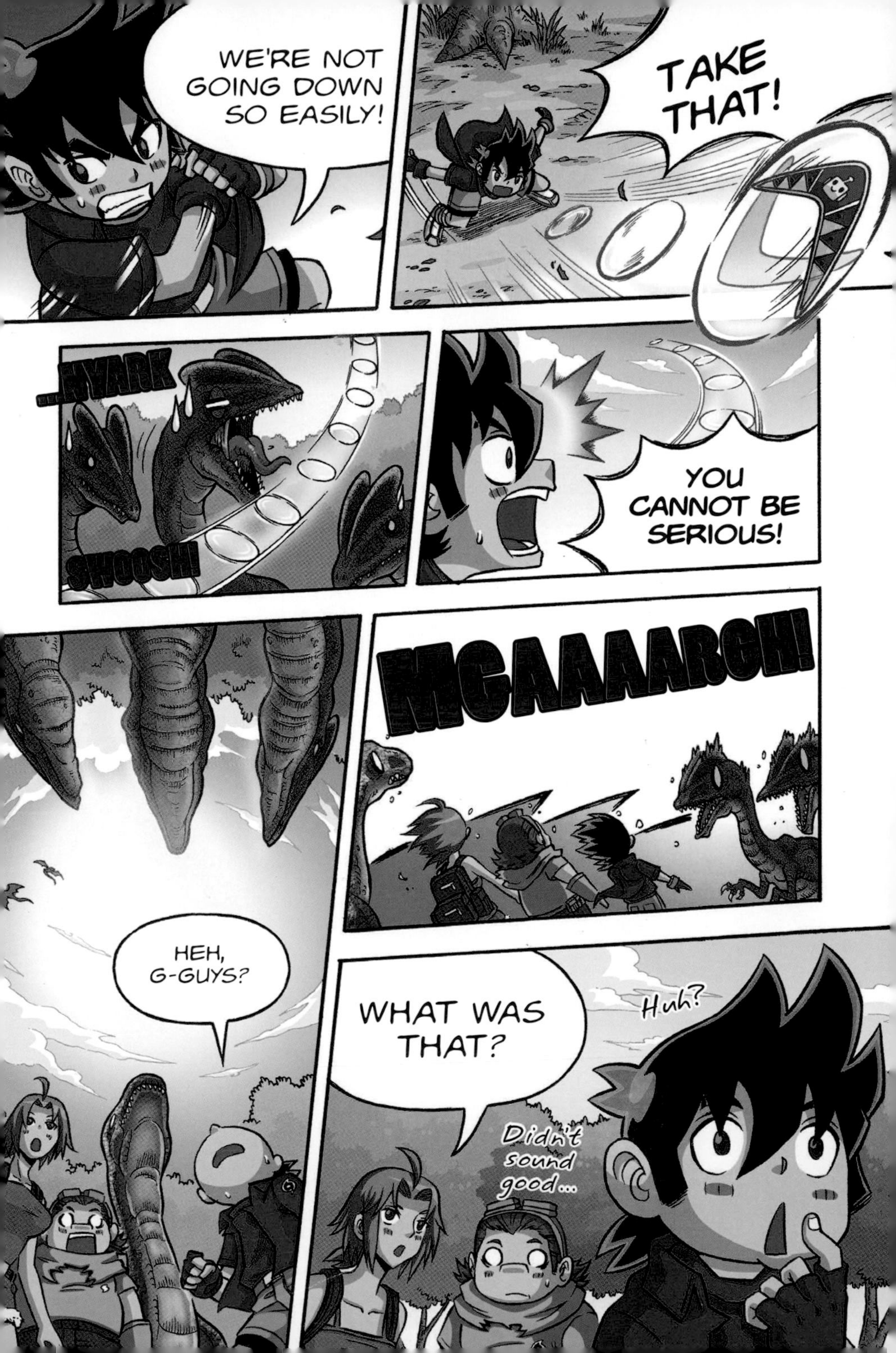
WE'RE NOT GOING DOWN SO EASILY!
TAKE THAT!
...NYARK
SWOOSH!
YOU CANNOT BE SERIOUS!
MGAAAAARCH!
HEH, G-GUYS?
WHAT WAS THAT?
Huh?
Didn't sound good...

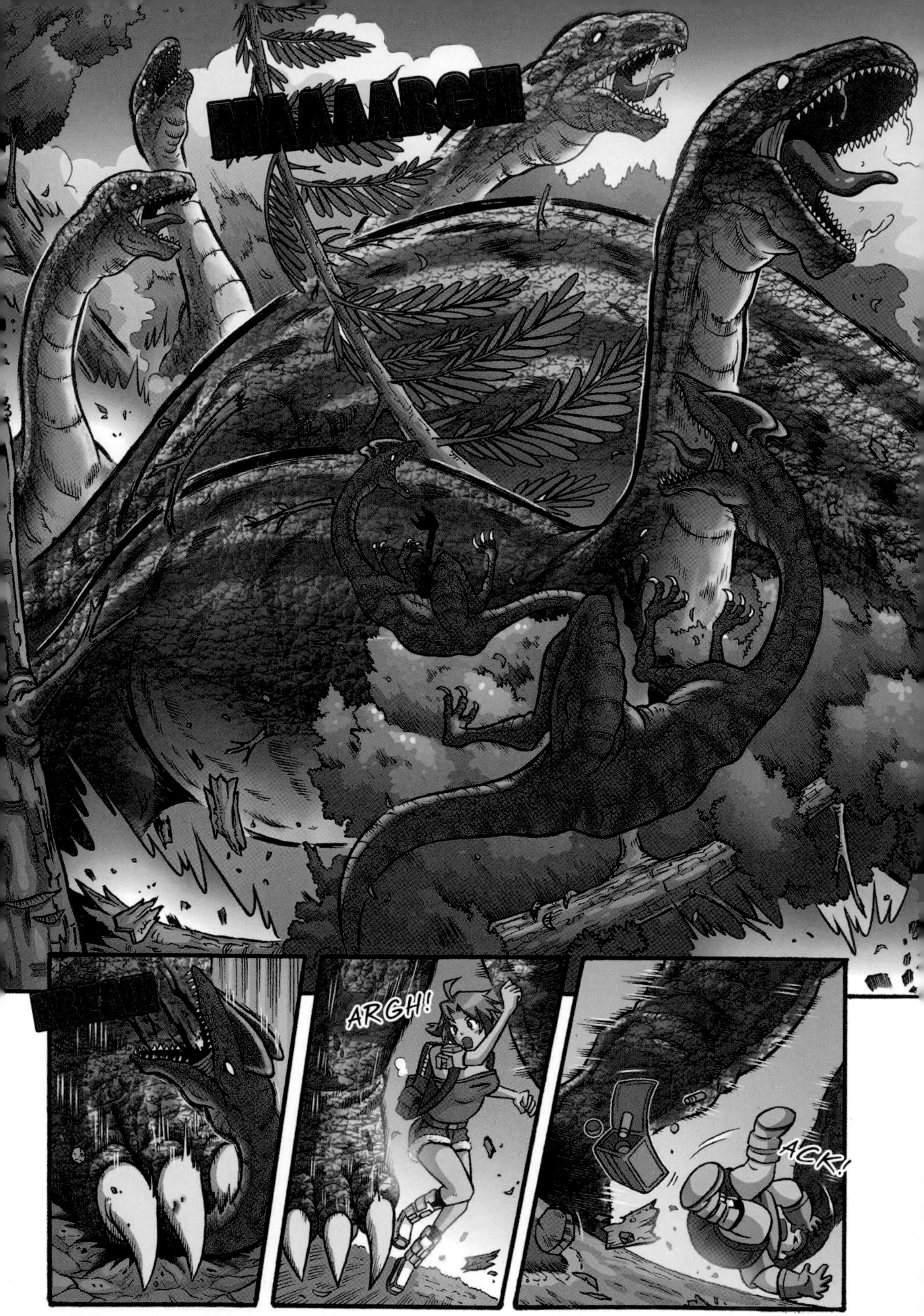
ARGH!
ACK!

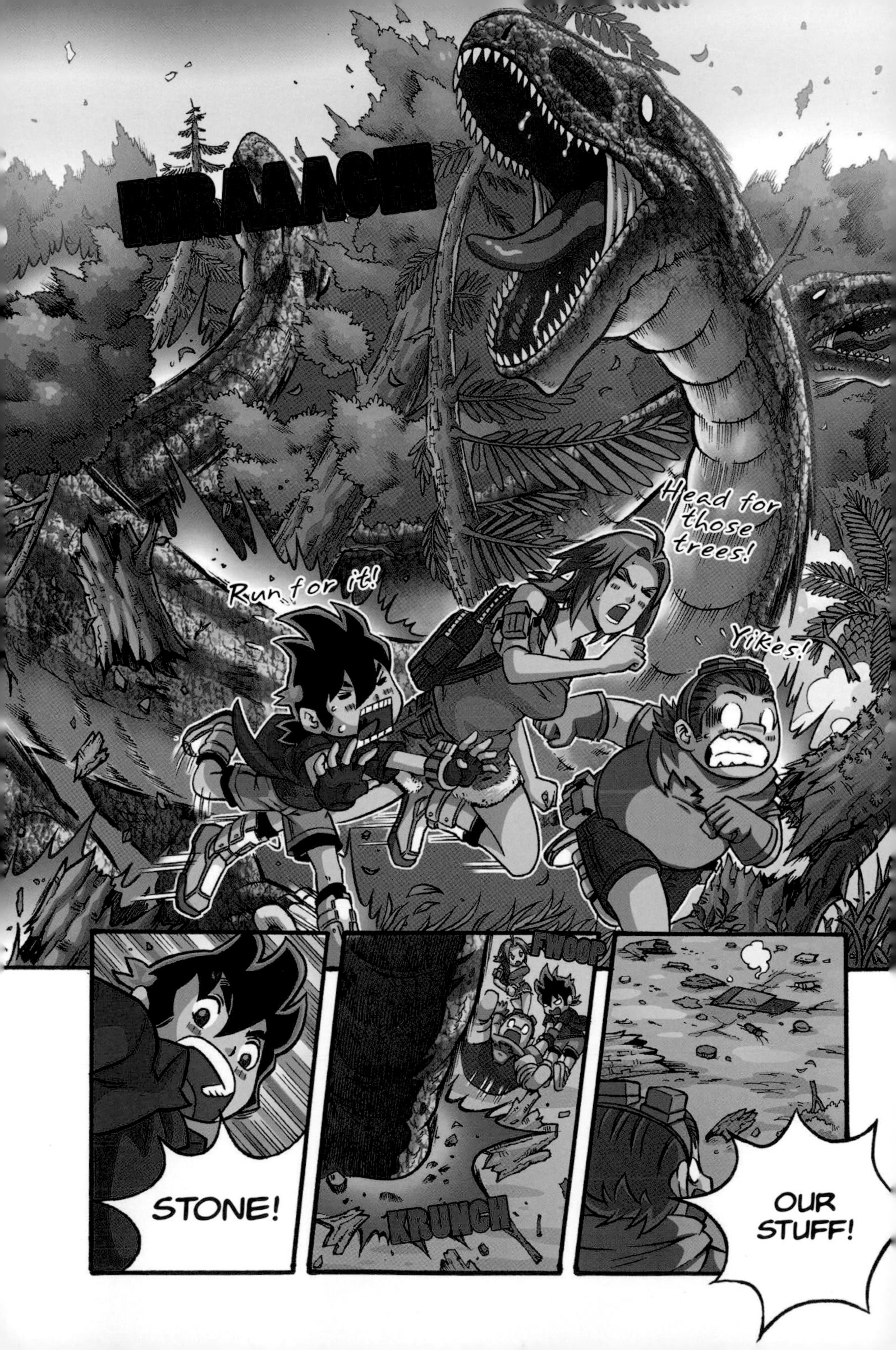
HRAAACH
Run for it!
Head for those trees!
Yikes!
STONE!
KRUNCH
FWOOP
OUR STUFF!

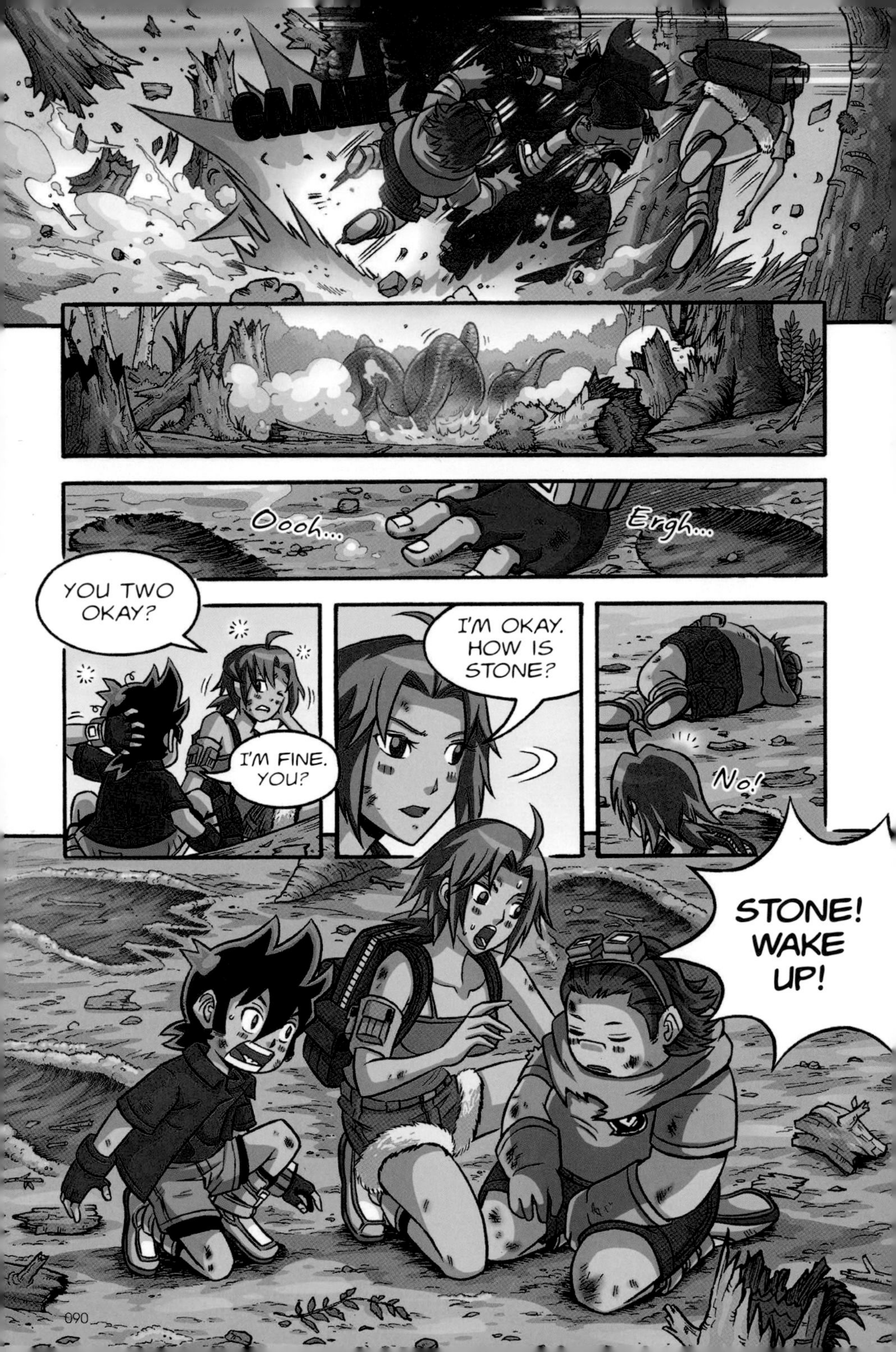
Oooh...
Ergh...
YOU TWO OKAY?
I'M FINE. YOU?
I'M OKAY. HOW IS STONE?
No!
STONE! WAKE UP!

Dilophosaurus

Dilophosaurus was an early theropod; its name was derived from the V-shaped crest on its head ("Dilophosaurus" means "two-crested lizard" in Greek). Though it looked cool, the inner bone structure was actually quite weak, and as such it is believed that it was used to attract females rather than serve any practical purpose. In any case, it had more than enough advantages already–powerful legs for speed, sharp, clawed limbs for hunting, and strong jaws. All these made it one of the early Jurassic's most terrifying predators.

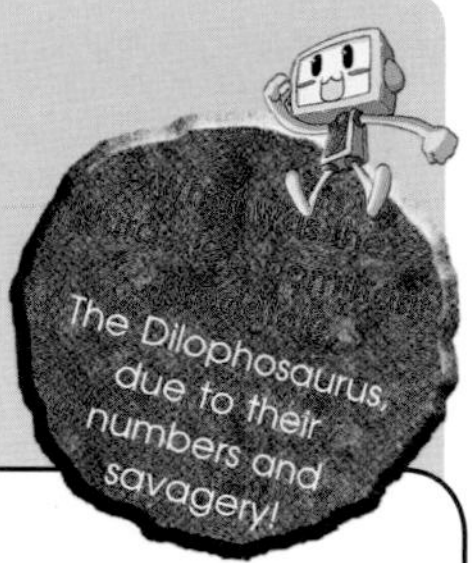
The Dilophosaurus,
due to their
numbers and
savagery!

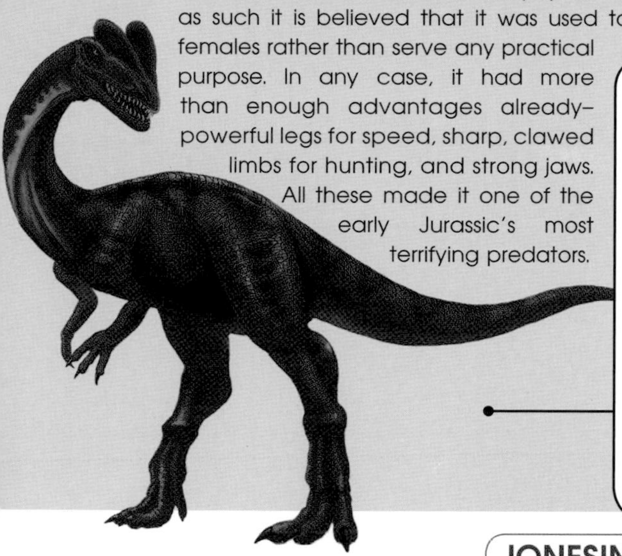

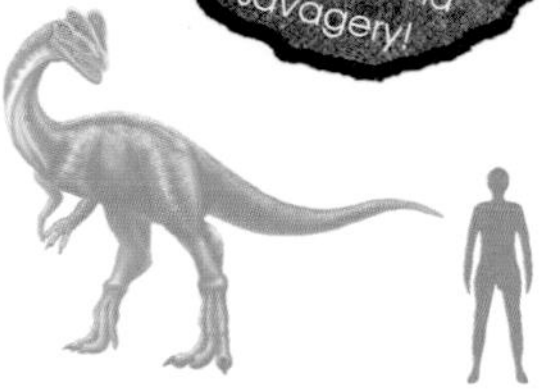

Scientific name: Dilophosaurus
Length: 19.6 feet
Diet: Carnivorous
Habitat: Large forests and jungles
Discovered: North America and China
Era: Early Jurassic

Cryolophosaurus

Cryolophosaurus once lived on the continent that would become the Antarctic. While it was not that cold back then, its weather was far from the near-eternal summer of the Jurassic. As such, scientists believe that Cryolophosaurus might have been warm-blooded. The crest on top of its head was weak, and might have served to attract mates and nothing more.

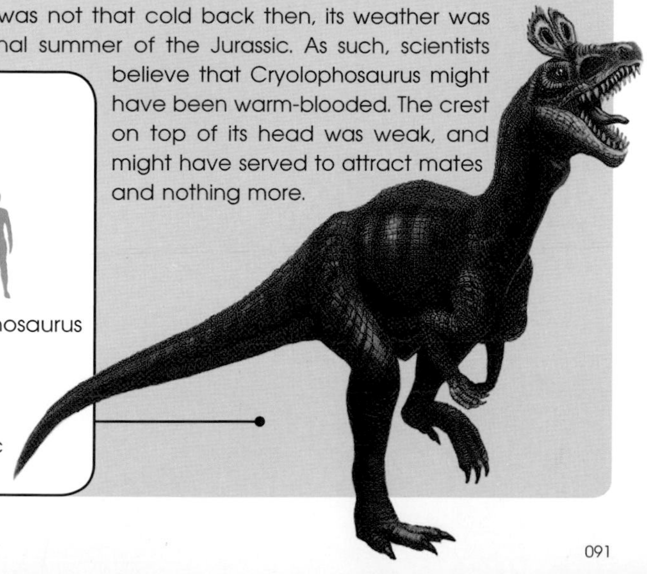

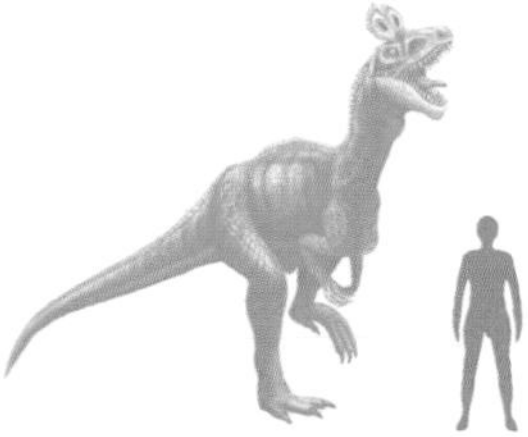

Scientific name: Cryolophosaurus
Length: 19.6 feet
Diet: Carnivorous
Habitat: Colder regions
Discovered: The Antarctic
Era: Early Jurassic

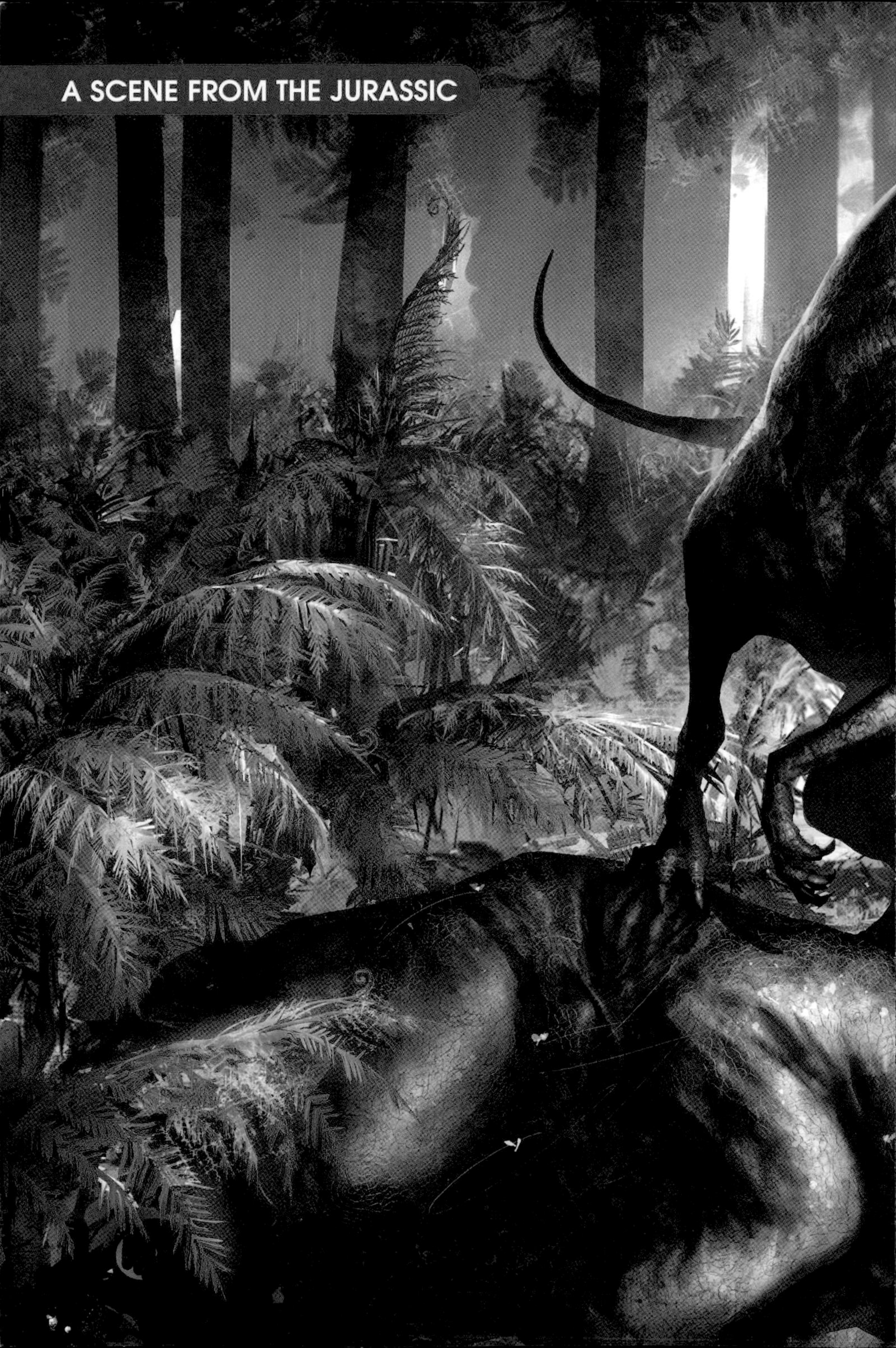
A SCENE FROM THE JURASSIC

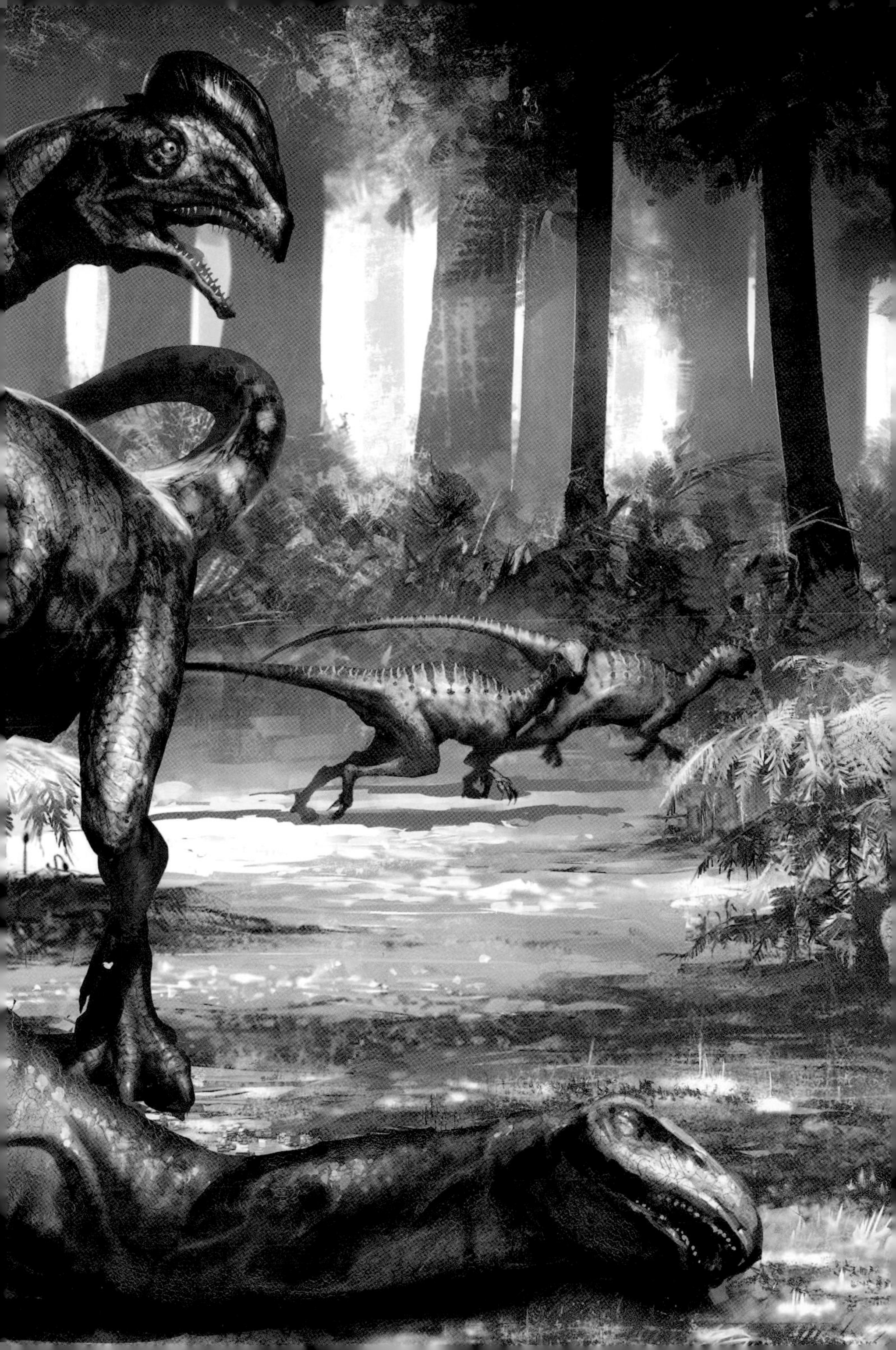

JONESING FOR THE JURASSIC

Barapasaurus

Scientific name: Barapasaurus
Length: 59 feet
Diet: Herbivore
Habitat: Flatlands
Discovered: India
Era: Early Jurassic

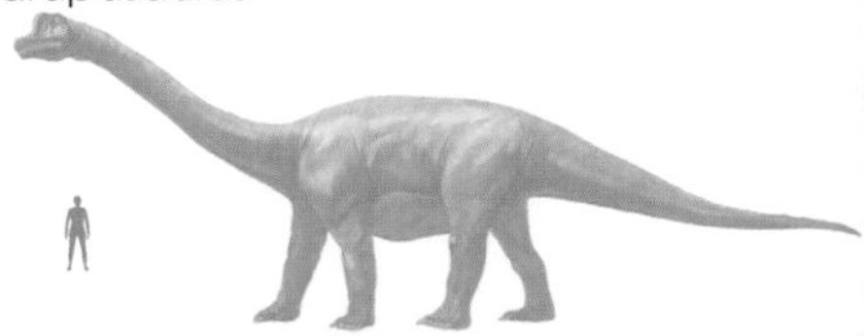

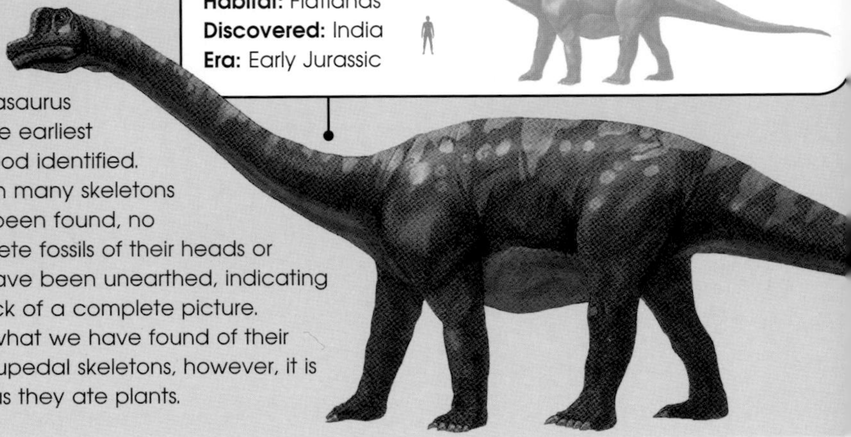

Barapasaurus was the earliest sauropod identified. Though many skeletons have been found, no complete fossils of their heads or feet have been unearthed, indicating the lack of a complete picture. From what we have found of their quadrupedal skeletons, however, it is obvious they ate plants.

JONESING FOR THE JURASSIC

Tazoudasaurus

Tazoudasaurus was one of the earliest sauropods we know of. It was closely related to Vulcanodon, differing only in caudal vertebrae features. Like the Vulcanodon, it used its saw-toothed teeth to cut (instead of grind, like modern herbivores) leaves up before swallowing.

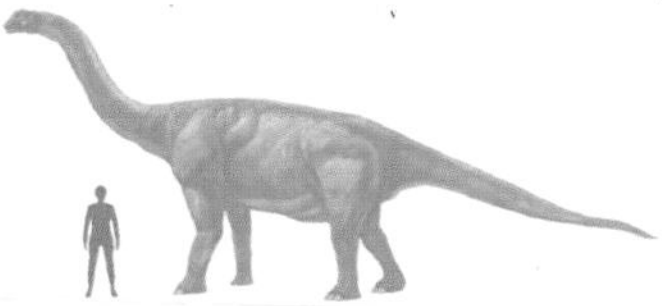

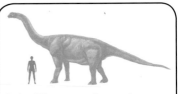

Scientific name: Tazoudasaurus
Length: 29.5 feet
Diet: Herbivore
Habitat: Equatorial jungles
Discovered: North Africa
Era: Early Jurassic

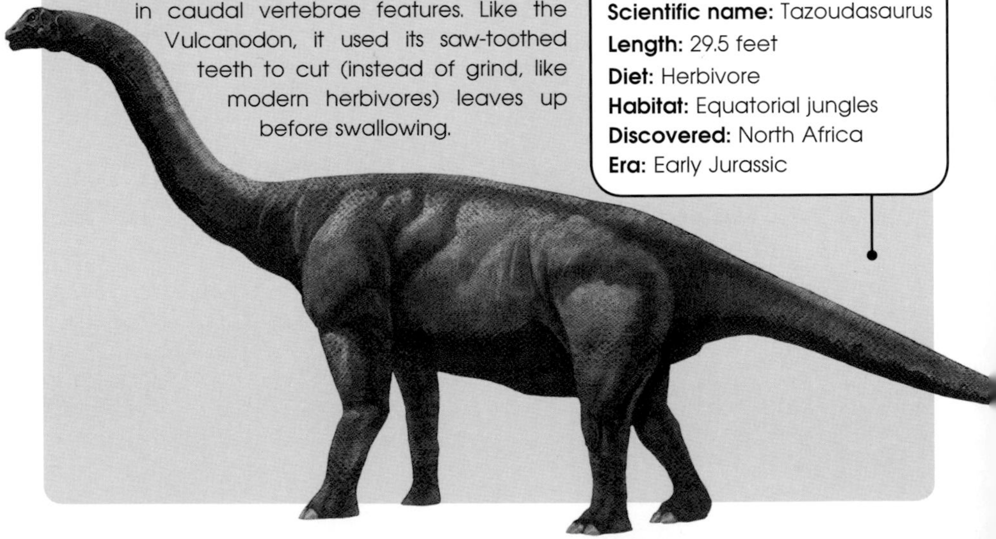

CHAPTER 5
THE WALKING WOUNDED

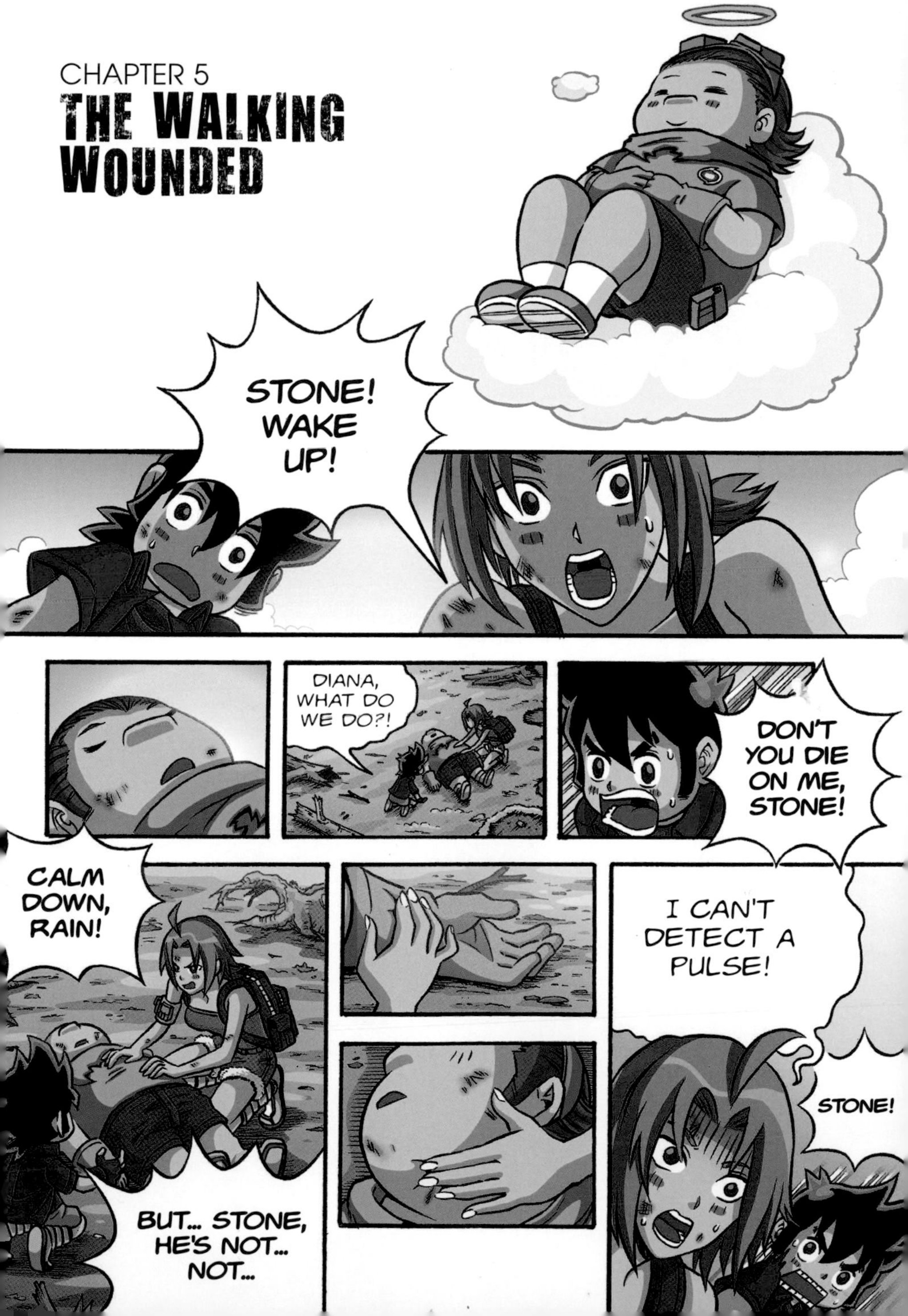
STONE! WAKE UP!
DIANA, WHAT DO WE DO?!
DON'T YOU DIE ON ME, STONE!
CALM DOWN, RAIN!
BUT... STONE, HE'S NOT... NOT...
I CAN'T DETECT A PULSE!
STONE!

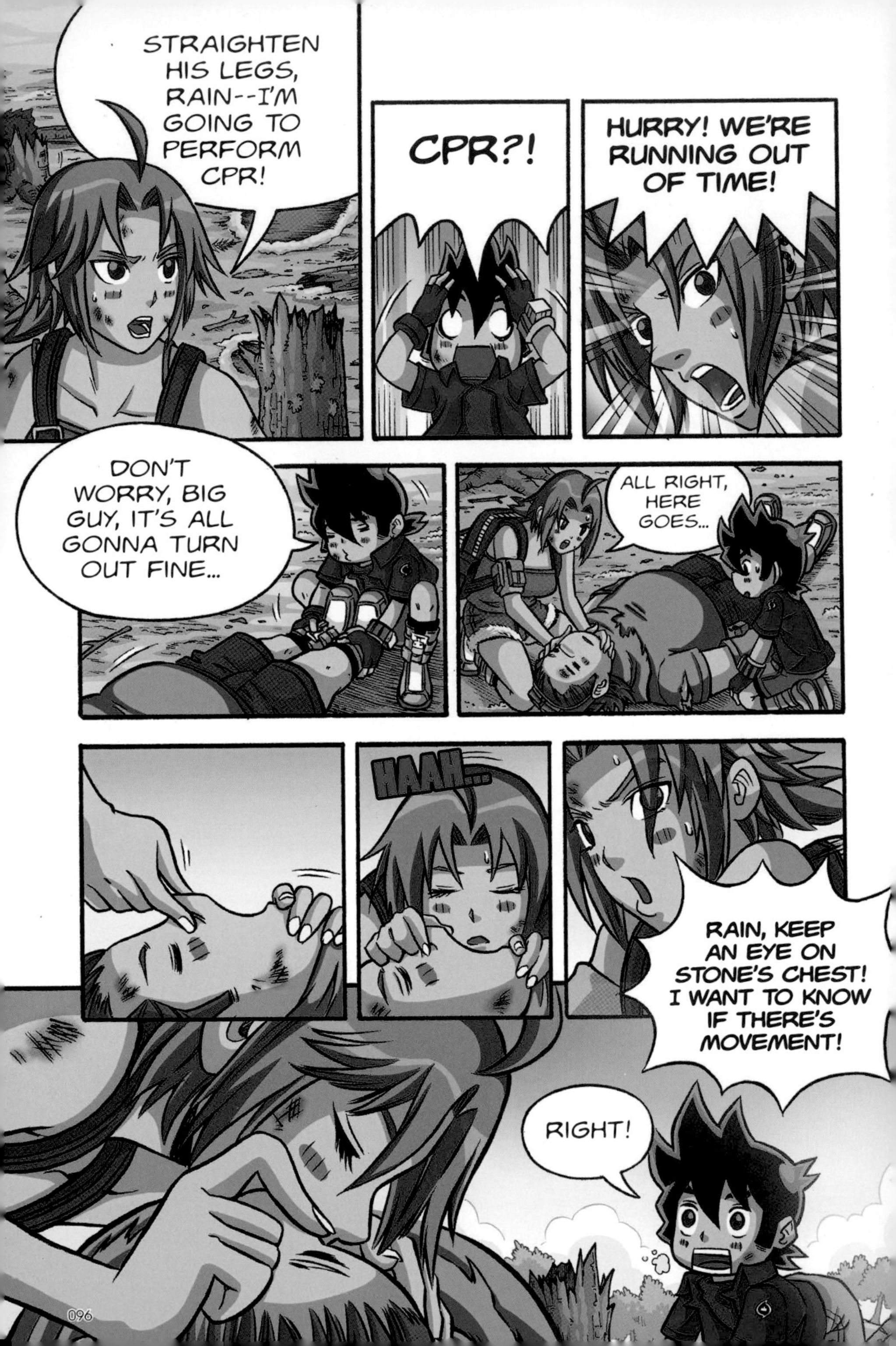
STRAIGHTEN HIS LEGS, RAIN--I'M GOING TO PERFORM CPR!
CPR?!
HURRY! WE'RE RUNNING OUT OF TIME!
DON'T WORRY, BIG GUY, IT'S ALL GONNA TURN OUT FINE...
ALL RIGHT, HERE GOES...
HAAH...
RAIN, KEEP AN EYE ON STONE'S CHEST! I WANT TO KNOW IF THERE'S MOVEMENT!
RIGHT!

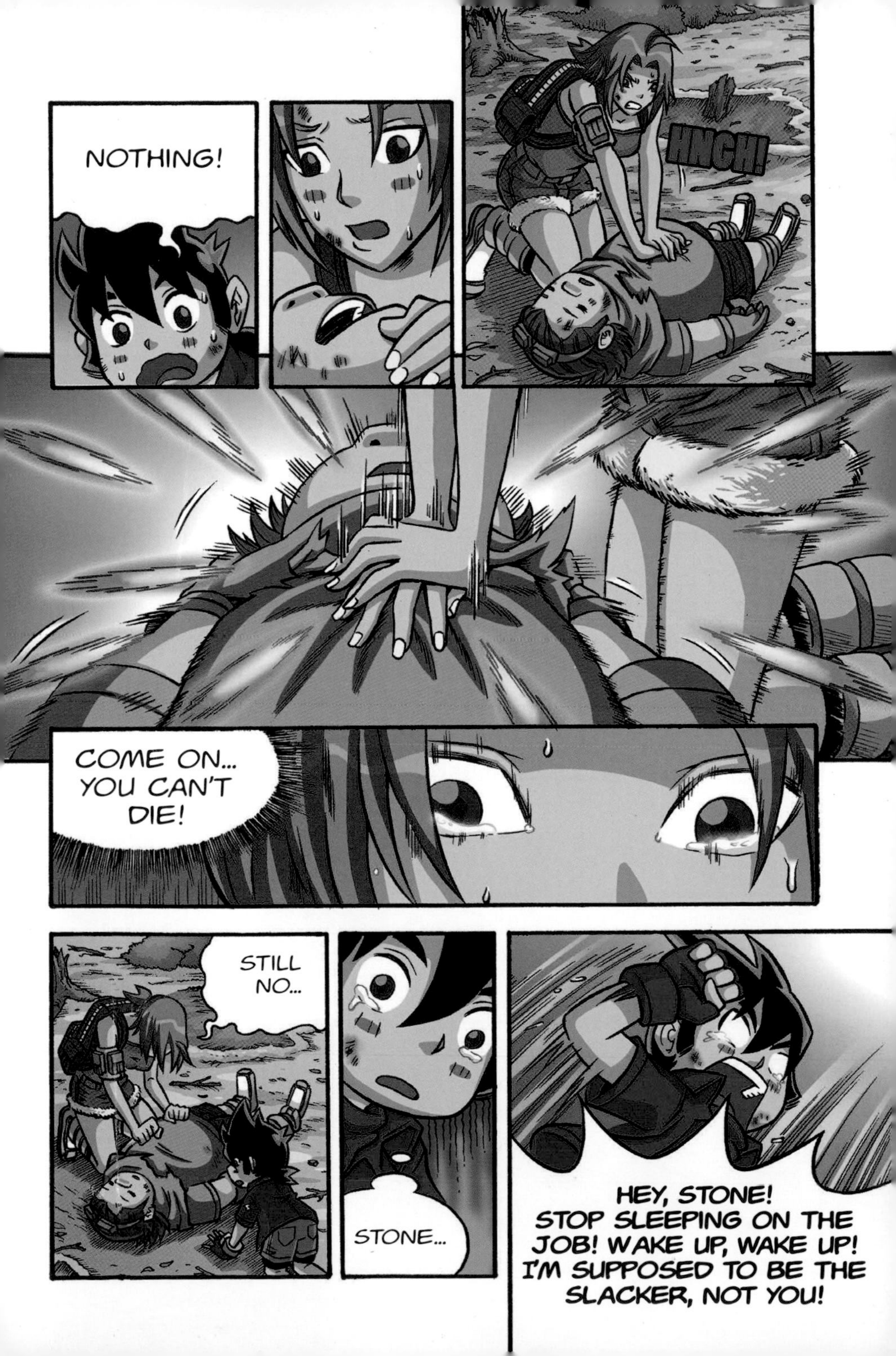
NOTHING!
HNGH!
COME ON... YOU CAN'T DIE!
STILL NO...
STONE...
HEY, STONE! STOP SLEEPING ON THE JOB! WAKE UP, WAKE UP! I'M SUPPOSED TO BE THE SLACKER, NOT YOU!

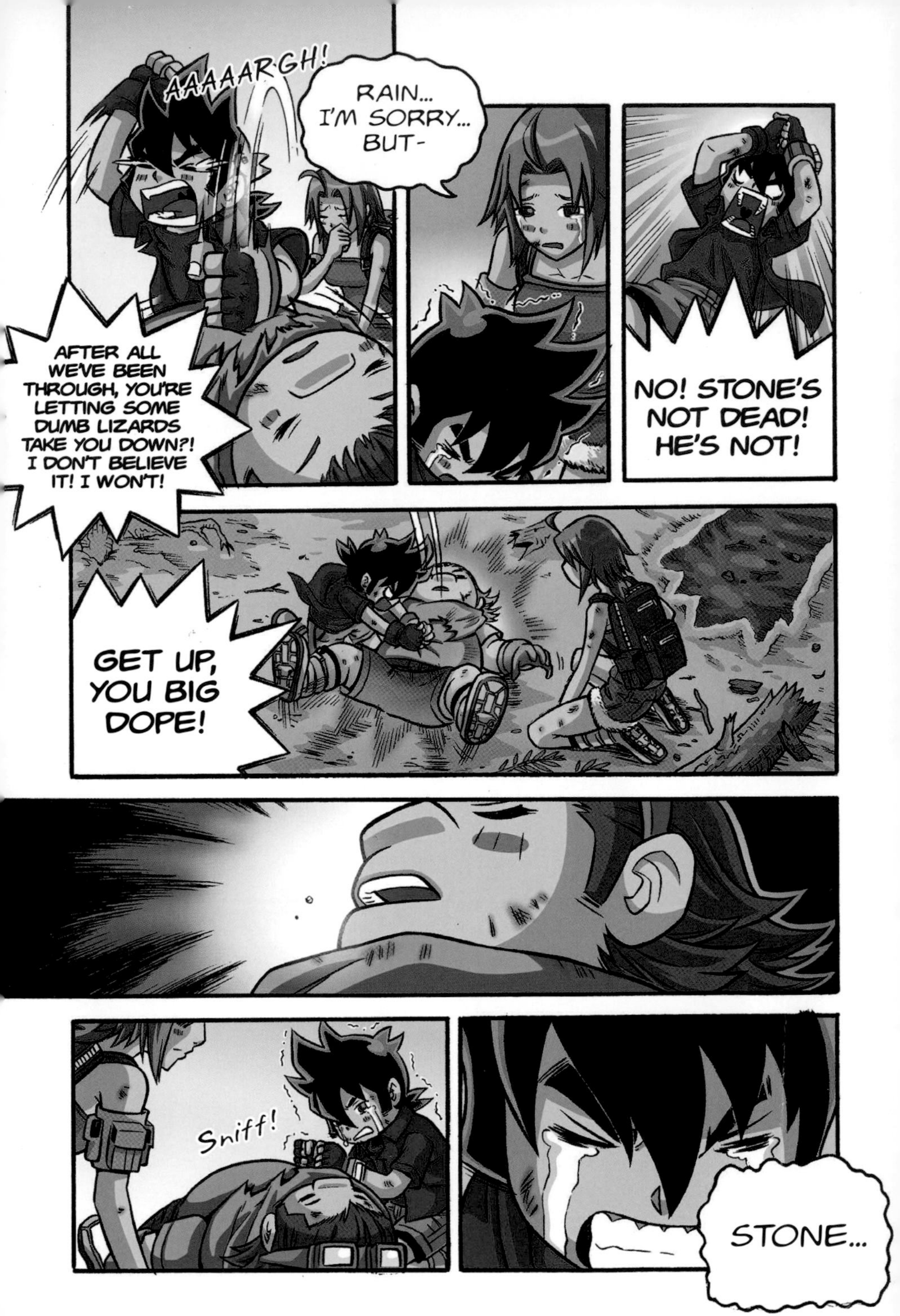
AAAAARGH!
RAIN... I'M SORRY... BUT-
AFTER ALL WE'VE BEEN THROUGH, YOU'RE LETTING SOME DUMB LIZARDS TAKE YOU DOWN?! I DON'T BELIEVE IT! I WON'T!
NO! STONE'S NOT DEAD! HE'S NOT!
GET UP, YOU BIG DOPE!
Sniff!
STONE...

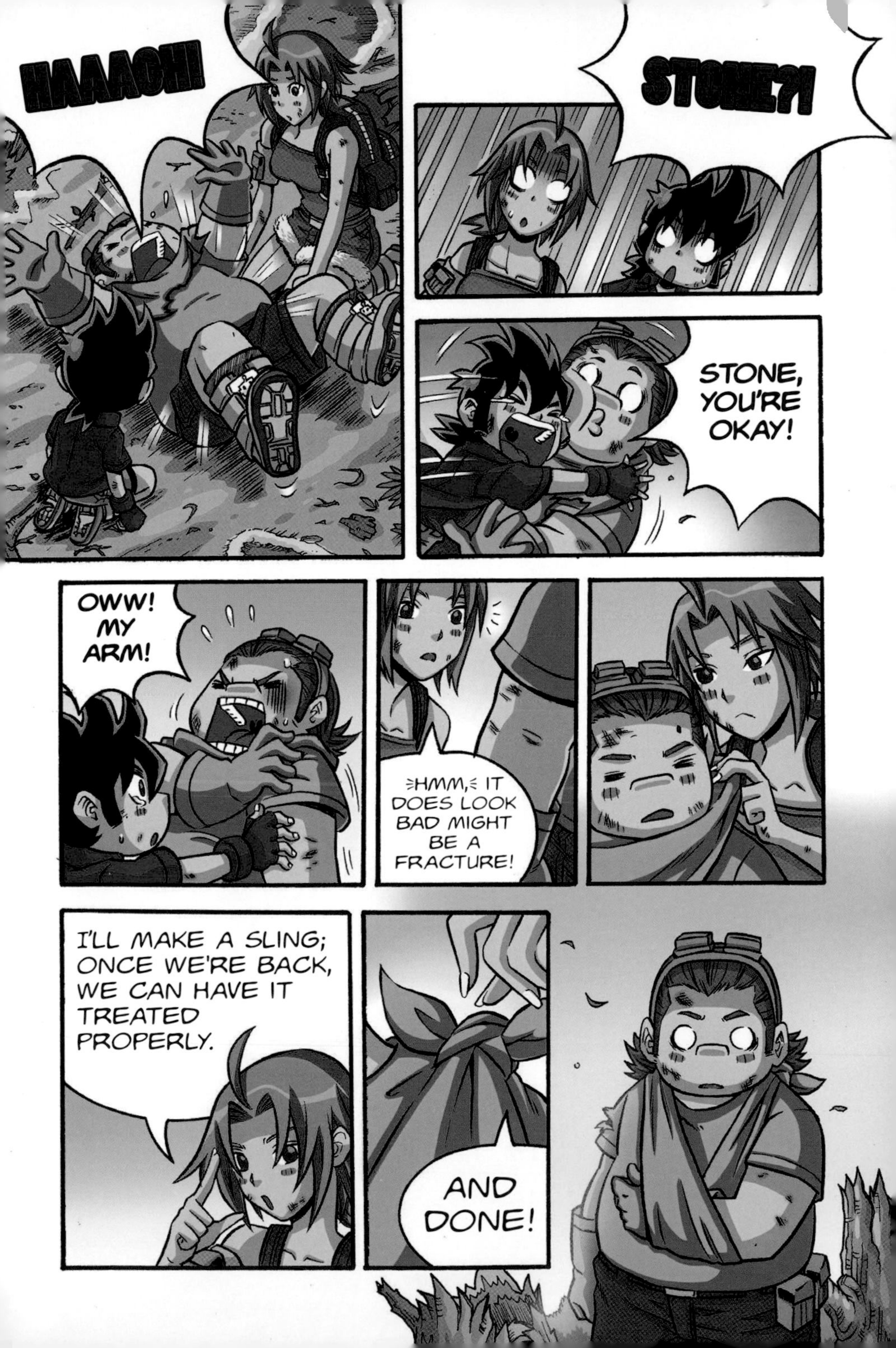
HAAACH!
STONE?!
STONE, YOU'RE OKAY!
OWW! MY ARM!
HMM, IT DOES LOOK BAD MIGHT BE A FRACTURE!
I'LL MAKE A SLING; ONCE WE'RE BACK, WE CAN HAVE IT TREATED PROPERLY.
AND DONE!

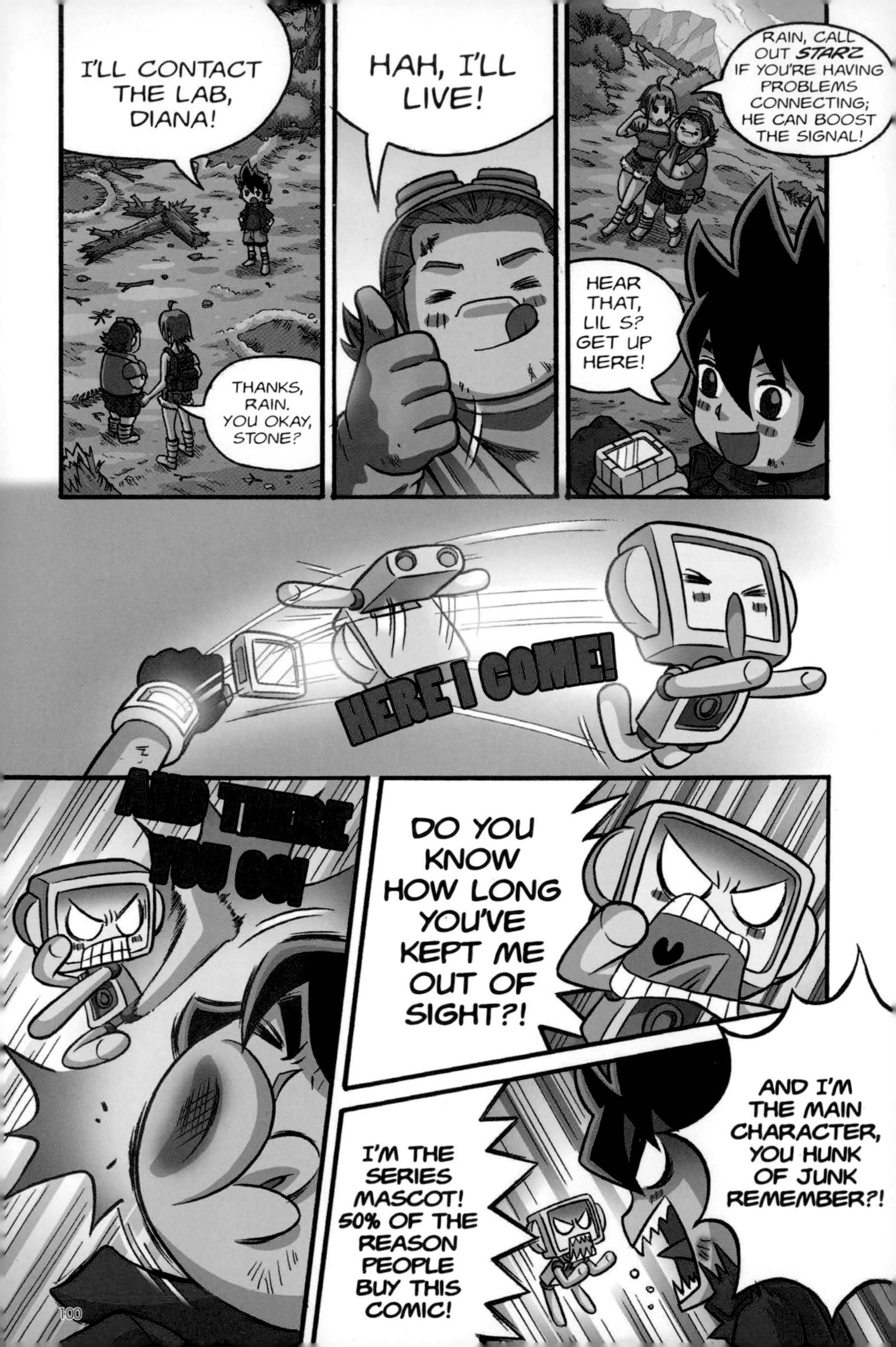
I'LL CONTACT THE LAB, DIANA!
THANKS, RAIN. YOU OKAY, STONE?
HAH, I'LL LIVE!
RAIN, CALL OUT STARZ IF YOU'RE HAVING PROBLEMS CONNECTING; HE CAN BOOST THE SIGNAL!
HEAR THAT, LIL S? GET UP HERE!
HERE I COME!
AND THERE YOU GO!
DO YOU KNOW HOW LONG YOU'VE KEPT ME OUT OF SIGHT?!
I'M THE SERIES MASCOT! 50% OF THE REASON PEOPLE BUY THIS COMIC!
AND I'M THE MAIN CHARACTER, YOU HUNK OF JUNK REMEMBER?!

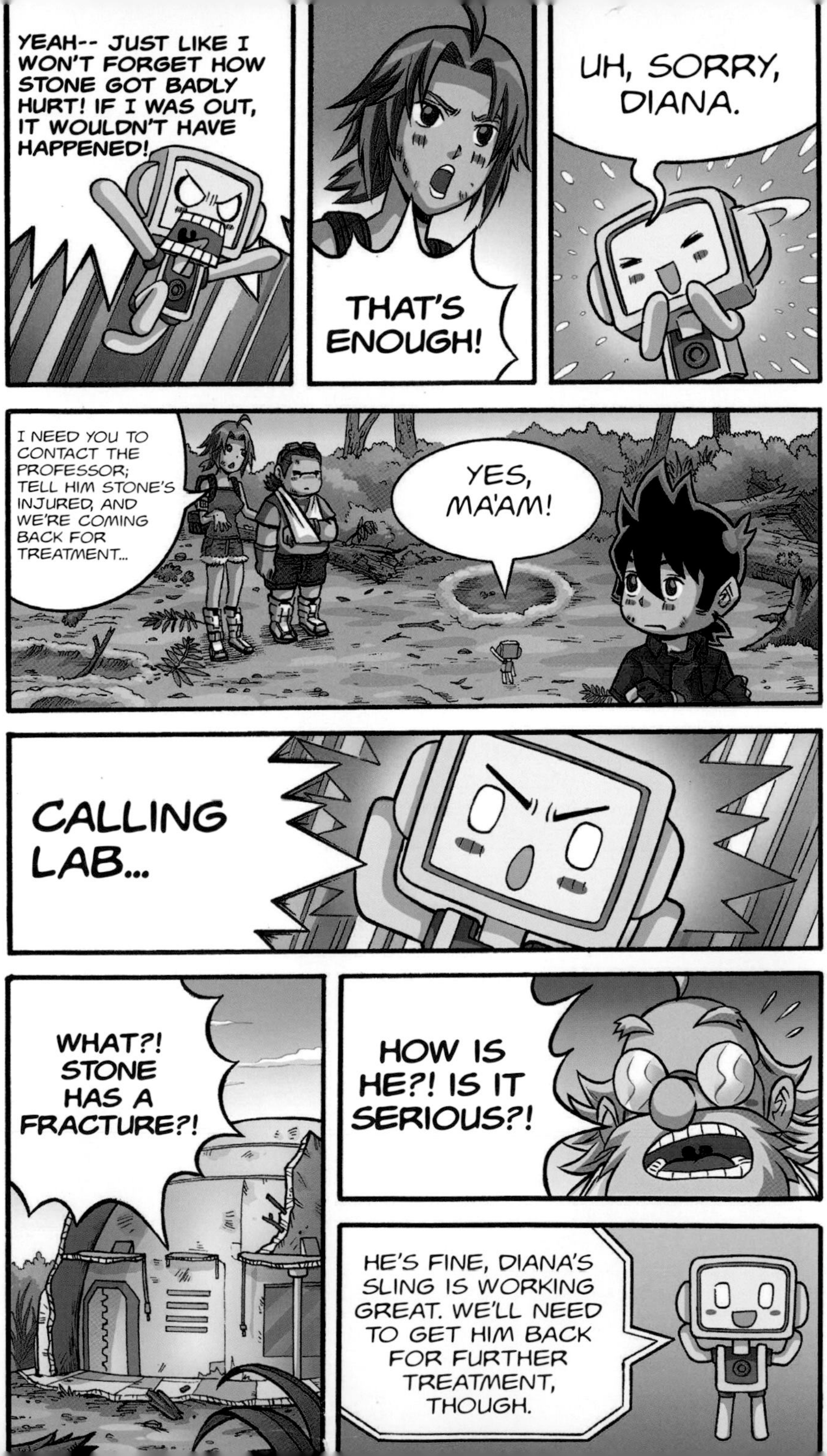

YEAH-- JUST LIKE I WON'T FORGET HOW STONE GOT BADLY HURT! IF I WAS OUT, IT WOULDN'T HAVE HAPPENED!
THAT'S ENOUGH!
UH, SORRY, DIANA.
I NEED YOU TO CONTACT THE PROFESSOR; TELL HIM STONE'S INJURED, AND WE'RE COMING BACK FOR TREATMENT...
YES, MA'AM!
CALLING LAB...
WHAT?! STONE HAS A FRACTURE?!
HOW IS HE?! IS IT SERIOUS?!
HE'S FINE, DIANA'S SLING IS WORKING GREAT. WE'LL NEED TO GET HIM BACK FOR FURTHER TREATMENT, THOUGH.

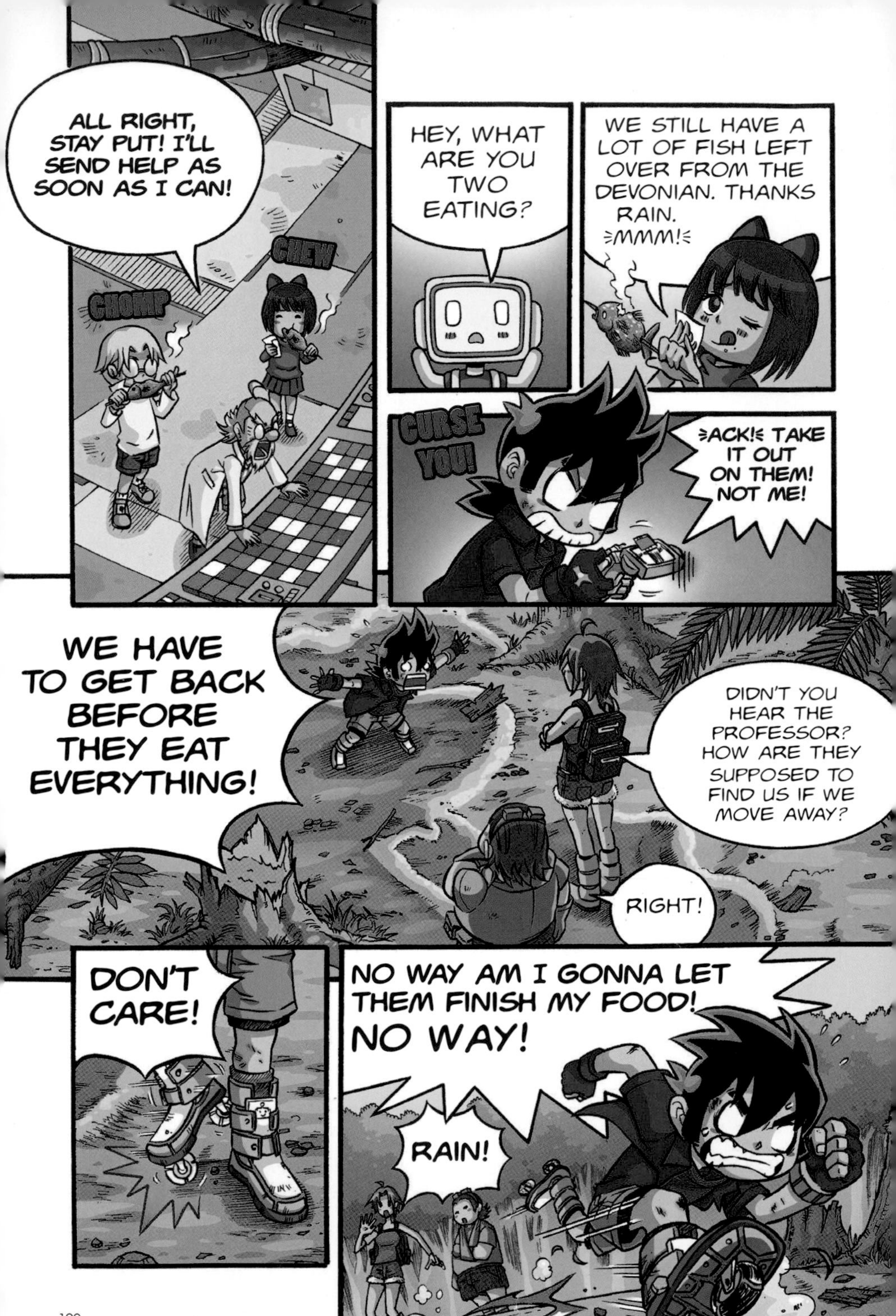
ALL RIGHT, STAY PUT! I'LL SEND HELP AS SOON AS I CAN!
CHEW
CHOMP
HEY, WHAT ARE YOU TWO EATING?
WE STILL HAVE A LOT OF FISH LEFT OVER FROM THE DEVONIAN. THANKS RAIN.
MMM!
CURSE YOU!
ACK! TAKE IT OUT ON THEM! NOT ME!
WE HAVE TO GET BACK BEFORE THEY EAT EVERYTHING!
DIDN'T YOU HEAR THE PROFESSOR? HOW ARE THEY SUPPOSED TO FIND US IF WE MOVE AWAY?
RIGHT!
DON'T CARE!
NO WAY AM I GONNA LET THEM FINISH MY FOOD!
NO WAY!
RAIN!

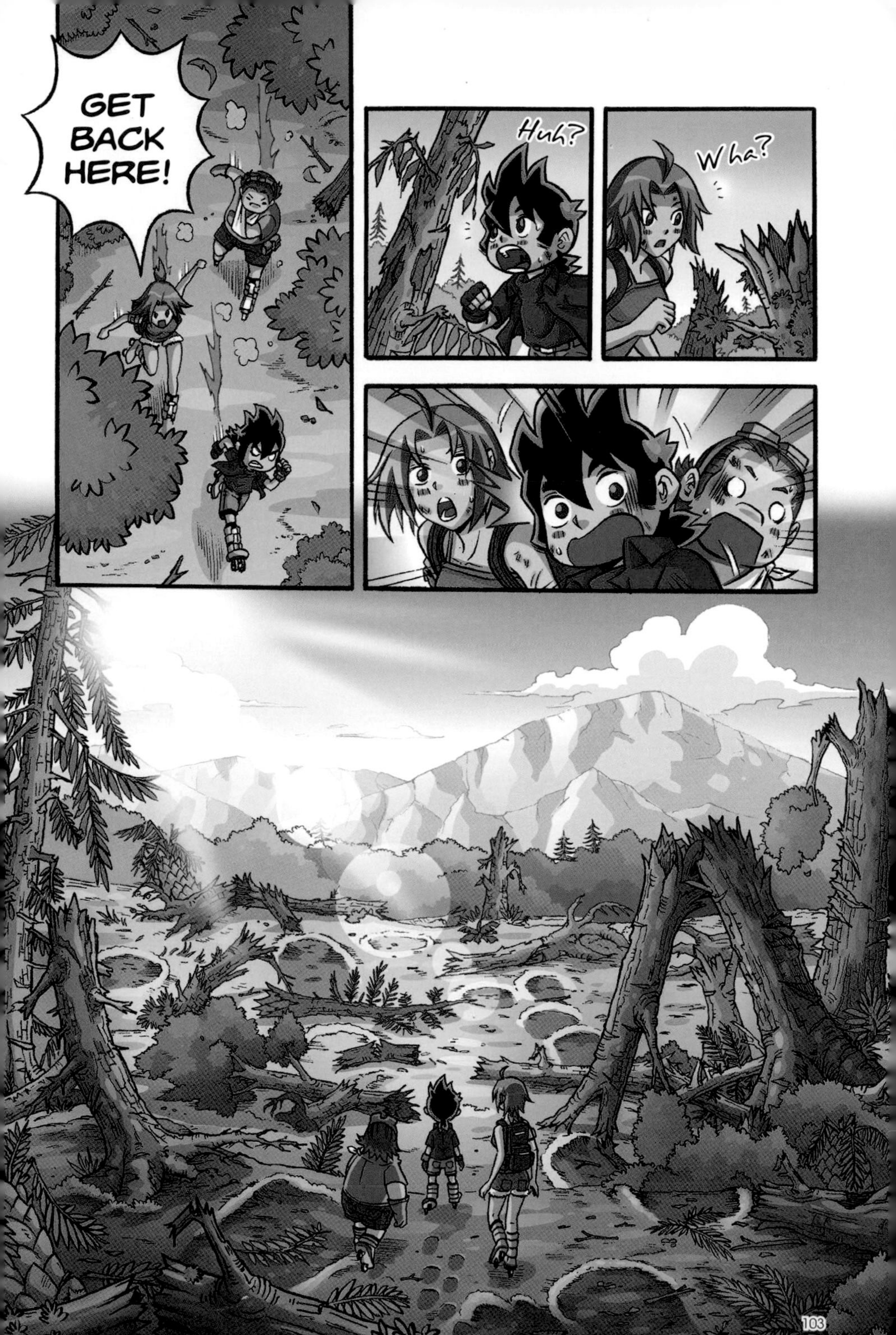
GET BACK HERE!
Huh?
Wha?

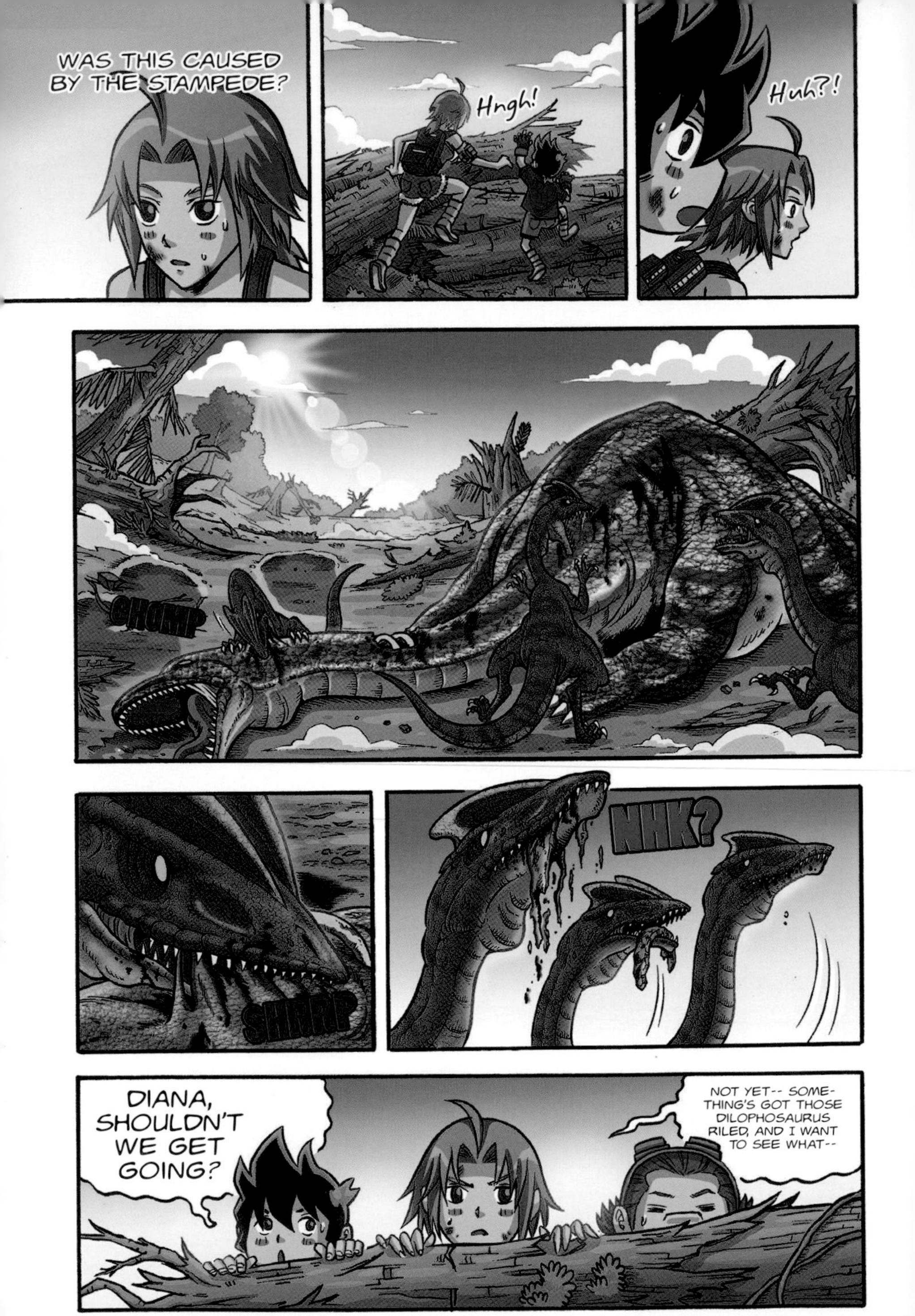

WAS THIS CAUSED BY THE STAMPEDE?
Hngh!
Huh?!
CHOMP
NHK?
DIANA, SHOULDN'T WE GET GOING?
NOT YET-- SOMETHING'S GOT THOSE DILOPHOSAURUS RILED, AND I WANT TO SEE WHAT--

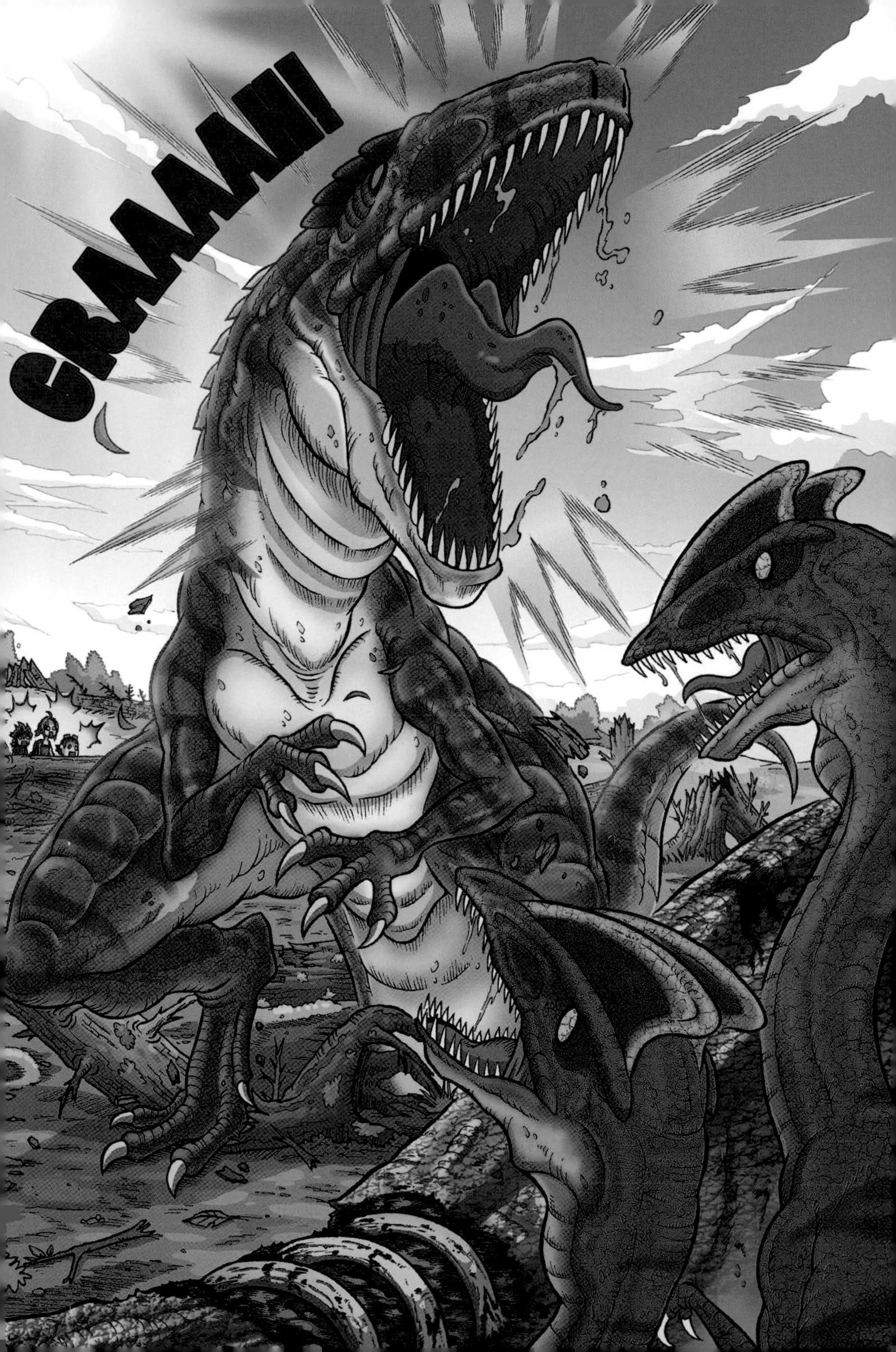
GRAAAAH!!

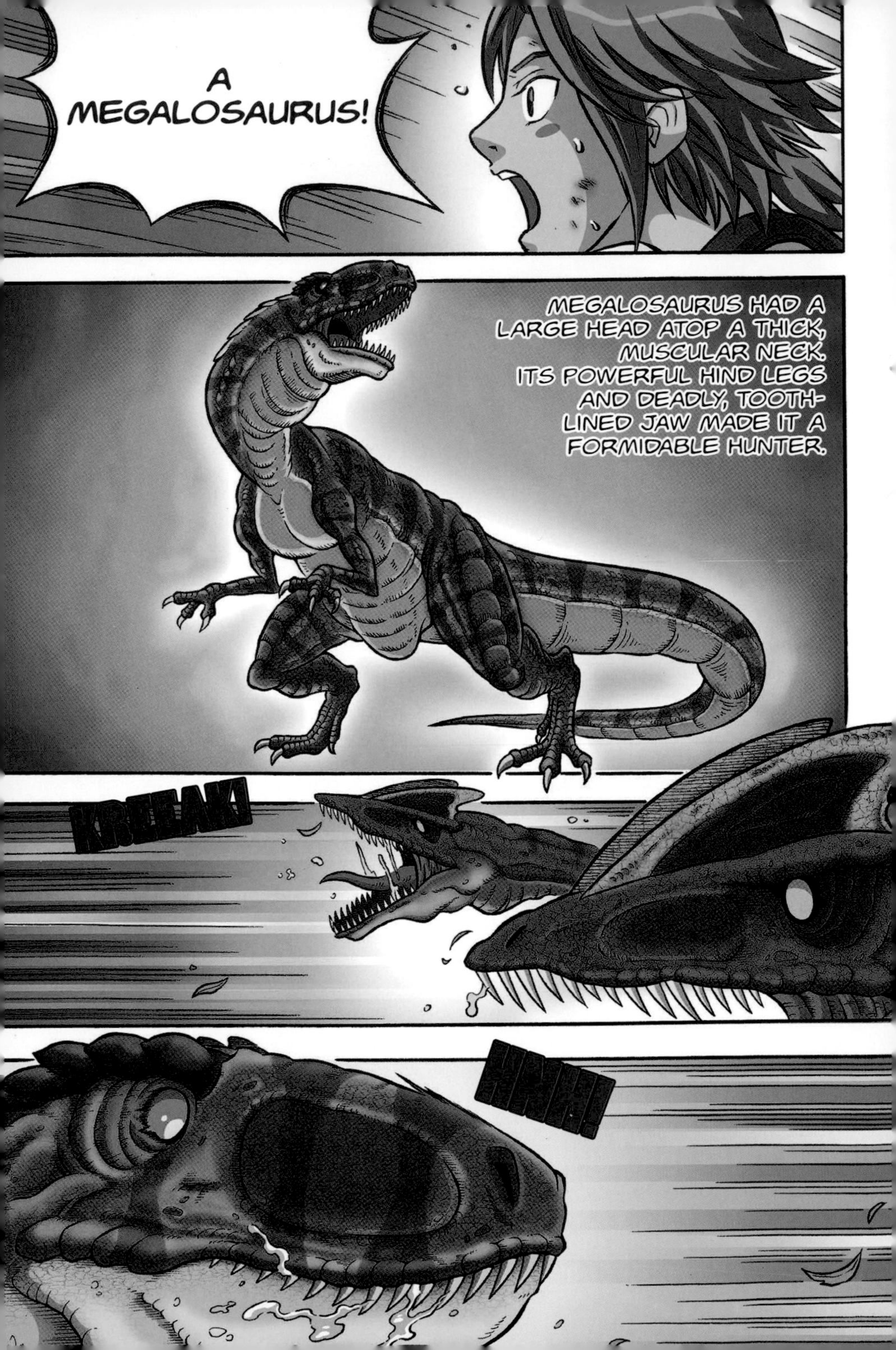
A MEGALOSAURUS!
MEGALOSAURUS HAD A LARGE HEAD ATOP A THICK, MUSCULAR NECK. ITS POWERFUL HIND LEGS AND DEADLY, TOOTH-LINED JAW MADE IT A FORMIDABLE HUNTER.
KREEAK!

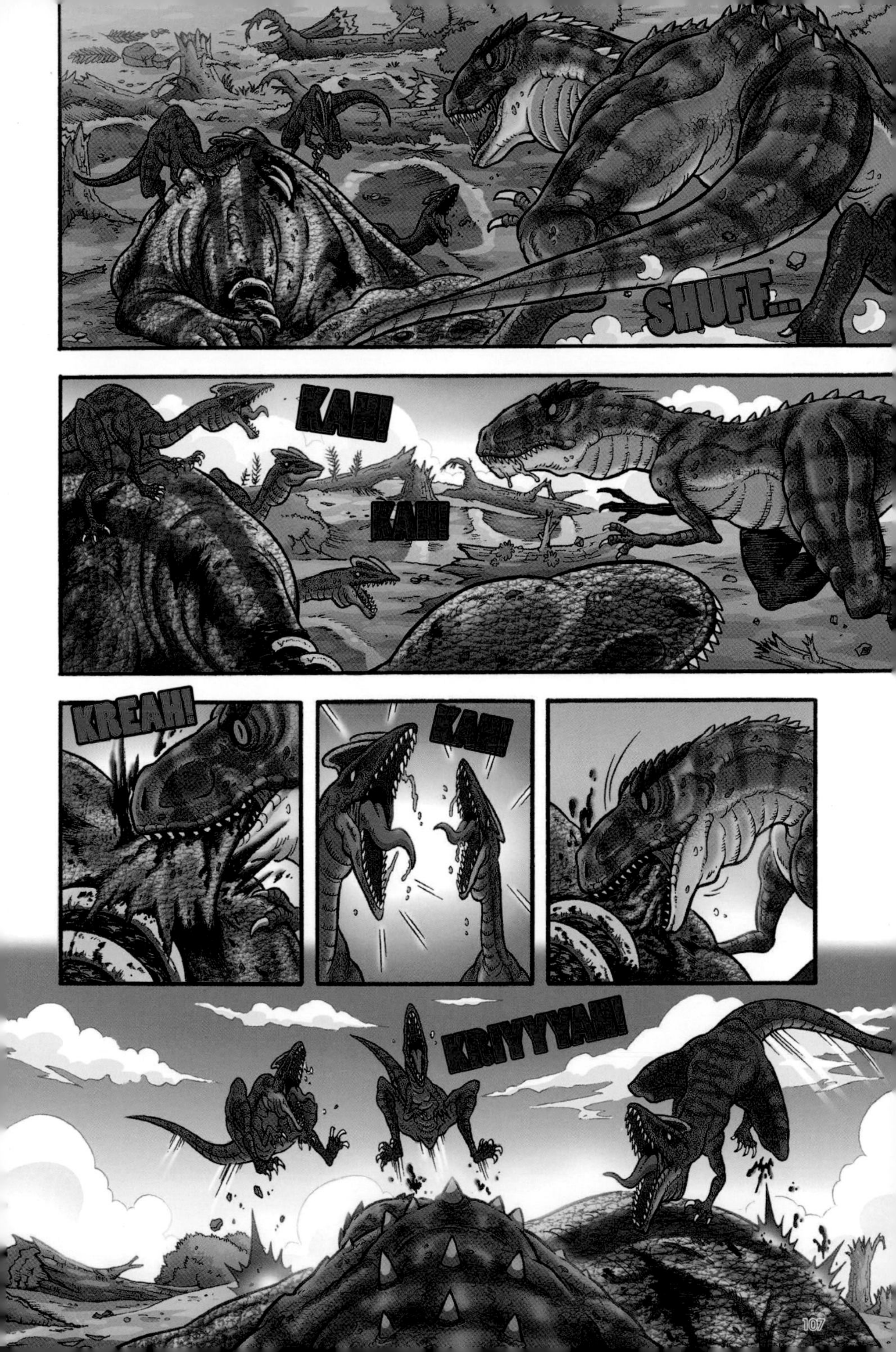
SHUFF...
KAH!
KAH!
KREAH!
KAH!
KRIYYYAH!

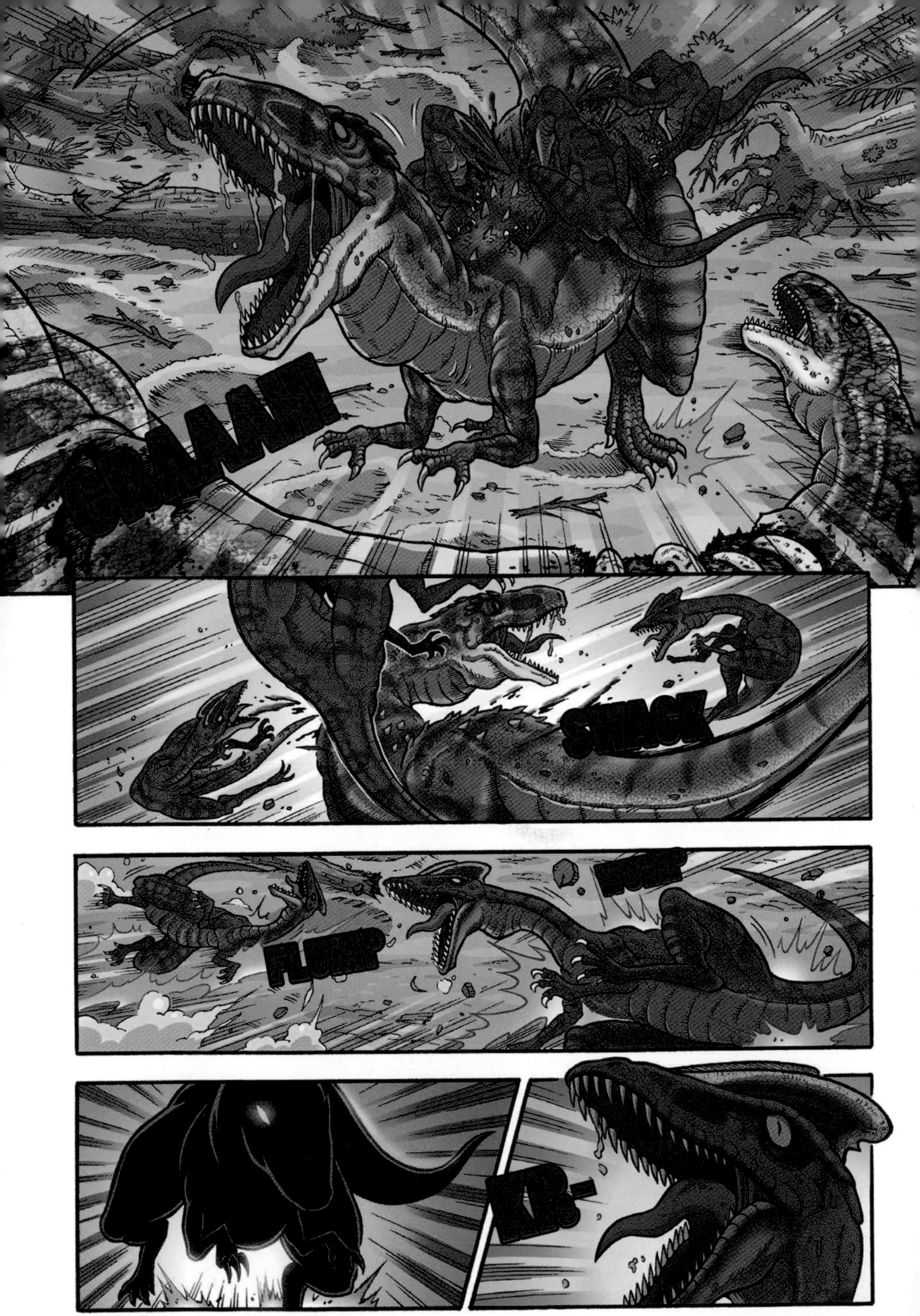
SWACK
KR-

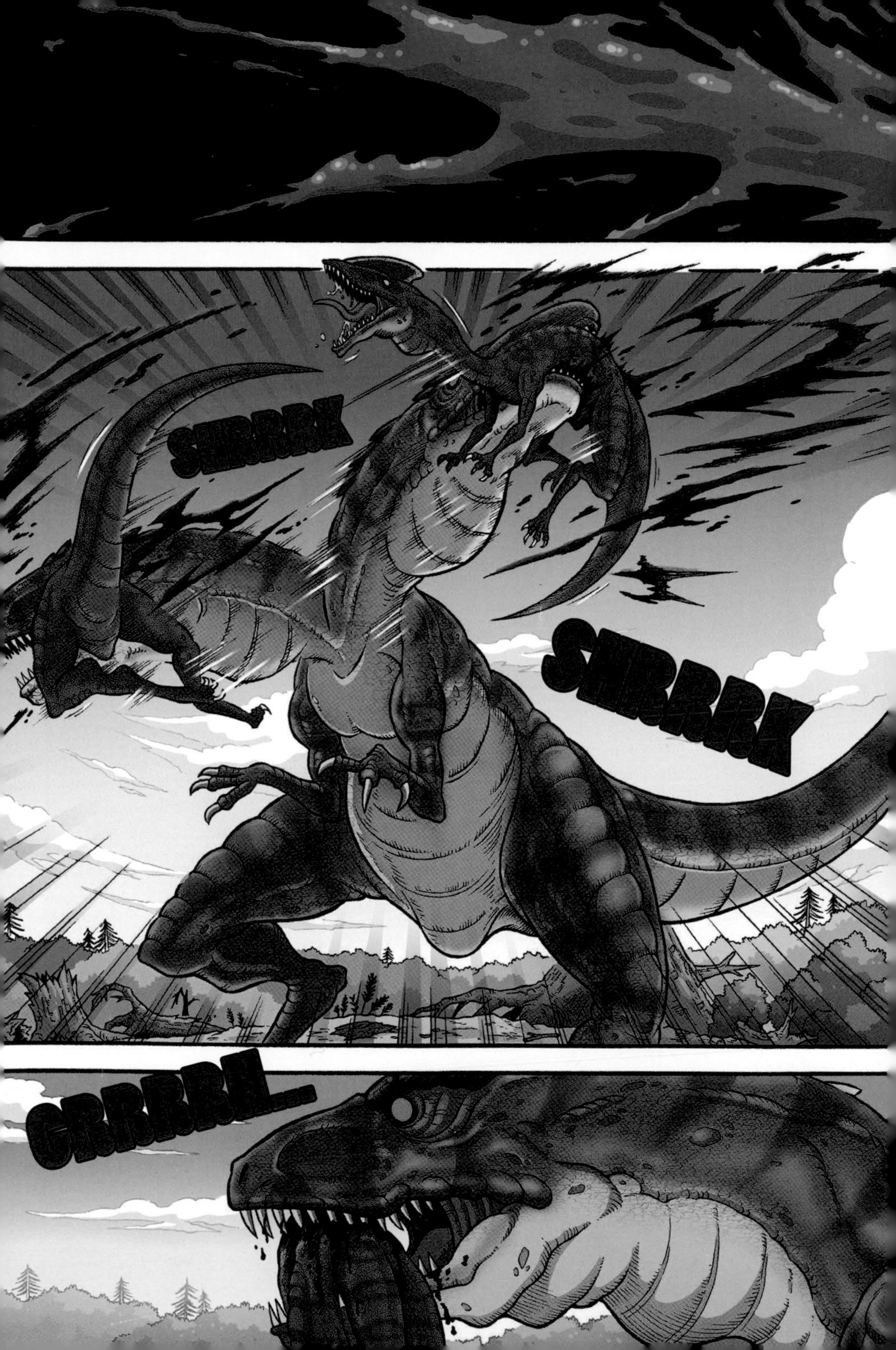
SHRRRK
SHRRRK
GRRRRL...

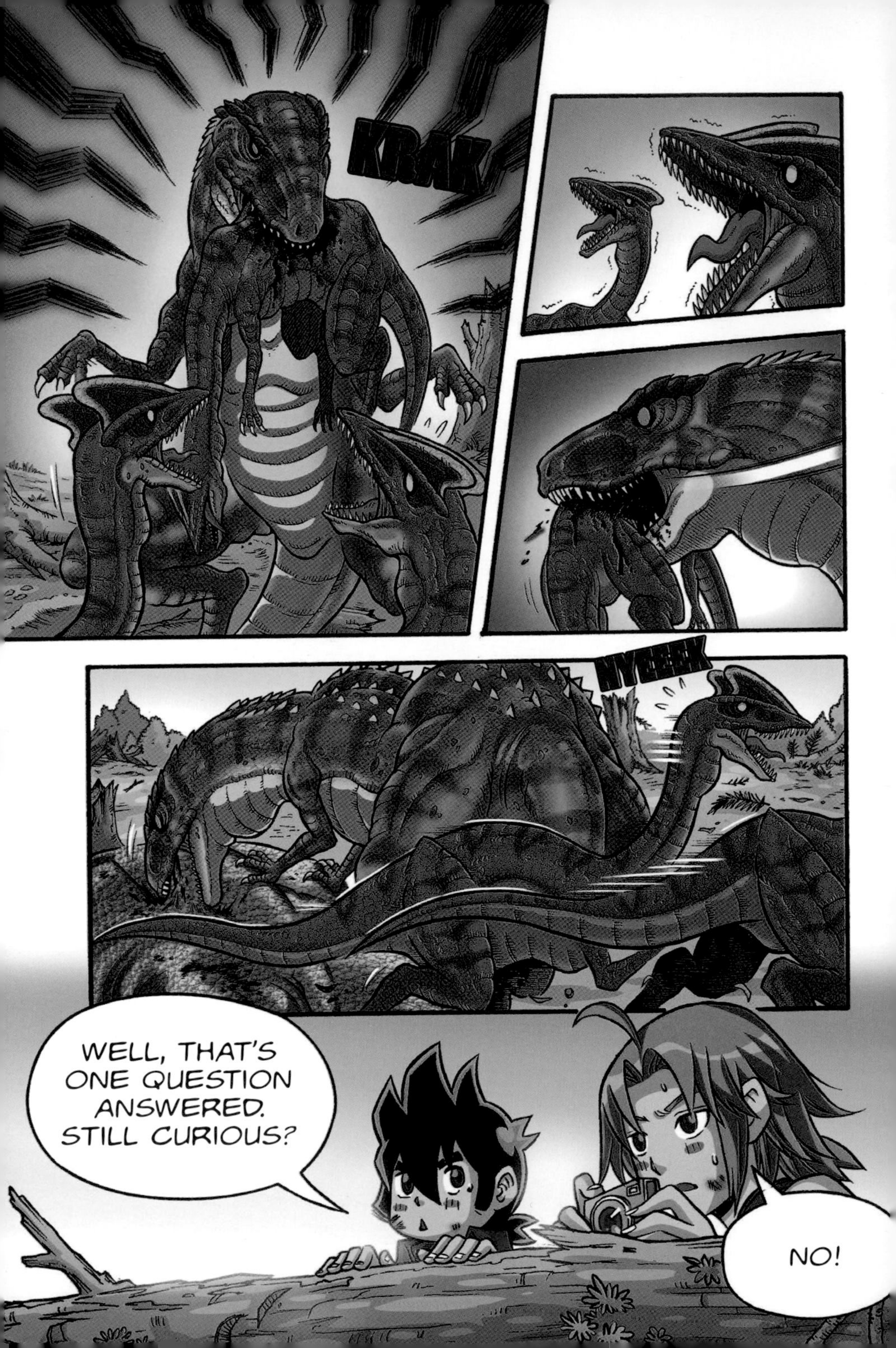
KRAK
NYEEK
WELL, THAT'S ONE QUESTION ANSWERED. STILL CURIOUS?
NO!

Megalosaurus

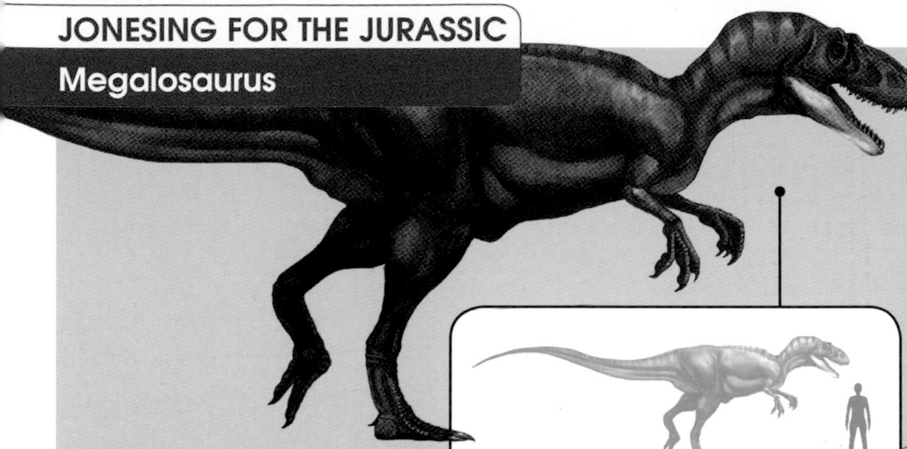

Megalosaurus was the first dinosaur to be described in scientific literature. A carnivorous therapod, it was found to possess a rather flexible neck, facilitating predation upon fleet-footed prey. Its tail was used for balance, and its powerful legs allowed it to move quickly.

Scientific name: Megalosaurus
Length: 29.5 feet
Diet: Carnivore
Habitat: Forest
Discovered: United Kingdom
Era: Late Jurassic

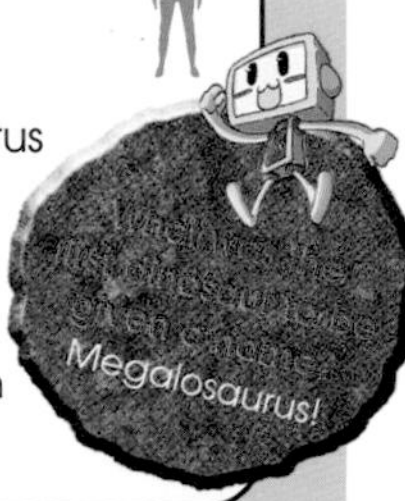
Megalosaurus!

Huayangosaurus

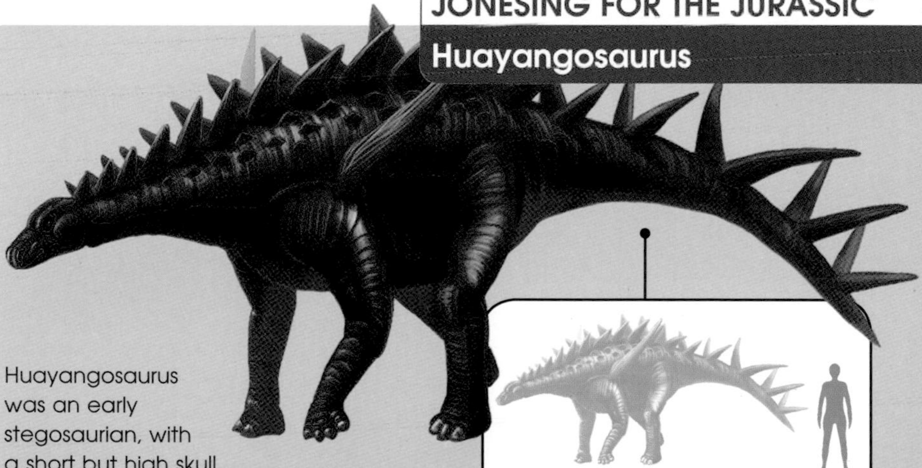

Huayangosaurus was an early stegosaurian, with a short but high skull, antorbital fenestral openings and toothed upper jaws. Though one of the smallest known stegosaurians, its distinctive double row of spiky plates, haunch spines and spiked tail were formidable defenses.

Scientific name: Huayangosaurus
Length: 14.7 feet
Diet: Herbivore
Habitat: Near rivers
Discovered: China
Era: Early to Mid-Jurassic

ORNITHISCHIAN CLADOGRAM

The ornithischians were one of two major dinosaur groups. They included the armored stegosaurians, the horned ceratopsids and the crowned hadrosaurs. Apart from their birdlike hip structures (hence their name, which means "bird hipped") Ornithischians were characterized by strong jaws and teeth.

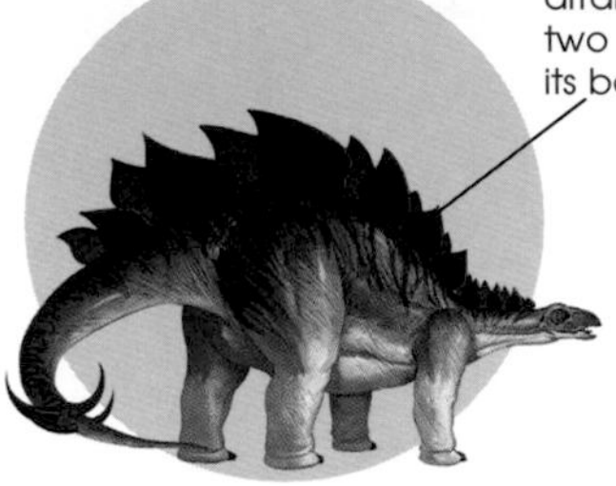

Stegosaurian plates were arranged in two rows along its back.

Thyreophora

Ornithischians are believed to have descended from the Lesothosaurus.

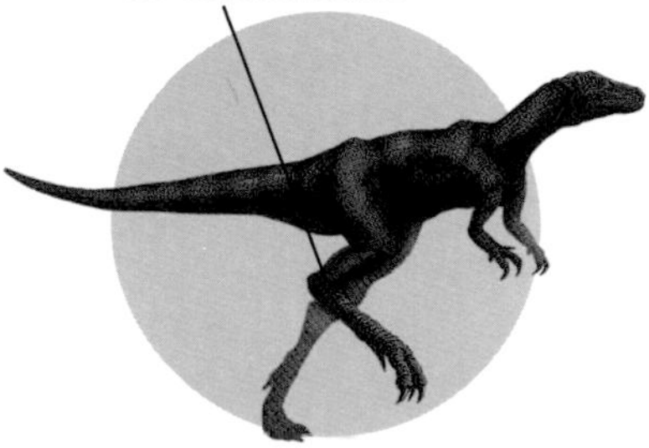

Lesothosaurus

Bony plates across its back gave it great protection.

Edmontonia from the Cretaceous

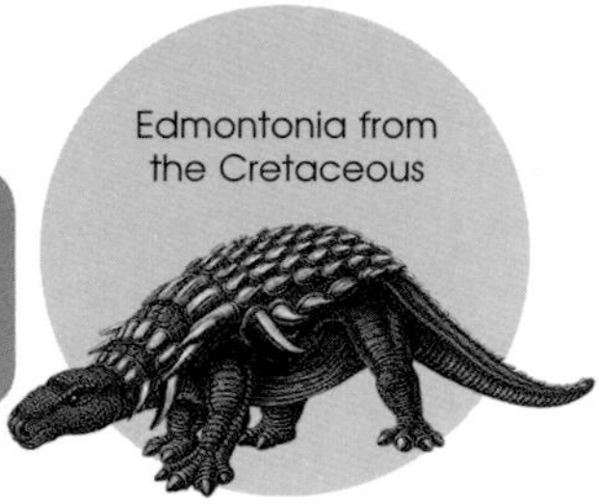

Genasauria's teeth were buried in its jaws.

A Jurassic Heteroaontosaurus skull and jaw

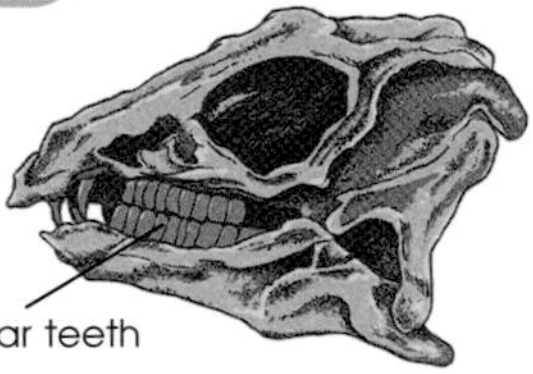

molar teeth

Ornithischian predentary bone

The predentary bone is a bone located at the end of the lower jaw, extending it. Ornithischian predentary bones were capable of moving on their own, and this helped them snap off plant matter facilitating consumption.

Ouranosaurus (from the Cretaceous) skull and jawbone.

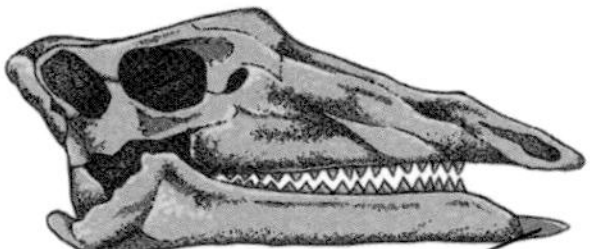

The predentary is shaped like a "U"; it formed a hard "beak" for the dinosaurs which had it.

Mighty molars:
Genasauria had powerful molar teeth to grind their food, as well as pits on either side of its skull.

Triceratops

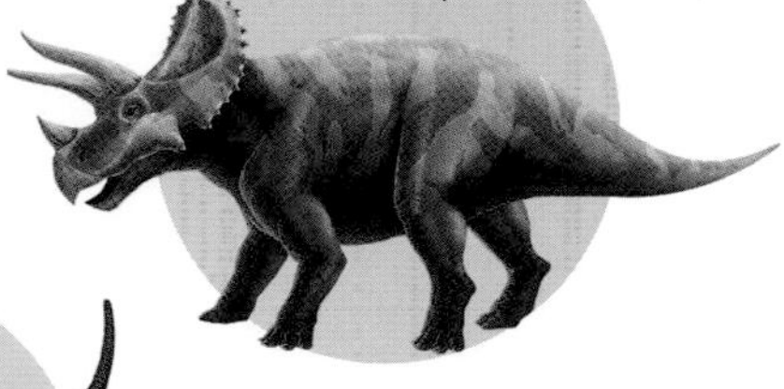

Pachycephalosaurs had thick, dome-shaped skulls that might have been used to show off for mates, or to fight.

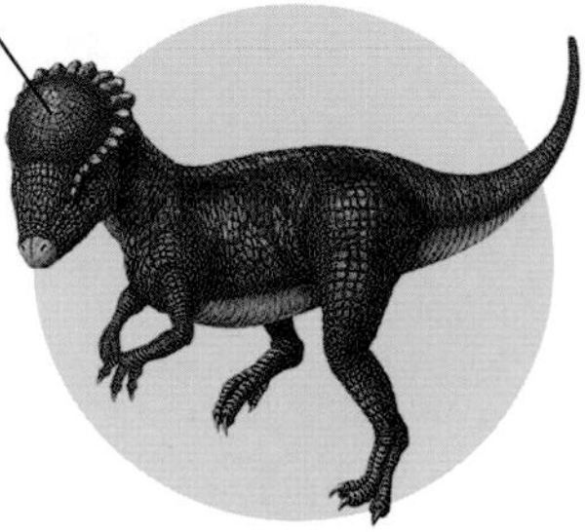

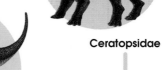

Ceratopsidae

Iguanadons and similar dinosaurs were ornithopods ("bird-legged"); though they were adept at walking on only two legs, and were comfortable with eating leaves on high branches, they still used all four limbs to walk.

Ceratopsidae (Dinosaurs with bony frills and horns) had "beaks" of their own, making them a unique group.

Pachycephalosauridae

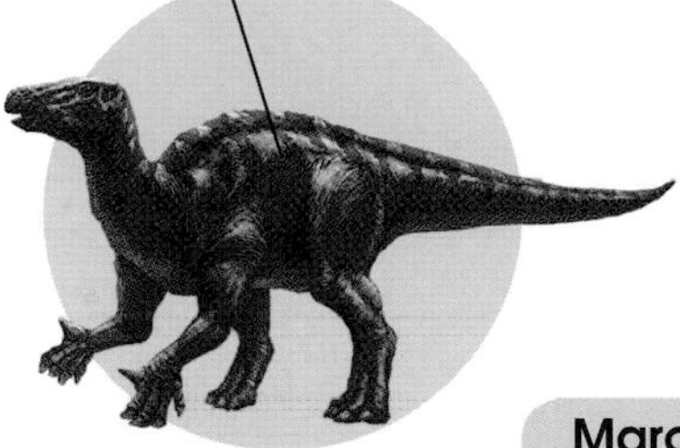

Ornithopoda

Marginocephalia: Have bony ridges or frills at the back of their skulls.

Cerapoda teeth are unevenly coated by enamel.

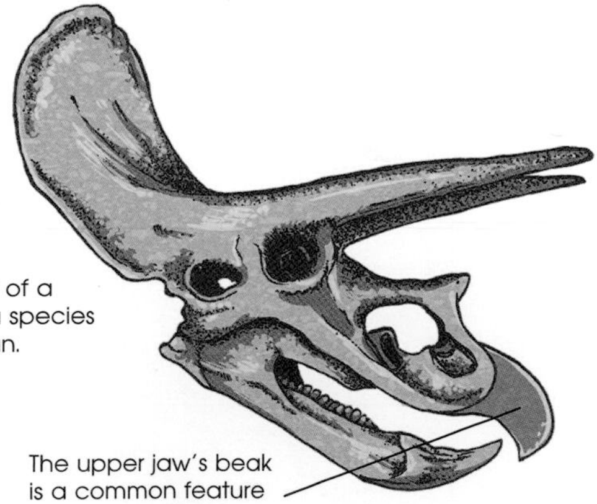

Skull and jaw of a Triceratops, a species of ceratopsian.

The upper jaw's beak is a common feature among ceratopsians.

JONESING FOR THE JURASSIC

Scelidosaurus

Scelidosaurus was one of the earliest thyreophores (armored dinosaur), and its back was covered by raised bony scales embedded in its skin. This coverage was incomplete, however, and as such, its head was only covered by hard keratin.

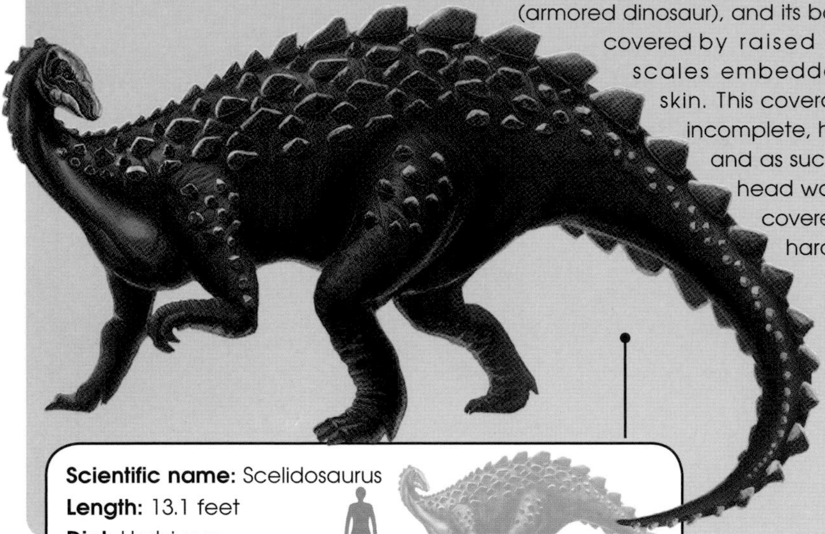

Scientific name: Scelidosaurus
Length: 13.1 feet
Diet: Herbivore
Habitat: River valleys
Discovered: United Kingdom, America
Era: Early to Late Jurassic

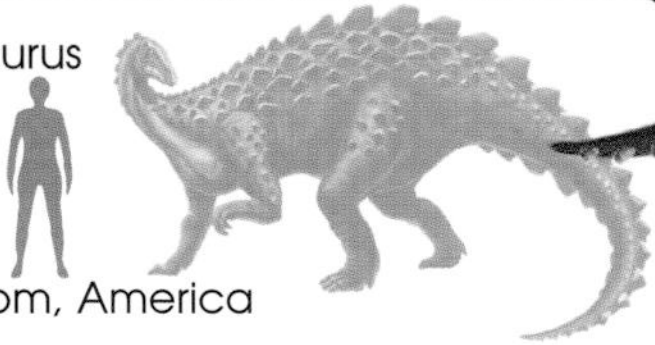

JONESING FOR THE JURASSIC

Morganucodon

Morganucodon might have been one of the earliest mammals in existence. Resembling a modern mouse, its descendants would eventually form the basis of modern mammals – humans included!

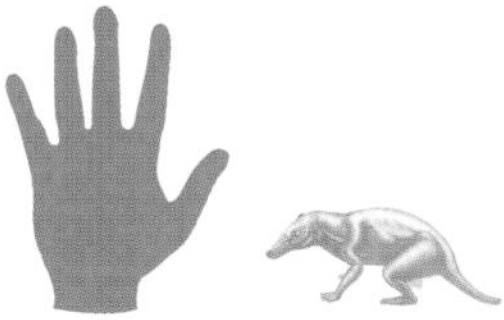

Scientific name: Morganucodon
Length: 3.9 inches
Diet: Carnivore
Habitat: Forests and jungles
Discovered: China, United Kingdom
Era: Late Triassic to Early Jurassic

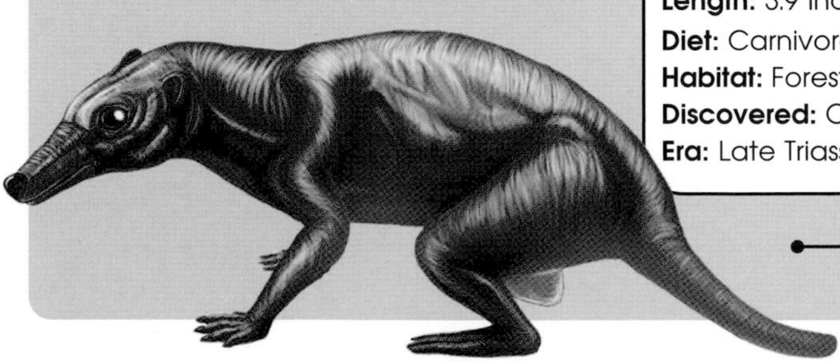

CHAPTER 6
RELENTLESS ASSAULT

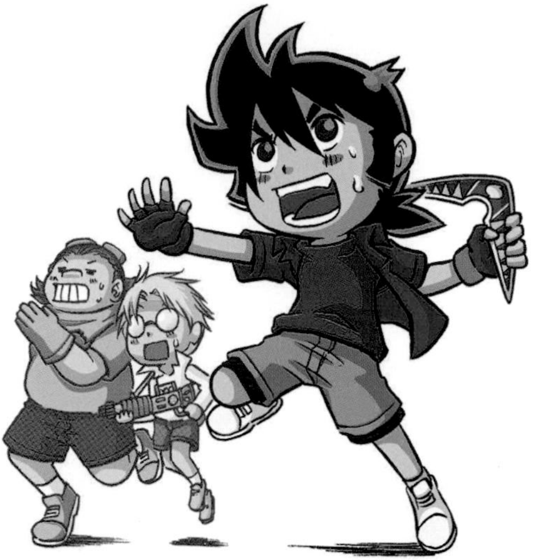

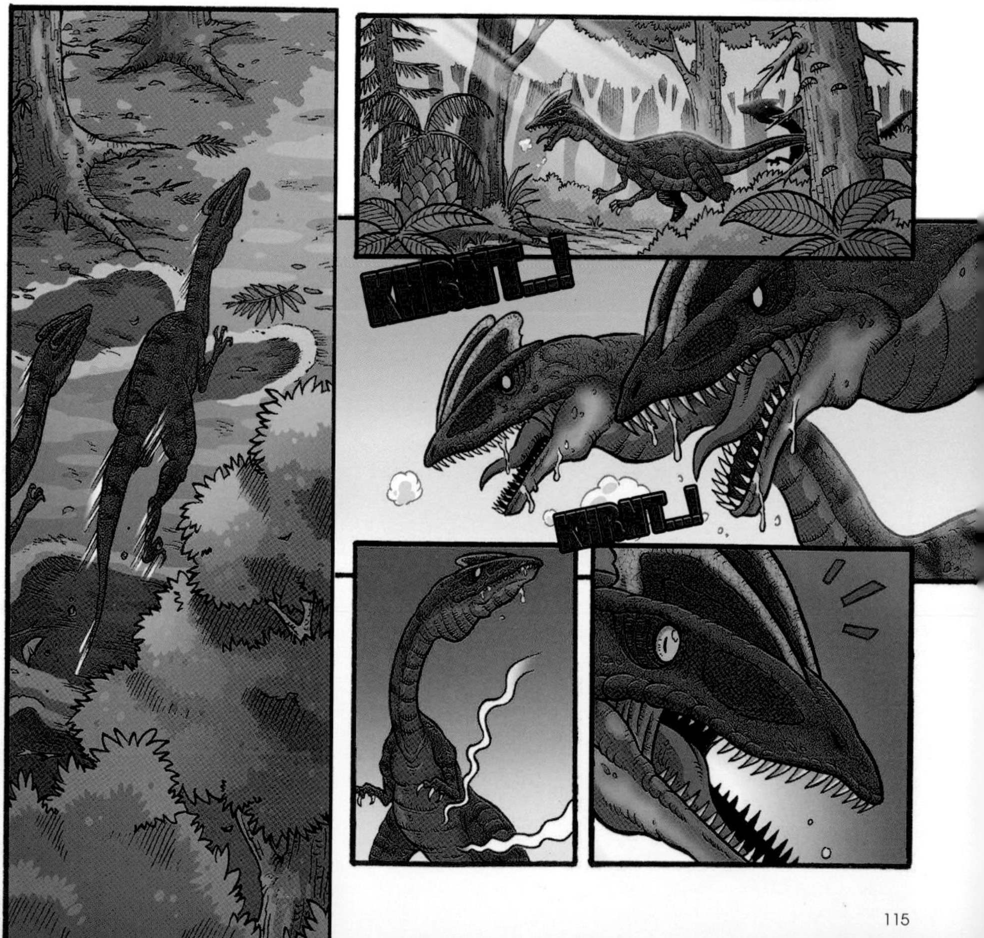
KHRNT...!
KHRNT..!

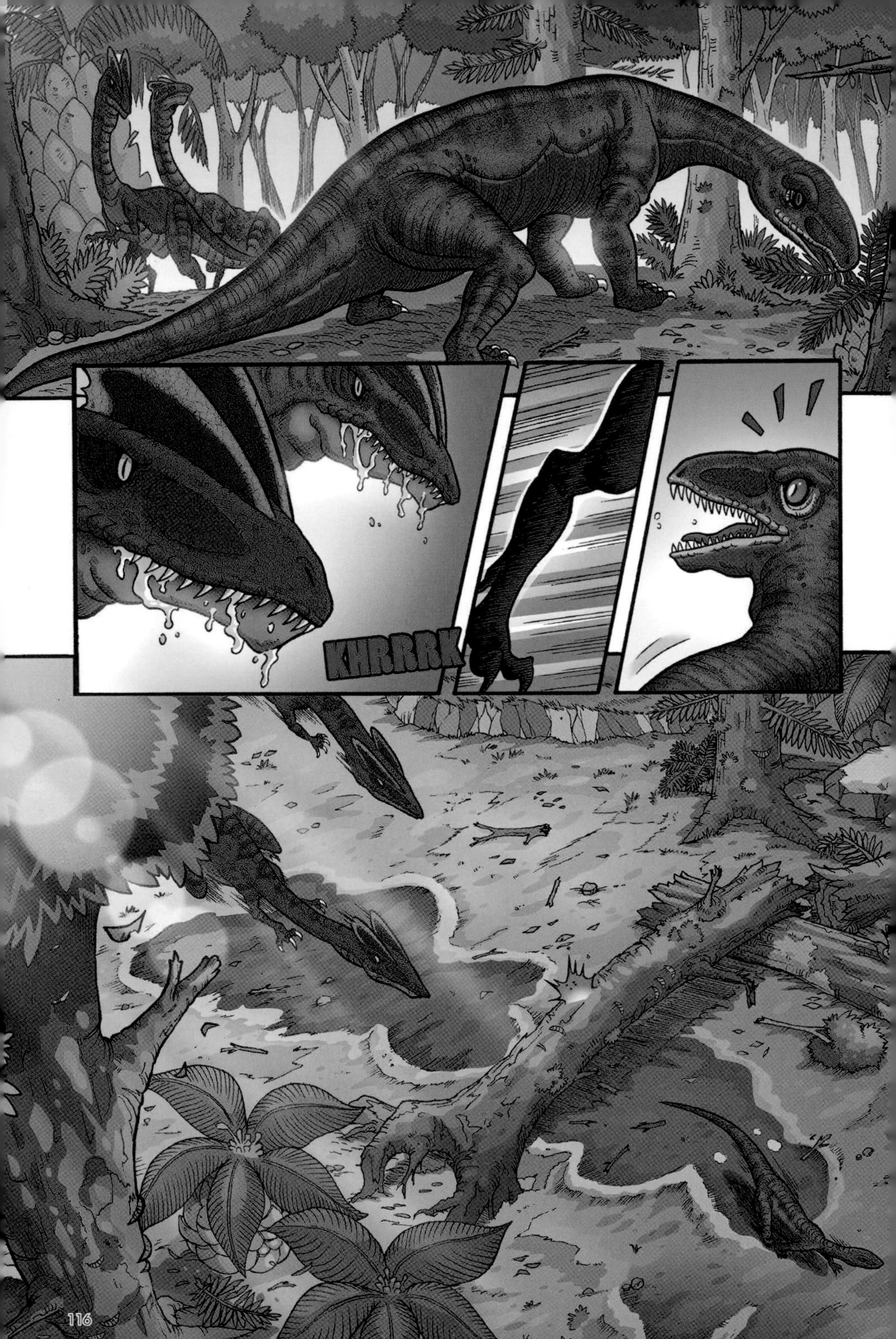
KHRRRK

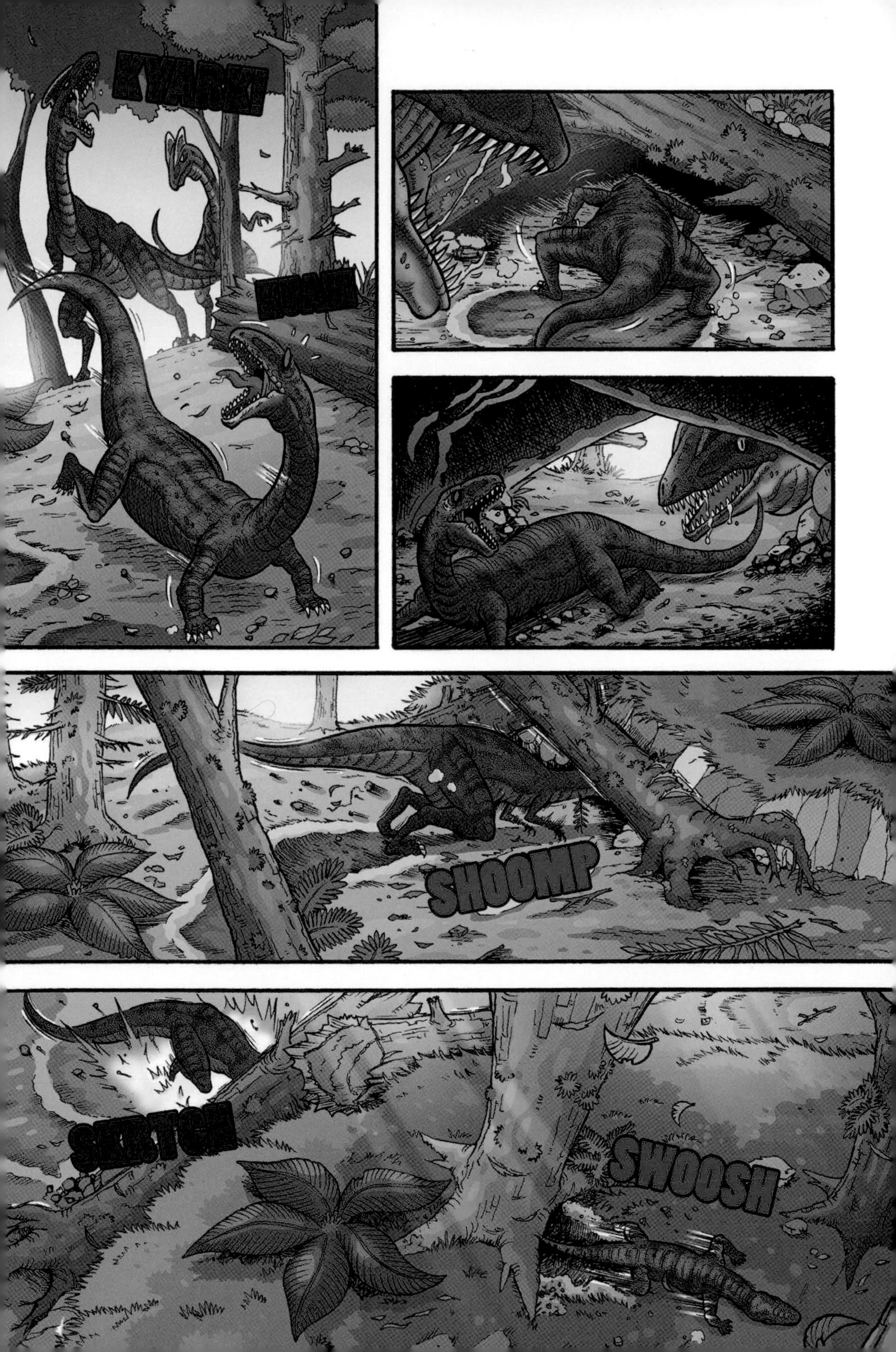
KYARK!
SHOOMP
SKRTCH
SWOOSH

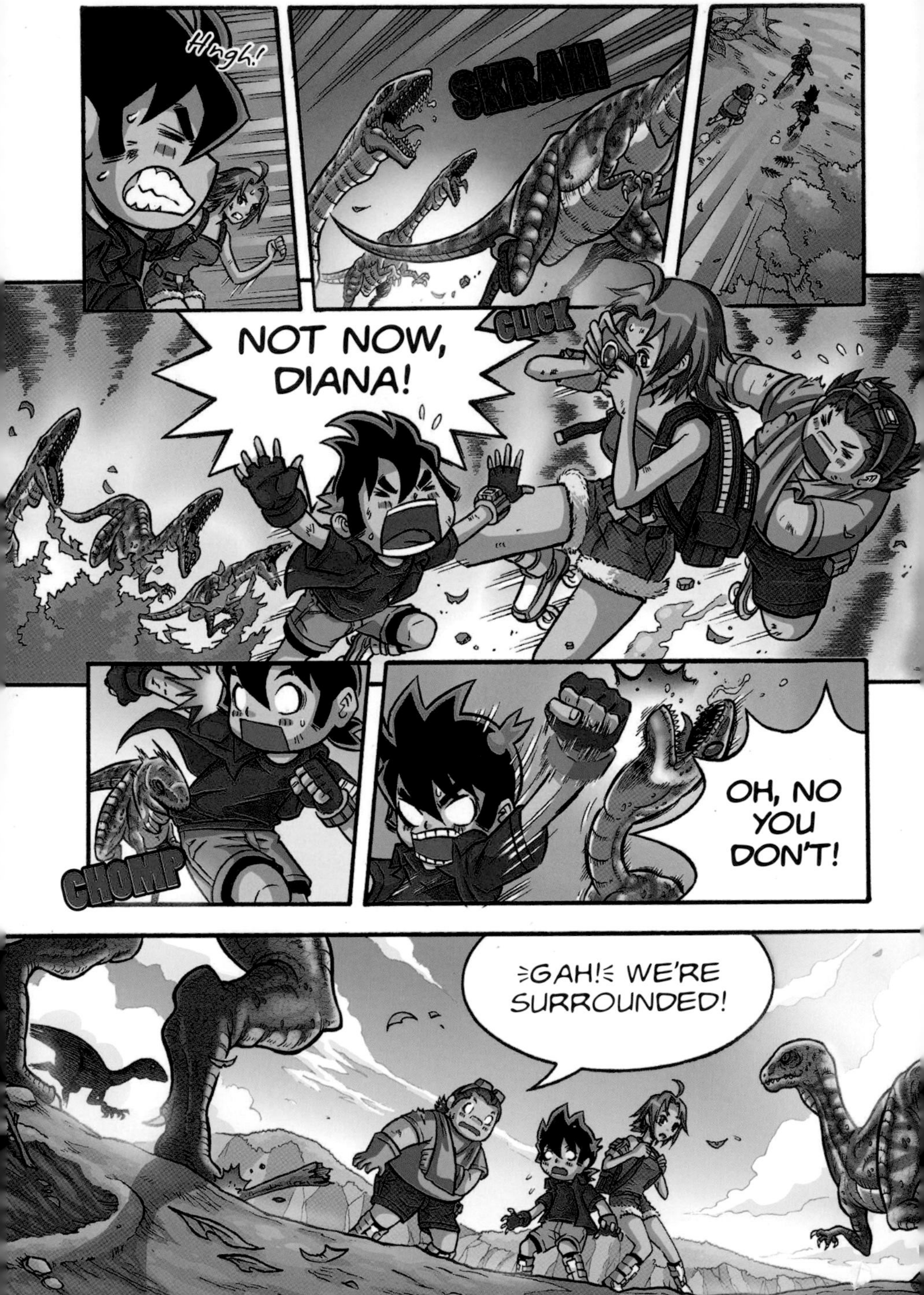
Hngh!
SKRAH!
CLICK
NOT NOW, DIANA!
CHOMP
OH, NO YOU DON'T!
GAH! WE'RE SURROUNDED!

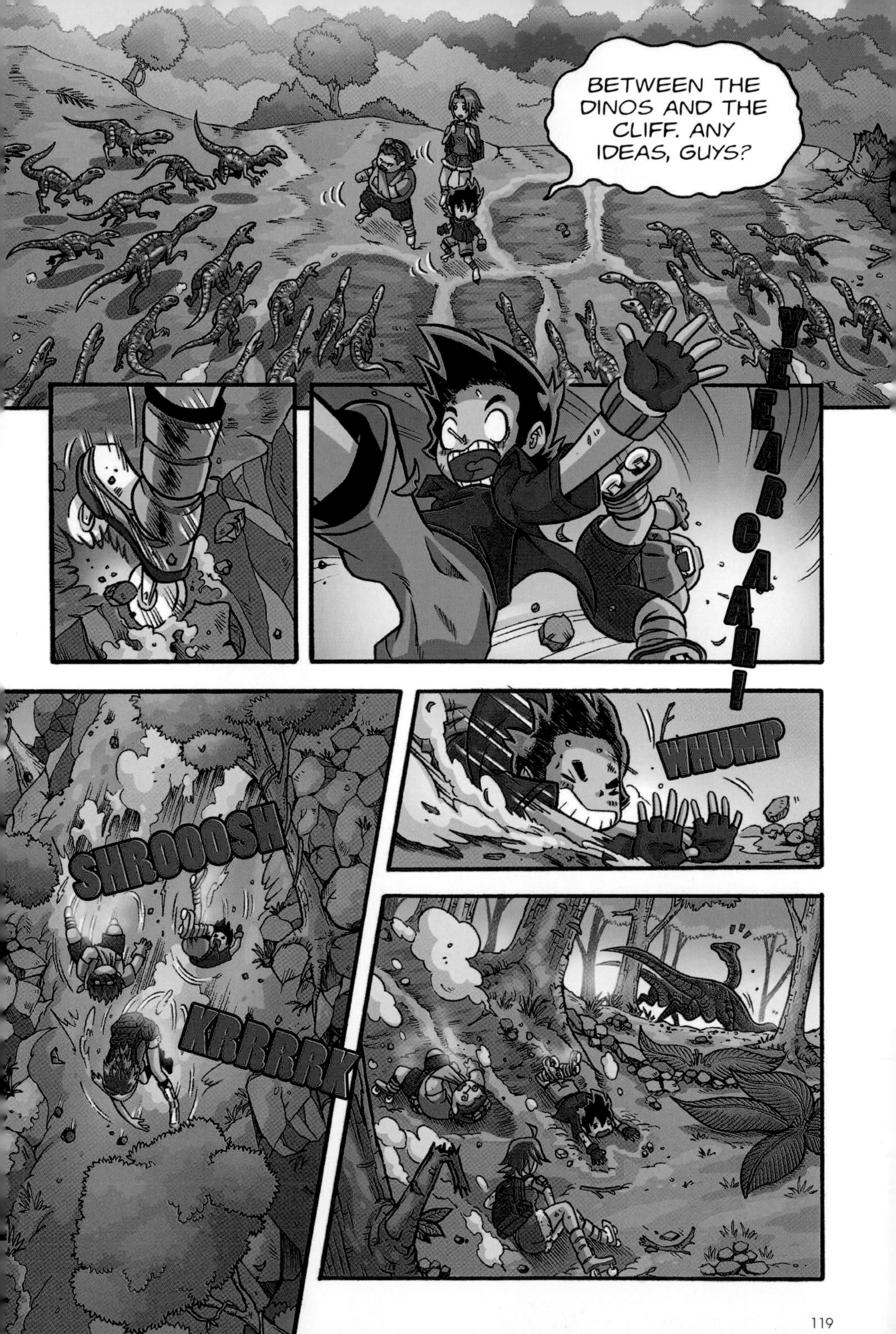
BETWEEN THE DINOS AND THE CLIFF. ANY IDEAS, GUYS?
YEEEARRGAAAH!
WHUMP
SHROOOOSH
KRRRRRK

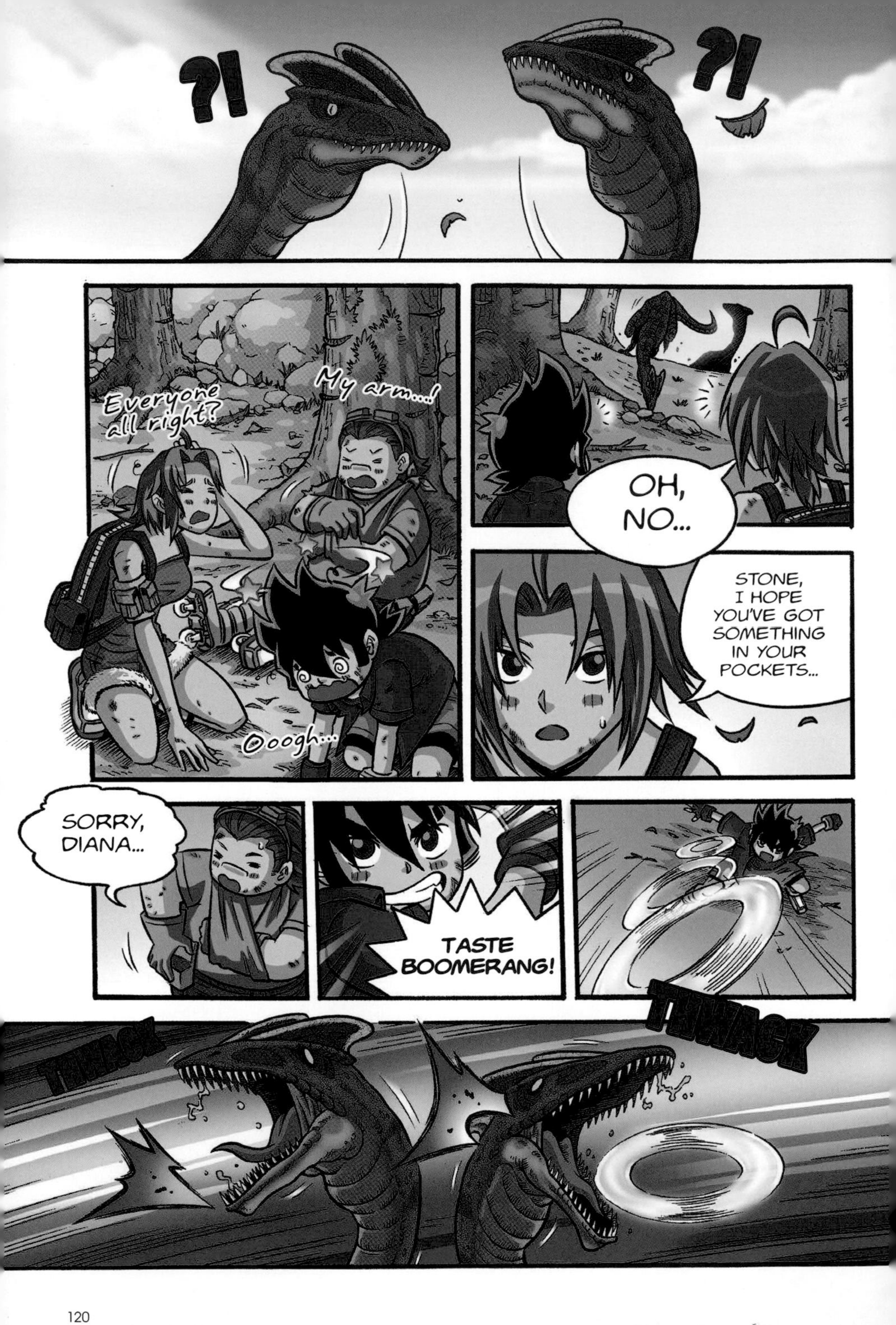
?!
?!
Everyone all right?
My arm...!
Ooogh...
OH, NO...
STONE, I HOPE YOU'VE GOT SOMETHING IN YOUR POCKETS...
SORRY, DIANA...
TASTE BOOMERANG!
THWACK
THWACK

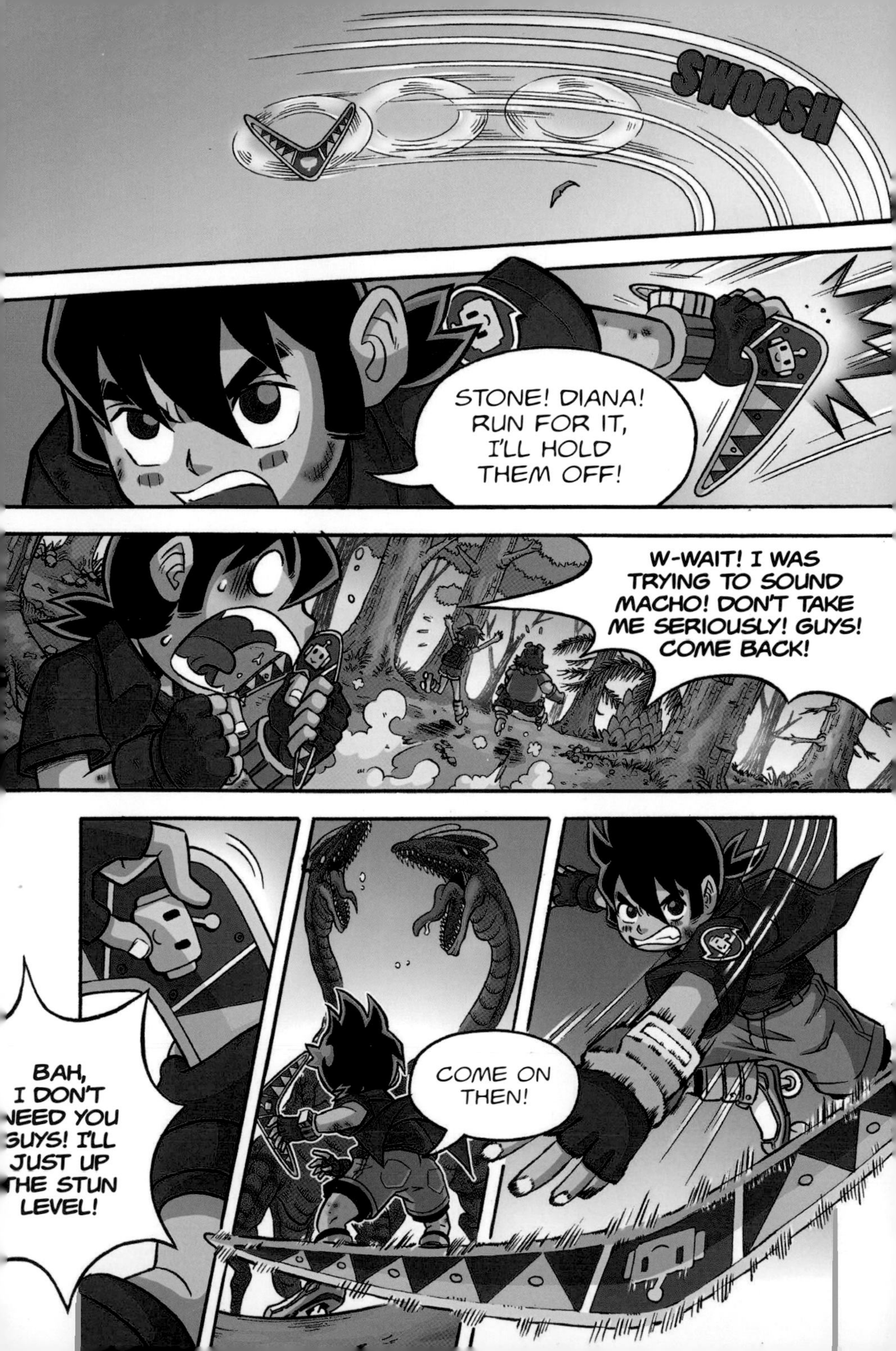
SWOOSH
STONE! DIANA! RUN FOR IT, I'LL HOLD THEM OFF!
W-WAIT! I WAS TRYING TO SOUND MACHO! DON'T TAKE ME SERIOUSLY! GUYS! COME BACK!
BAH, I DON'T NEED YOU GUYS! I'LL JUST UP THE STUN LEVEL!
COME ON THEN!

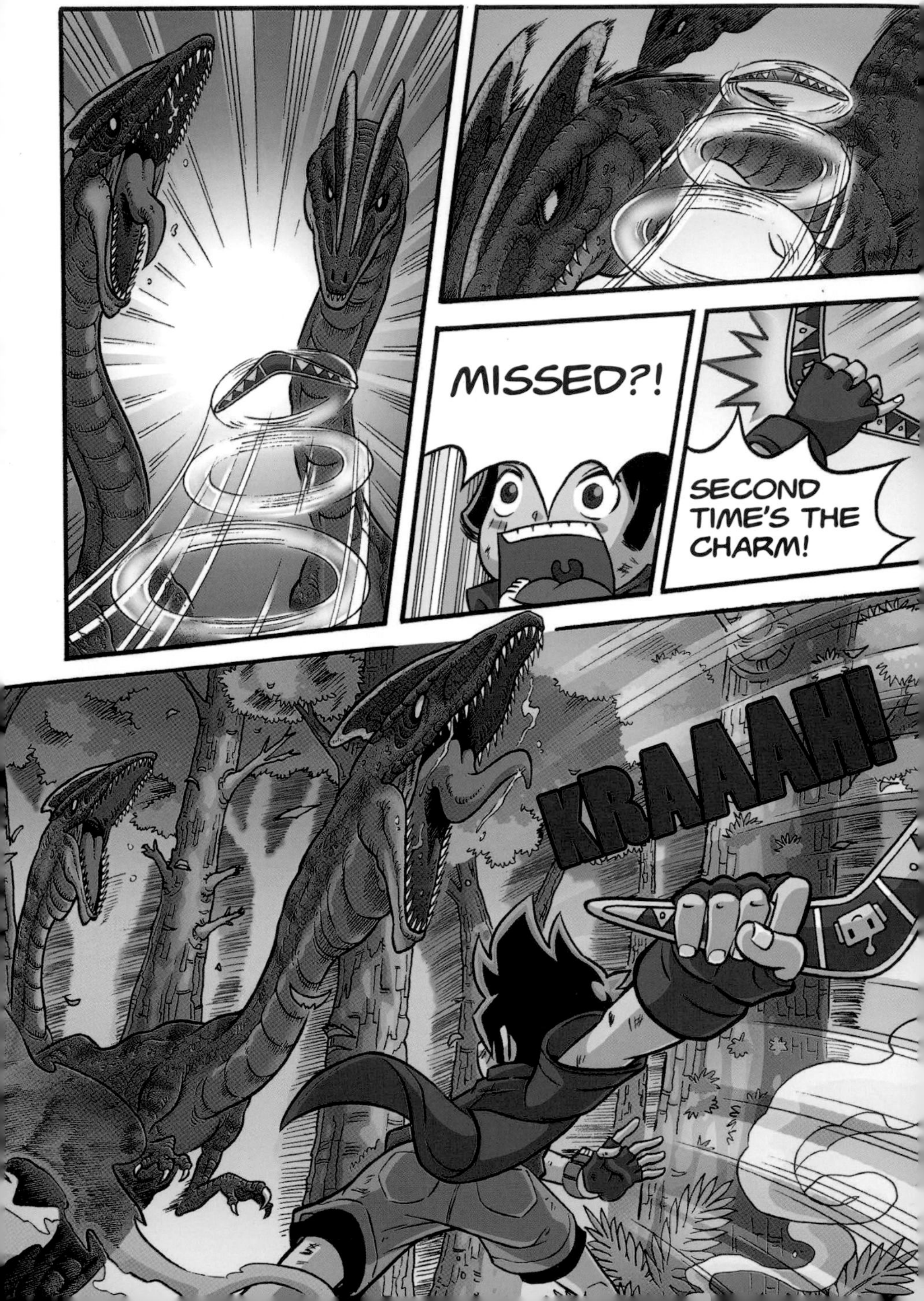
MISSED?!
SECOND TIME'S THE CHARM!
KRAAAH!

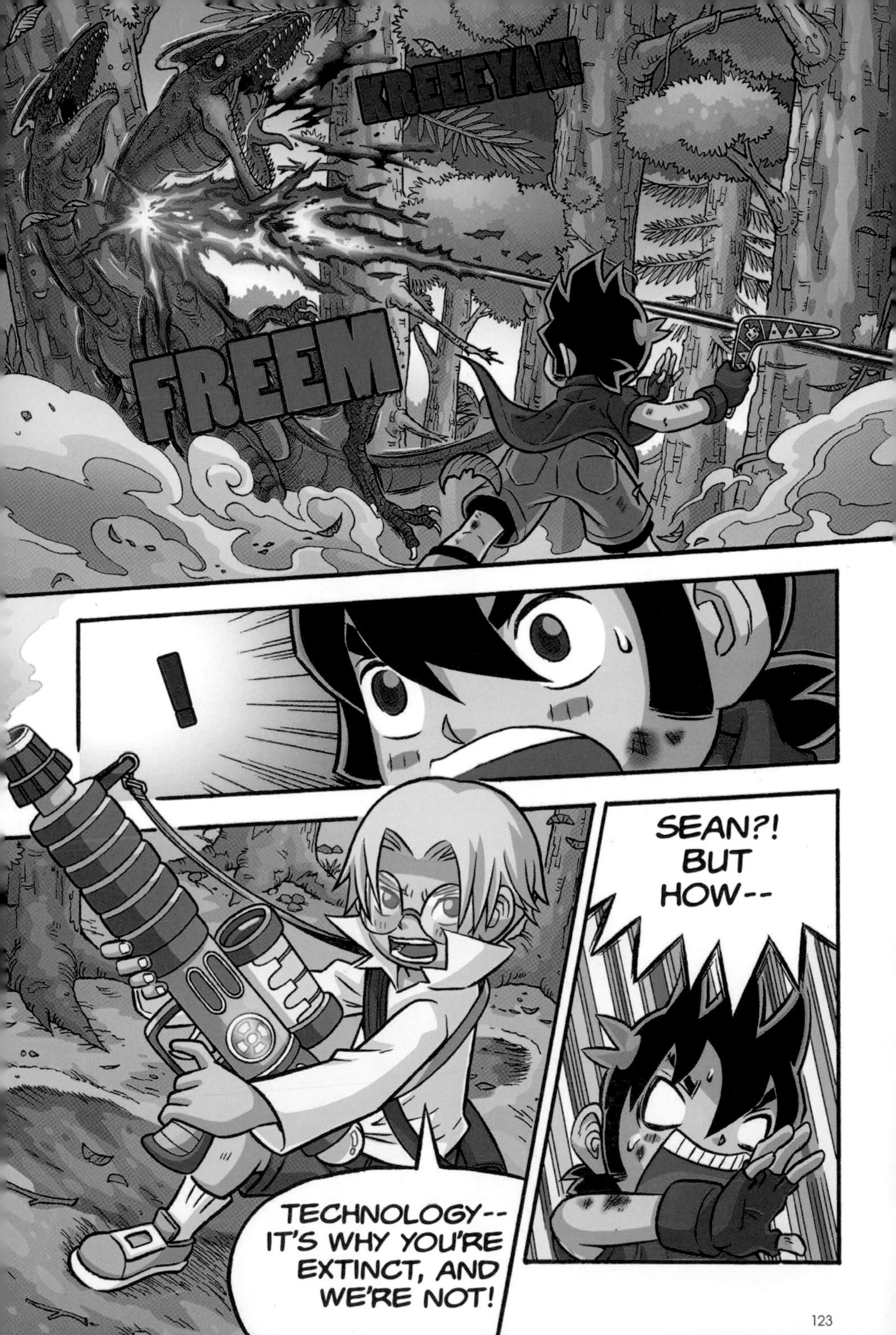
KREEEYAK!
FREEM
!
SEAN?! BUT HOW--
TECHNOLOGY-- IT'S WHY YOU'RE EXTINCT, AND WE'RE NOT!

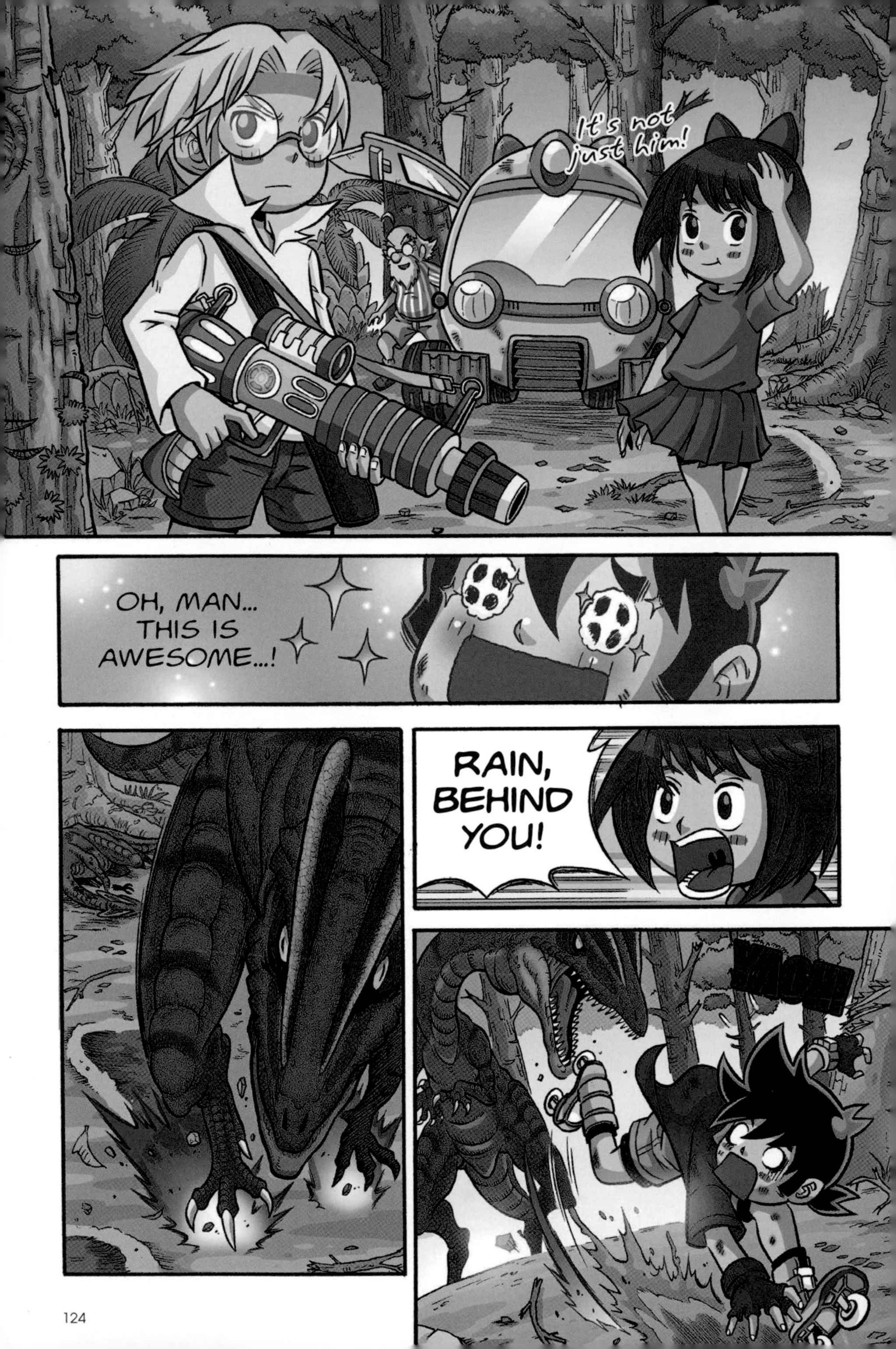
It's not just him!
OH, MAN... THIS IS AWESOME...!
RAIN, BEHIND YOU!

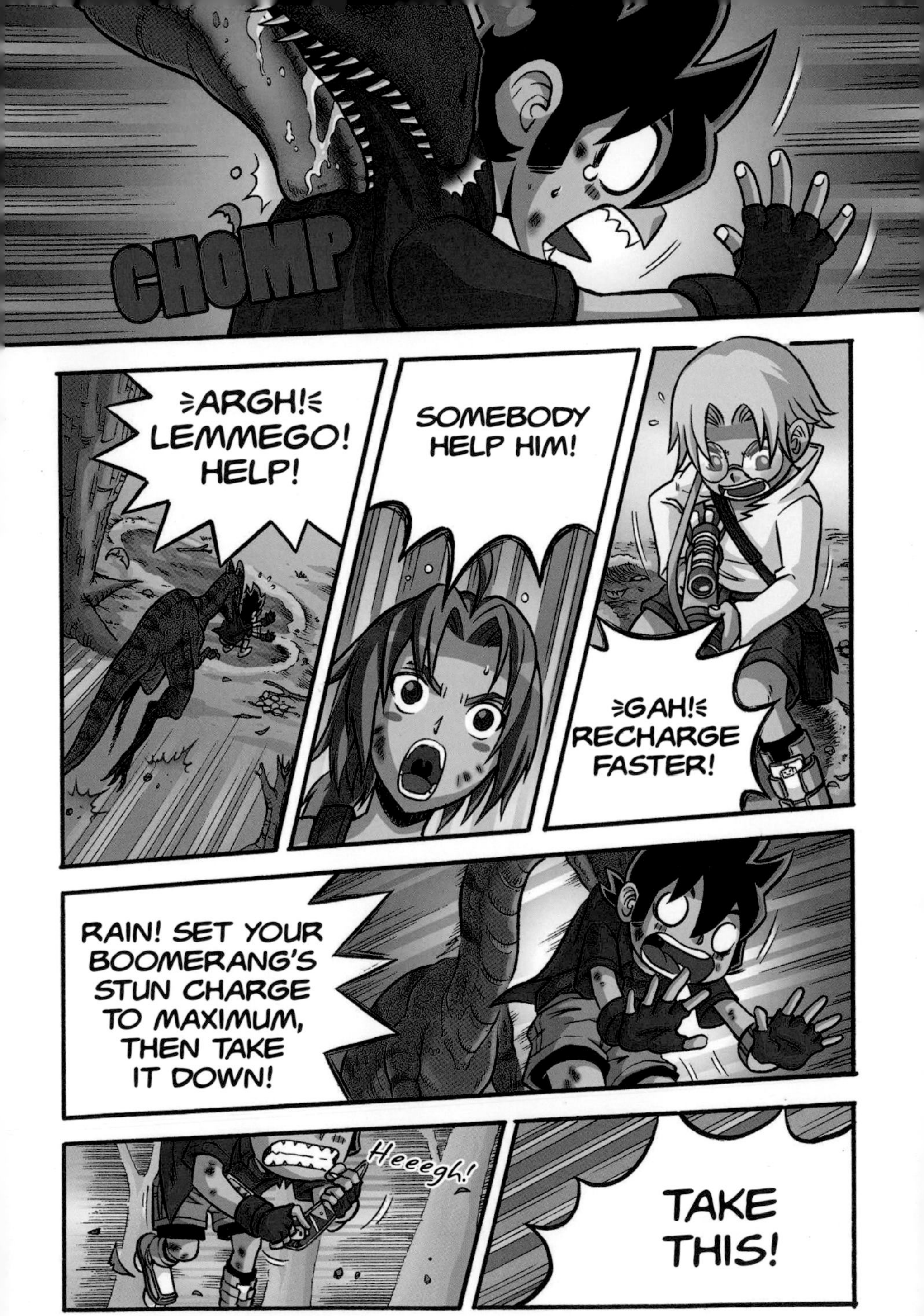
CHOMP
ARGH! LEMMEGO! HELP!
SOMEBODY HELP HIM!
GAH! RECHARGE FASTER!
RAIN! SET YOUR BOOMERANG'S STUN CHARGE TO MAXIMUM, THEN TAKE IT DOWN!
Heeeegh!
TAKE THIS!

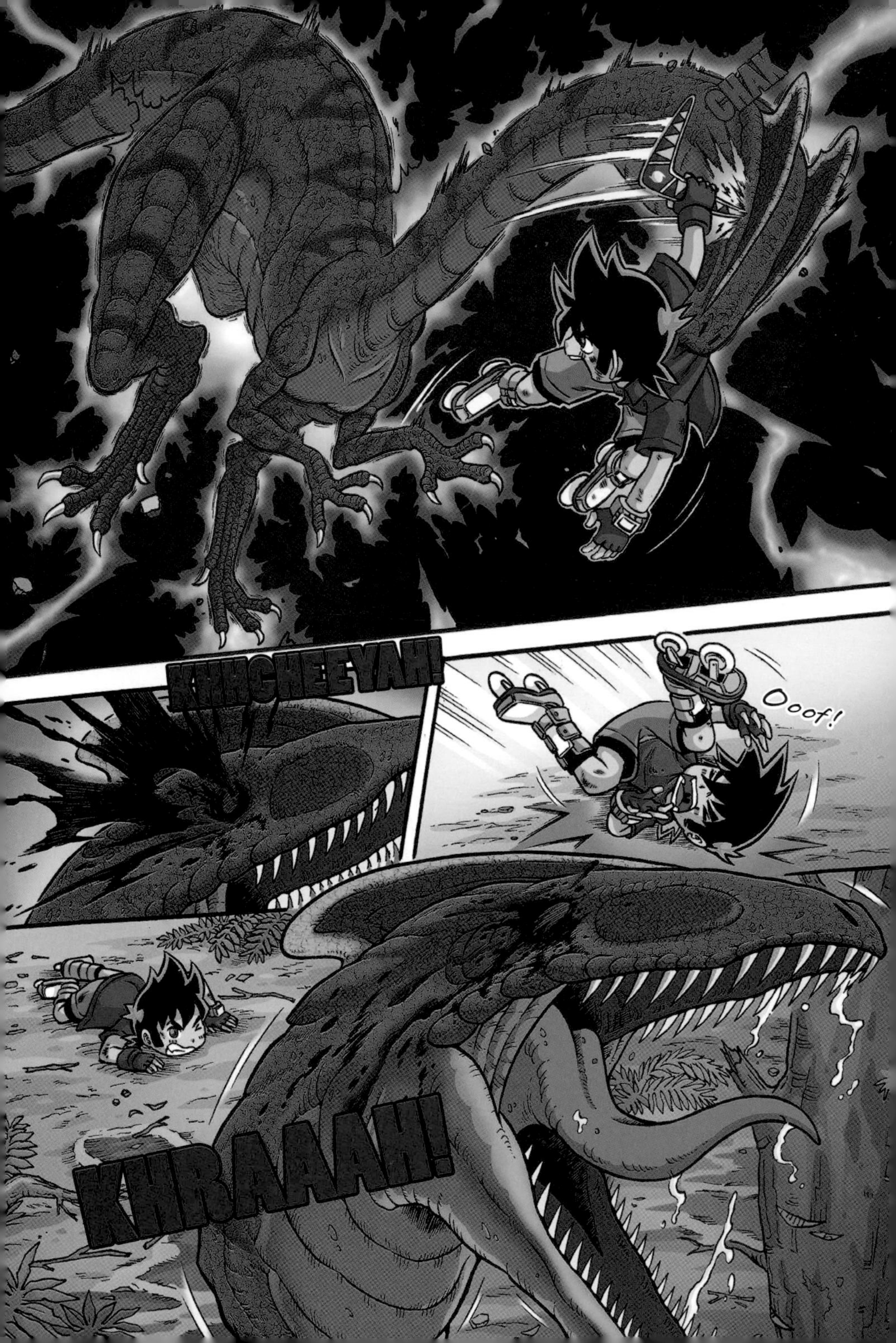
CHAK
KHHCHEEYAH!
Ooof!
KHRAAAAH!

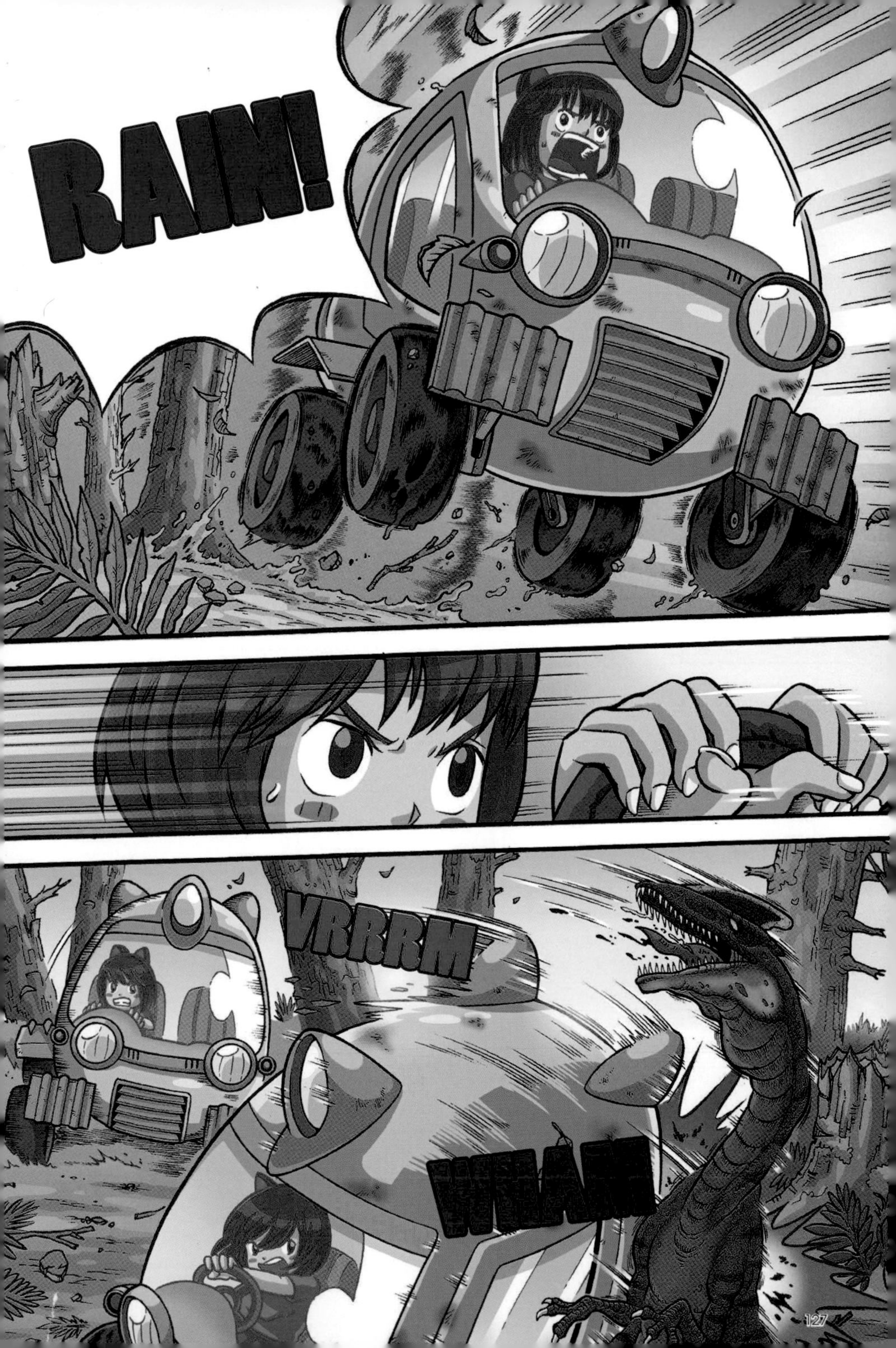
RAIN!
VRRRM

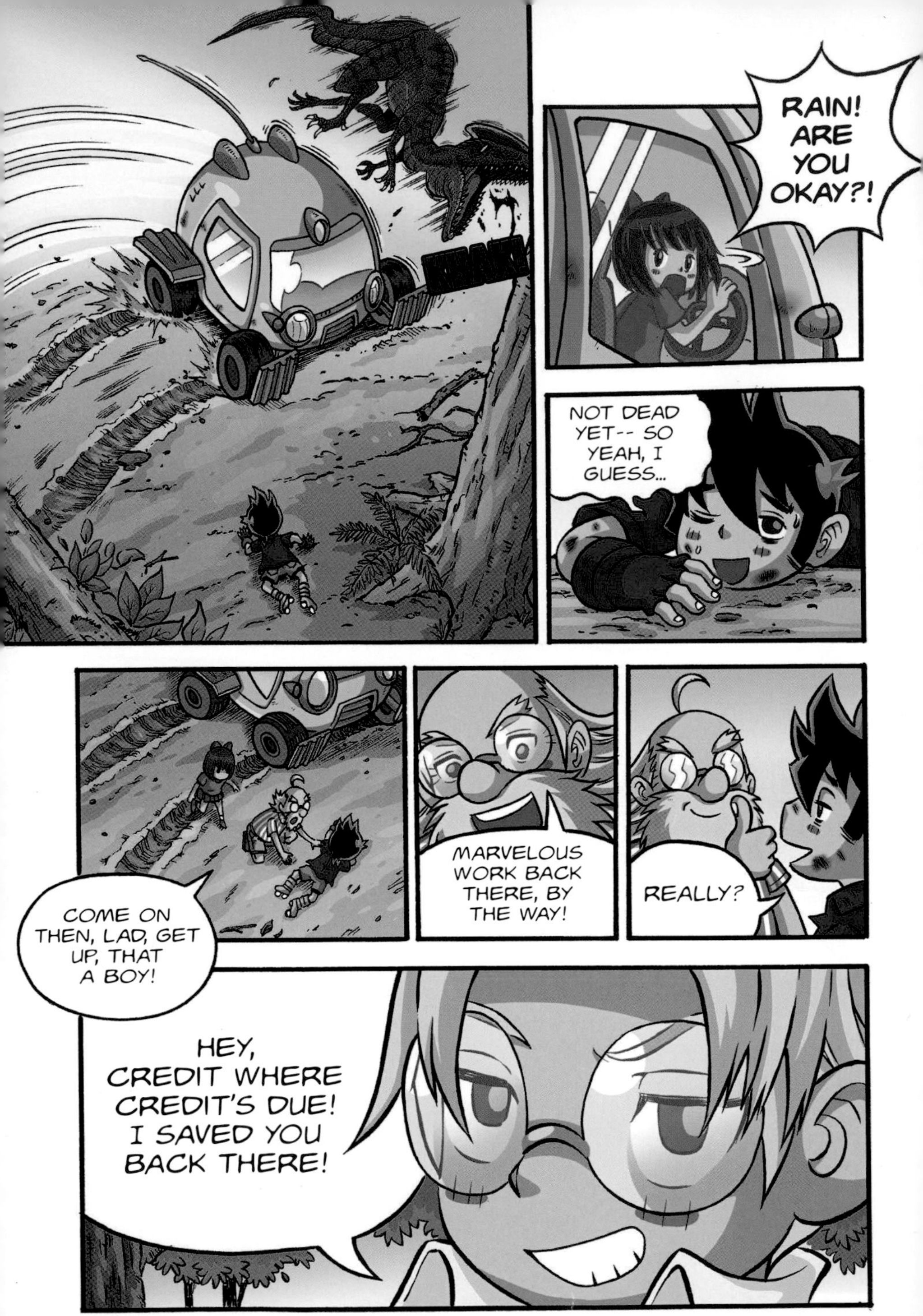
RAIN! ARE YOU OKAY?!
NOT DEAD YET-- SO YEAH, I GUESS...
COME ON THEN, LAD, GET UP, THAT A BOY!
MARVELOUS WORK BACK THERE, BY THE WAY!
REALLY?
HEY, CREDIT WHERE CREDIT'S DUE! I SAVED YOU BACK THERE!

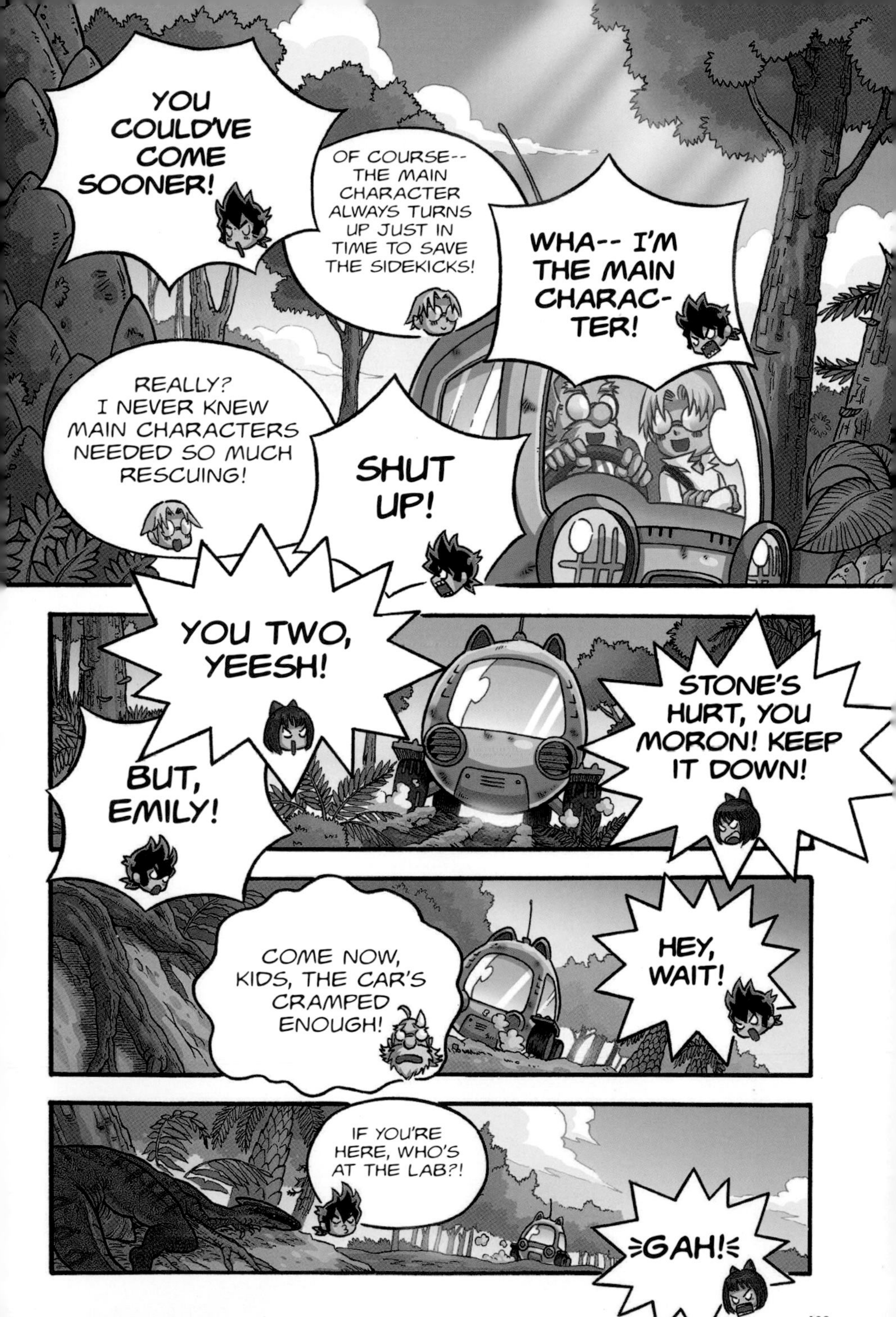
YOU COULD'VE COME SOONER!
OF COURSE-- THE MAIN CHARACTER ALWAYS TURNS UP JUST IN TIME TO SAVE THE SIDEKICKS!
WHA-- I'M THE MAIN CHARAC-TER!
REALLY? I NEVER KNEW MAIN CHARACTERS NEEDED SO MUCH RESCUING!
SHUT UP!
YOU TWO, YEESH!
BUT, EMILY!
STONE'S HURT, YOU MORON! KEEP IT DOWN!
COME NOW, KIDS, THE CAR'S CRAMPED ENOUGH!
HEY, WAIT!
IF YOU'RE HERE, WHO'S AT THE LAB?!
GAH!

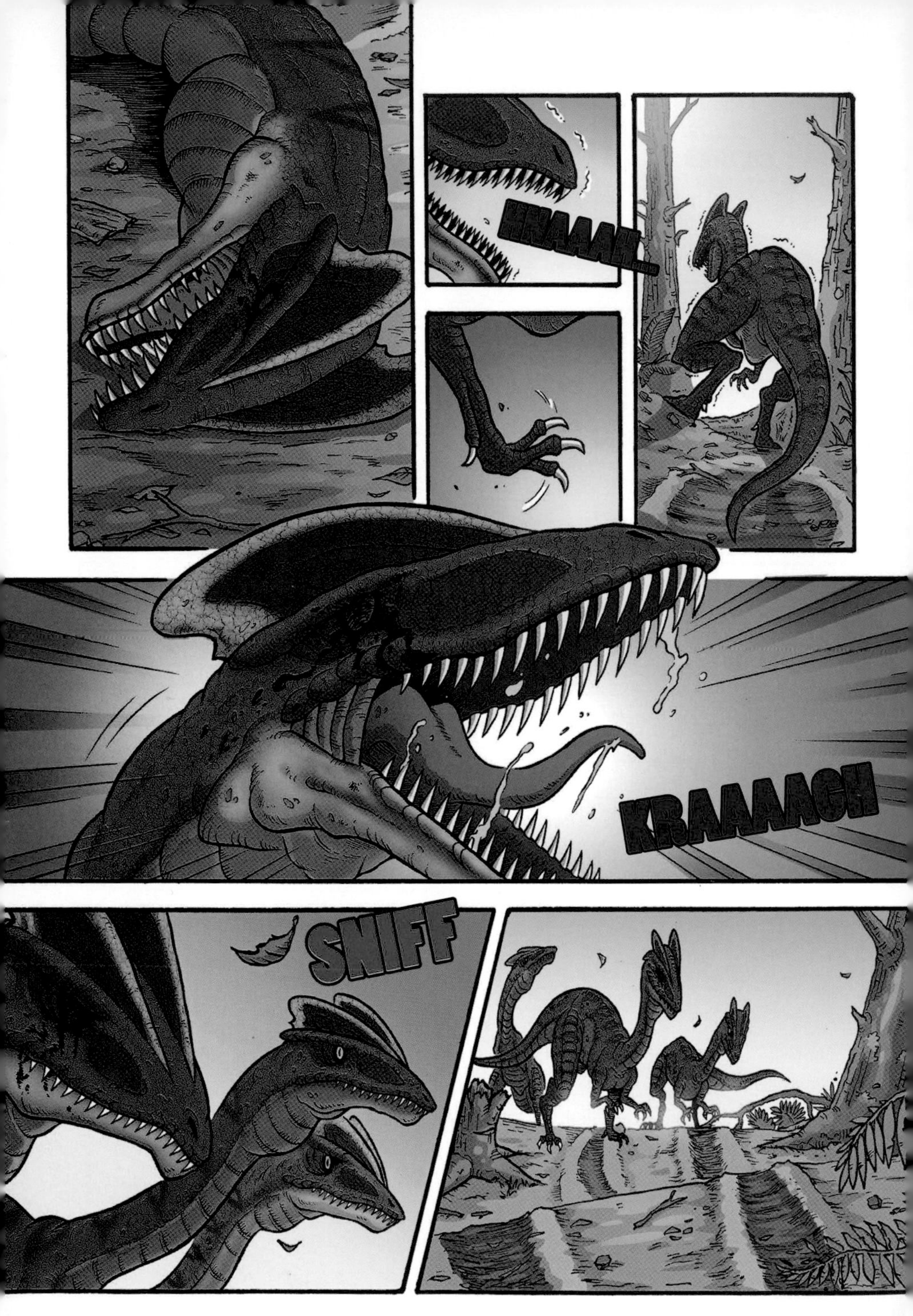
HRAAAAH...
KRAAAACH
SNIFF

JONESING FOR THE JURASSIC

Anchisaurus

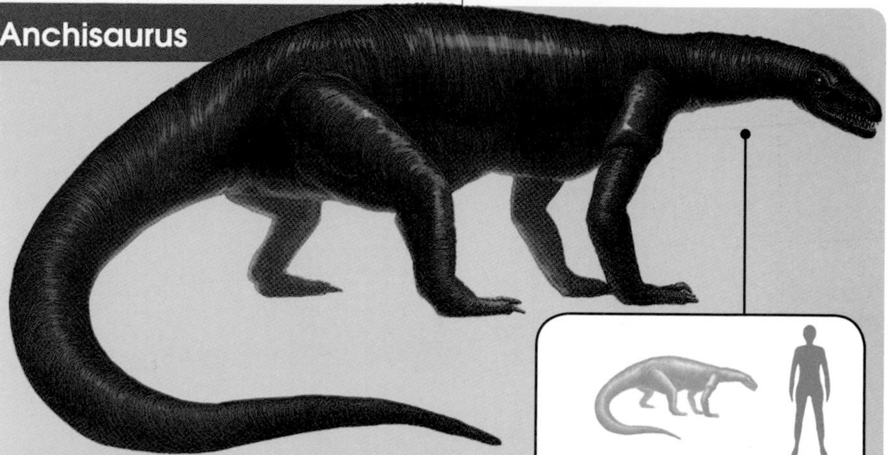

Scientific name: Anchisaurus
Length: 5.5-8.2 feet
Diet: Herbivore
Habitat: Forest outskirt
Discovered: North America, South Africa
Era: Early Jurassic

Anchisaurus had a near-triangular head and a long, delicate snout. It also had a long neck, body, and tail. The curved claws on its forelimbs are believed to have been used to dig up plant roots. It usually walked on all fours, but stood fully upright in order to reach higher vegetation.

JONESING FOR THE JURASSIC

Lesothosaurus

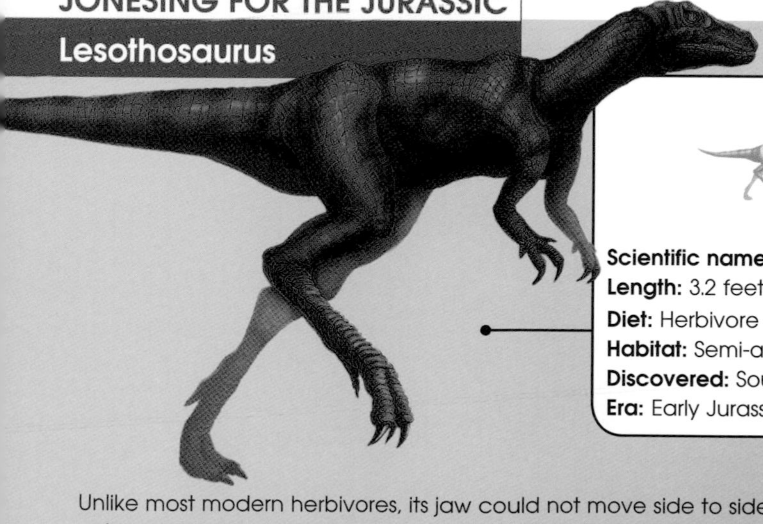

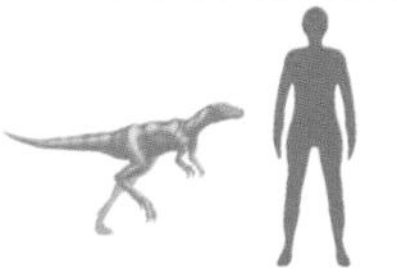

Scientific name: Lesothosaurus
Length: 3.2 feet
Diet: Herbivore
Habitat: Semi-arid areas
Discovered: South Africa
Era: Early Jurassic

Unlike most modern herbivores, its jaw could not move side to side to grind food, only up and down. Its pointed, grooved teeth, however, were great for chewing plant matter. Its hindlimbs were very long, especially for a dinosaur of its size–making it an exceedingly fast runner.

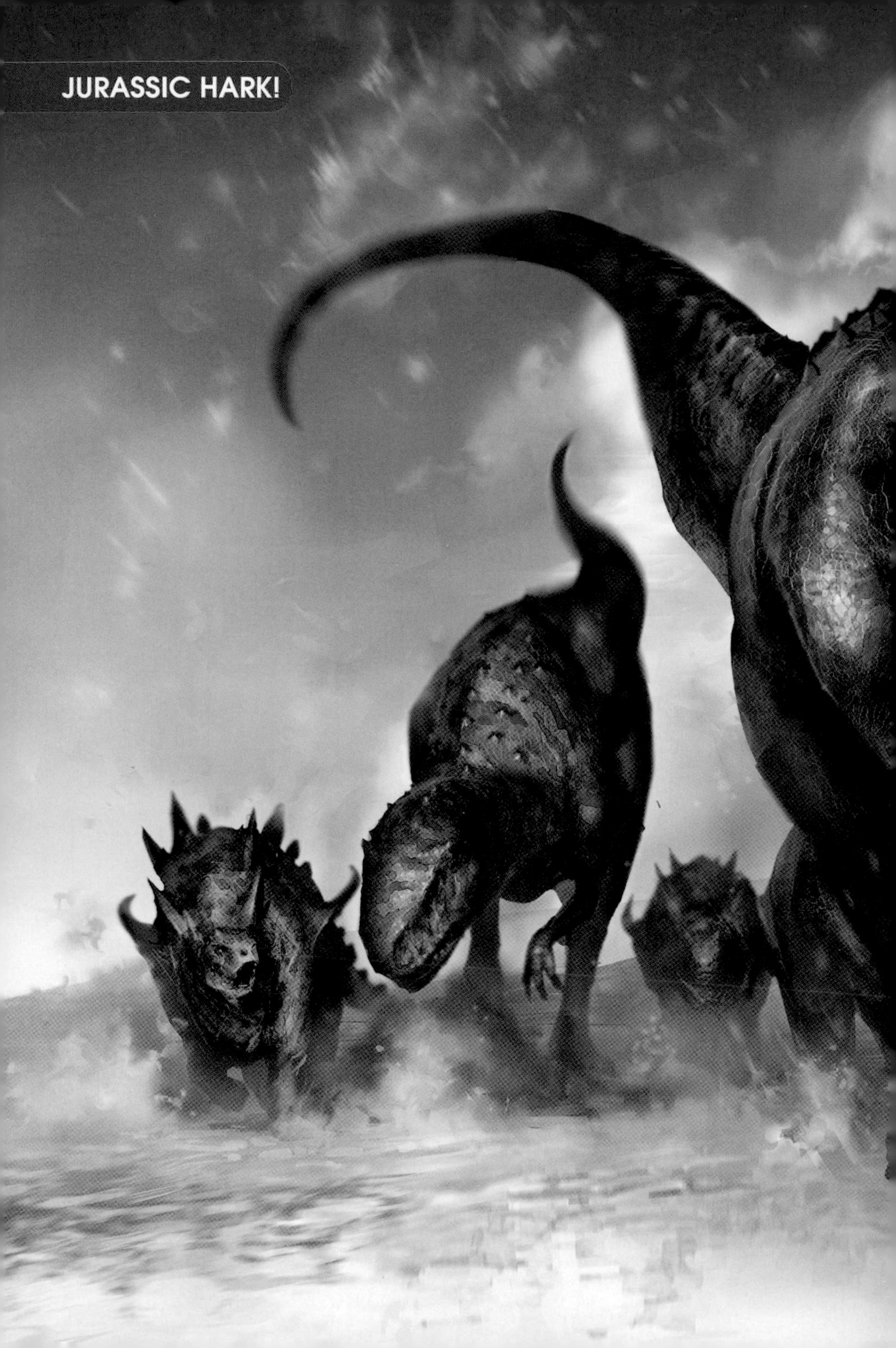

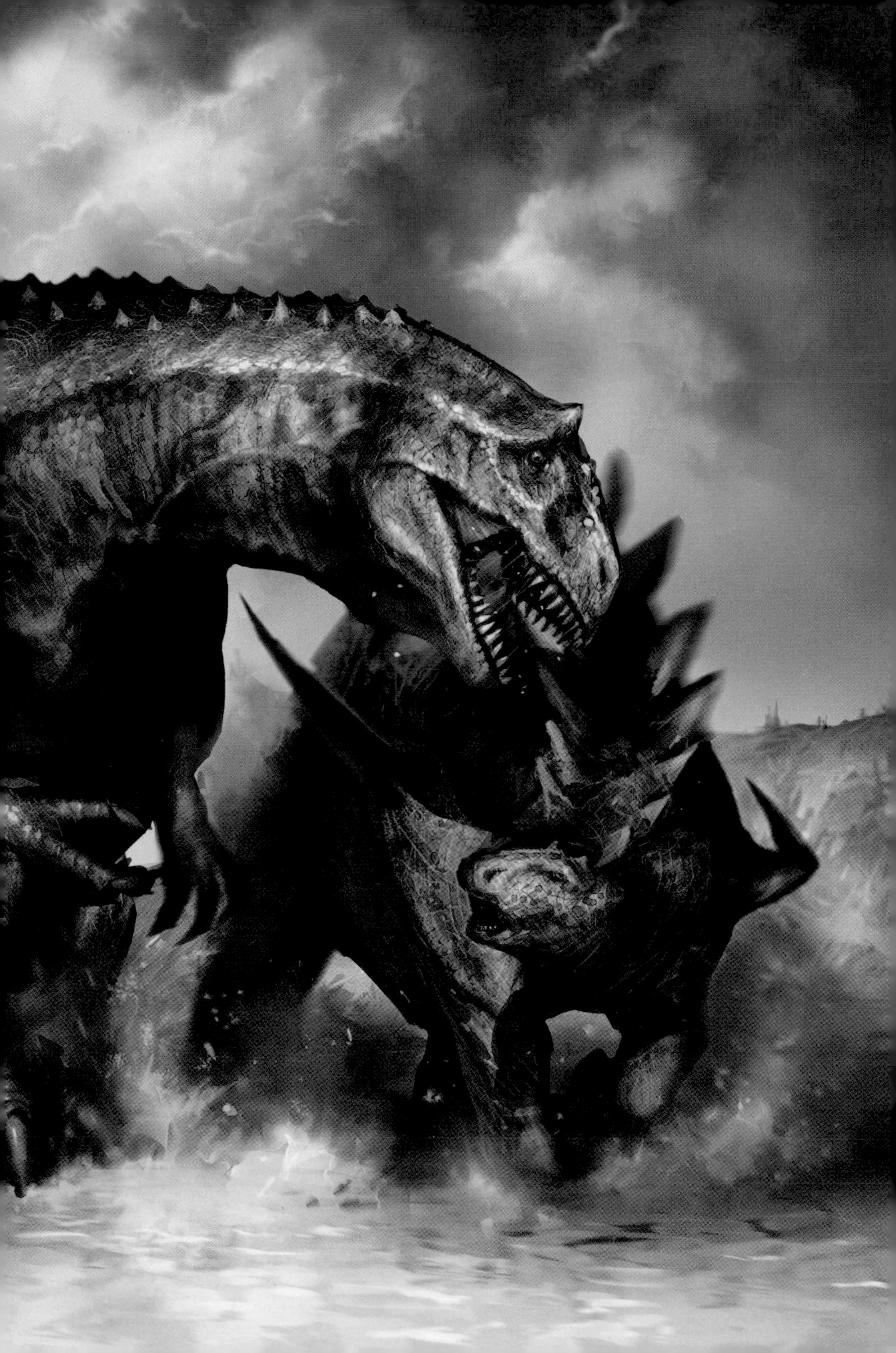

Bipedal (two-legged) skeletal structure

Bipedal dinosaurs used their forelimbs to defend themselves and search for food. They also often had long legs in order to maximize running potential and maneuverability.

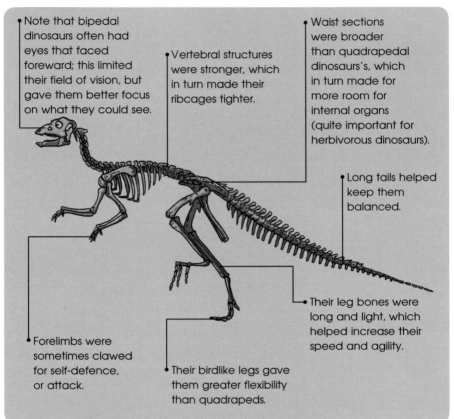

• Note that bipedal dinosaurs often had eyes that faced foreward; this limited their field of vision, but gave them better focus on what they could see.

• Vertebral structures were stronger, which in turn made their ribcages tighter.

• Waist sections were broader than quadrapedal dinosaurs's, which in turn made for more room for internal organs (quite important for herbivorous dinosaurs).

• Long tails helped keep them balanced.

• Forelimbs were sometimes clawed for self-defence, or attack.

• Their birdlike legs gave them greater flexibility than quadrapeds.

• Their leg bones were long and light, which helped increase their speed and agility.

Dinosaur skeleton

Dilophosaurus

Massopondylus

Jaw joints and teeth were located on the same level, giving its jaws a scissor-like quality that made it easy to cut and slice flesh.

The jaw joint is located behind its teeth. Their clamplike jaws crushed and squeezed the leaves they ate.

Quadruped (four-legged) dinosaur skeleton

The vertebral bones were connected with structural tissues, ensuring body weight could be evenly distributed.

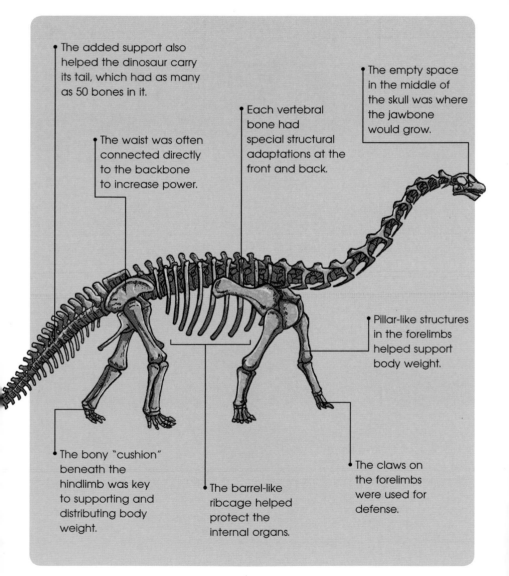

The added support also helped the dinosaur carry its tail, which had as many as 50 bones in it.

The empty space in the middle of the skull was where the jawbone would grow.

The waist was often connected directly to the backbone to increase power.

Each vertebral bone had special structural adaptations at the front and back.

Pillar-like structures in the forelimbs helped support body weight.

The bony "cushion" beneath the hindlimb was key to supporting and distributing body weight.

The barrel-like ribcage helped protect the internal organs.

The claws on the forelimbs were used for defense.

JONESING FOR THE JURASSIC

Fabrosaurus

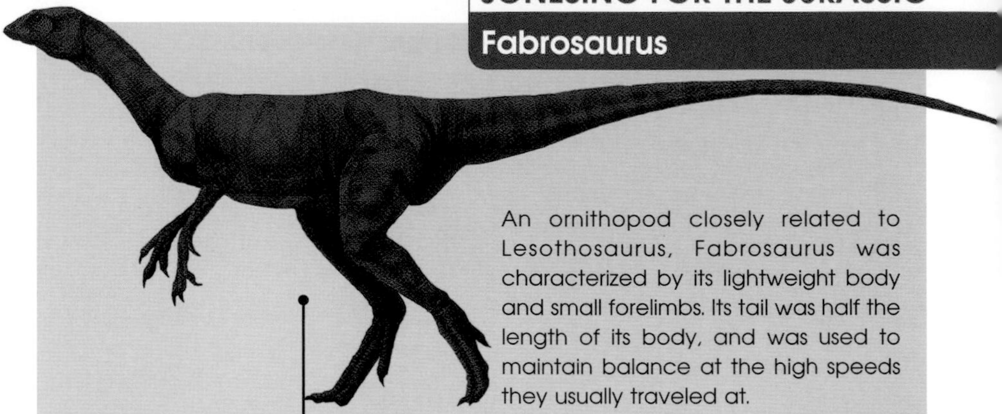

An ornithopod closely related to Lesothosaurus, Fabrosaurus was characterized by its lightweight body and small forelimbs. Its tail was half the length of its body, and was used to maintain balance at the high speeds they usually traveled at.

Scientific name: Fabrosaurus
Length: 3.2 feet
Diet: Herbivore
Habitat: Arid areas
Discovered: South Africa, China
Era: Early to Mid-Jurassic

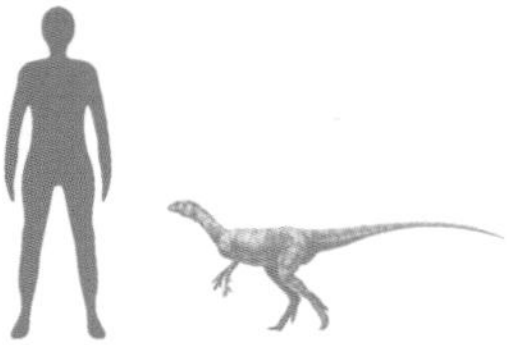

JONESING FOR THE JURASSIC

Scutellosaurus

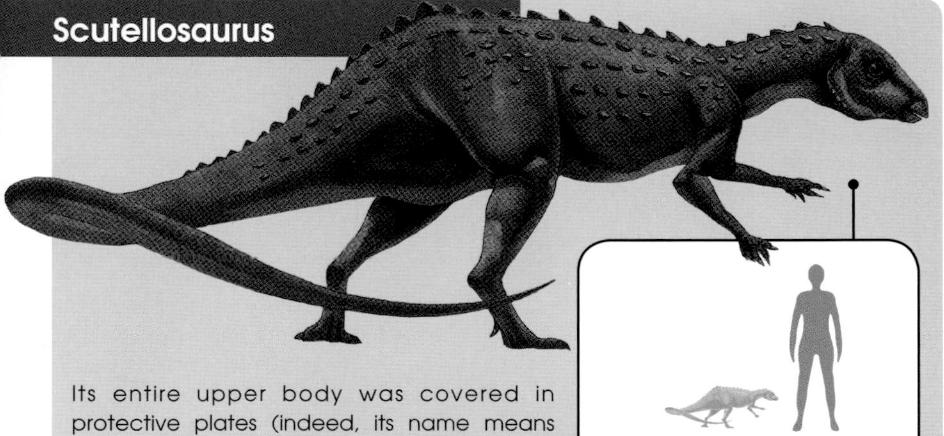

Its entire upper body was covered in protective plates (indeed, its name means "little-shielded lizard"); as such, was classified as a thyreophore ("shieldbearer"). A close relative was Scelidosaurus. The main difference between the two was that the Scutellosaurus could walk on two legs, while Scelidosaurus could only manage on all fours.

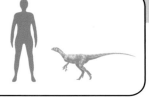

Scientific name: Scutellosaurus
Length: 3.9 feet
Diet: Herbivore
Habitat: Unknown
Discovered: North America
Era: Early Jurassic

CHAPTER 7

INVASION!

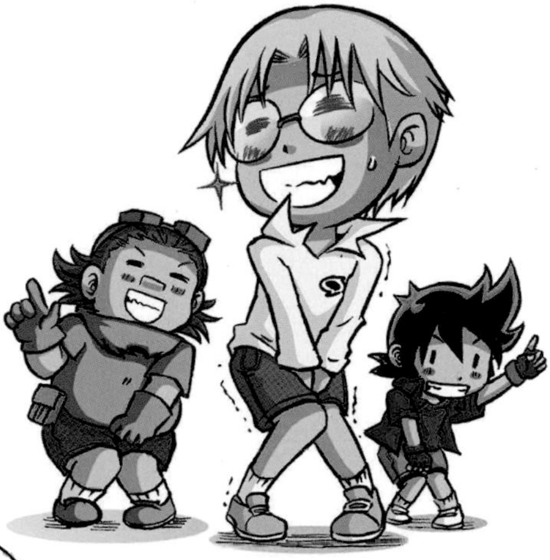

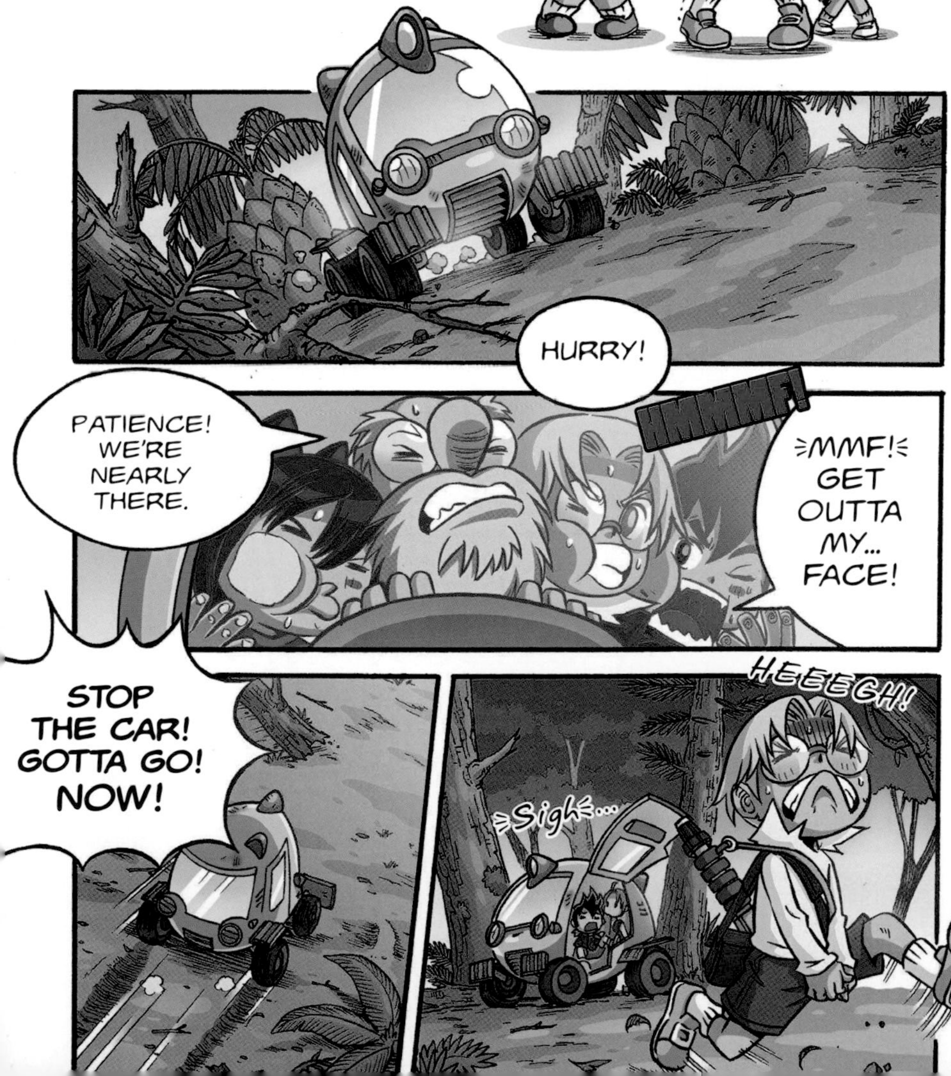
HURRY!
HMMMF!
PATIENCE! WE'RE NEARLY THERE.
MMF! GET OUTTA MY... FACE!
STOP THE CAR! GOTTA GO! NOW!
HEEEEGH!
Sigh...

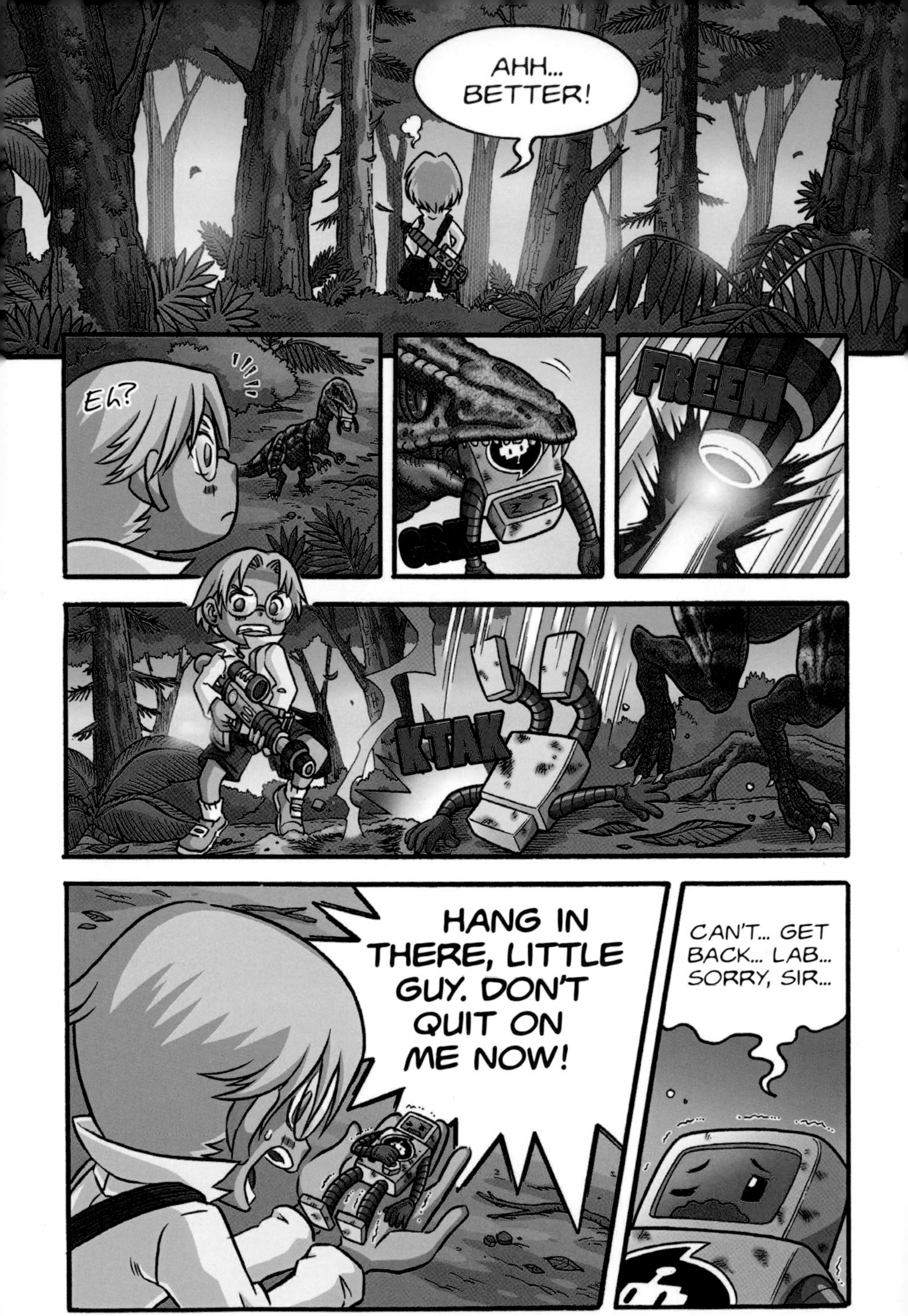

AHH... BETTER!
Eh?
FREEM
KTAK
HANG IN THERE, LITTLE GUY. DON'T QUIT ON ME NOW!
CAN'T... GET BACK... LAB... SORRY, SIR...

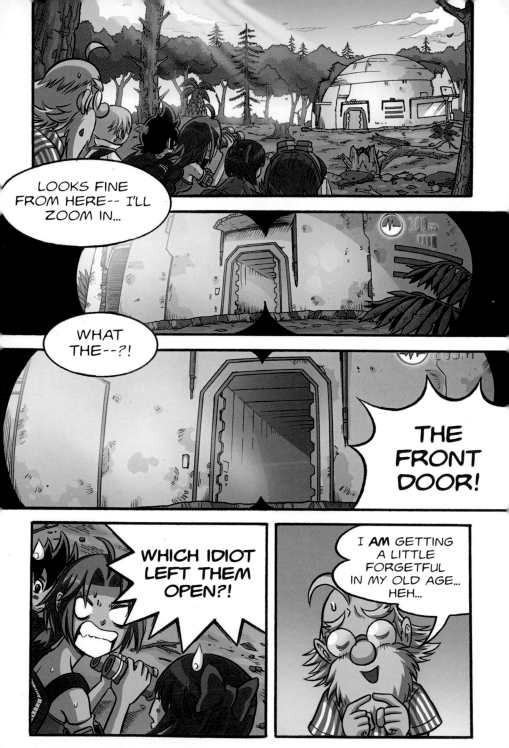

LOOKS FINE FROM HERE-- I'LL ZOOM IN...

WHAT THE--?!

THE FRONT DOOR!

WHICH IDIOT LEFT THEM OPEN?!

I **AM** GETTING A LITTLE FORGETFUL IN MY OLD AGE... HEH...

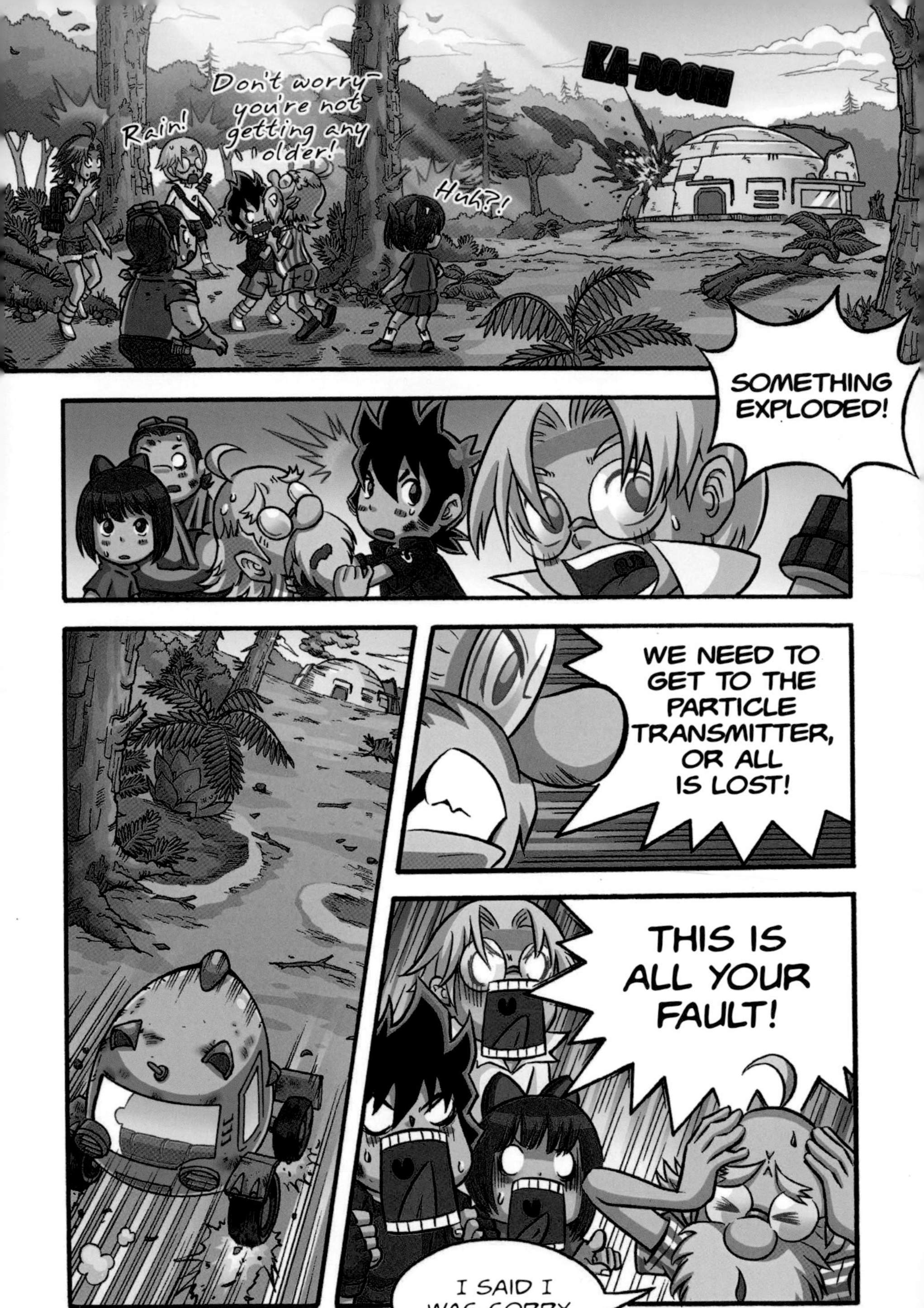
Rain!
Don't worry- you're not getting any older!
Huh?!
KA-BOOM
SOMETHING EXPLODED!
WE NEED TO GET TO THE PARTICLE TRANSMITTER, OR ALL IS LOST!
THIS IS ALL YOUR FAULT!
I SAID I WAS SORRY...

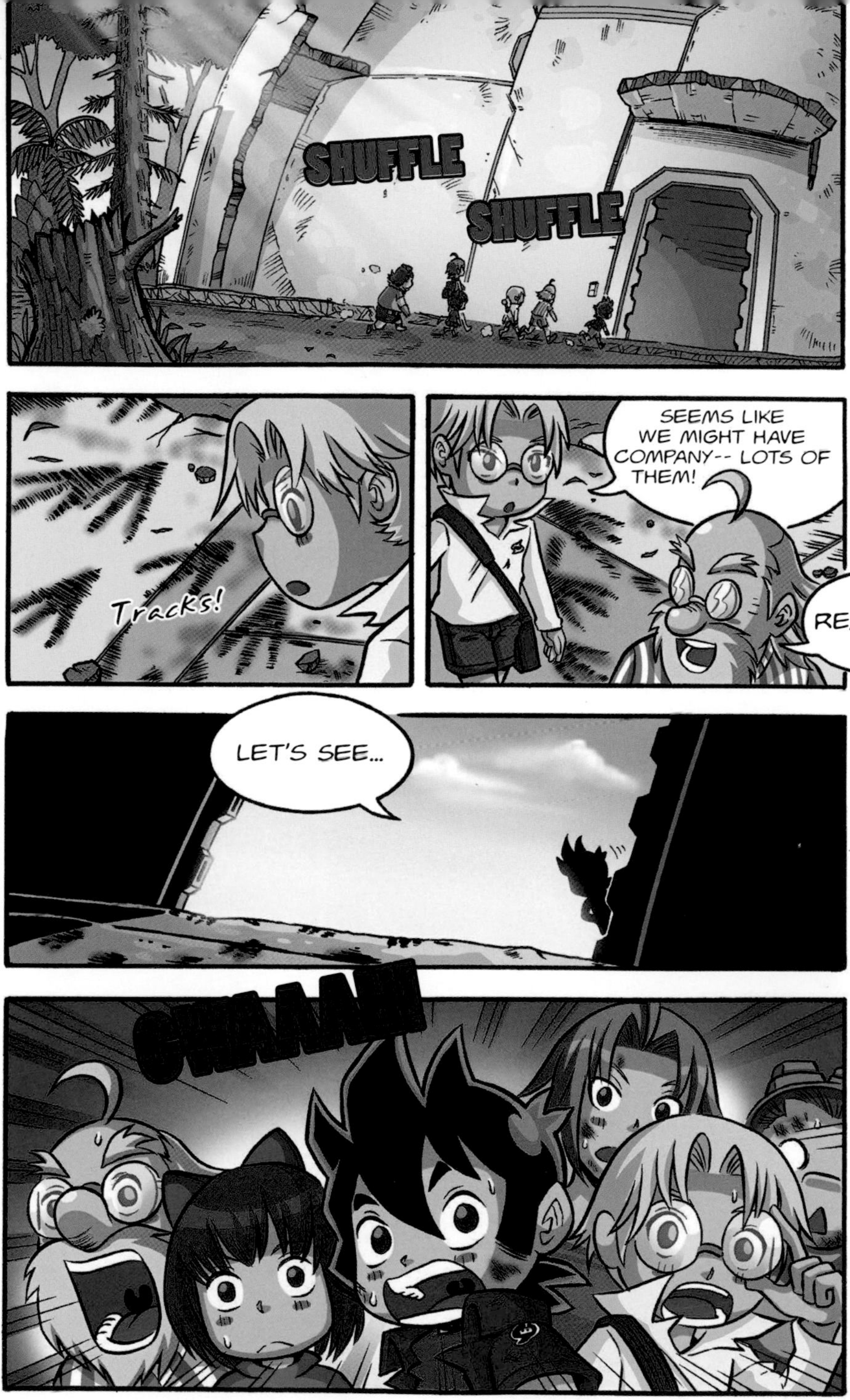
SHUFFLE
SHUFFLE
Tracks!
SEEMS LIKE WE MIGHT HAVE COMPANY-- LOTS OF THEM!
REALLY?
LET'S SEE...

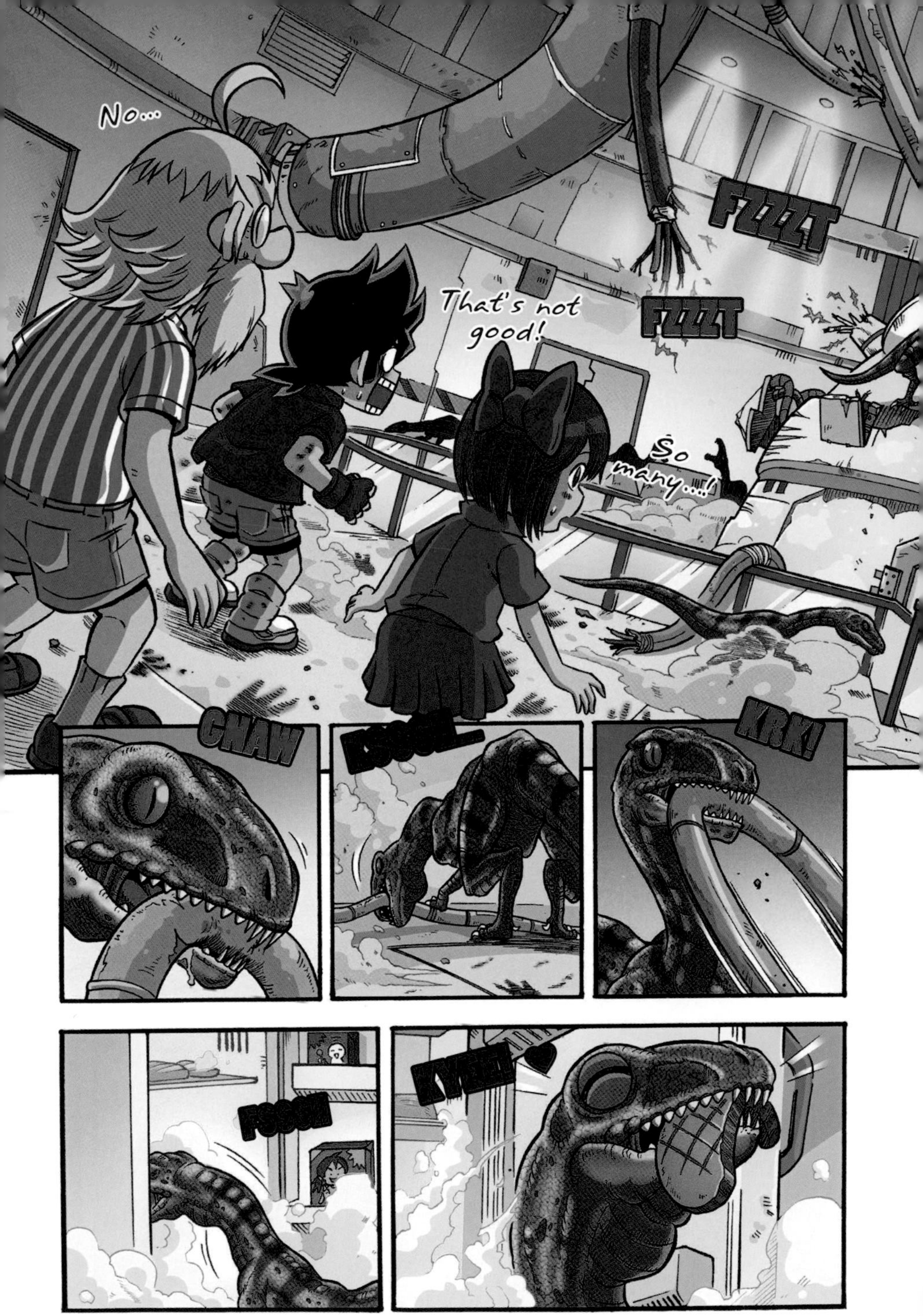
No...
FZZZT
FZZZT
That's not good!
So many...!
GNAW
KRK!

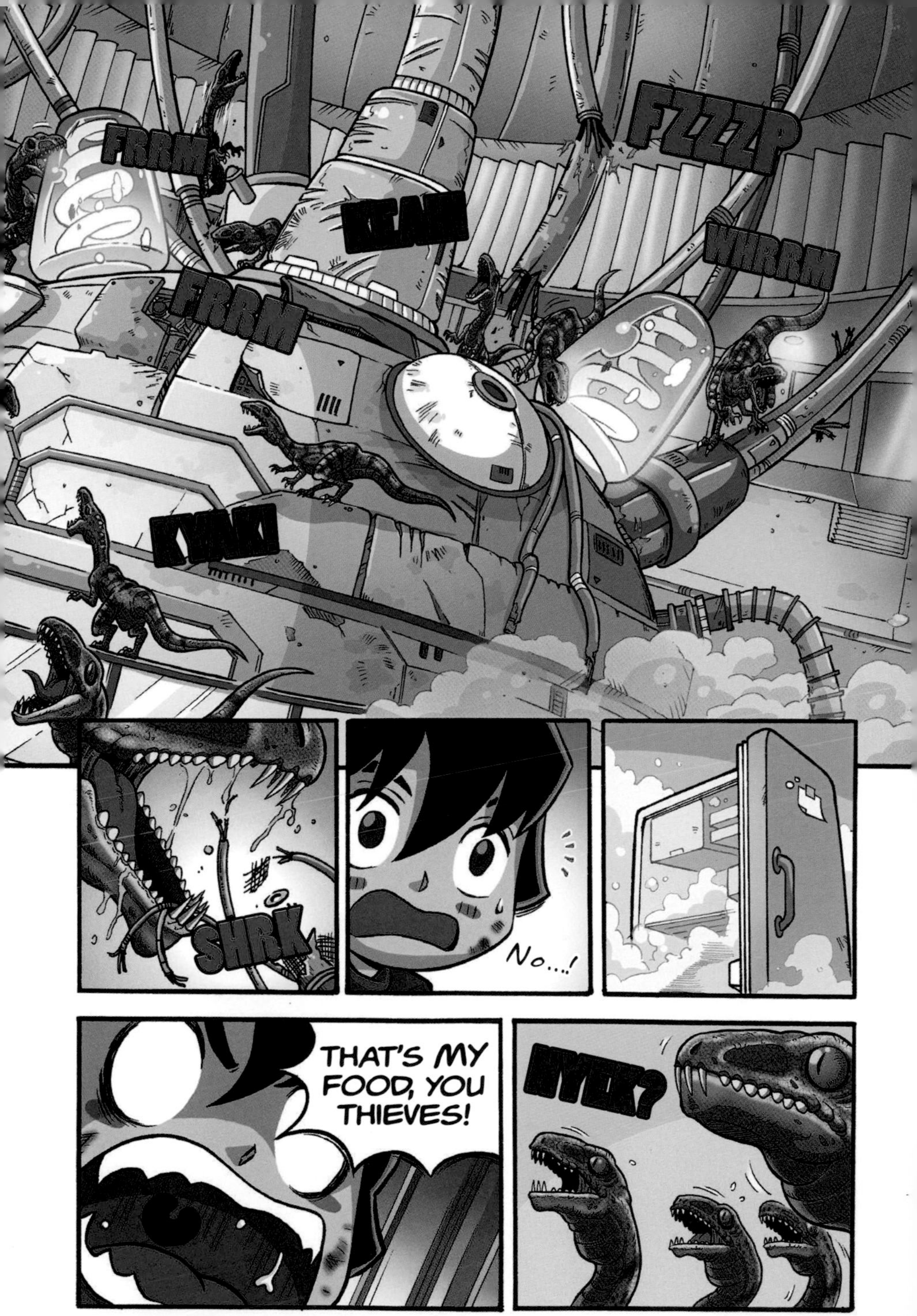
FRRM
FZZZP
WHRRM
FRRM
KYAK!
SHRK
No...!
THAT'S MY FOOD, YOU THIEVES!
NYEK?

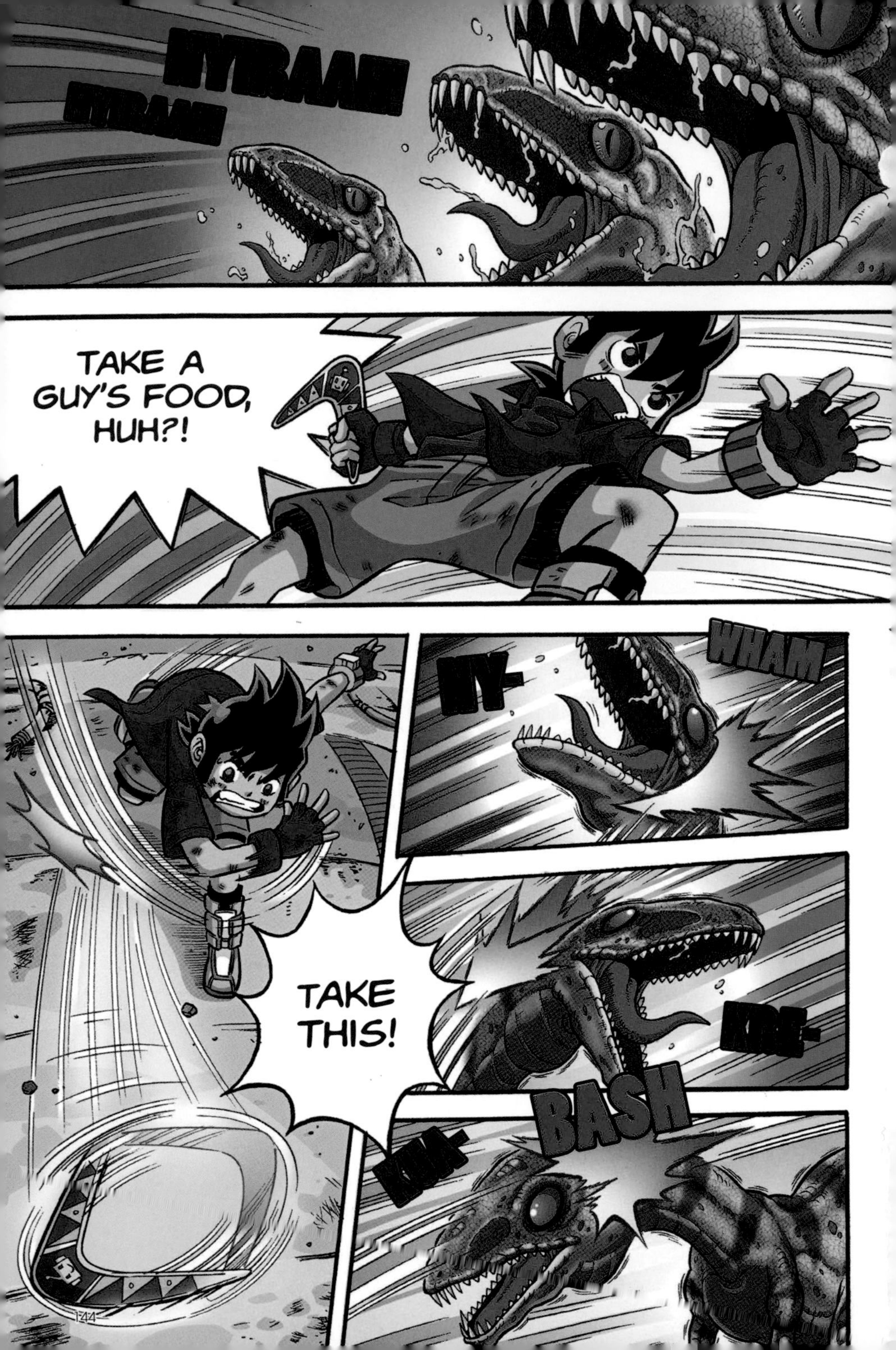
HYRAAAH!
HYRAAH
TAKE A GUY'S FOOD, HUH?!
HY-
WHAM
TAKE THIS!
KRE-
BASH
KRA-

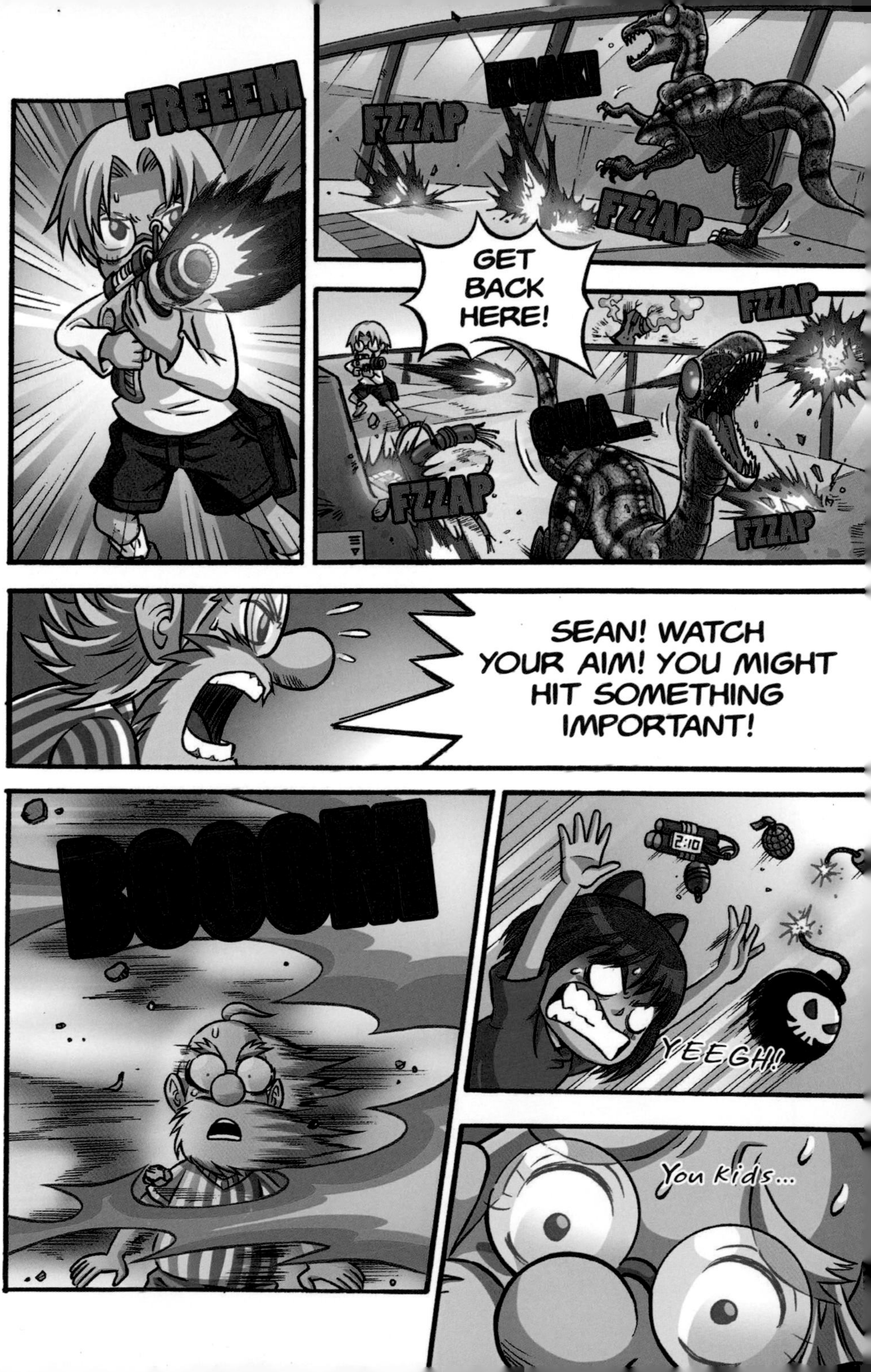
FREEEM
FZZAP
FZZAP
GET BACK HERE!
FZZAP
FZZAP
FZZAP
SEAN! WATCH YOUR AIM! YOU MIGHT HIT SOMETHING IMPORTANT!
2:10
YEEGH!
You kids...

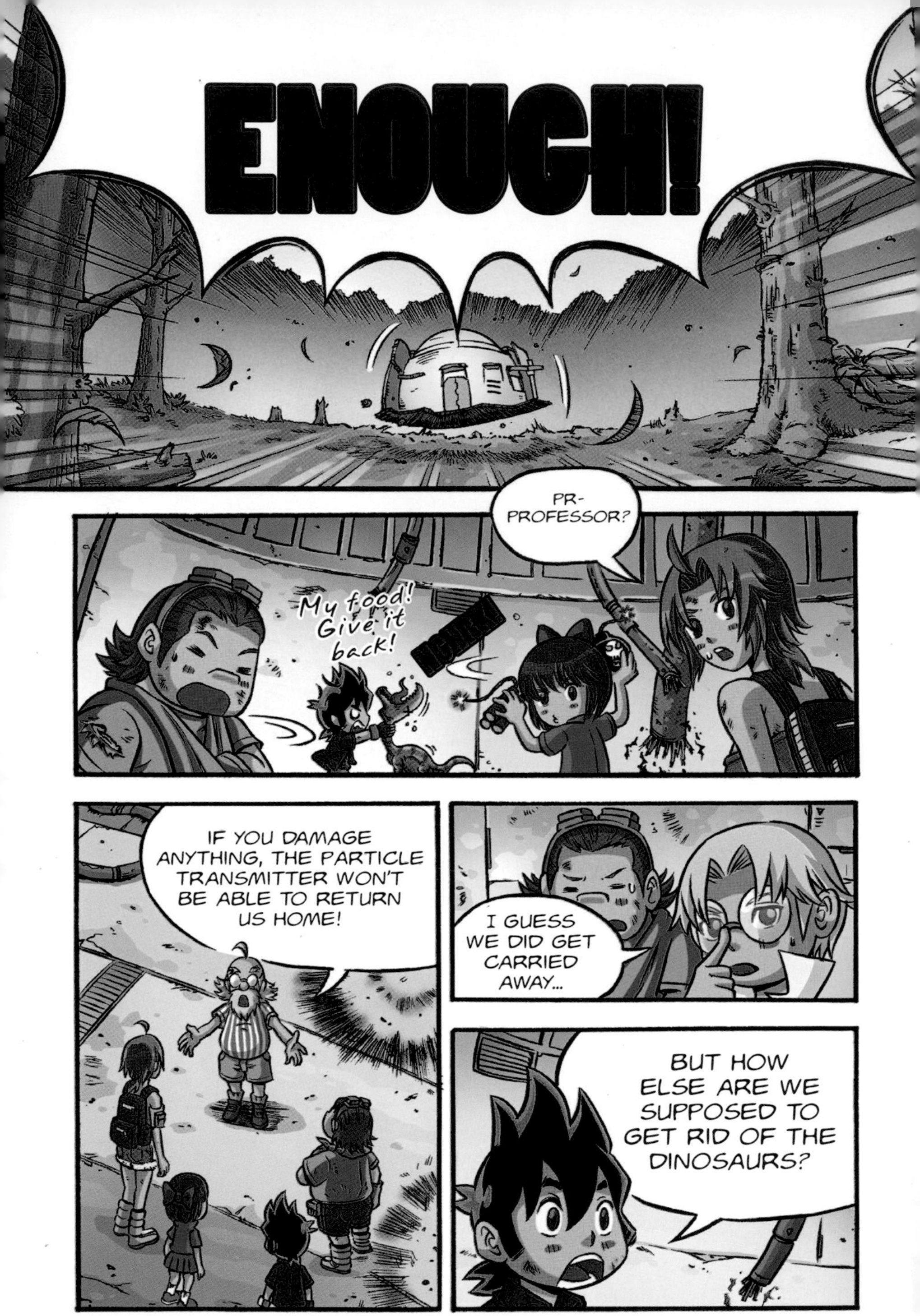
ENOUGH!
PR-
PROFESSOR?
My food! Give it back!
IF YOU DAMAGE ANYTHING, THE PARTICLE TRANSMITTER WON'T BE ABLE TO RETURN US HOME!
I GUESS WE DID GET CARRIED AWAY...
BUT HOW ELSE ARE WE SUPPOSED TO GET RID OF THE DINOSAURS?

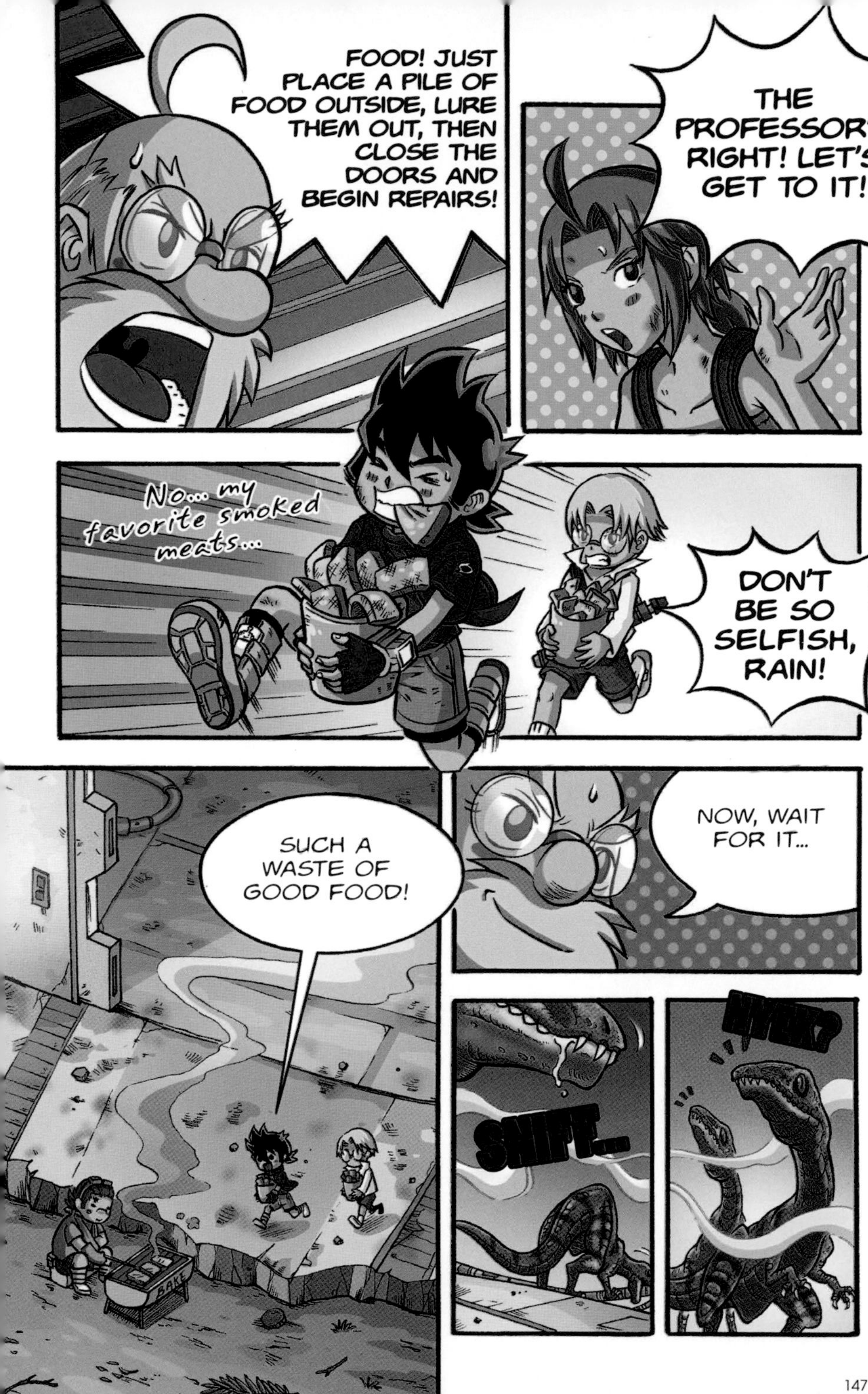
FOOD! JUST PLACE A PILE OF FOOD OUTSIDE, LURE THEM OUT, THEN CLOSE THE DOORS AND BEGIN REPAIRS!
THE PROFESSOR'S RIGHT! LET'S GET TO IT!
No... my favorite smoked meats...
DON'T BE SO SELFISH, RAIN!
SUCH A WASTE OF GOOD FOOD!
NOW, WAIT FOR IT...
SNIFF...

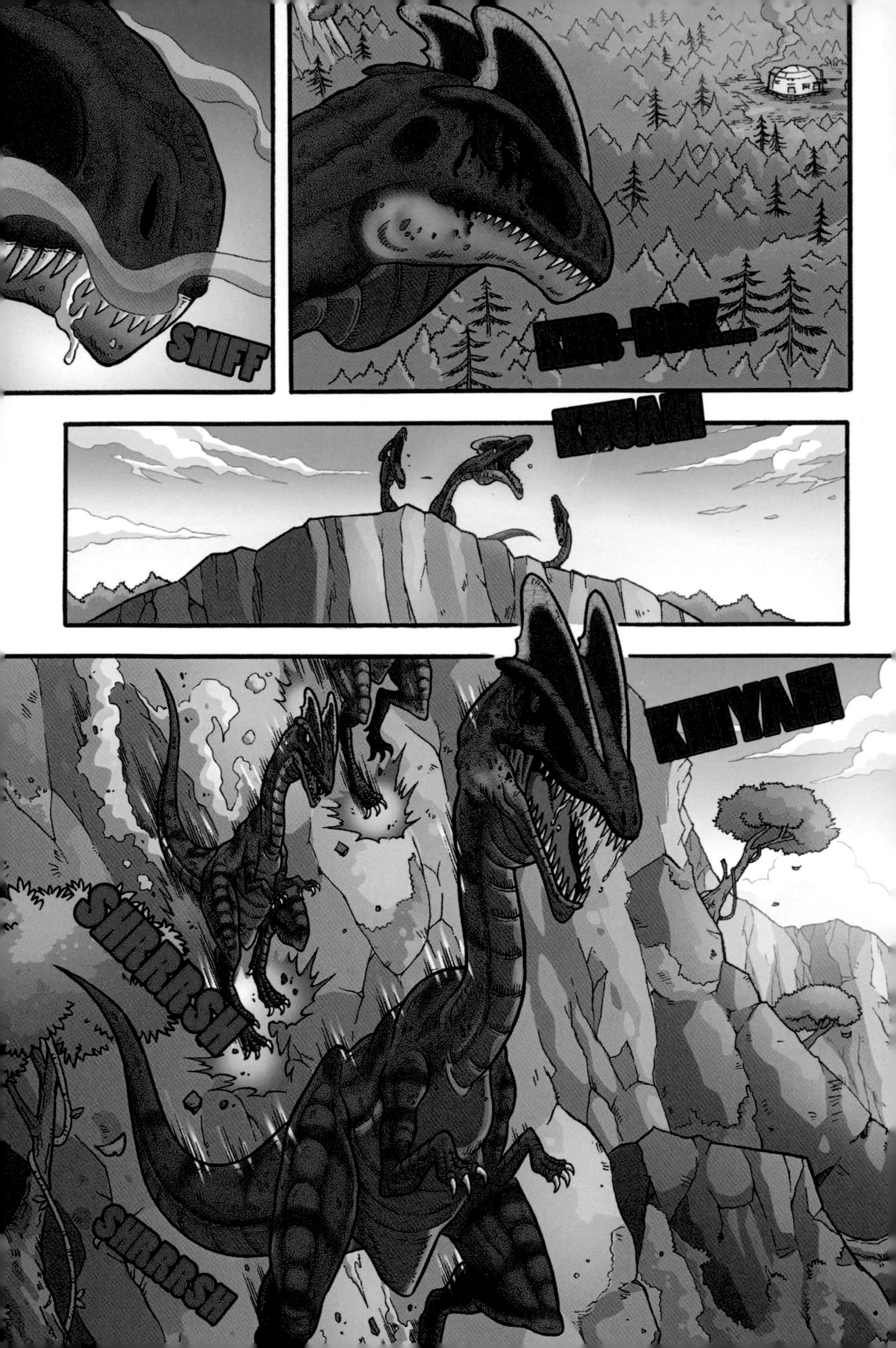
SNIFF
KRR-RRK...
KRUAH!
KRIYAH!
SHRRRSH
SHRRRSH

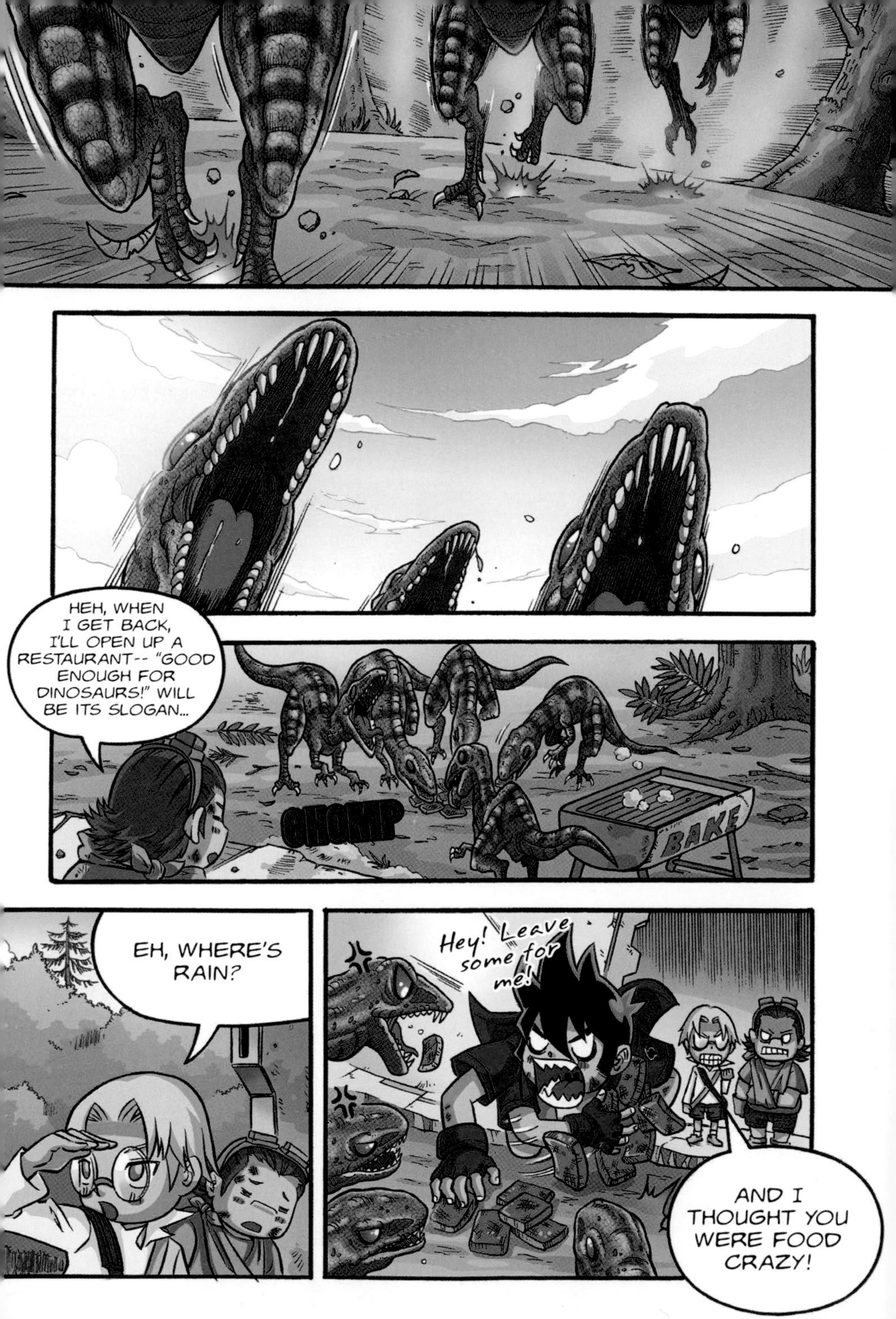
HEH, WHEN I GET BACK, I'LL OPEN UP A RESTAURANT-- "GOOD ENOUGH FOR DINOSAURS!" WILL BE ITS SLOGAN...
CHOMP
BAKE
EH, WHERE'S RAIN?
Hey! Leave some for me!
AND I THOUGHT YOU WERE FOOD CRAZY!

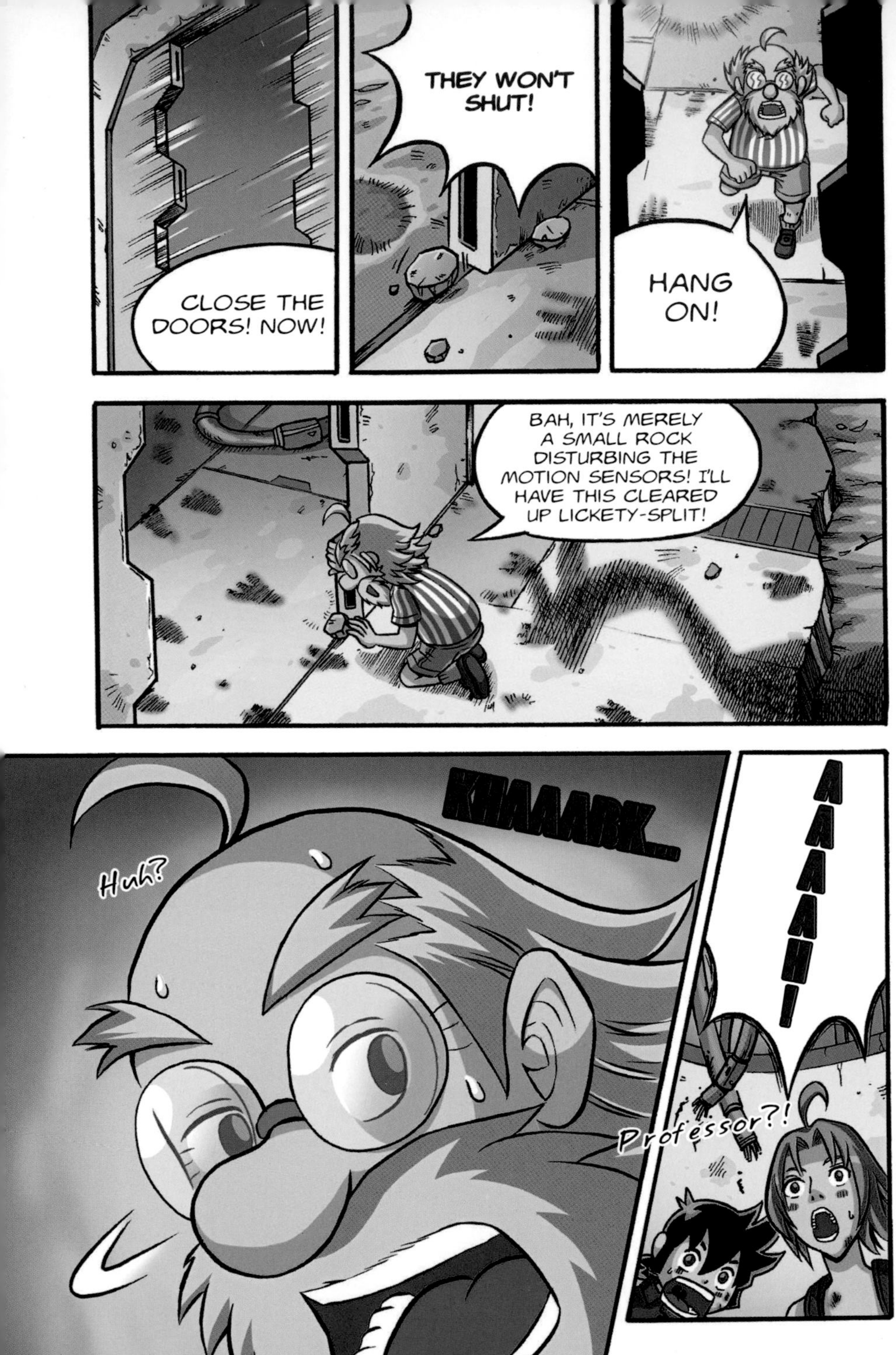
CLOSE THE DOORS! NOW!
THEY WON'T SHUT!
HANG ON!
BAH, IT'S MERELY A SMALL ROCK DISTURBING THE MOTION SENSORS! I'LL HAVE THIS CLEARED UP LICKETY-SPLIT!
KHAAARK...
Huh?
AAAAAH!
Professor?!

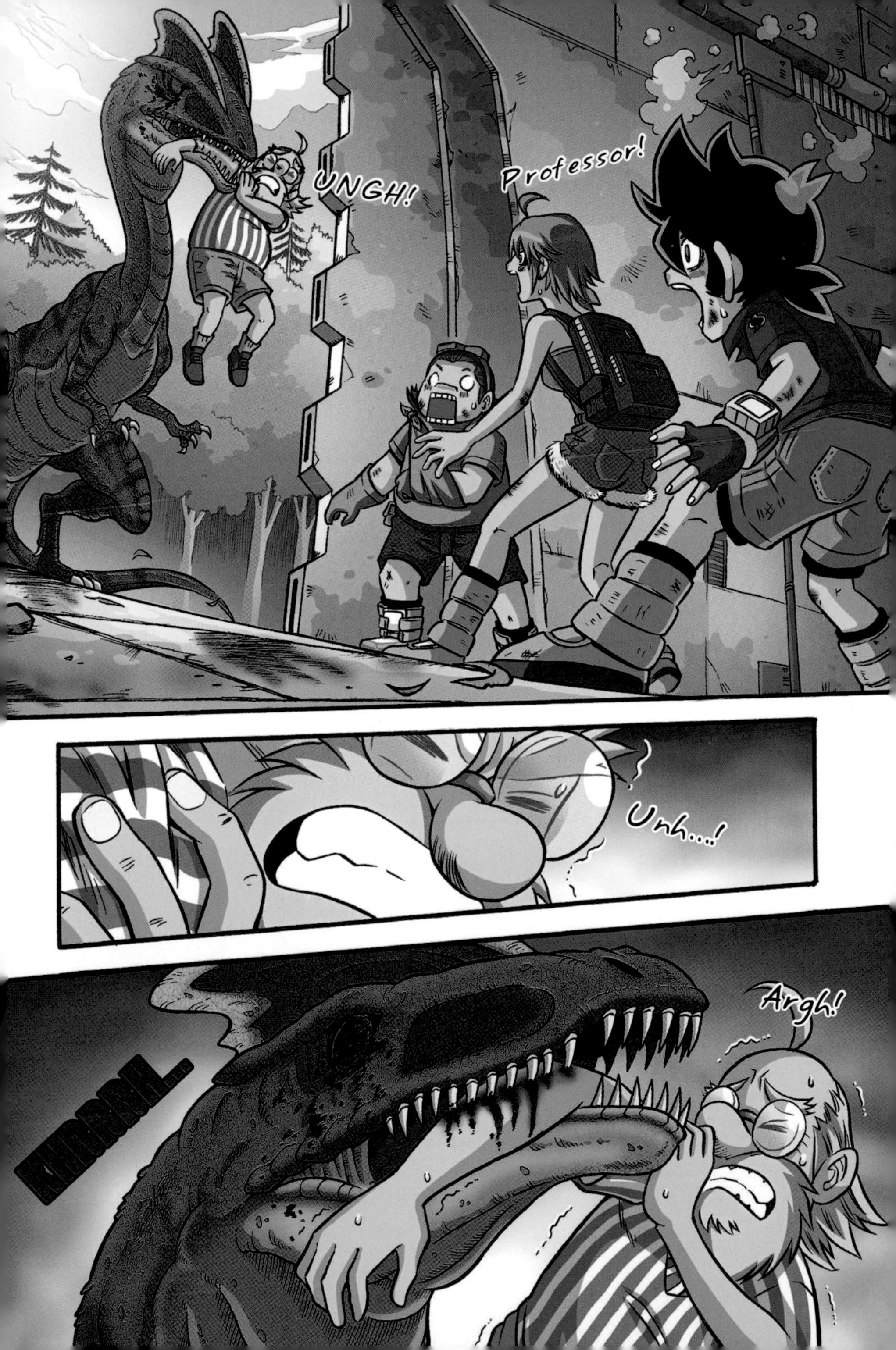
UNGH!
Professor!
Unh...!
Argh!

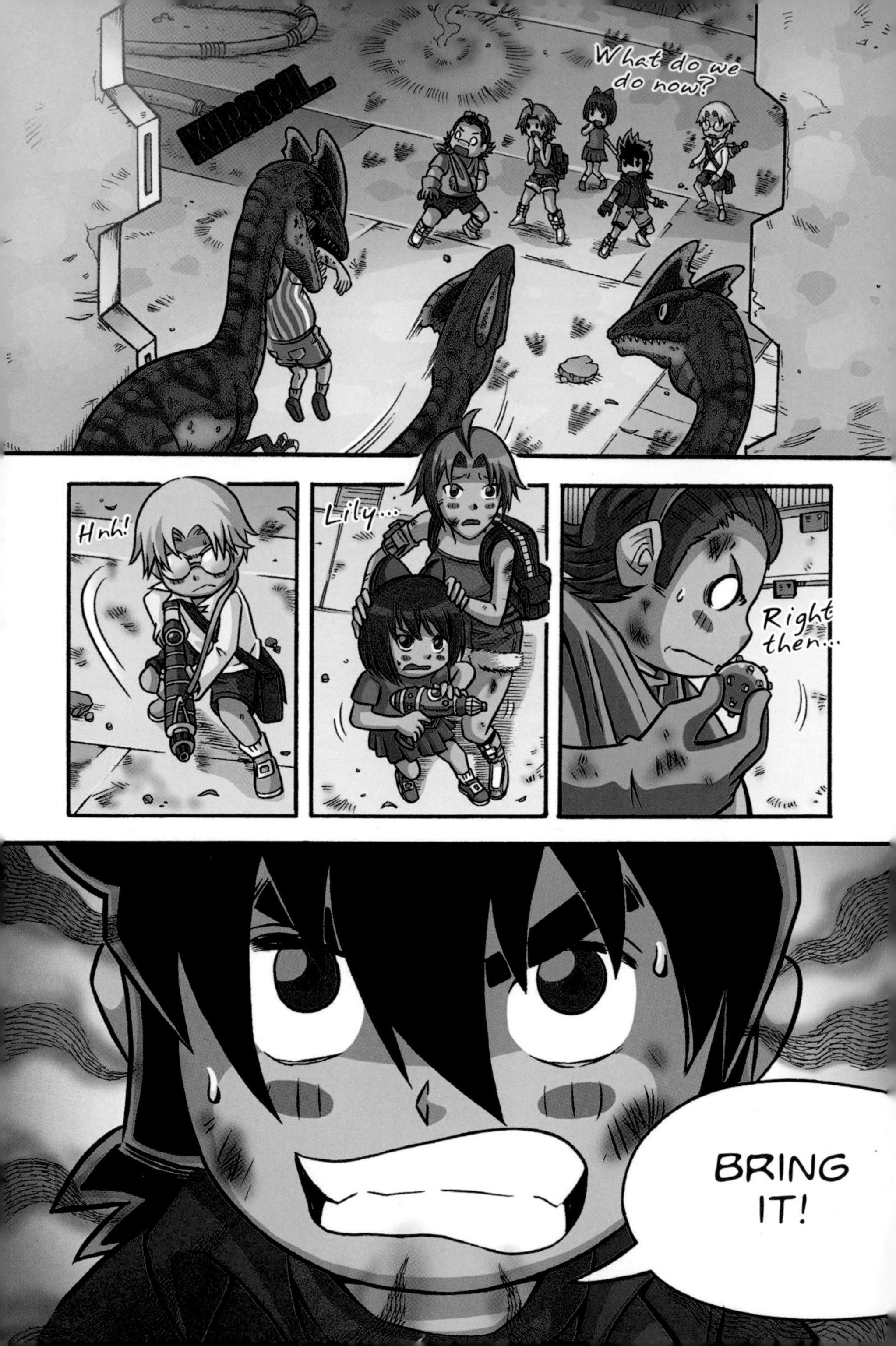
What do we do now?
KRRRH...
Hnh!
Lily...
Right then...
BRING IT!

JONESING FOR THE JURASSIC

Heterodontosaurus

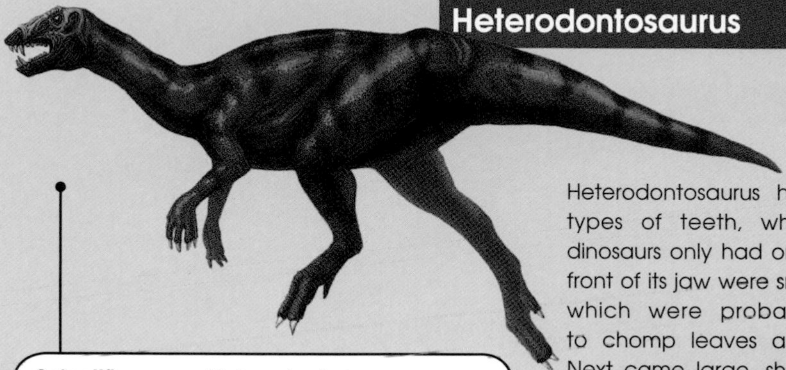

Heterodontosaurus had three types of teeth, while other dinosaurs only had one. At the front of its jaw were small teeth which were probably used to chomp leaves and stems. Next came large, sharp fangs that might have been used to attract mates and/or attack enemies. Finally, came a set of grinding teeth. These distinct teeth have led some to theorize that the Heterodontosaurus was an omnivore.

Scientific name: Heterodontosaurus
Length: 3.9 feet
Diet: Herbivore (theoretically an omnivore)
Habitat: Arid areas
Discovered: South Africa
Era: Early Jurassic

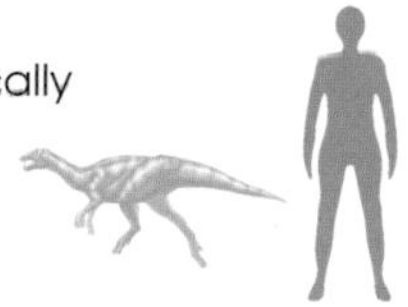

JONESING FOR THE JURASSIC

Piatnitzkysaurus

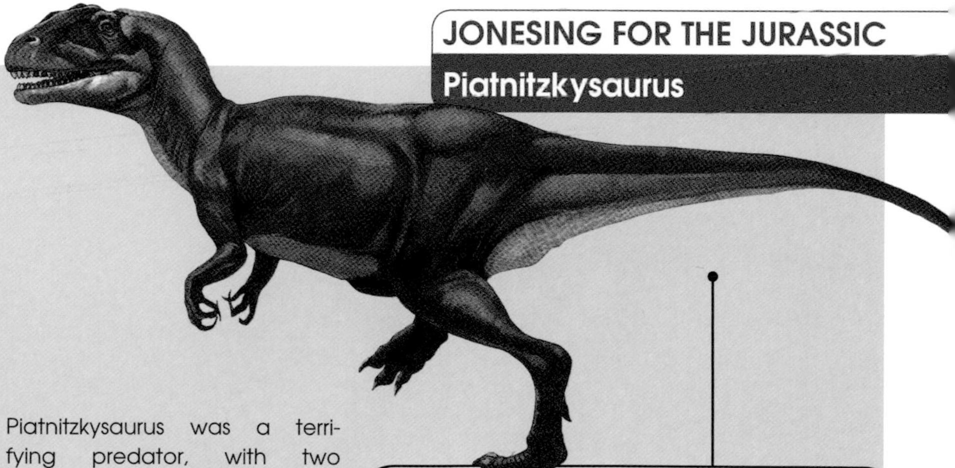

Piatnitzkysaurus was a terrifying predator, with two powerful, clawed arms. While it is currently classified as tetanurae (a kind of therapod), the fact that only two sets of Piatnitzkysaurus fossils have been found thus far means that its proper classification, however, is still being debated.

Scientific name: Piatnitzkysaurus
Length: 14.1 feet
Diet: Carnivore
Habitat: Forest
Discovered: Argentina
Era: Mid-Jurassic

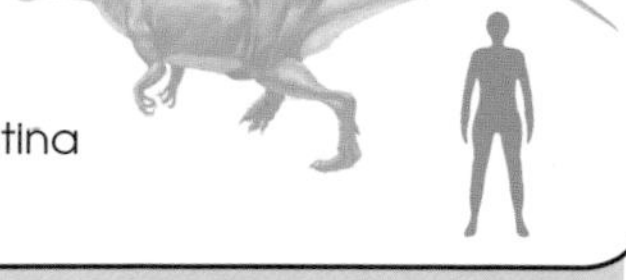

JONESING FOR THE JURASSIC

Liopleurodon

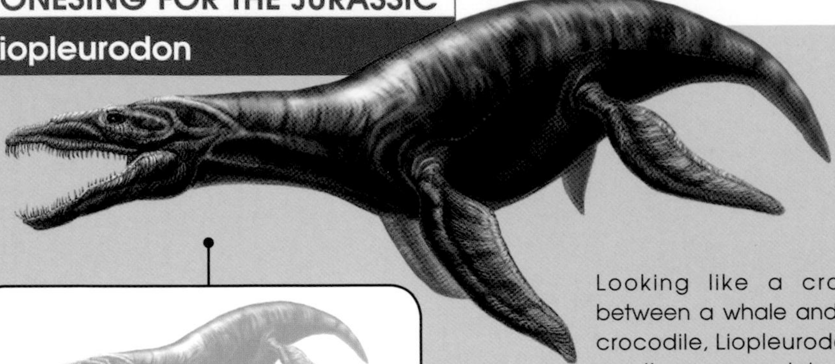

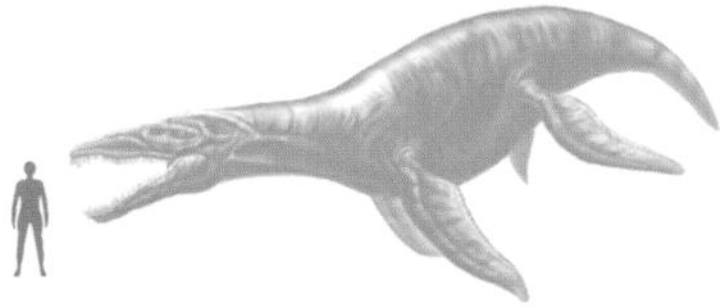

Scientific name: Liopleurodon
Length: 82 feet
Diet: Carnivore
Habitat: Oceans
Discovered: England, France, and Russia
Era: Mid to Late Jurassic

Looking like a cross between a whale and a crocodile, Liopleurodon was the apex predator of the Jurassic seas. Paleontologists believe that its unique inner nose structure allowed it to smell and track prey through the water. As their eyes were on top of their heads, they might have also been ambush predators like crocodiles, attacking their prey from below.

JONESING FOR THE JURASSIC

Cryptoclidus

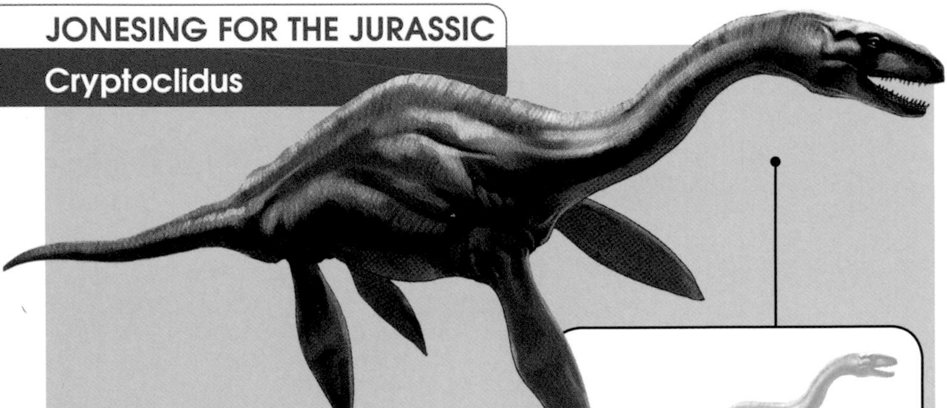

Cryptoclidus was the typical long-necked plesiosauroid of the middle to late Jurassic seas, its neck reaching 6.5 feet in length, consistling of 30 inflexible vertebrae. Armed with around 100 needle-like teeth, a deadly "cage" was formed, trapping smaller organisms such as small fish, and prawns, which comprised its diet.

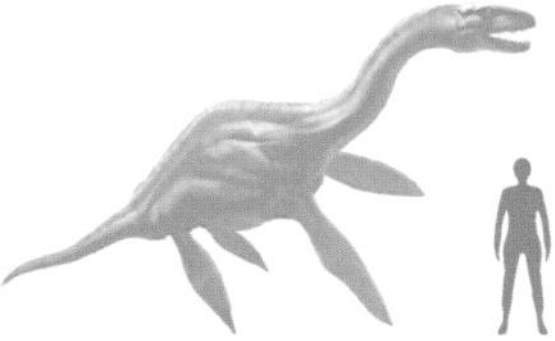

Scientific name: Cryptoclidus
Length: 13.1 feet
Diet: Carnivore
Habitat: Oceans
Discovered: England and France
Era: Mid-Jurassic

CHAPTER 8
JURASSIC JUMP-OUT

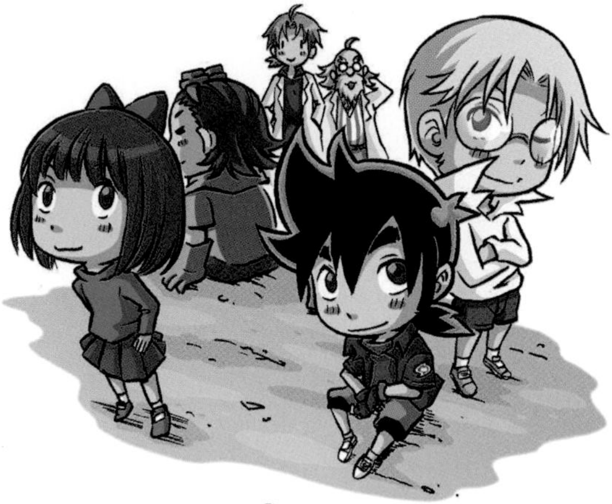

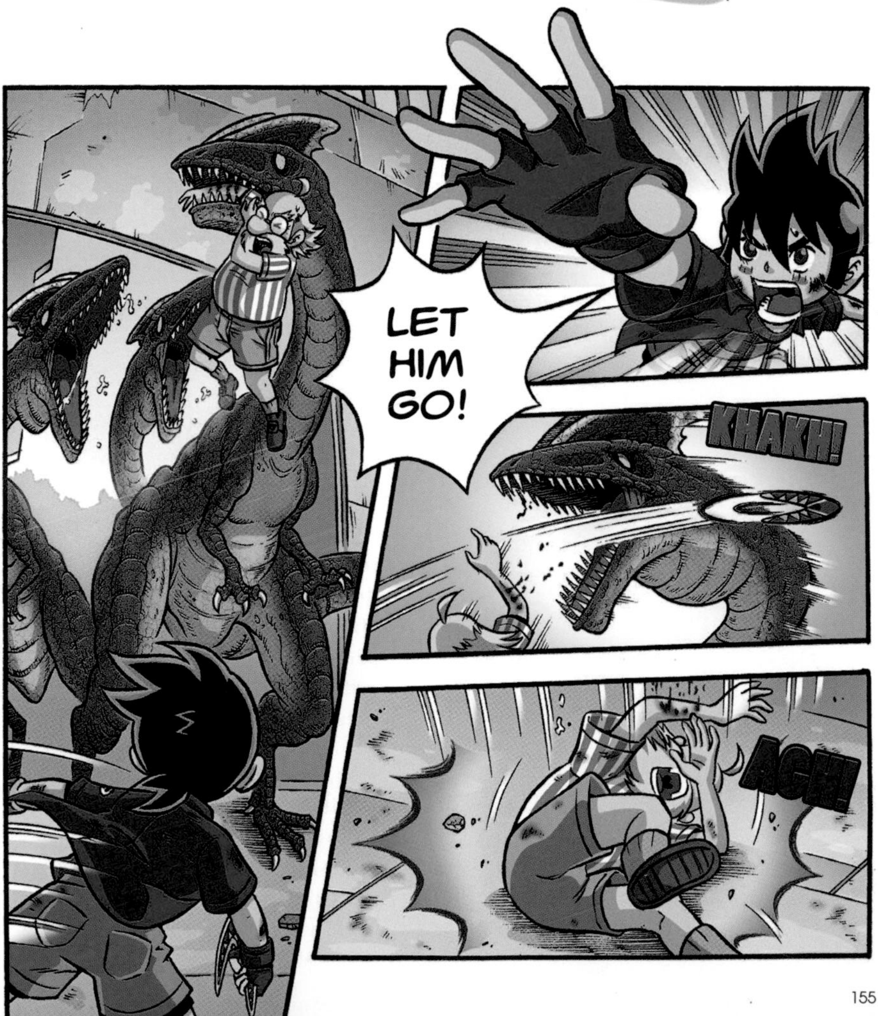
LET HIM GO!
KHAKH!
ACH!

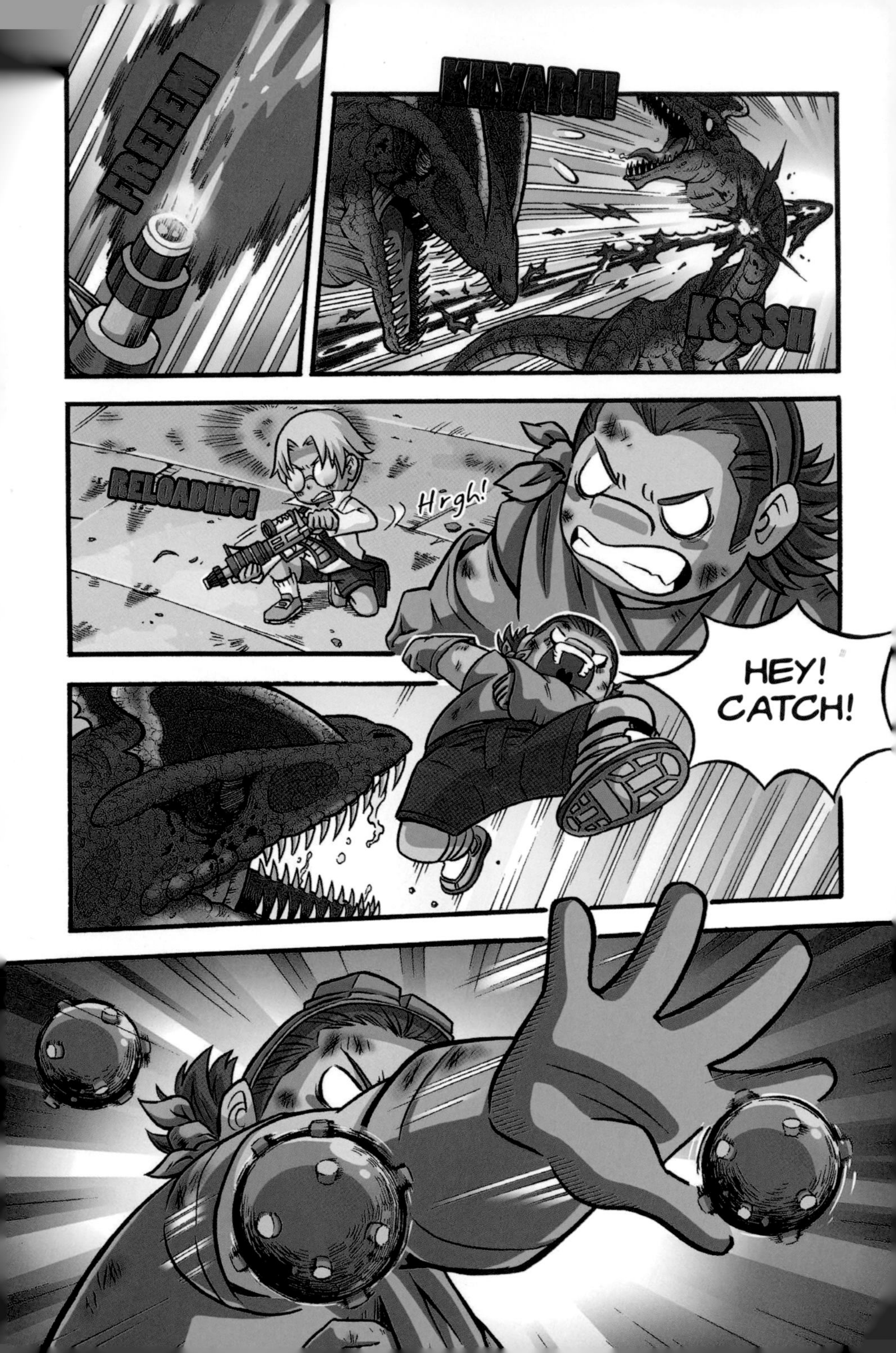
FREEEM
KHYARH!
KSSSH
RELOADING!
Hrgh!
HEY! CATCH!

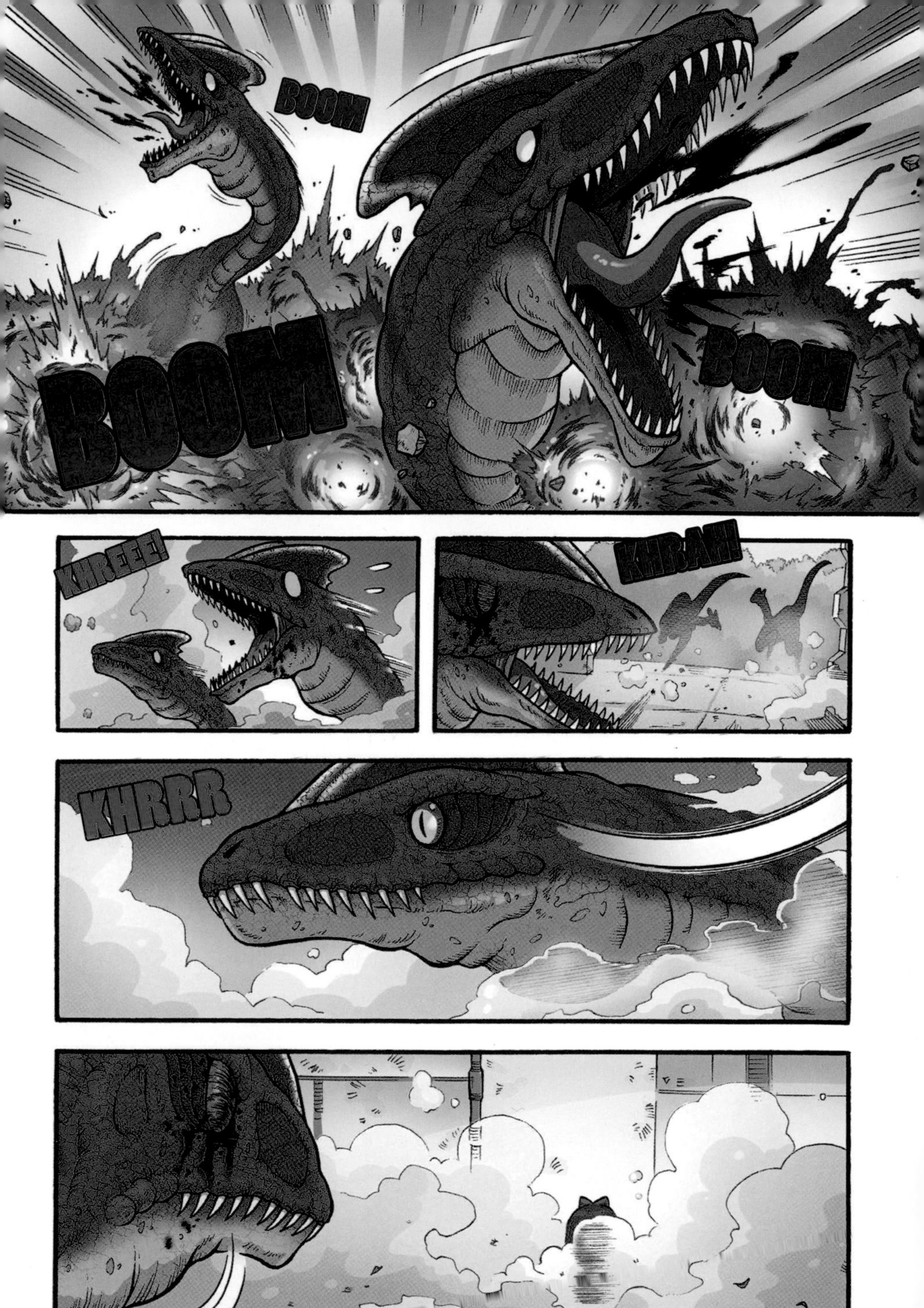
BOOM
BOOM
BOOM
KHREEE!
KHRAH!
KHRRR

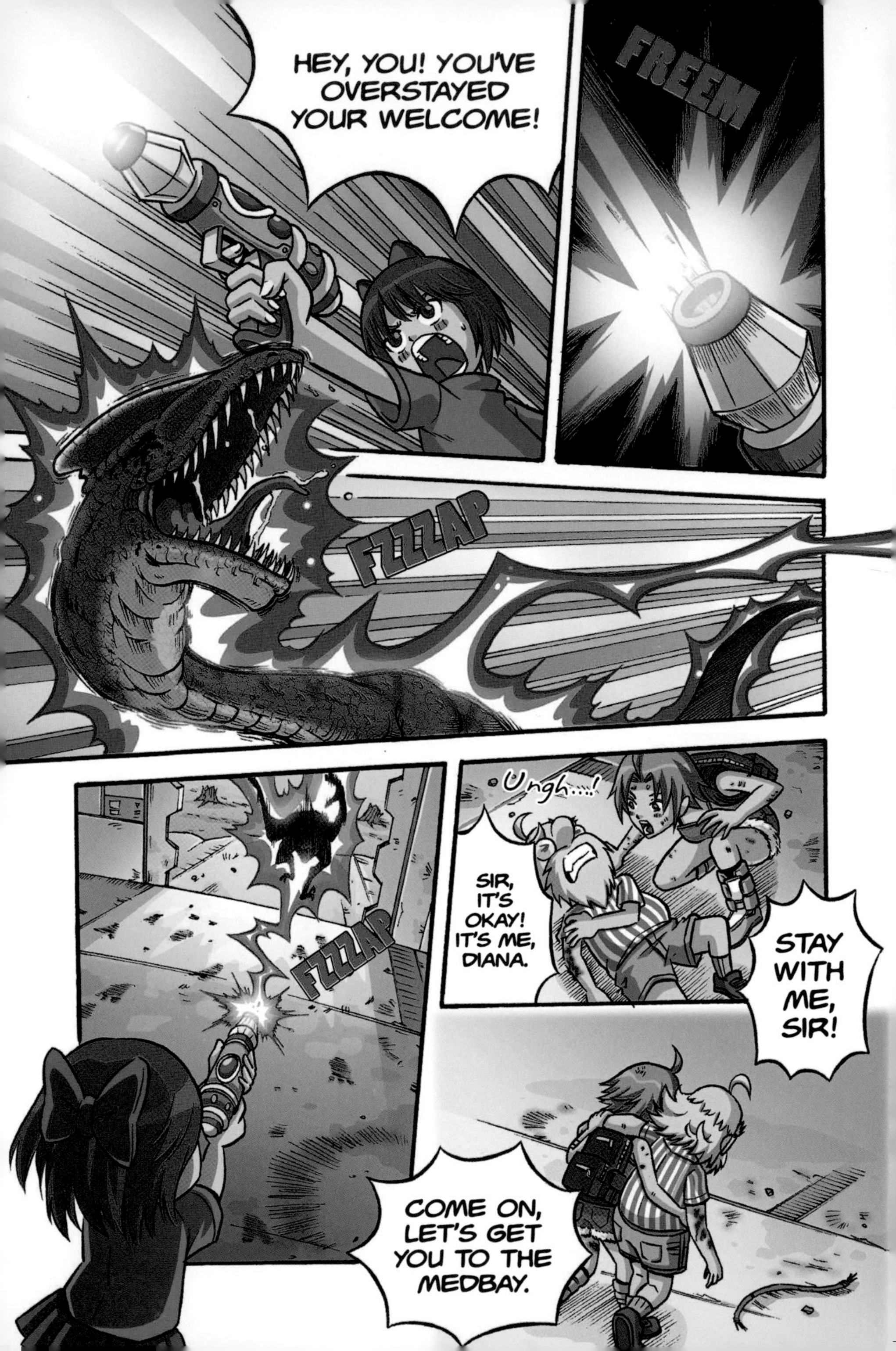
HEY, YOU! YOU'VE OVERSTAYED YOUR WELCOME!
FREEM
FZZZAP
FZZZAP
Ungh...!
SIR, IT'S OKAY! IT'S ME, DIANA.
STAY WITH ME, SIR!
COME ON, LET'S GET YOU TO THE MEDBAY.

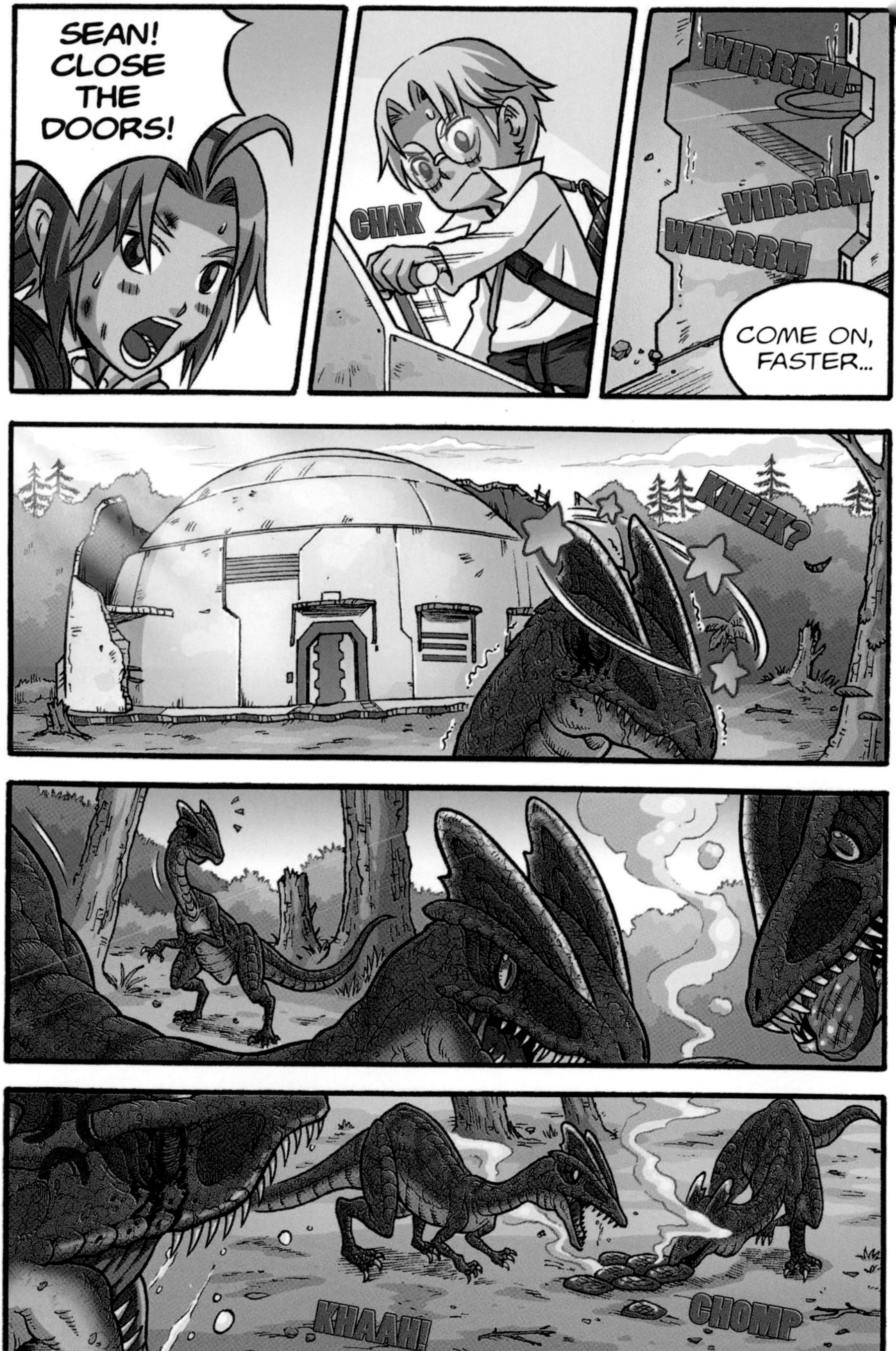
SEAN! CLOSE THE DOORS!
CHAK
WHRRRM
WHRRRM
WHRRRM
COME ON, FASTER...
KHEEK?
KHAAH!
CHOMP

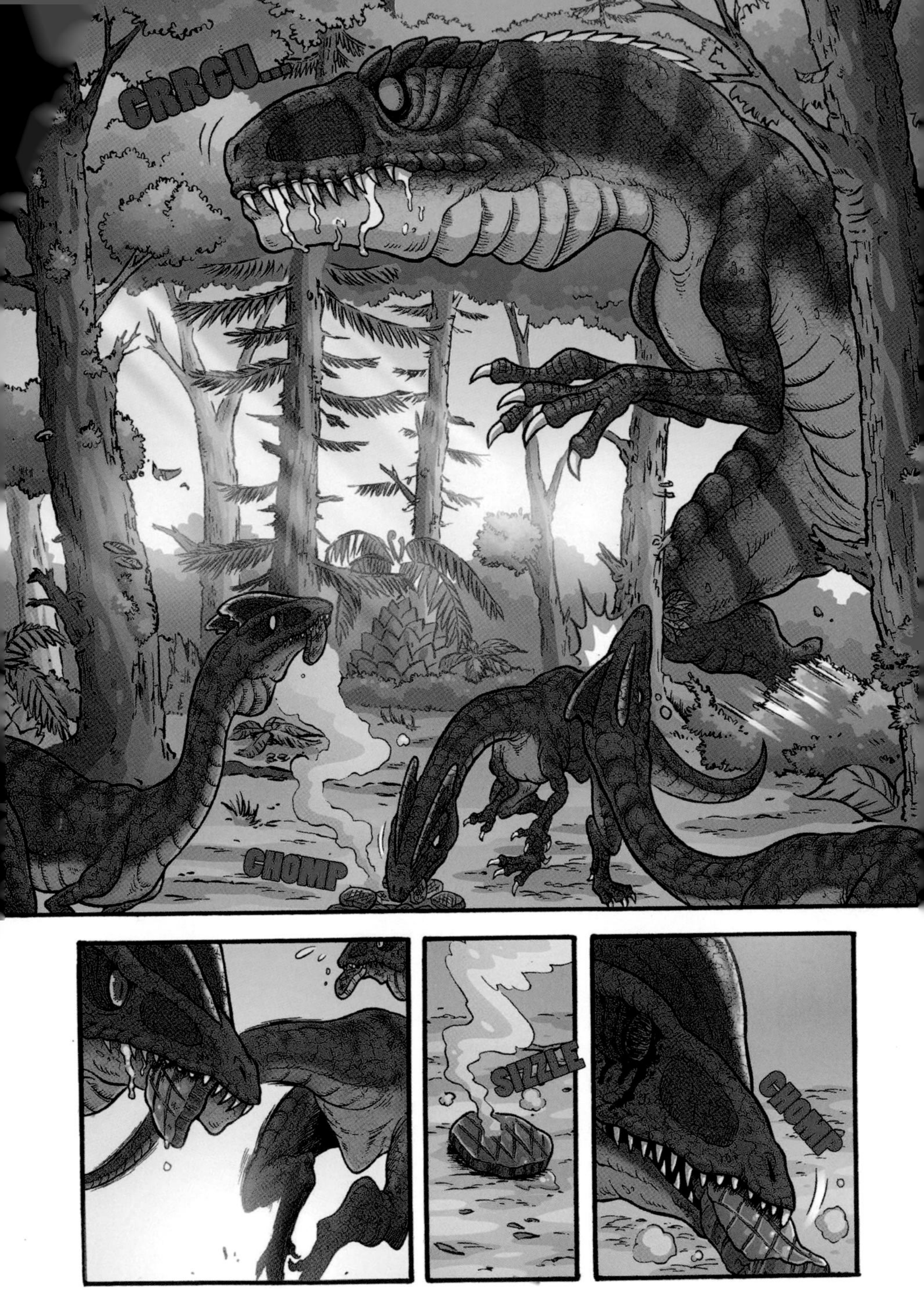
CRRCU...
CHOMP
SIZZLE
CHOMP

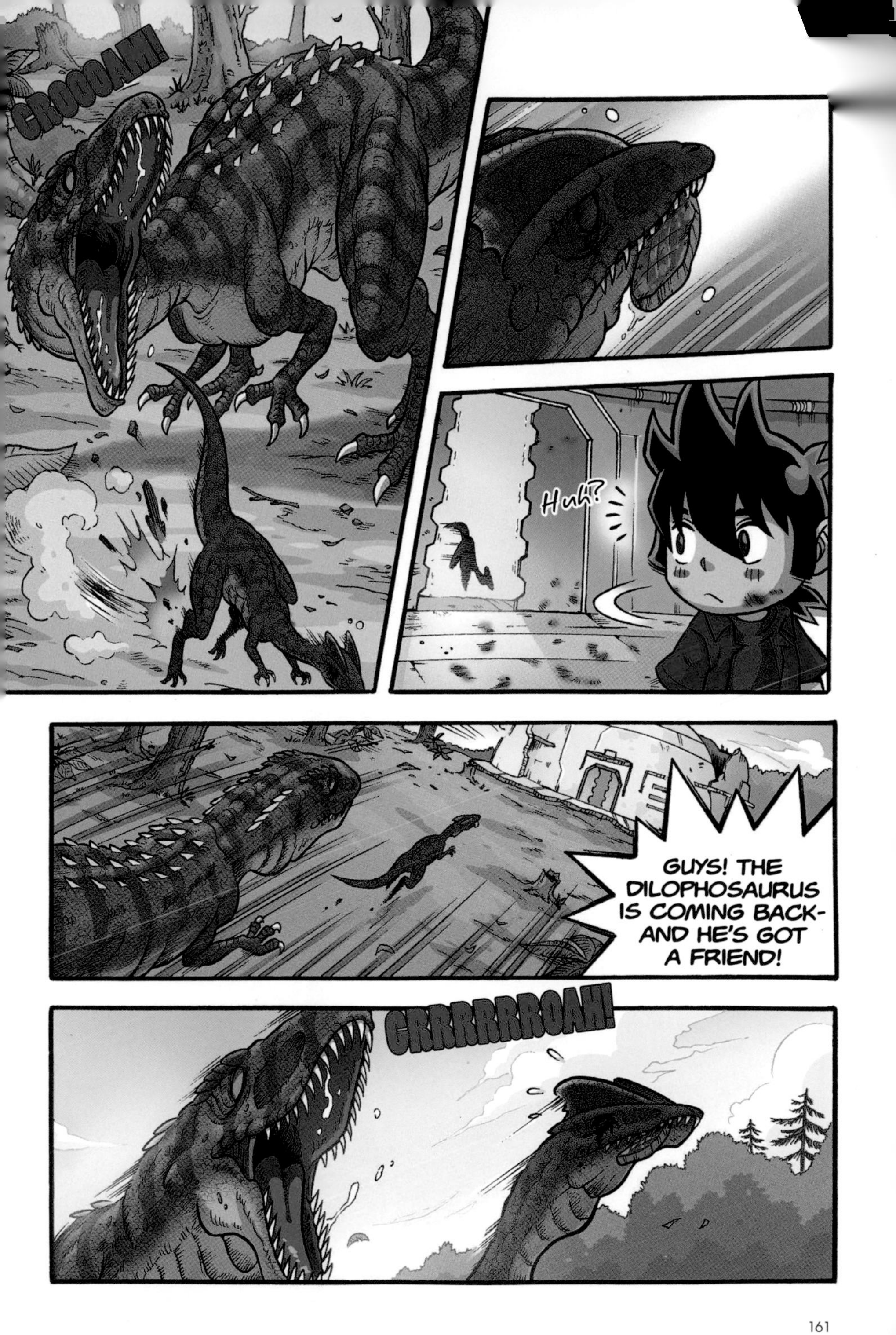
CROOOAM!
Huh?
GUYS! THE DILOPHOSAURUS IS COMING BACK- AND HE'S GOT A FRIEND!
CRRRRRROAH!

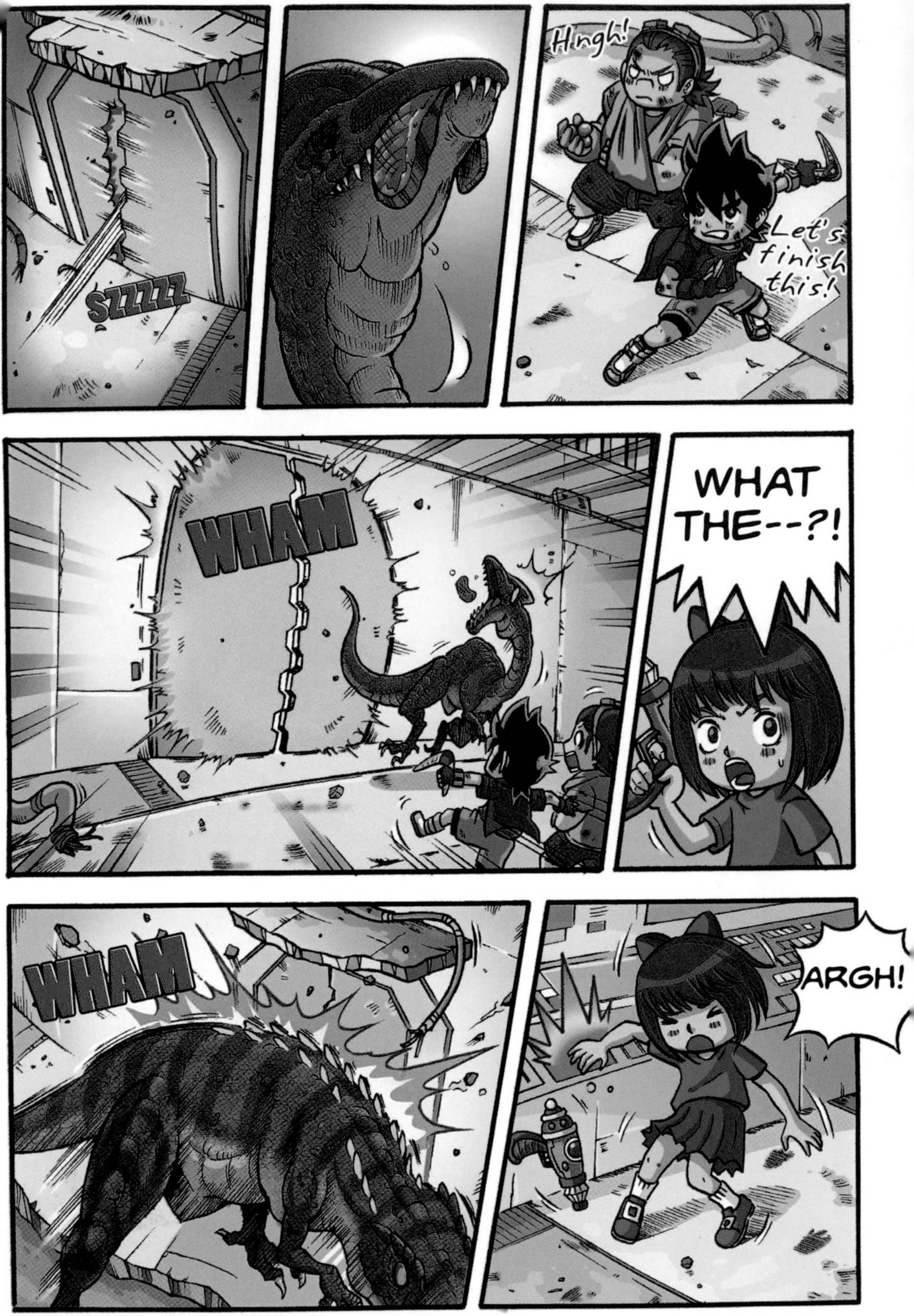
SZZZZZ
Hngh!
Let's finish this!
WHAM
WHAT THE--?!
WHAM
ARGH!

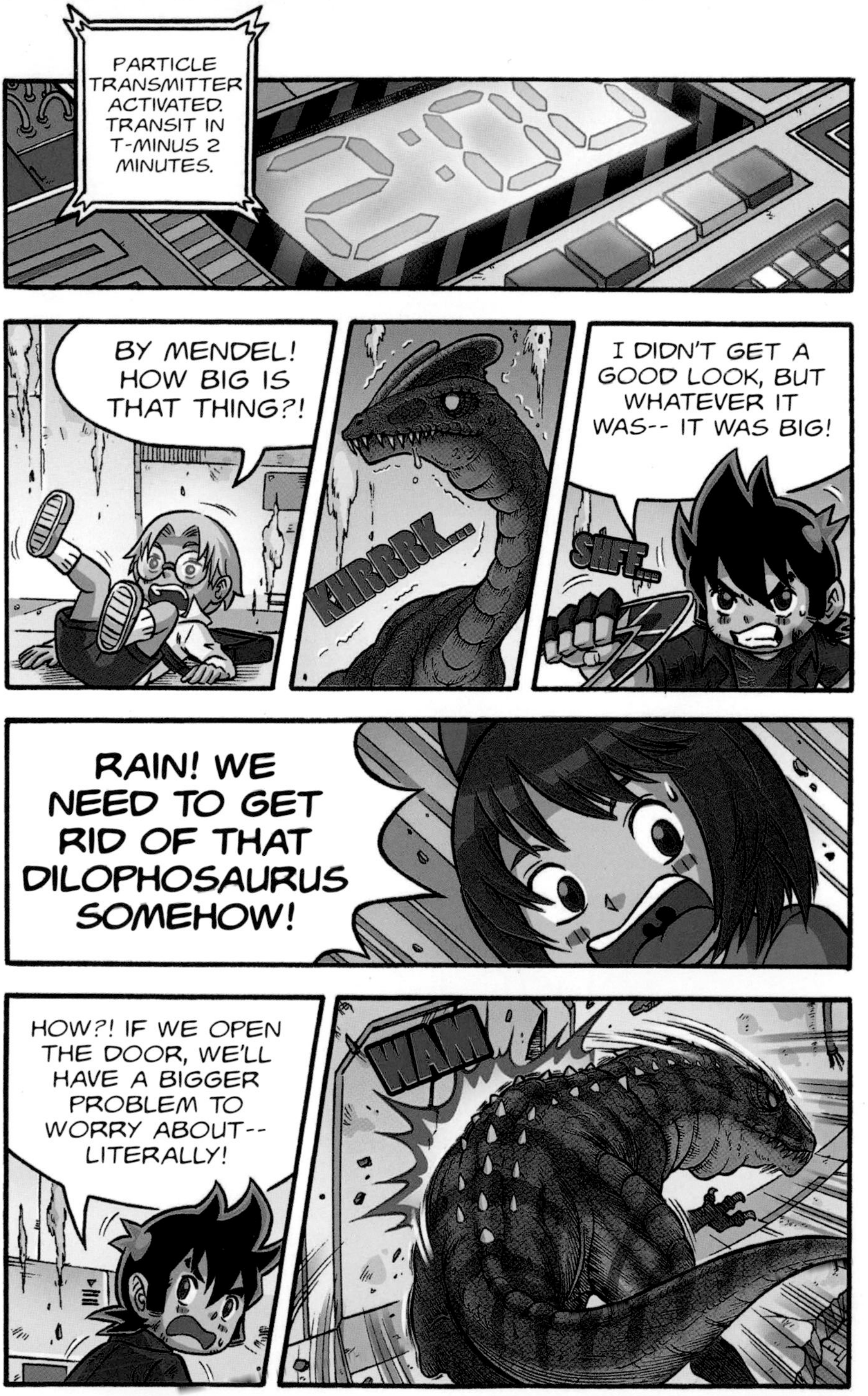
PARTICLE TRANSMITTER ACTIVATED. TRANSIT IN T-MINUS 2 MINUTES.
BY MENDEL! HOW BIG IS THAT THING?!
KHRRRK...
I DIDN'T GET A GOOD LOOK, BUT WHATEVER IT WAS-- IT WAS BIG!
SHFF...
RAIN! WE NEED TO GET RID OF THAT DILOPHOSAURUS SOMEHOW!
HOW?! IF WE OPEN THE DOOR, WE'LL HAVE A BIGGER PROBLEM TO WORRY ABOUT-- LITERALLY!
WAM

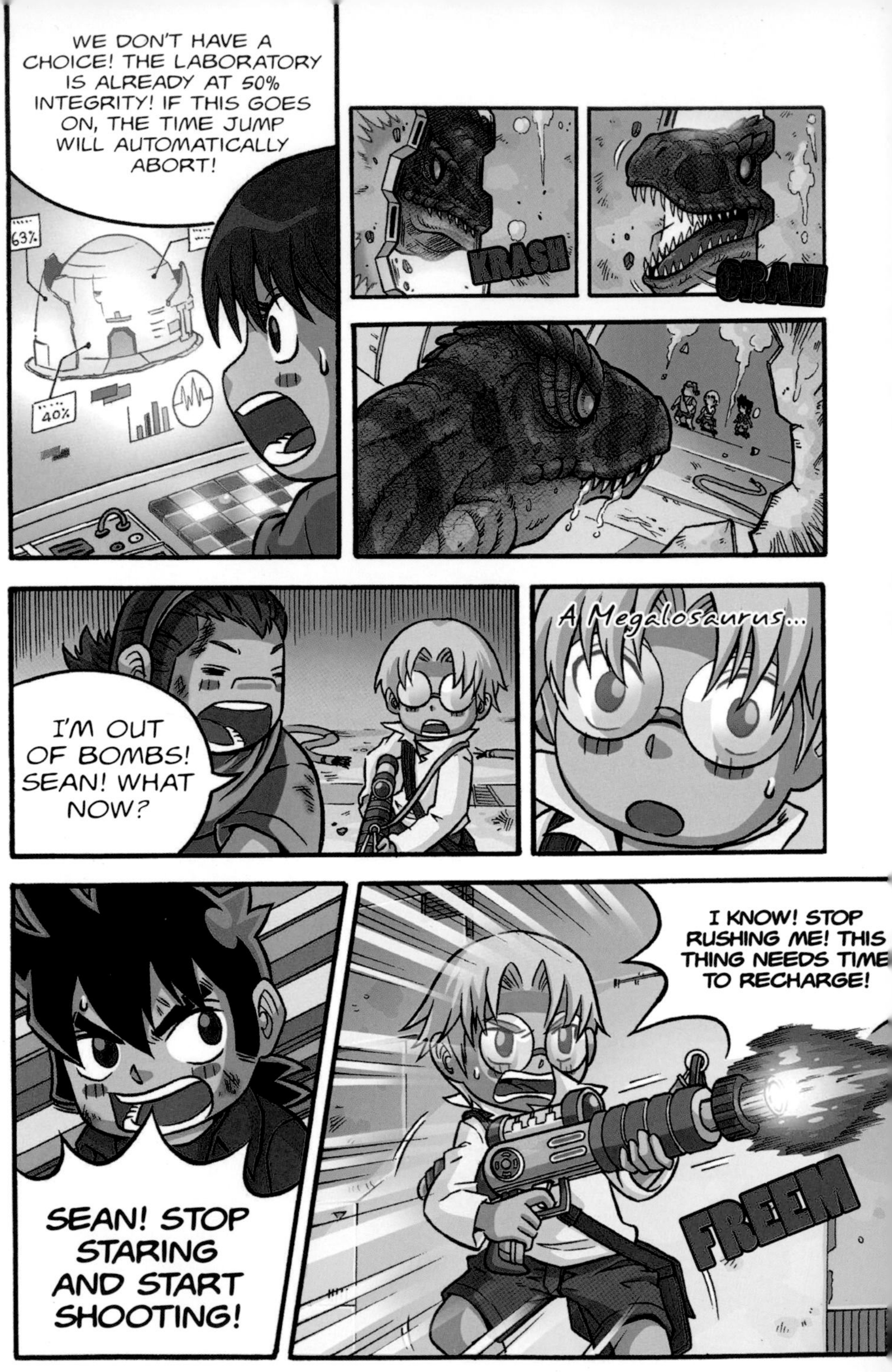
WE DON'T HAVE A CHOICE! THE LABORATORY IS ALREADY AT 50% INTEGRITY! IF THIS GOES ON, THE TIME JUMP WILL AUTOMATICALLY ABORT!
63%
40%
KRASH
GRAH!
A Megalosaurus...
I'M OUT OF BOMBS! SEAN! WHAT NOW?
SEAN! STOP STARING AND START SHOOTING!
I KNOW! STOP RUSHING ME! THIS THING NEEDS TIME TO RECHARGE!
FREEM

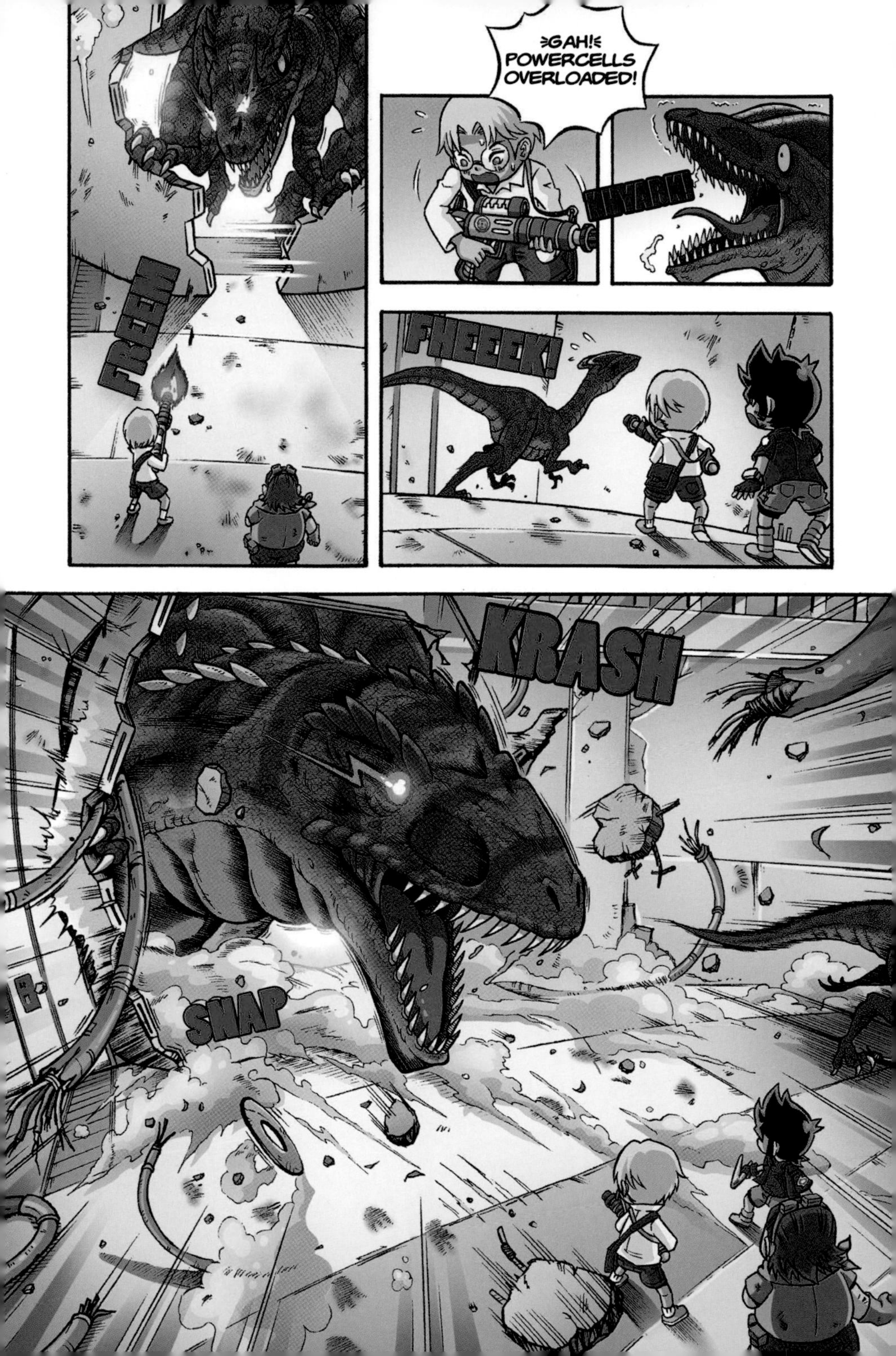
FREEEM
GAH! POWERCELLS OVERLOADED!
KHYARK!
FHEEEK!
KRASH
SNAP

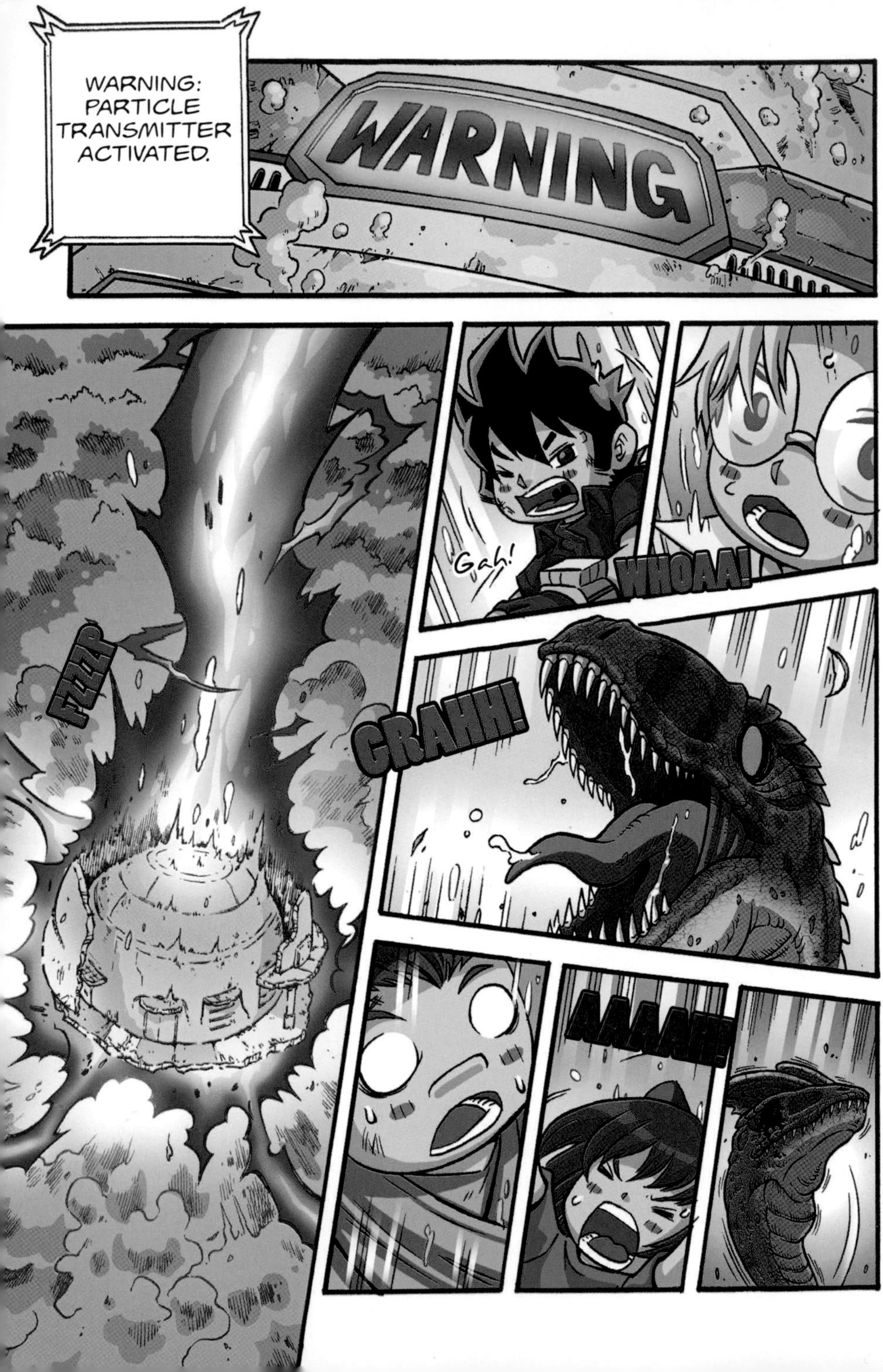
WARNING: PARTICLE TRANSMITTER ACTIVATED.
WARNING
FZZZP
Gah!
WHOAA!
CRAHH!
AAAAAH!

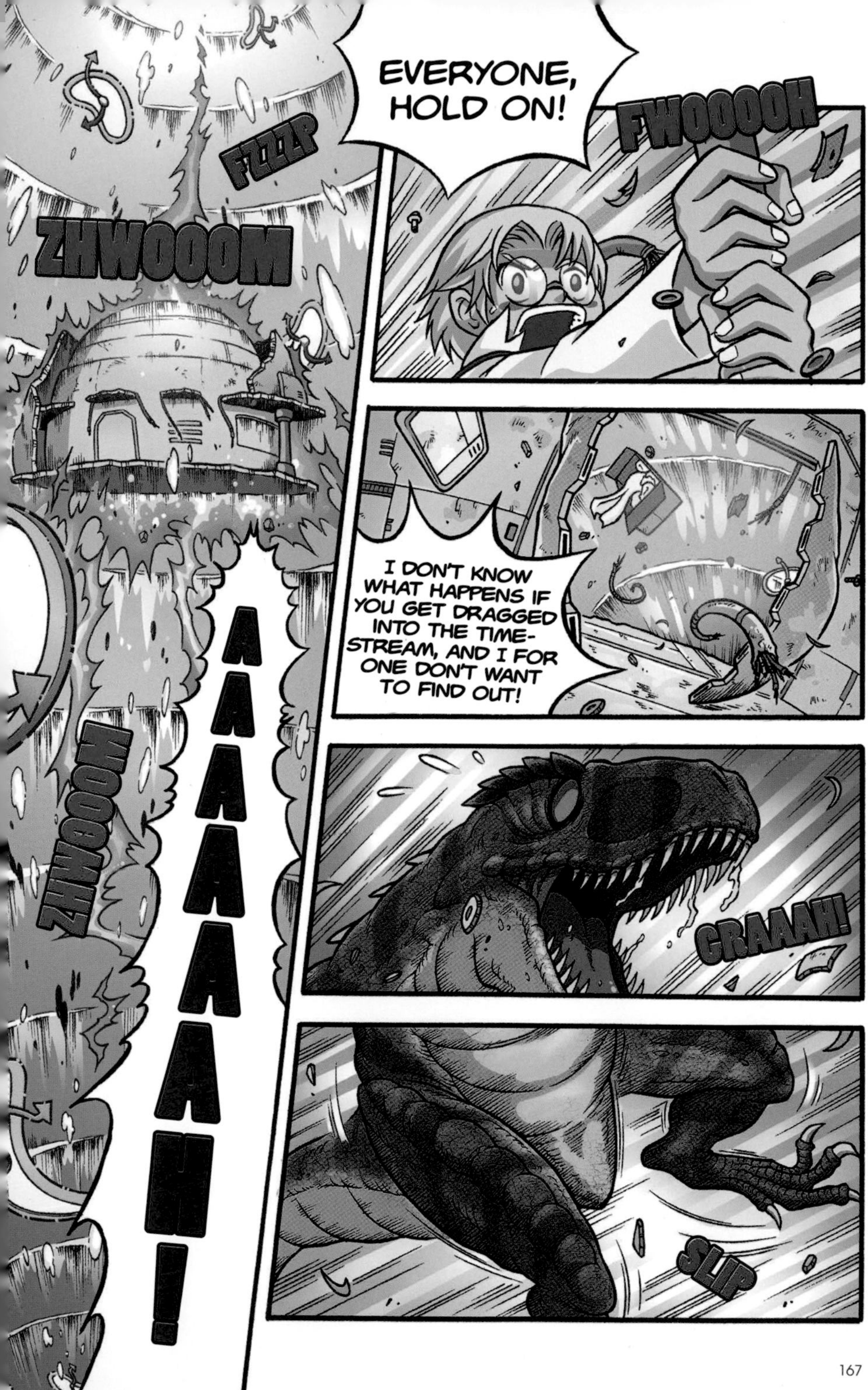
EVERYONE, HOLD ON!
FZZZZP
ZHWOOOM
FWOOOOH
I DON'T KNOW WHAT HAPPENS IF YOU GET DRAGGED INTO THE TIME-STREAM, AND I FOR ONE DON'T WANT TO FIND OUT!
ZHWOOOM
AAAAAAAAAAHH!
GRAAAH!
SLIP

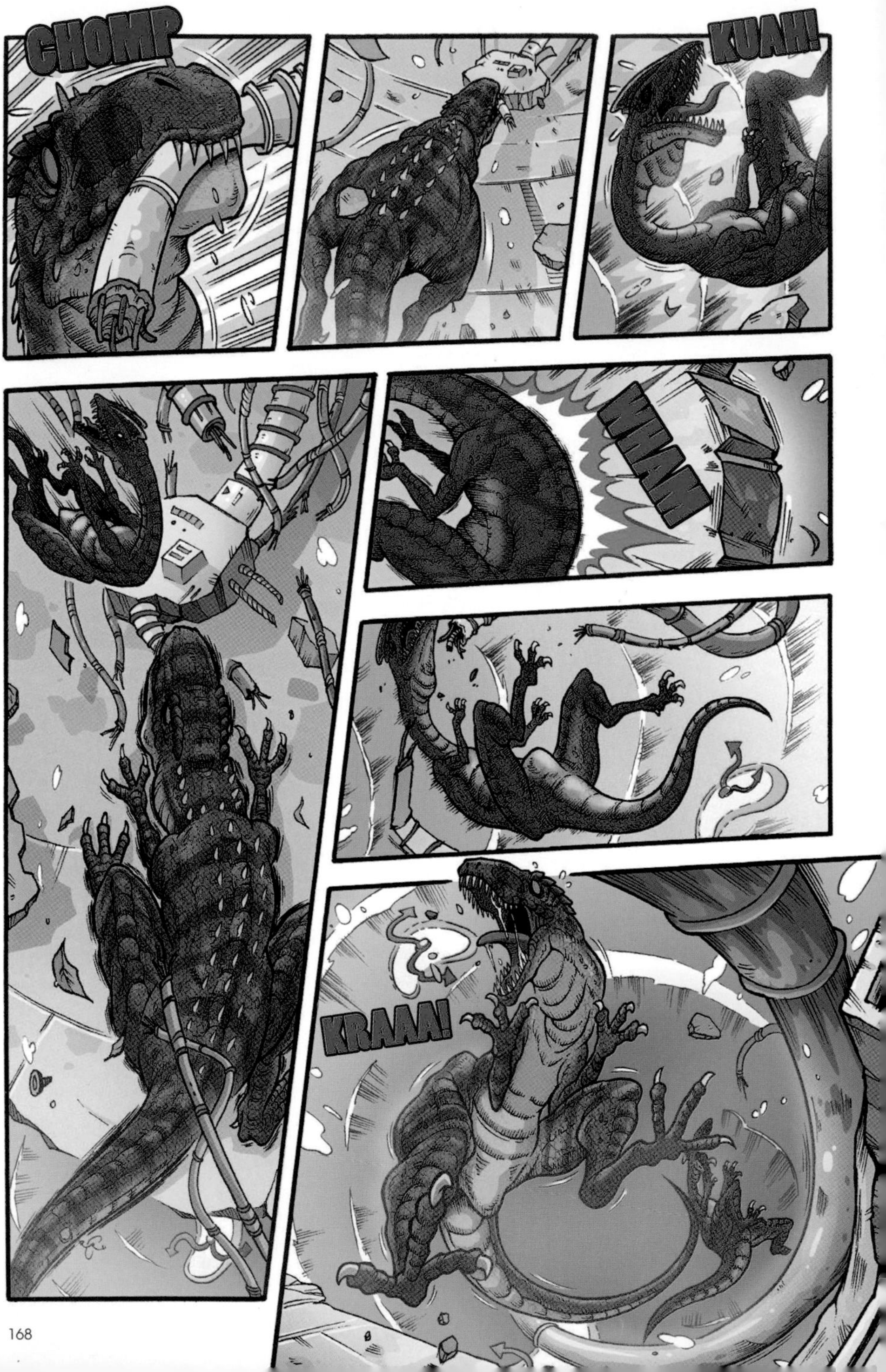
CHOMP
KUAH!
WHAM
KRAAA!

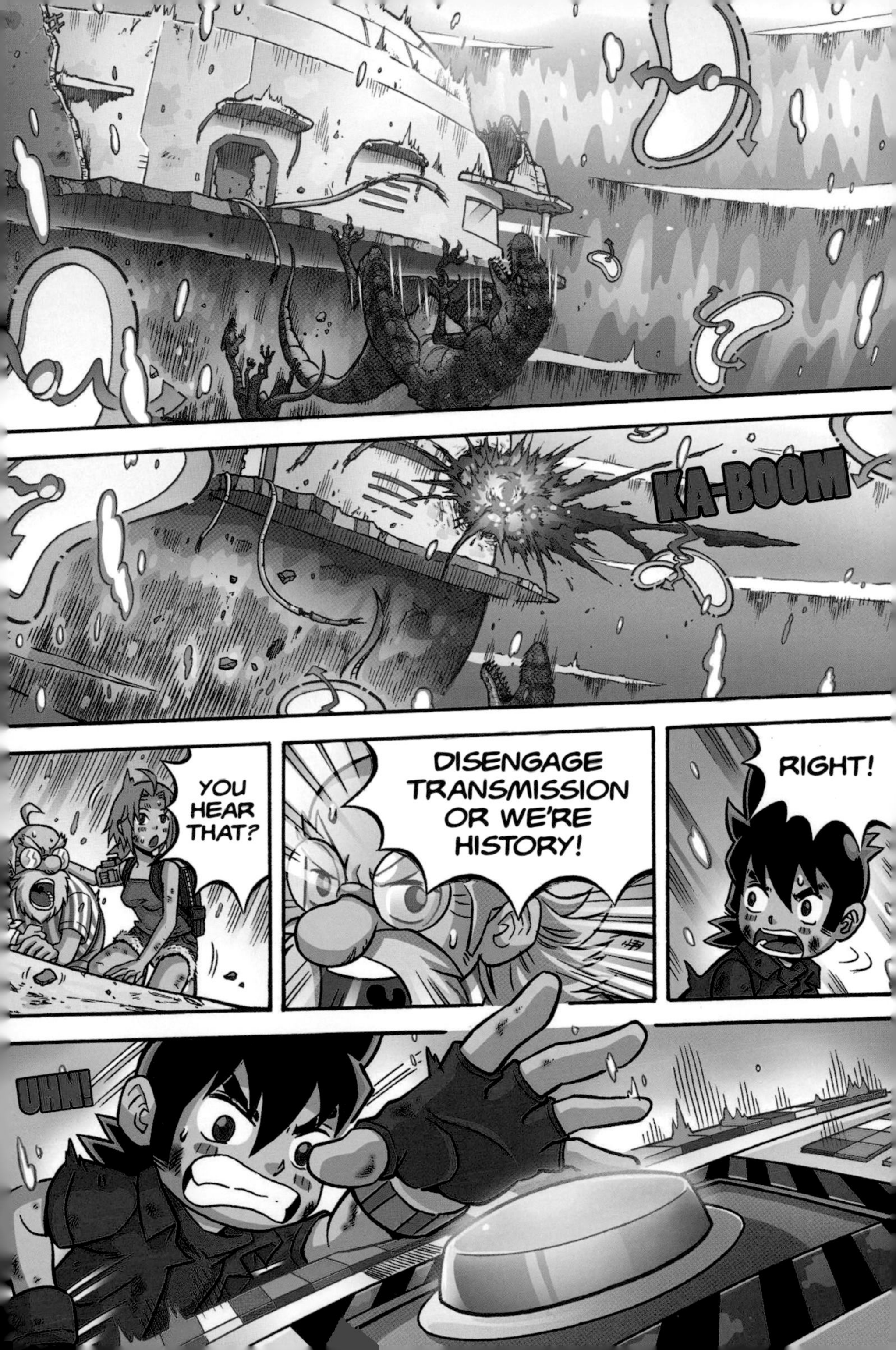
KA-BOOM
YOU HEAR THAT?
DISENGAGE TRANSMISSION OR WE'RE HISTORY!
RIGHT!
UHN!

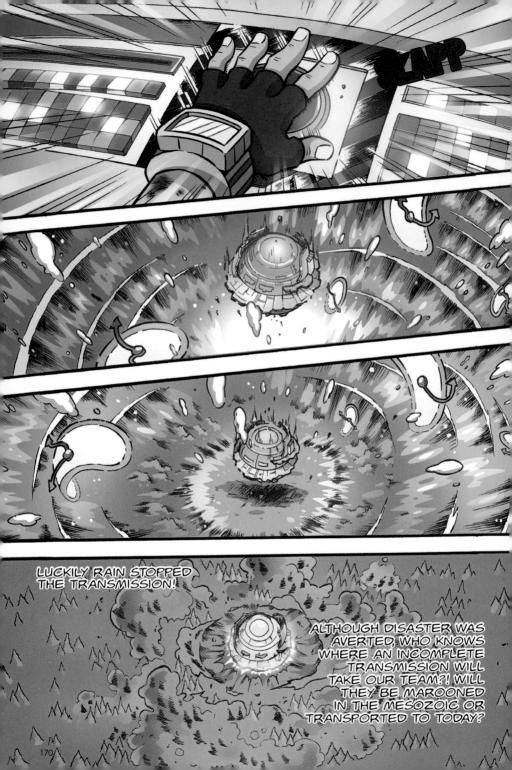

LUCKILY RAIN STOPPED THE TRANSMISSION!

ALTHOUGH DISASTER WAS AVERTED, WHO KNOWS WHERE AN INCOMPLETE TRANSMISSION WILL TAKE OUR TEAM?! WILL THEY BE MAROONED IN THE MESOZOIC OR TRANSPORTED TO TODAY?

Shunosaurus

Shunosaurus was a sauropod the size of a female elephant. As it was slow, it relied on its spiked tail to defend itself. This weapon was quite effective, and was fully capable of killing an attacker.

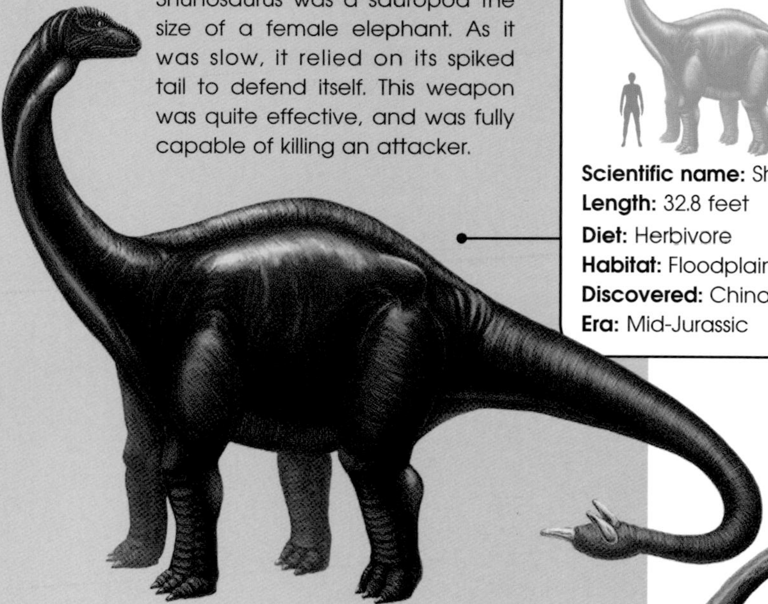

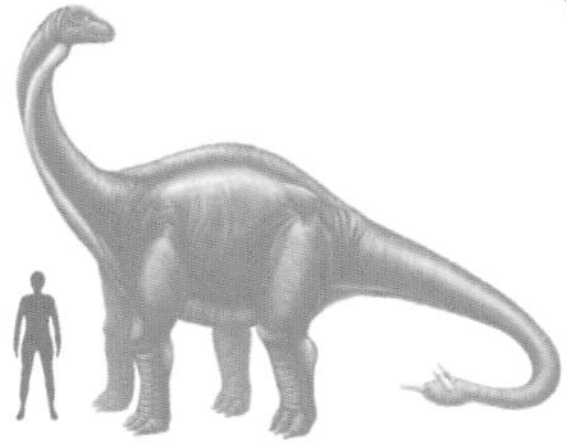

Scientific name: Shunosaurus
Length: 32.8 feet
Diet: Herbivore
Habitat: Floodplains
Discovered: China
Era: Mid-Jurassic

JONESING FOR THE JURASSIC

Omeisaurus

Omeisaurus was a large sauropod; its longer than average neck had 17 bone segments. Another oddity compared to other sauropods was the fact that its waist was higher than its shoulders, due to its stumpy front legs, which were clawed to help it dig up roots and tubers. Some paleontologists believe it had a clublike mass on the end of its tail for defense.

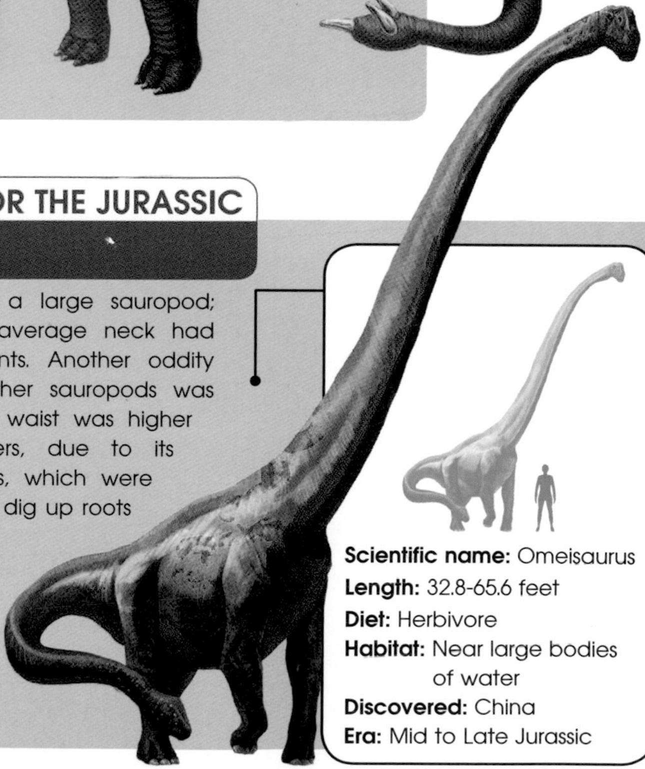

Scientific name: Omeisaurus
Length: 32.8-65.6 feet
Diet: Herbivore
Habitat: Near large bodies of water
Discovered: China
Era: Mid to Late Jurassic

JONESING FOR THE JURASSIC

Tanystropheus

With a neck longer than its body and tail, Tanystropheus was an ambush predator. It had to hunt like this due to its size. Its neck alone was around 9.8 feet long and composed of 10 neck vertebrae.

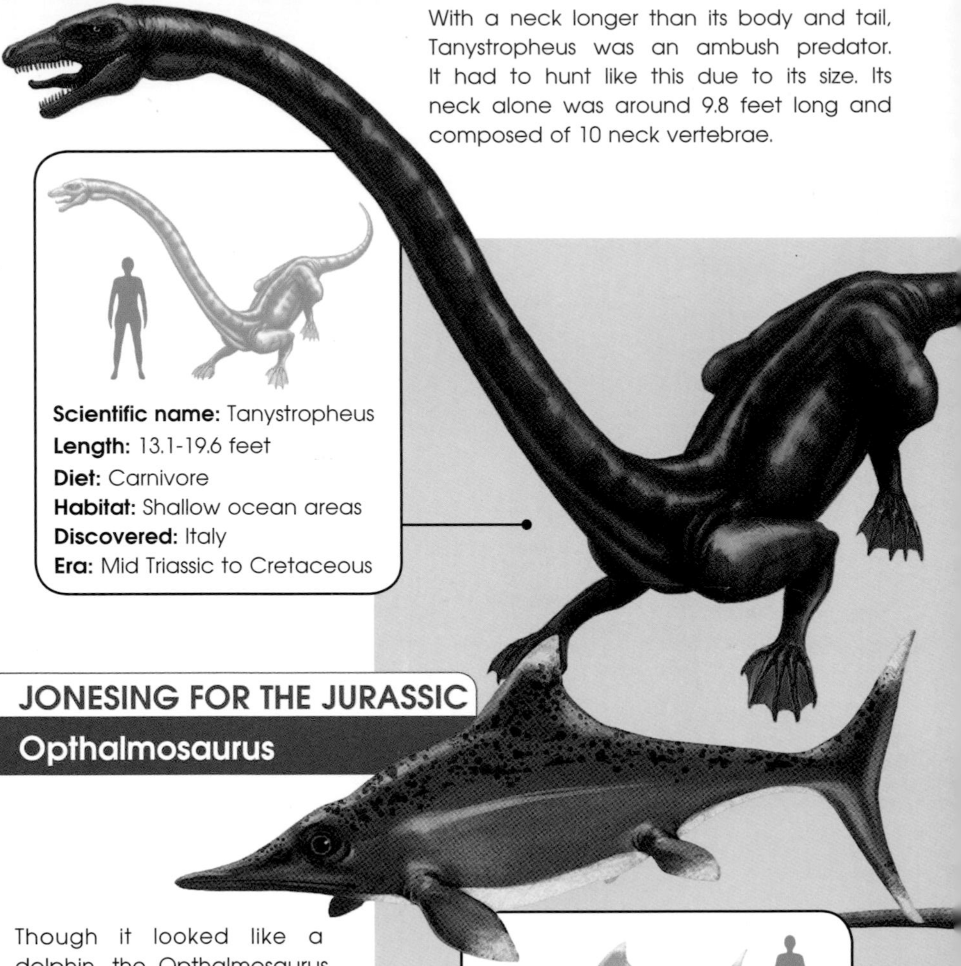

Scientific name: Tanystropheus
Length: 13.1-19.6 feet
Diet: Carnivore
Habitat: Shallow ocean areas
Discovered: Italy
Era: Mid Triassic to Cretaceous

JONESING FOR THE JURASSIC

Opthalmosaurus

Though it looked like a dolphin, the Opthalmosaurus was a vastly different creature. For one, it was a reptile while dolphins are mammals. It did share a streamlined body shape and powerful tail, however, to propel it through the water. The Opthalmosaurus had massive eyes (its name means "eye lizard") which probably helped it hunt in dark places or at night.

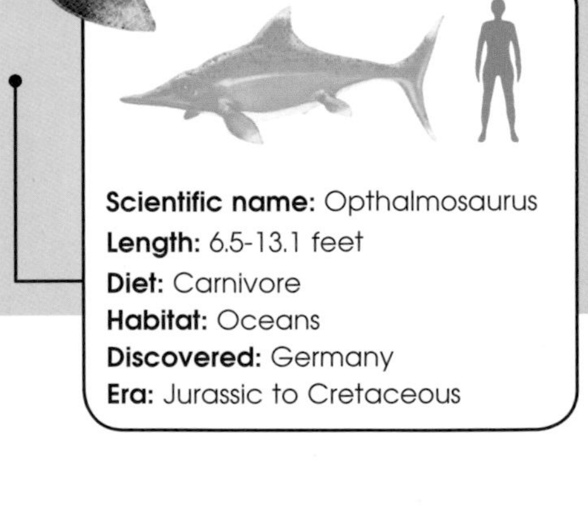

Scientific name: Opthalmosaurus
Length: 6.5-13.1 feet
Diet: Carnivore
Habitat: Oceans
Discovered: Germany
Era: Jurassic to Cretaceous

JONESING FOR THE JURASSIC

Geosaurus

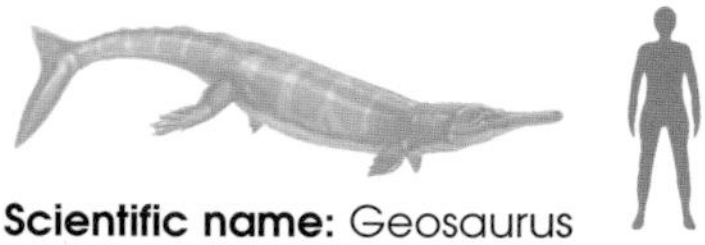

Scientific name: Geosaurus
Length: 9.8 feet
Diet: Carnivore
Habitat: Shallow ocean areas
Discovered: England, France, Switzerland, Argentina, Cuba and Mexico
Era: Jurassic

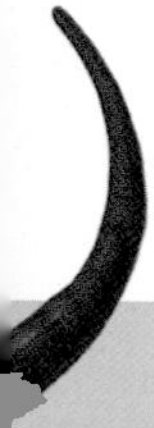

The slim, small Geosaurus was a proto-crocodile which seemed fully adapted for speed. Not only was its body extremely streamlined (from the narrow nose to the daggerlike tail), fossil records lack evidence of armor plating, a trait posessed even by modern crocodiles. It was probably as flexible as it was fast, relying on its adaptations to hunt and survive unlike the armored juggernauts that were the rest of its kind.

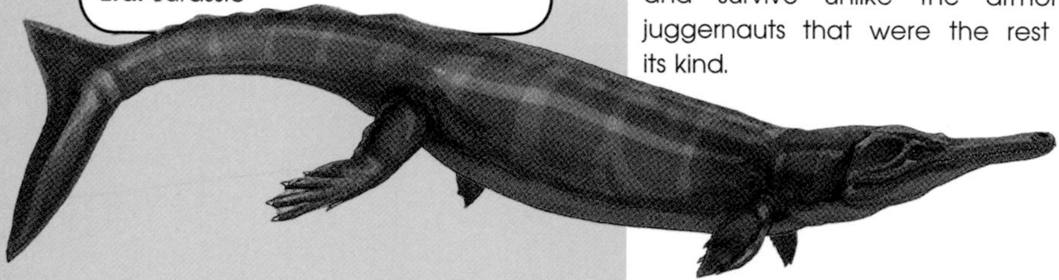

JONESING FOR THE JURASSIC

Yandusaurus

Scientific name: Yandusaurus
Length: 3.2-5.2 feet
Diet: Omnivore
Habitat: Jungles and forests
Discovered: China
Era: Early Jurassic

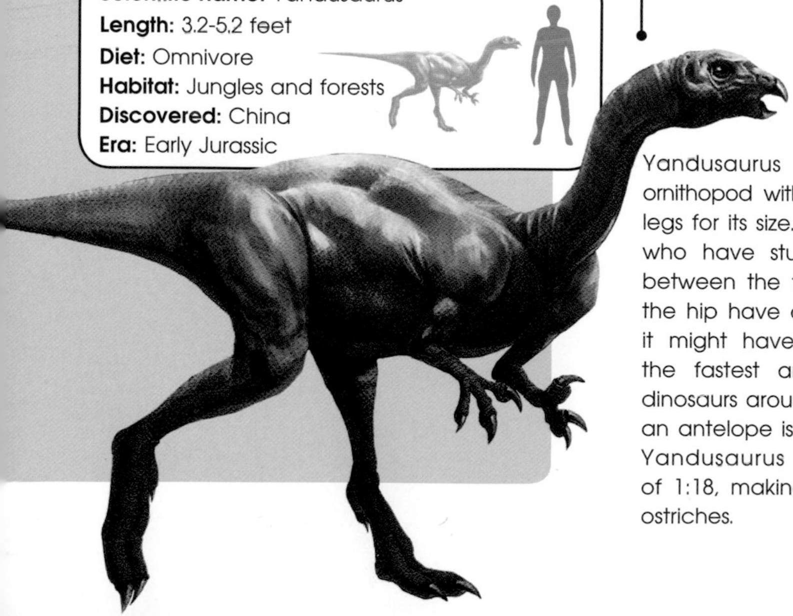

Yandusaurus was a small ornithopod with powerful hind legs for its size. Paleontologists who have studied the ratio between the tibia bone and the hip have concluded that it might have been one of the fastest and most agile dinosaurs around; the ratio for an antelope is 1:25, while the Yandusaurus had a ratio of 1:18, making it faster than ostriches.

JURASSIC LARK!

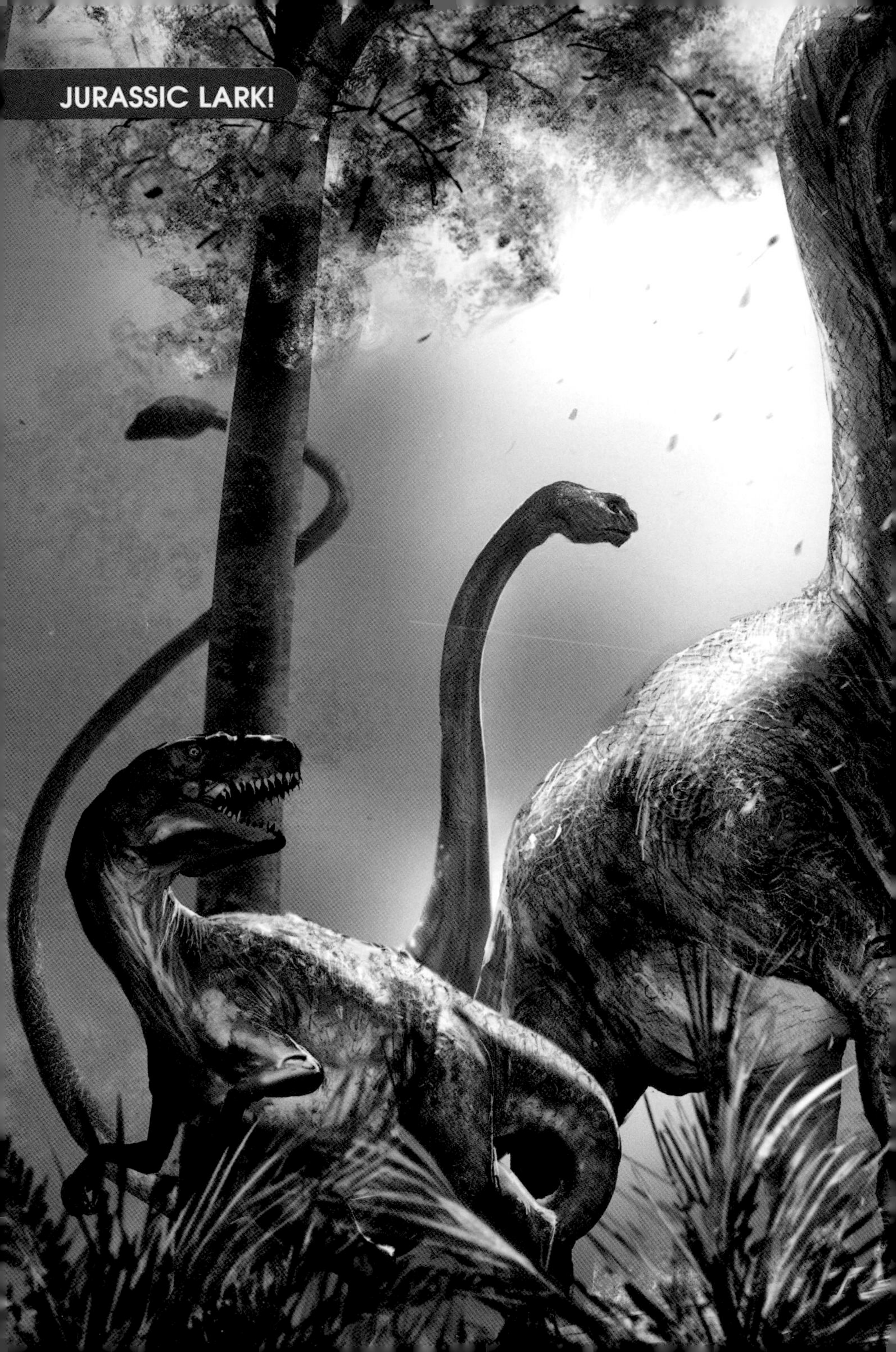

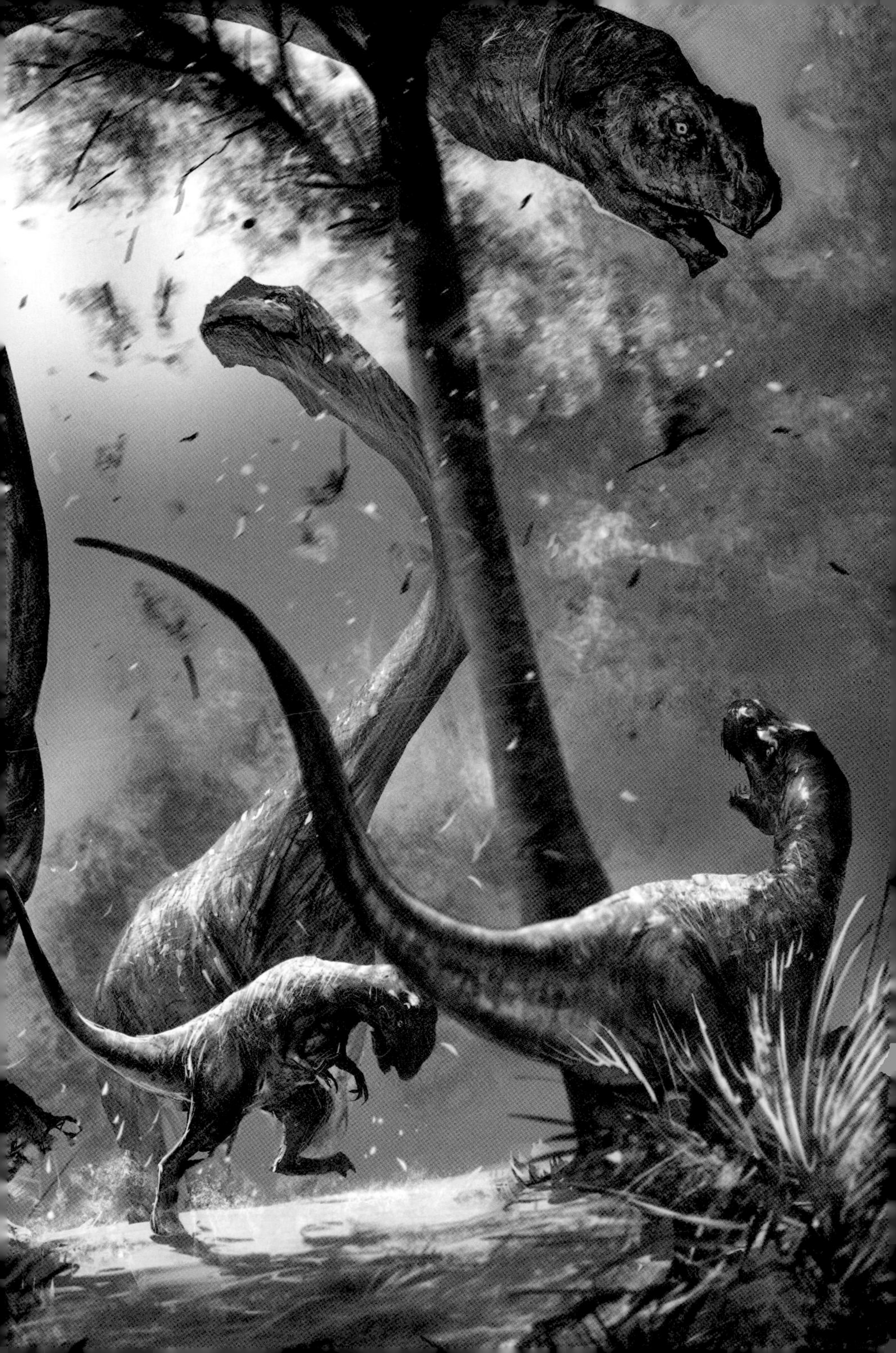

WATCH OUT FOR PAPERCUT𝗭

Welcome to Jurassic—Oops! I'm such a dinosaur! I almost mentioned that famous movie that tries to recreate the Jurassic Age as a theme park. I edited the comics based on that film many years ago, but not nearly as long ago as the Jurassic era itself. So, let me start over...

Welcome to the frightening, fact-filled fifth DINOSAUR EXPLORERS graphic novel by Redcode and Albie, writers, and Air Team, artists, from Papercutz, those dinosaur nerds dedicated to publishing great graphic novels for all ages. I'm Jim Salicrup, the Editor-in-Chief and mostly preserved in amber, here to share a little behind-the-scenes info regarding DINOSAUR EXPLORERS and Papercutz...

For those of you who read all the small print on page 2, otherwise known as "the copyright page," you already know that DINOSAUR EXPLORERS is created in Malaysia and was originally called "X-VENTURE™ X-PLORERS." The adventures we're publishing are called the Dinosaur Kingdom series. "Lost in the Jurassic" is the fifth of 12 graphic novels in the Dinosaur Kingdom series.

Redcode is responsible for storyboarding the X-VENTURE Dinosaur Kingdom Series (which means laying out all the comics pages), as well as assisting in illustrations and storylines.

Albie began planning the X-VENTURE series in 2009, and is responsible for research, story, and editing.

Air Team is Kino, Samu, Neko, Esther, and Vezill, and they are the artists behind the X-VENTURE Dinosaur Kingdom series, each bringing their special talents and skills to the project. From visualizing a scene, to creating the awesome scenic backgrounds and character designs, each of them has left their personal mark on this amazing series.

If you're just joining us, you don't know what you've been missing, so allow me to bring you up to speed...

DINOSAUR EXPLORERS #1 "Prehistoric Pioneers" – This one sets the stage for the entire series. The DINOSAUR EXPLORERS – Rain, Sean, Stone, Diana, Emily, Starz, and Dr. Da Vinci – wind up trapped in the Precambrian Era (570 million years ago), and have to fix their temperamental time machine (the Particle Transmitter). But try finding electricity in an era where humans have yet to exist. And to make matters worse, the locals – prehistoric creatures who existed before the dinosaurs – don't take kindly to these visitors from the future.

DINOSAUR EXPLORERS #2 "Puttering in the Paleozoic" – A funny thing happened on the way back to the present – our heroes can "only" travel so many centuries at a time and wind up in the Silurian Era (430 million years ago) – Rain somehow manages to enlist Emily in his scheme to collect ancient treasures. They find more than they bargained for, however, when a group of prehistoric shellfish decides to snack on them.

DINOSAUR EXPLORERS #3 "Playing in the Permian" – Next stop for our heroes is between the Permian and Carboniferous eras (around 350 million years ago). It is here that they encounter the much, much larger ancestors of many much, much smaller creatures of today. In other words, they face such delightful critters as giant spiders!

DINOSAUR EXPLORERS #4 "Trapped in the Triassic" – Things seems to get progressively more difficult for our heroes when they wind up in the Triassic Era. They're even fighting among themselves and split up. But who gets to drive the newly built "Divvy," a super-cool vehicle created by Dr. Da Vinci and who has to walk?

And after this graphic novel (#5), the DINOSAUR EXPLORERS wind up next in the late Jurassic period! Don't miss the excitement coming soon in #6 "Exploring the Jurassic."

Thanks, *Jim*

STAY IN TOUCH!

EMAIL:	salicrup@papercutz.com
WEB:	papercutz.com
TWITTER:	@papercutzgn
INSTAGRAM:	@papercutzgn
FACEBOOK:	PAPERCUTZGRAPHICNOVELS
FAN MAIL:	Papercutz, 160 Broadway, Suite 700, East Wing, New York, NY 10038

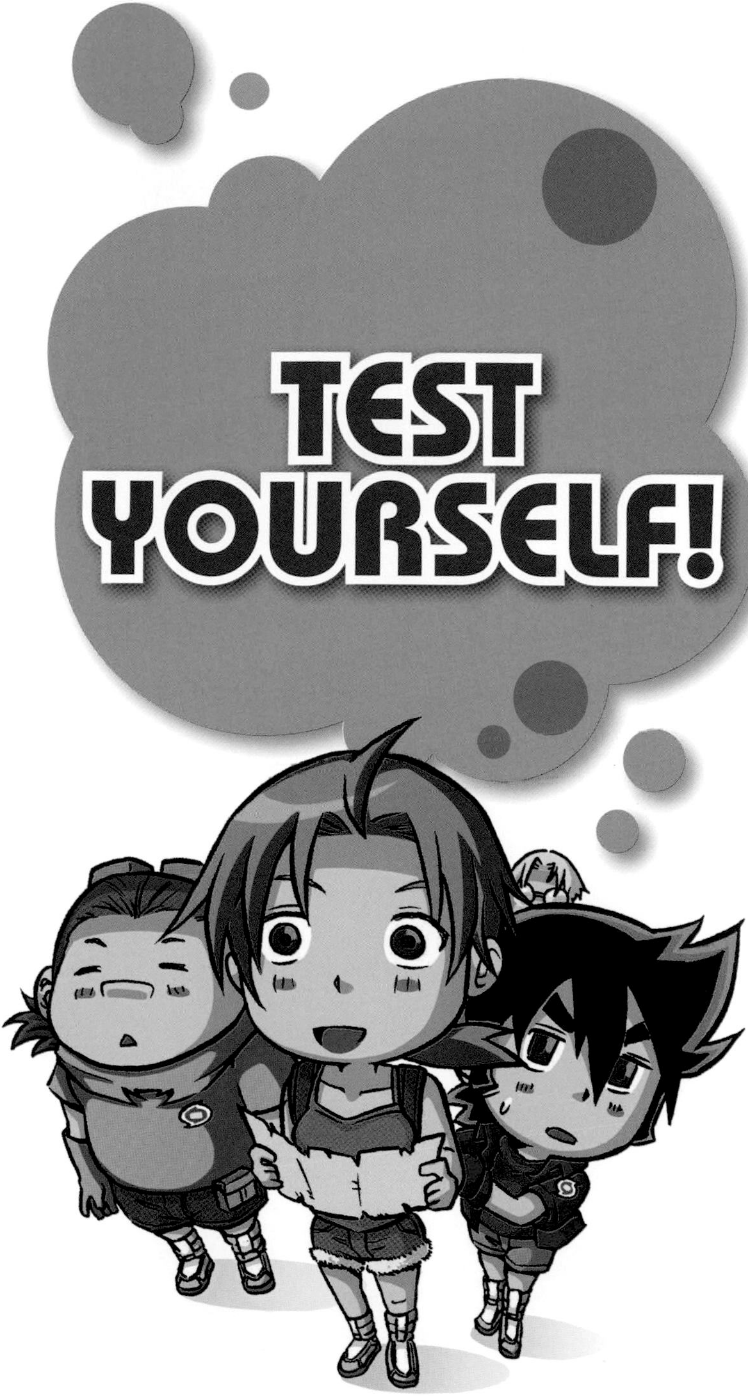
TEST
YOURSELF!

ABOUT THE JURASSIC...

01 **The Jurassic was a period in which era?**

A - Paleozoic

B - Mesozoic

C - Cenozoic

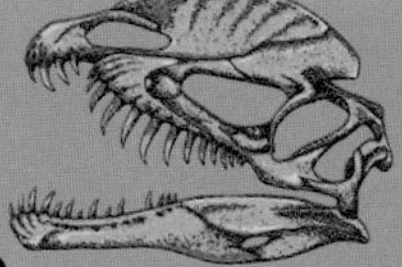

02 **What kind of dinosaur might have had the skull above?**

A - Carnivore

B - Herbivore

C - Omnivore

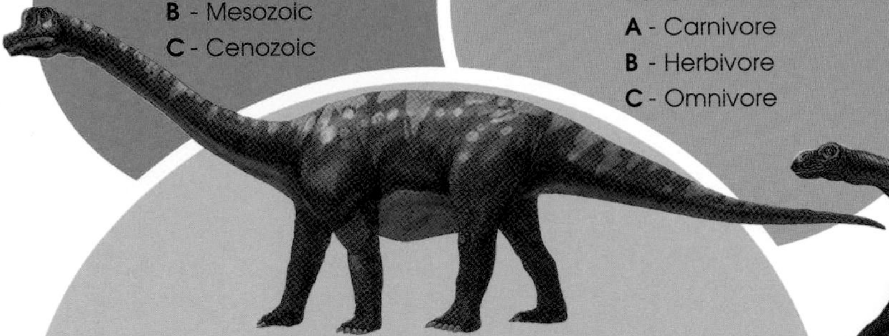

A Tazoudasaurus

03 **Which of these was the earliest sauropod that we're aware of?**

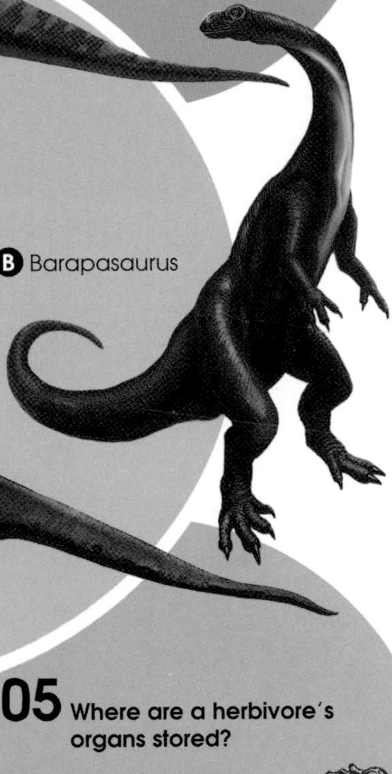

B Barapasaurus

C Massospondylus

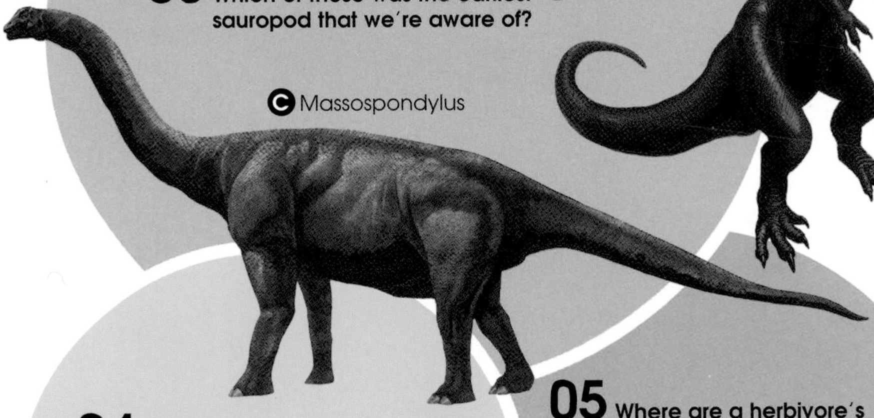

04 **What is one major ornithischian trait?**

A - Long necks and index finger on the hands

B - Beaks on the upper jaw

C - Strong jaw and tooth structures

05 **Where are a herbivore's organs stored?**

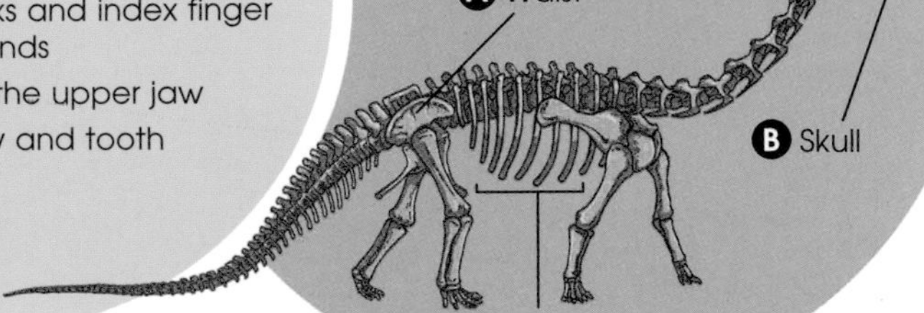

A Waist

B Skull

C Chest

06 Which of these is considered the apex predator of the Jurassic seas?

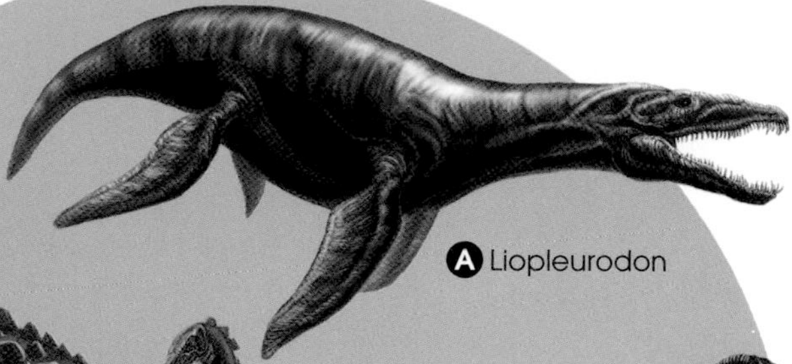

A Liopleurodon

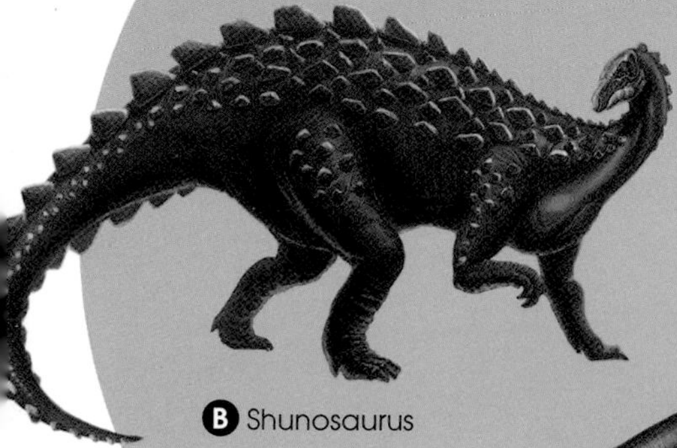

B Shunosaurus

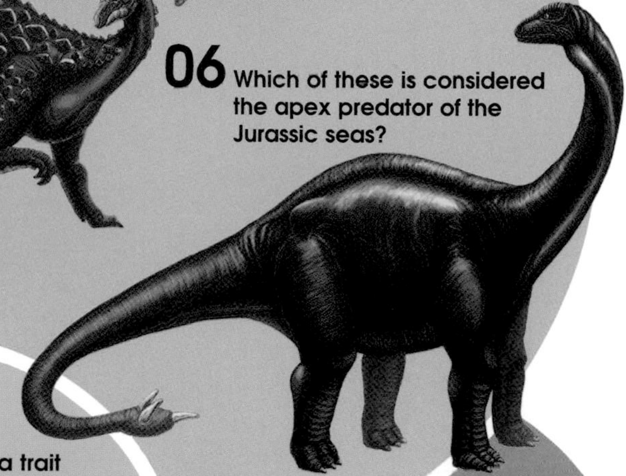

C Scelidosaurus

07 Which of these is a trait usually possessed by qudrapedal (four-legged) dinosaurs?

A - Shorter front limbs to catch food or defend itself

B - Four limbs of equal length and strength to support its weight

C - High speed and agility

08 Massospondylus; What is this dinosaur's genus?

A - Prosauropod

B - Tetrapod

C - Sauropod

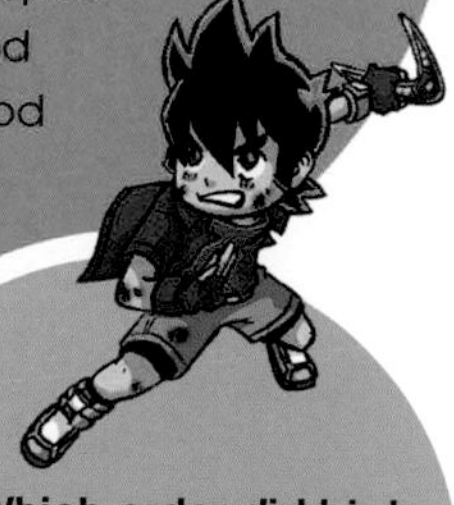

09 Which order did birds evolve from?

A - Ornithischians

B - Saurischians

C - Theropods

A

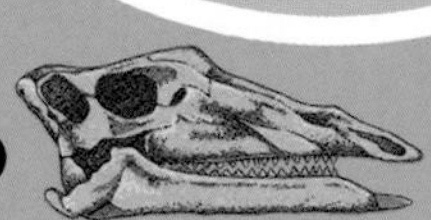

B

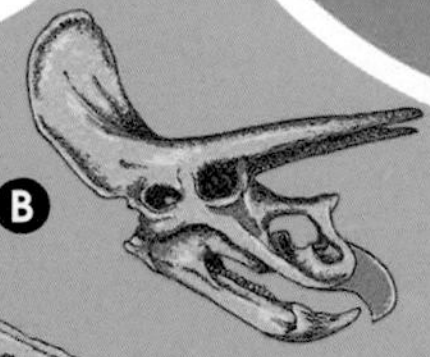

C

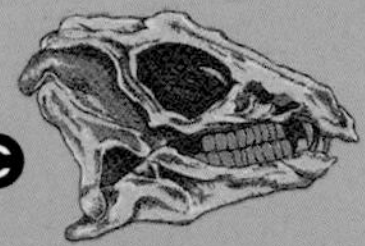

10 Which of these is a ceratopsid skull?

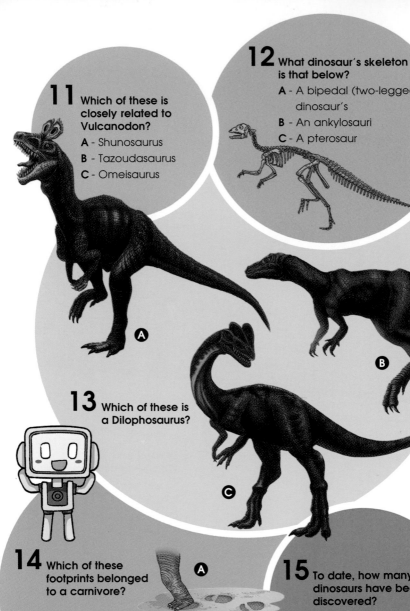

11 **Which of these is closely related to Vulcanodon?**

A - Shunosaurus

B - Tazoudasaurus

C - Omeisaurus

12 **What dinosaur's skeleton is that below?**

A - A bipedal (two-legged) dinosaur's

B - An ankylosauri

C - A pterosaur

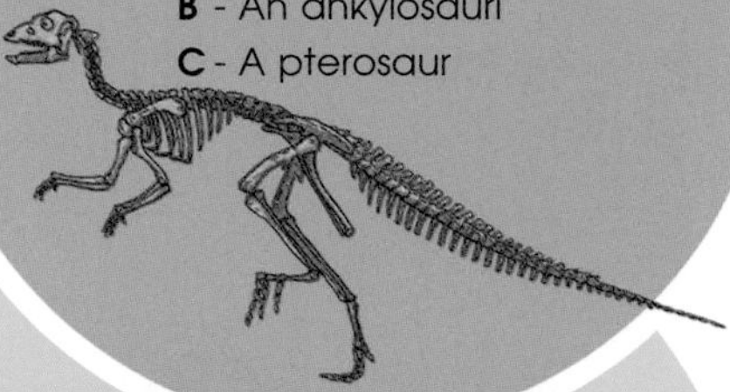

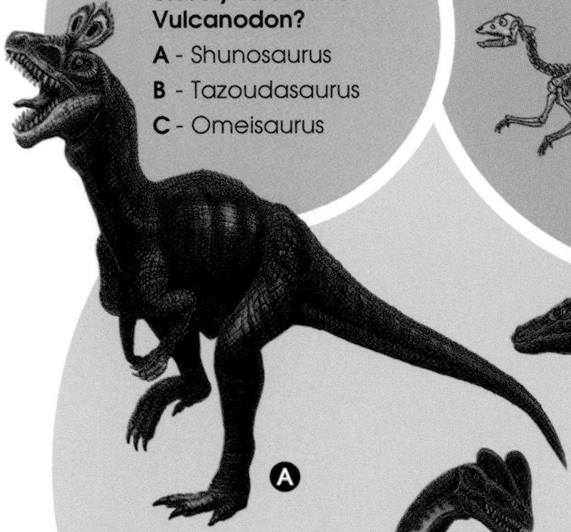
A

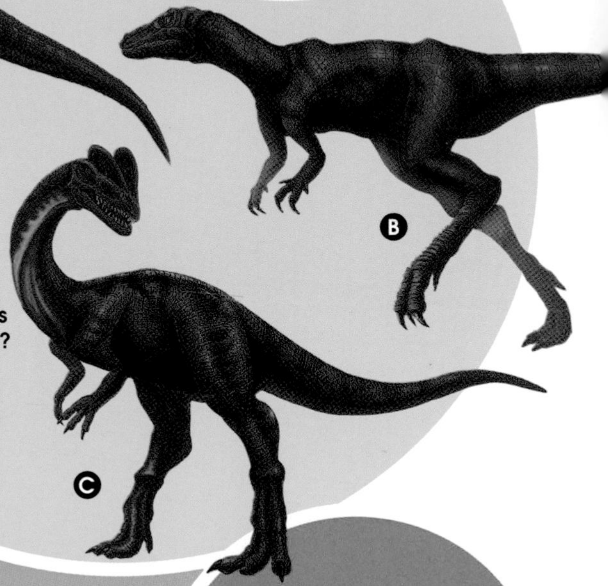
B
C

13 **Which of these is a Dilophosaurus?**

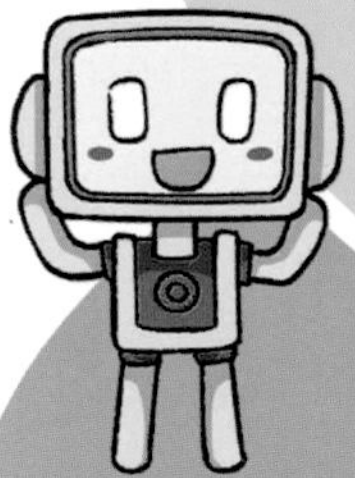

14 **Which of these footprints belonged to a carnivore?**

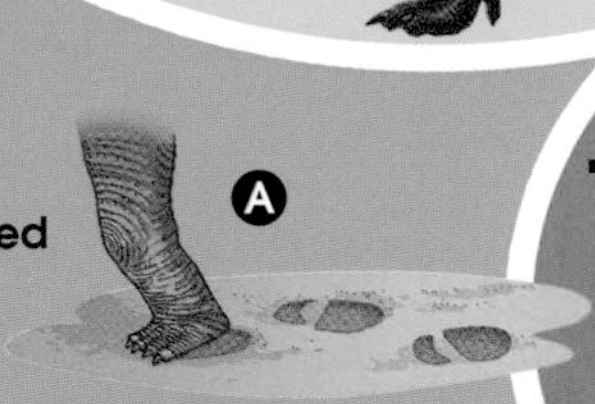
A

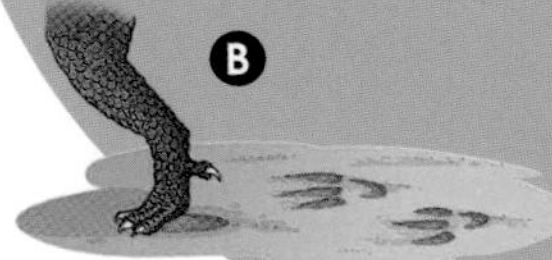
B

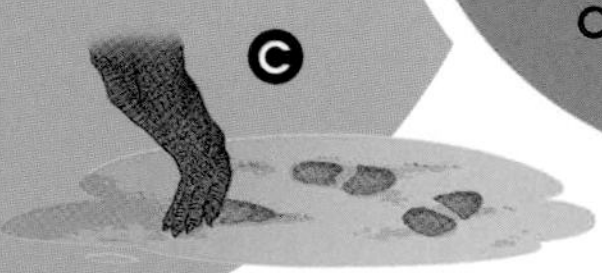
C

15 **To date, how many dinosaurs have been discovered?**

A - 100

B - More than 200

C - Not more than 200

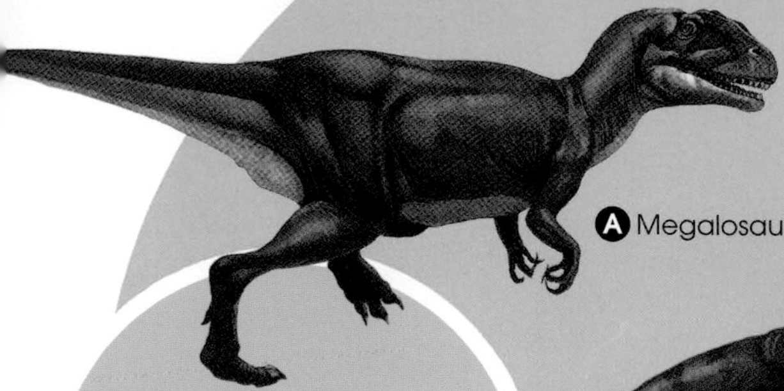

16 **Which of these was the first dinosaur to be named?**

A Megalosaurus

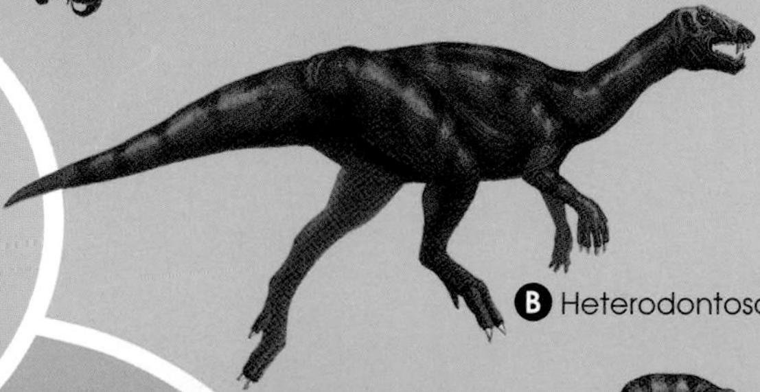

B Heterodontosaurus

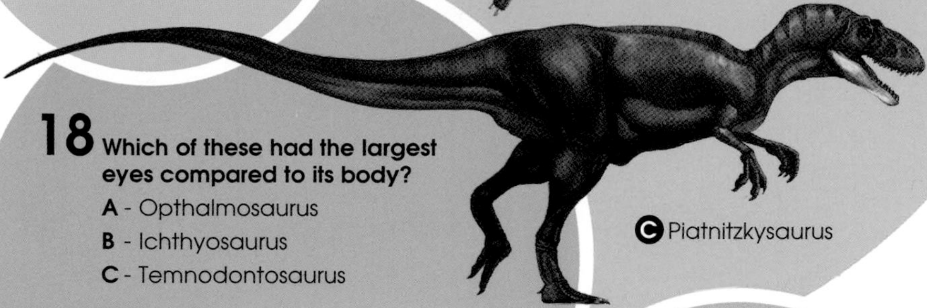

C Piatnitzkysaurus

17 **The Jurassic was which period in the Mesozoic?**

A - Second

B - Third

C - Fourth

18 **Which of these had the largest eyes compared to its body?**

A - Opthalmosaurus

B - Ichthyosaurus

C - Temnodontosaurus

19 **Which of these was a common saurischian trait?**

A - Long necks and index fingers

B - Beaked upper jaws

C - Strong tooth and jaw structures

20 **Which of these three is a Thyreophoran?**

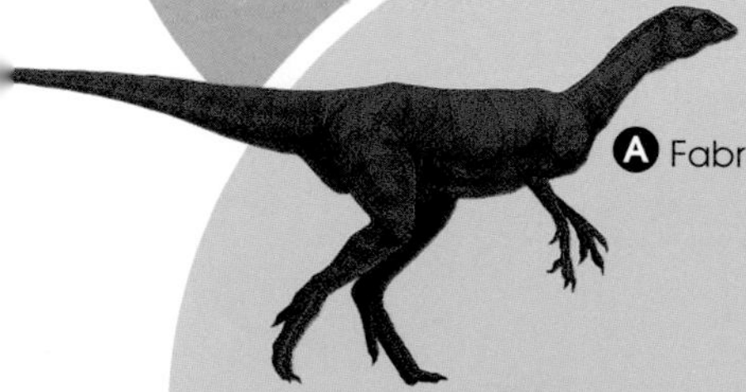

A Fabrosaurus

B Scelidosaurus

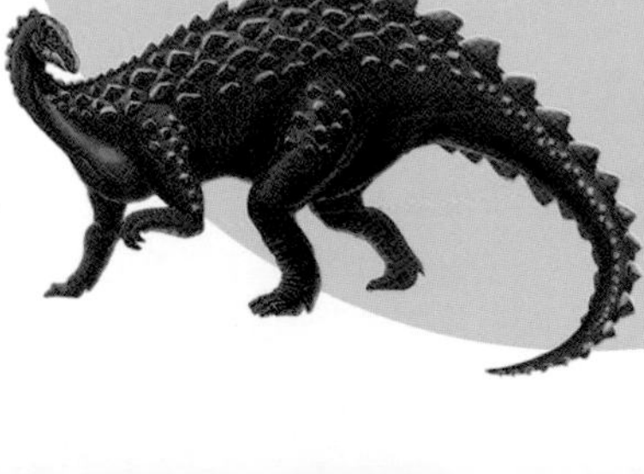

C Anchisaurus

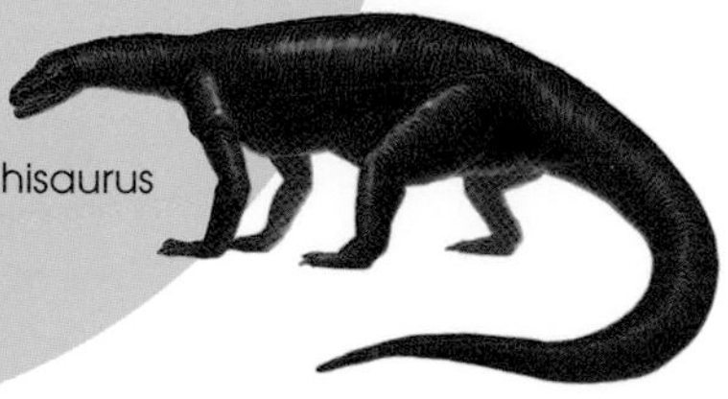

ANSWERS

01 B	02 A	03 A	04 C	05 C
06 A	07 B	08 A	09 B	10 B
11 B	12 A	13 C	14 B	15 B
16 A	17 A	18 A	19 A	20 B

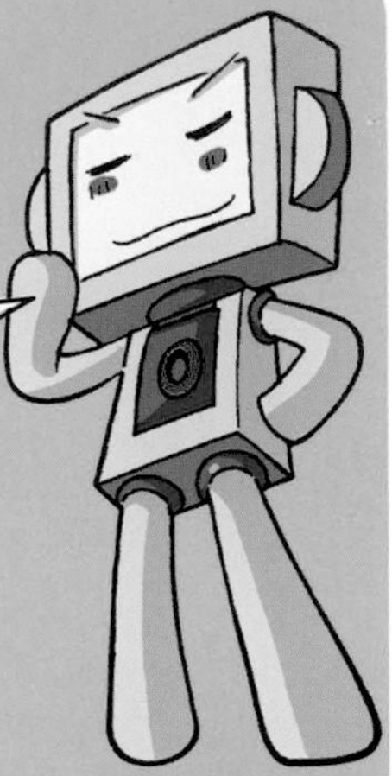

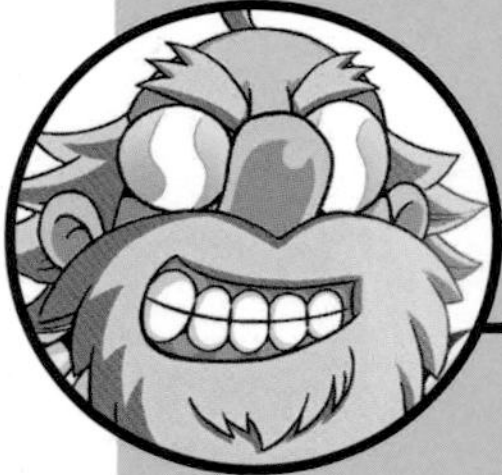

All correct?

Congrats! You're as smart as I am! I think.

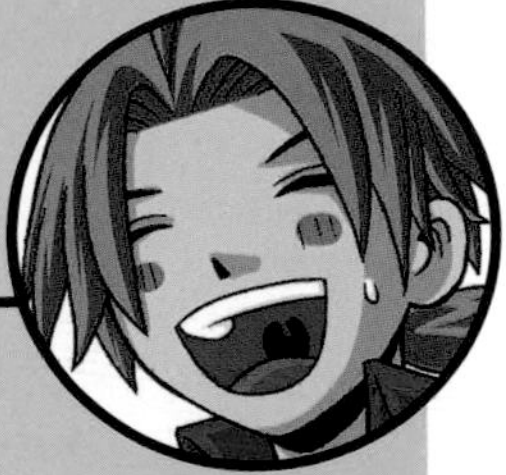

16 – 19 correct?

I'm actually smarter than the Doctor! Don't tell anyone!

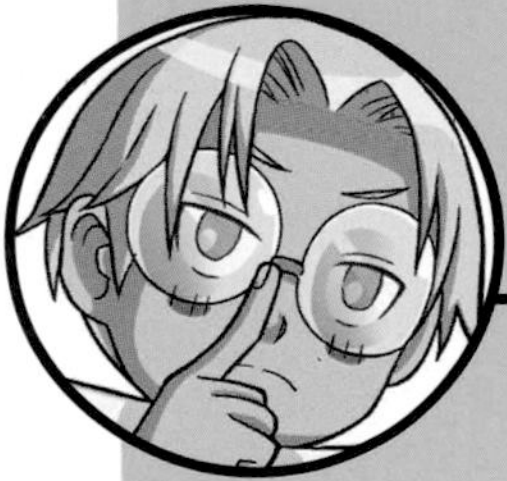

12 -15 correct?

Don't just take in knowledge – apply it to real life!

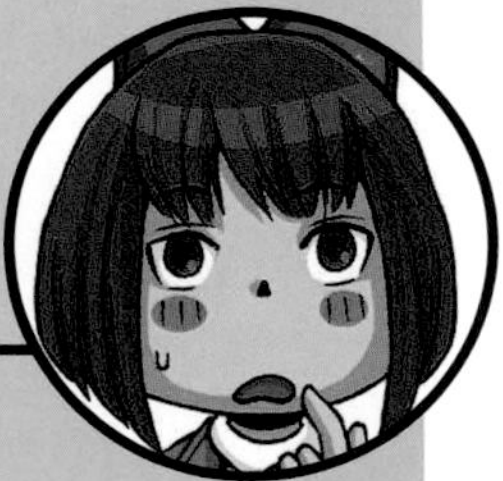

8 - 11 correct?

What? You're smarter than me? Impossible!

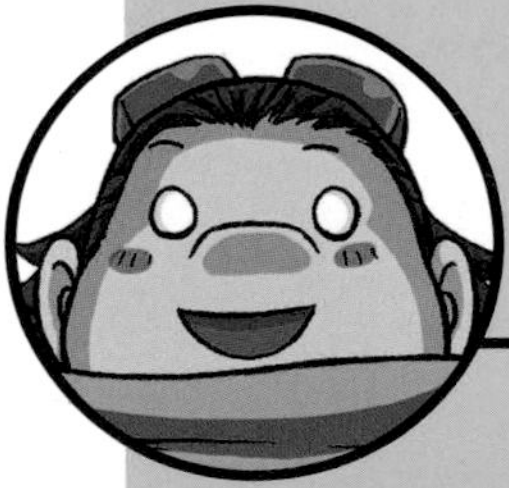

4 – 7 correct?

Huh, looks like we both can use some work! Let's go to the library! Studying's better with friends!

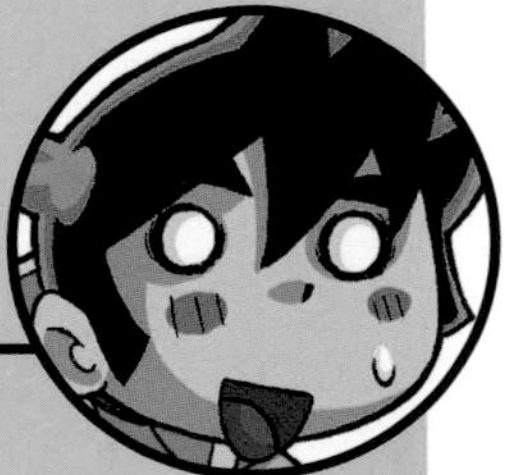

0 - 3 correct?

Don't worry, you're as S-M-R-T smart as me!

TRAVEL BACK IN TIME WITH THE DINOSAUR EXPLORERS

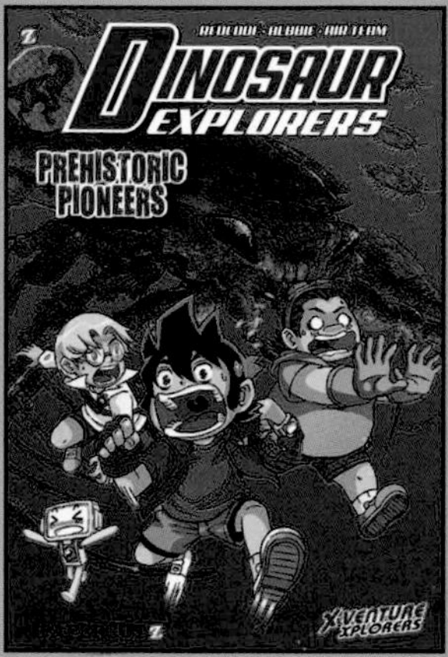
REDCODE · ALBBIE · AIR TEAM
DINOSAUR EXPLORERS
PREHISTORIC PIONEERS
X-VENTURE EXPLORERS

DINOSAUR EXPLORERS #1
"PREHISTORIC PIONEERS"

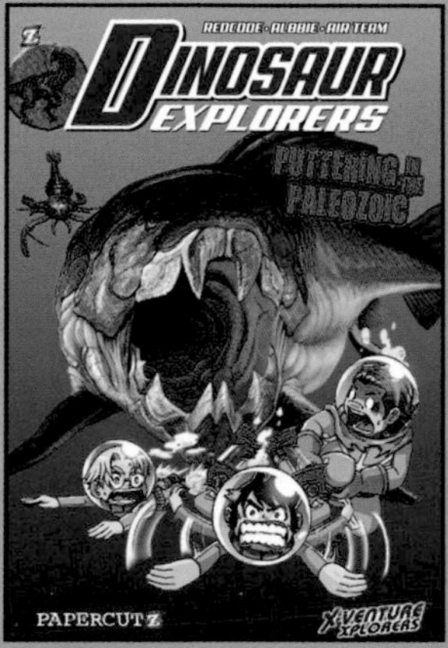
REDCODE · ALBBIE · AIR TEAM
DINOSAUR EXPLORERS
PUTTERING IN THE PALEOZOIC
PAPERCUTZ
X-VENTURE EXPLORERS

DINOSAUR EXPLORERS #2
"PUTTERING IN THE PALEOZOIC"

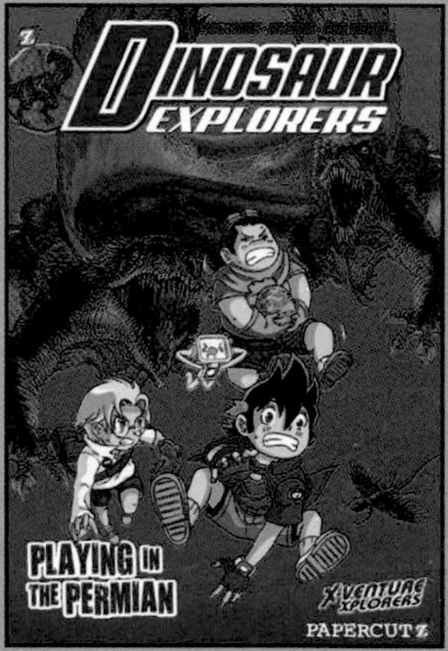
DINOSAUR EXPLORERS
PLAYING IN THE PERMIAN
X-VENTURE EXPLORERS
PAPERCUTZ

DINOSAUR EXPLORERS #3
"PLAYING IN THE PERMIAN"

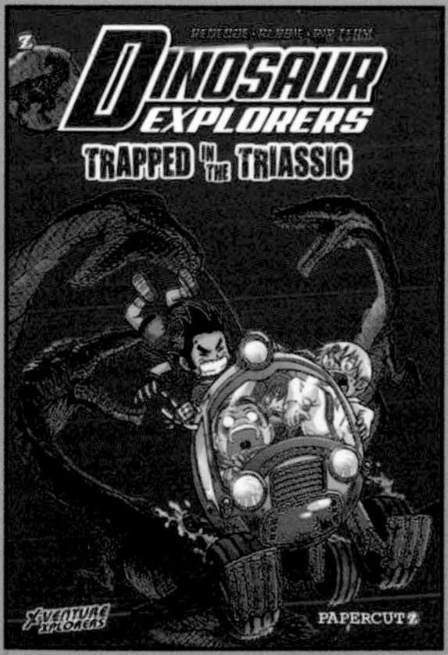
DINOSAUR EXPLORERS
TRAPPED IN THE TRIASSIC
X-VENTURE EXPLORERS
PAPERCUTZ

DINOSAUR EXPLORERS #4
"TRAPPED IN THE TRIASSIC"

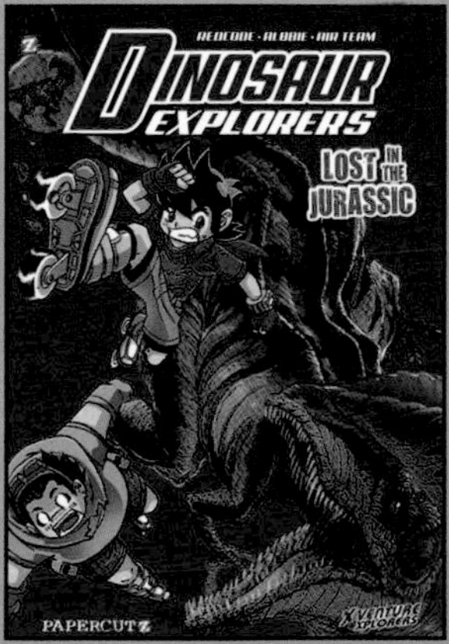
REDCODE · ALBBIE · AIR TEAM
DINOSAUR EXPLORERS
LOST IN THE JURASSIC
PAPERCUTZ
X-VENTURE EXPLORERS

DINOSAUR EXPLORERS #5
"LOST IN THE JURASSIC"

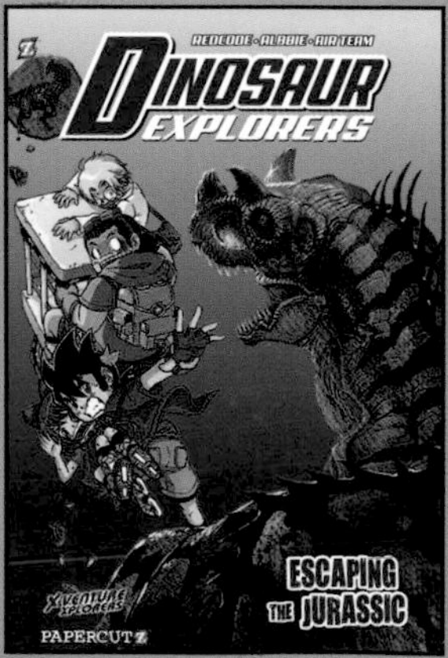
REDCODE · ALBBIE · AIR TEAM
DINOSAUR EXPLORERS
X-VENTURE EXPLORERS
ESCAPING THE JURASSIC
PAPERCUTZ

COMING SOON!
DINOSAUR EXPLORERS #6
"ESCAPING THE JURASSIC"

DINOSAUR EXPLORERS graphic novels are available for $12.99 each in paperback and $16.99 each in hardcover. Available from booksellers everywhere. You can order online from www.papercutz.com. Or call 1-800-866-1223, Monday through Friday, 9-5 EST. MC, Visa, and AmEx accepted. To order by mail, please add $5.00 for postage and handling for first book ordered, $1.00 for each additional book, and make check payable to NBM Publishing. Send to: Papercutz, 160 Broadway, Suite 700, East Wing, New York, NY 10038.

DINOSAUR EXPLORERS are also available digitally wherever e-books are sold.

www.papercutz.com